Return

By

A.J. Messenger

First Print Edition December 2018

ISBN-13: 9781791322533

Cover images credit:

Annie Spratt | istockphoto.com

Books by A.J. Messenger

The Guardian Series
(a paranormal angel romance series):

Guardian (Book One)

Fallen (Book Two)

Revelation (Book Three)

Return (Book Four)

More titles from A.J. Messenger coming soon

Sign up for A.J.'s "*new release newsletter*" at
ajmessenger.com or **facebook.com/ajmessengerauthor**

A message to readers about Return

Dear Reader,

I originally planned for the *Guardian Series* to end with book three, *Revelation*. Some of you wrote to me because you wished to read about how Declan and Alexander rediscover each other and reconnect with their past. That helped inspire me to write *Return*, which brings the *Guardian Series* full circle so that now you can find out how Declan and Alexander come together once more, and also what happens next for everyone involved.

I hope you enjoy it!

A. J. Messenger

Table of Contents

"There are no endings, only new beginnings."

– Anonymous

"But the eyes are blind. One must look with the heart."

– Antoine de Saint-Exupéry

Preface

As the waves of pain become overwhelming, I begin to lose focus. I know if I fail, there'll be no hope for rescue and the stakes extend far beyond my suffering alone.

At first I was fighting back, but now I'm simply hanging on.

As I feel my life force slipping away, I remember Uncle Finn's hypothesis. It was an alluring fancy, but I'm afraid what may have looked promising was only as good as junk after all.

As darkness seeps in and consciousness fades to nothingness, I console myself with the fact that after I'm gone, the ones I love can no longer be used as targets and cudgels.

Because how can you threaten someone who no longer exists?

Chapter One

Dany

"This is crazy," I mutter aloud, for what must be the tenth time as I make my way up Highway 280 to San Francisco in my trusty little Prius. As I pass through Hillsborough, I'm momentarily distracted by the enormous monument to Junipero Serra perched on a short hill beside the freeway. It was carved with soft, simple edges and few details, and one of my co-workers told me her son thought it was a statue of a man bowling. He's in a robe, posed on one knee and pointing west, dramatically, across eight lanes of zooming traffic. The practical girl in me ponders the wisdom of placing a giant statue next to a busy freeway that points *away* from where drivers should be looking when they're going 80 miles per hour.

I glance at the speedometer and ease up on the gas. *Take it easy, Dany, you're not in a hurry. You're not even sure if you should be going at all.*

For the hundredth time I wonder if I should turn around and beg off with an excuse. Who would blame me after the day I just had?

But I remind myself what my favorite teacher, Mr. Angelides, always used to say: When you do something you know is the right thing to do, even when you don't want to (in fact, especially when you don't want to), you meet the kind of person you are. I catch my reflection in the rearview mirror and make a face. Hello there, dummy. Your honorable refusal to cancel plans at the last minute may end up ruining the sweetest friendship you ever had.

Oh, cut the dramatics, grumbles my inner drill sergeant, and I chuckle. She's right but I'm still uneasy. I don't know why I have so many butterflies in my stomach over this.

My thoughts drift back to when I left Australia. I knew my father's posting with his company was never meant to be permanent. We moved from Kansas to Australia when I was seven and my sister Karin was ten, and by the time we went back to Kansas three years later, she was in prime teenage mode and itching to get home to her friends. Maybe my parents were tired of her begging every day to go back, or maybe they were just as eager—it was no secret they missed Kansas, too. I was the lone holdout hoping we'd stay.

"Xander and Dany. Best friends forever." I can still picture the words that I wrote in my journal in large block letters and colored in with every shade of crayon I could find as I tried to assert control against forces that were out of my hands. My childish proclamation, surprisingly, turned out to be true. Well, sort of … it was true in that it wasn't completely off the mark.

Xander and I have stayed in touch. It started out as childhood pen pals exchanging short dispatches on wide-ruled paper and turned into lengthy, handwritten letters throughout the years—always sent via old school snail mail. Odd, I know, (or people tell me) but for some reason we started this habit and kept it up. You could call it quaint and dutiful inertia. For the past few years we've exchanged only about one letter a year, but neither of us has seemed to want to let the connection fall away completely.

So why am I so nervous about seeing him again?

It can't be just the spectacularly awful day I've had. I think it's that I've come to rely on the steadfastness of our friendship. What if we don't connect like we used to? I mean, let's be real—it's been almost fifteen years. We used to go exploring, hang out by the river, and search for frogs, and I'm pretty sure none of those things are on the itinerary tonight.

When Xander wrote to me weeks ago to say he was coming to San Francisco for a conference and suggested we meet for dinner, I agreed, happily. But now I'm full of hesitation. What if our easy compatibility as kids isn't there anymore? What if we run out of things to say after the initial hellos and catching up?

It could end up being great or it could lead to severing the string of our friendship for good.

The thought makes my stomach heavy.

When I reach the address, I drive up and down the block and around in circles, searching for an open spot to park. Finally I see someone pulling out. After parking and continuing to procrastinate for several more minutes, I get out and tread down the steep hill to the restaurant. On the way, I distract myself by second-guessing my blue dress and sandals the entire time. Too dressy? Too casual? Who cares? What am I so nervous about?

I pause halfway to shake out my arms and bounce off my toes, left and right like a boxer before a match, to release nervous energy. What the heck is wrong with me? Anyone watching me right now must think I'm a lunatic.

It's just Xander, for Pete's sake, my childhood chum. *Get a grip, Jameson.*

I take a deep breath and walk the rest of the way and pause when I reach the restaurant. Two tall, thick glass doors with "Rubicon" stenciled across them offer entry. I take another deep breath, pull on the handle, and as I step inside and let the weighty door slowly close behind me, I peruse the interior scene. Xander said he'd be waiting at the bar. Only, the last time I saw him he was ten years old. I expected I would recognize him by his dark hair and green eyes and the smile I remember, but now I'm questioning that assumption. I'm sure I could pick him out by his laugh, but it's not likely he'll be sitting by himself laughing like a mental case, so I try to conjure up his boyish face in my mind and scan for suspects.

My eyes trail over the long bar, searching. Had I known how many dark-haired, twenty-something potentials would be here, I might have asked him to bring a red rose or wear something distinctive like they do in the movies. Before I finish scanning, however, one of the men turns and meets my eyes and that's when everything else falls away.

No more conversational din, no more clinking glasses, no more rushed hubbub of a busy hotspot. For a brief moment as our gazes connect, the clamor just ... *stops*. Then the man slowly smiles and his eyes (are they green?) crinkle in an irresistible way that feels ... warm ... and familiar. I peer over my shoulder to ensure the true source of his attention—presumably a tall, willowy supermodel—doesn't exist, and then I turn back. Nope, gorgeous guy's eyes are still on me.

Please, oh please, if there's any kindness in the universe at all for a girl who's had a very bad day, please let this heavenly specimen be my Xander River.

Five Months Earlier

Chapter Two
Dany

I'm fumbling with my earbud as I hustle through the casino and attempt to hear the caller on the other end of the phone.

"…you back here." I manage to get one earbud in properly. *Ah,* now I can hear actual words over the unrelenting electronic dings from the rows of slots and poker machines.

"What was that?" I answer as I continue to thread my way through the crowd.

"Angus is sick. We need you back here at the booth, Dany."

The wind deadens abruptly from my sails and I halt at the elevator banks. "Sick?" I ask. "Or hung over?"

I don't even listen for the answer because I already know. The locations change, but some version of this story always ends with me filling in for some sales guy who partied too hard. Good ol' Dany Jameson who can go 12 hours without as much as a bathroom break. Or, for that matter, a day off in almost two years.

After all day on the expo floor for the Open Tech Universe (OTU) conference in Las Vegas, all I was thinking about was getting up to my hotel room, putting my feet up, and ordering a giant burger from room service, or maybe a pizza. Or both. And I was dreaming of seeing natural light and eating French fries and lying on a bed—or even on the floor would be fine at this point. To say I'm starving doesn't begin to describe the shriveled, pleading state of my stomach. Now David is calling to tell me that Angus, one of his fellow reps—who was supposed to relieve me at our booth four hours ago—can't work even the last two hours of his shift that remains.

Typical.

I hang up with David when another call comes in.

"Hey, where are you?" asks Becca.

"Your boyfriend is barfing his guts out," I reply.

"Who?"

"Dream boy, Angus. Hurling his guts into a trash can. Again."

She laughs. "One date with that idiot and you'll never let me live it down."

"Just wanted to make sure you realize you didn't give up on a hidden gem there."

She laughs. "Where are you, then?"

"Headed back to the booth. I don't have much choice." Elevator doors for the Mirage open as we're talking and I glumly watch as they start to close again. I want to step in, but how is it going to look to potential customers—and investors—if our company is being represented by Mr. "I'm the party" Angus? Resentment emerges from my throat as a frustrated growl.

"Jared and I have a meeting with an angel investor in an hour," Becca says. "Or else I'd try to give you a break."

"No worries. If we don't get the funding, none of it will matter eventually anyway."

"See you at 8:00 then? For dinner?"

Dinner. The thought of food makes me practically weep. "Yep. See you then."

I hang up, turn around, and start to walk back towards the expo. But after one step forward, I stop. I know I have to go back, but do I have to go back *immediately*?

Continuing forward will take me back to our booth … and lovely Angus. Turning around, on the other hand, leads to the elevators and my room on the 27th floor with a fluffy pillow-top mattress.

C'mon, will it kill anyone if I just go lay flat on my back for five lovely minutes? Or ten? And maybe scarf down a Snickers from the mini bar while I'm at it? Is that too much to ask?

"No. It's not," I grumble defiantly as I spin around and punch the call button for the elevators again. For once I'm putting the pillow-top first. For ten minutes, tops, but it's a start.

I lean against the wall of the elevator, taking the weight off my impaled-on-nailbeds feet as I enjoy the whoosh of being propelled upwards. When the elevator opens at my floor, I hesitate. I feel guilty. I really should have gone straight back to the expo.

But I've come this far … I may as well give myself a break and lie down for a minute. Maybe Jared will be there. Becca said their next meeting wasn't for an hour. Hopefully we'll secure the next round of funding. It's make or break time for Synsa, our company. Of course it always seems that way when you're working for a startup, but this influx truly could take us to the next level. It's why we've all been working so hard for so long. And why Jared's been so stressed lately. Synsa is his baby and I want this to work for him … and for us. I put my heart and soul into the company for the past two years, too. Jared's enthusiasm has always been contagious—it's why I accepted the job in the first place. And it's one of the reasons I fell for him soon after.

I press my keycard to the door and open it swiftly. The sweet relief I feel as I kick off my shoes in the hallway and walk towards the waiting king-size bed nearly manifests as giddy tears. When I round the corner, however, I let out an involuntary yelp. I stop short, unsteady, and try to focus my eyes.

Jared is here in our room.

But he's not alone.

My eyes eventually absorb why my brain is stuck in a hanging, confused reboot.

There's a girl in bed with him.

And it's Becca. My best friend.

Chapter Three
Mira

"Your birthday is coming." Grandpa Edwin says the words in his usual matter-of-fact way as we eat our eggs. Since I started living in the cottage in his back yard it's become a routine to join him in the main house for breakfast at least once a week. Throughout college and graduate school I had been living with my nan and Grandpa Mark, but when I was ready to get my own apartment, Grandpa Edwin convinced me to move into his cottage. One of the perks he touted was breakfasts like this. Having ready access to a washer and dryer was another. But the biggest perk, of course, was free rent. Who can say no to that? Even if my new cottage apartment is only two houses down (and across the street) from where I grew up, it still feels like a step up in independence and perhaps a sign of everyone loosening the reins a little.

"My *birthday*? Isn't it a little early to be talking about that?"

"You're going to be twenty-five." The deep register of Grandpa Edwin's voice is normally soothing, but I sense an underlying tension today.

I lower the forkful of eggs in my hand back to my plate. "And?"

"Twenty-five is a momentous year," he says as he stirs his tea slowly.

"More so than twenty-four? Or any other?"

He sets his spoon down. "Yes. It's a transformative year. It's important to remain focused and ... vigilant."

"Vigilant? What the heck does that mean? Are you trying to scare me or is this leading to another one of your rules?"

Ever since I can remember, Grandpa Edwin has always had a list of rules for me: from the mundane that all kids follow like not giving my full name to strangers, to the quite odd like never shaking hands and avoiding certain people entirely. As I grew up, the rules changed over time—some new ones added, some old ones dropped—but for the most part I've always abided by them. Mostly because the memory of the one time I didn't still makes me shudder. Suffice it to say I don't love all the rules, but Grandpa Edwin is persuasive and I pay attention, because he seems to sense things that others don't.

"I believe you should be vigilant about giving yourself the space and time to focus."

"To focus on what?"

"Discovery."

"Discovering what?"

"Yourself."

I stare at him, confused. "You mean discovering what I'm supposed to do?"

"Certainly," he replies with a nod.

Now we're on familiar terrain at least. All my life, I've had this nagging feeling that there's something I'm headed towards—some plan. And every time I think I've worked it out, like finishing my education and getting my job at the hospital, it always feels as if there's more, forever out of focus in the distance. Grandpa Edwin (and everyone else for that matter) has encouraged me to just keep following my instincts and that's what I've been doing, but the nagging feeling never goes away or feels complete.

"How is turning twenty-five going to help me all of a sudden?" I ask.

"You won't know unless you stay focused."

I glance at him skeptically. I can't see how turning twenty-five will do magical things for me, but it seems harmless to go along with the idea that it could be possible. "Okay, Grandpa, I'll focus … or be vigilant … although I have no idea what that means in terms of living my actual day-to-day life."

"May I suggest a new rule?"

"I *knew* it! I knew that's where this was going."

He ignores my outburst. "I'd like to suggest that, until your birthday, you refrain from dating anyone."

"*What?* Are you serious?"

He nods.

"Why?"

"You may encounter new people who enter your life this year but if you remain focused you'll be better able to follow your instincts and not get distracted."

I raise an eyebrow. "I think I've been pretty focused my whole life, Grandpa."

"Yes, but twenty-five is an important year." The look on his face is so serious it has me a little worried.

"You realize this is kind of crazy, don't you? Even as your rules go?"

He flashes a reassuringly sane-looking smile. "Humor me."

"My birthday isn't for more than six months."

His expression doesn't change.

I take a deep breath and exhale as I consider what he's asking. "It's not like I have a rip-roaring dating life anyway," I mutter.

"So you agree?"

I take another deep breath. Memories of Dusty, my last disaster date, swirl in my mind. "If you honestly think this will help me find the answers to all the questions in my head … then, what the heck, until my birthday, I'll agree."

He smiles. "Brilliant."

I let out a laugh, scoffing at myself for what I've just agreed to. "Grandpa, I can't decide sometimes if you're a little crazy or just eccentric and random."

He chuckles, but after a few moments his expression turns serious. "The most important thing to know is that I'm always looking out for you, Miracle." The tone of his voice and the use of my full name—something he does only when making a serious point—causes me to study his eyes as he sips his tea. He's frustratingly inscrutable, as usual.

We finish eating, and when I'm in my car and headed to work I continue to ponder my oddly persuasive grandpa and what his crazy rule (and the entire conversation for that matter) was really about. As usual, his instructions are so obtuse that, other than not dating, I'm not sure what I'm supposed to do exactly and why. When I was younger I used to think of him as a Jedi master whose vague instructions were meant for me to puzzle out—the more difficult they were to understand, the more important the message.

Now I wonder if he's just nuts.

Except that he's been right in the past.

Chapter Four

Dany

It feels peculiar to wake up every morning and not have a job with a never-ending list of Critical Things To Do. The last four weeks (is that how long it's been?) honestly feel like a fever dream. I blew up my life in spectacular form and speed, yet each decision seemed perfectly sane at the time:

1. Tell Jared he's a flaming pile of garbage. **Check.**

2. Throw the keys to our apartment in his stupid, shifty liar face and walk away with just a suitcase. *Hmmm, maybe a little extreme?*
   Who cares, let him deal with a bunch of stuff I don't need anyway. **Check.**

3. Quit job. *Understandable reaction... although perhaps a tad hasty without other employment in place?*
   Let it slide, I was on a roll. **Check.**

4. Get in the car and drive. *First vacation in two years is applauded, but having an actual destination in mind rather than just meandering across the country might be helpful at some point?*
   Perhaps, but right now distance is what I'm after. **Check.**

5. Burn the image of Jared and Becca in our hotel room out of my skull forever. *Ugh.* **Unable to check.**

I can't erase the initial sight or the immediate aftermath from playing over and over in my head: Becca's cool eyes and Jared's guilty shock followed immediately by what looked like an equal measure of relief, which was like a second sucker punch to the gut.

The life I had built (the illusion, anyway) tumbled down, one lying, betraying domino after another. Wresting out the details: how long, when, where, why, how, *how-could-you?*—the questions that twist your insides and make you feel like an idiot retroactively—just seemed pointless once I got all the answers.

What did it even matter? The bottom line is they're both lying schmuckface dirtbags.

And now you know, so you can move on to something real.

That's my consolation prize (or so I keep telling myself). No more wasting time and staying stagnant. More than two years in one place was at least one year too long, anyway. My peripatetic ways were always calling to me in the background but I kept tuning them out because of Jared. Boston was nice, but it wasn't my final stop. I always knew that on some level, didn't I? Or maybe I'm just making stuff up now to make myself feel better.

Regardless, the slow drive across country has been nice. Even the pit stop in Kansas where I visited my family was pleasant enough, although the whole time I had that familiar feeling in my gut that I needed to keep moving. I love my family and I know they love me, but I can't say that I've ever felt quite understood by any of them, and I'm sure the feeling goes both ways. When I hugged everyone goodbye and put my childhood home in the rearview mirror, I think everyone felt satisfied all the way around.

When I finally reached California and couldn't go farther west, I turned north and drove up the coast on Highway 1, enjoying the gentle curves and turns and the view of the endless blue ocean. Somehow, being on Hwy 1, not Hwy 90 or 40 or 66, but number *one*—the beginning, where it all starts—feels right. Last night I stayed along the central coast in Cambria, and now, hours later, I'm wondering where I might stop again when I reach a stretch of Highway 1 that becomes a main street running directly through a Northern California town. That's when I see the mural.

The entire side of the large rectangular concrete building to my right is painted with a large surf town mural in four simple colors. The background is red and there's a black silhouette of a girl in the middle on a beach cruiser holding a blue surfboard in her right hand as she rides her bike, carefree, and the wind blows her long hair back. The words "Welcome to San Mar," stretch across the top in bold white letters, and the girl's hair and surfboard partially obscure the "o," "S," and "a" in the middle. The rich, sky-blue color of her board perfectly matches the real blue sky above the building and all around. The cloudless perfection of the sky blurs where the mural ends and real life begins and I can't stop staring at it. I don't know why but I pull over and park.

I study the mural for a long time and then I decide to go into the building. It's a bike shop. As I look around, I notice a quote painted on the wall above the register: *"A good traveler has no fixed plans, and is not intent on arriving."* - *Lao Tzu*

"Hi, can I help you?" the young guy behind the counter calls out.

I surprise myself with my answer. "Yes, I'd like to buy a bike."

Chapter Five
Mira

When I get to the beach, I check in at the volunteer station under the large blue and white Healing Waves banner. From the looks of all the people and families, the turnout this year is bigger than ever. The blue sky is cloudless and the sun is warm and welcoming. Even the break looks ideal. The cooperation of the weather and the waves signal a perfect day for an event that couldn't be more deserving.

"Mira!"

I turn in the direction of the sweet little voice behind me. "Rafi!" I answer with equal enthusiasm. "You made it!" I tread through a maze of beach blankets to find my favorite pint-sized patient already suited up in a wetsuit and standing proudly with his parents, Sana and Sivar, on his towel in the sand. I bend down to give him a hug and he wraps his arms around my neck. "I'm so happy to see you. Are you ready to ride your first wave?" I ask.

Rafi nods excitedly. His gapped-tooth smile is so adorable and earnest it makes my heart ache to see him, but when I look up and catch his parents' eyes it's obvious they're nervous.

"This program has been going on since I was a kid," I assure them. "They know what they're doing." I turn to Rafi. "I'll be your tandem surfer today. It's going to be a lot of fun." I look back up at his mom and dad. "In addition to me, there'll be surfers on rescue boards on both sides."

"All these kids are like Rafi?" asks Sivar.

"No, but they all have physical or developmental challenges of some kind. Last year I worked with a girl who was blind and a little boy with autism. There's even a special surfboard with a chair on it for kids with paralysis."

"They're brave," Sana says as she surveys all the kids and their families across the beach.

"Very," I agree as I look down at Rafi. The only sign of the burns that cover half of his body is a small bit of taut skin peeking out from his wetsuit on the side of his neck. "Another one of my patients from the pediatric burn unit is here who I'm hoping Rafi can meet. I spoke with her parents and they'd like to meet you. She's a few years older—ten—and she's very sweet."

Sana smiles and reaches out to squeeze my hand. "Thank you, Mira. That would be lovely."

The next several hours are a blur of wet smiles, shrills of joy, and tearful thanks from parents who get to see their kids conquer fears, accomplish dreams, and enjoy surfing in the ocean just like any other kid. I manage to introduce my other patient, Maddy, to Rafi during the lunch break and later I see their parents exchanging numbers. I know firsthand that talking with other kids who understand what you're going through is just as important as physical therapy sessions.

On the last ride of the day I act as one of the four rescue boards for Henry, a smiling boy who loves dolphins and has cerebral palsy. Dale, a paramedic, is with him on the surfboard and the rest of us are all people I've teamed with before, except for a handsome blonde guy who has paddled in to act as the additional rescue board on my side. He smiles at me in the water and the brilliant azure blue of his eyes nearly stops my heart.

"I'm Charlie," he says with a pleasantly deep voice. At least that's what I think he said. I'm still mesmerized by his eyes and smile.

I nudge my wandering mind back to the moment and introduce myself and then we turn our focus to Henry. After careful prep with the team we're rewarded with his hoots of delight as he rides a wave. Several more times we work together until all of us have permanent smiles plastered on our faces as we bring him in and he rejoins his mom and dad.

Afterwards, on the beach, I say goodbye to a few friends who are leaving, and then I find my towel and bend over to shake out my hair and dry it off. When I'm finished I raise my head and flip the towel up onto my shoulder and I hear someone blurt, "Ow," and I'm startled to see Mr. Blue Eyes from the ride with Henry standing in front of me. He's out of his wetsuit now and he's in board shorts and an O'Neill t-shirt that stretches across his broad shoulders nicely. He's laughing while he rubs his chest with his fingers.

"Did I hit you with my towel?" I ask, confused.

"I think the edge of your towel flipped up something from the sand." He bends over to pick up what looks like a coin lying on the sand between us.

"Really? Oh my gosh, I'm sorry. Are you okay?"

He smiles. "I'm fine. It's just a penny."

"What year is it?"

He turns it over in his hand. "1981."

"That's lucky. You should keep it."

21

He raises an eyebrow. "1981 is lucky?"

"My Uncle Finn once told me that 1981 is the last year pennies were made of copper. So anything 1981 or earlier is lucky, because it's real."

"And now they're all fake?"

I shrug. "What would you call a lump of zinc masquerading around with a thin veneer of copper plating?"

"An abomination."

I laugh. "Not to mention a fraud."

"How dare they masquerade like that."

"Exactly." Our laughter fades until we're left staring at each other and smiling. He holds the penny out to me in his hand.

"What are you doing?"

"Giving it back to you."

"It's not mine."

"Well, even so, you just said it's lucky, so you might want it."

I shake my head. "I subscribe to fate more than luck."

He studies me for a moment. "I'm not sure fate and luck are all that different, but I'll keep it." He slips it into his pocket. "I'm feeling lucky today."

"You're feeling lucky after you just got hit by a flying penny?"

He laughs. "Can we start over?" He smiles disarmingly. "I'm Charlie. We helped Henry together."

I smile back. "I know. I'm Mira."

"I know."

His eyes meet mine and I get that same fluttery feeling I felt out on the ocean when I first saw him.

"Today was fun," he says. "Have you done this before?"

I nod. "Every year. It's a cliché, but I think the volunteers get more out of it than anyone."

"The kids really seemed to enjoy being out in the water."

"It's freeing," I say with a nod. "And to be able to share a little of the feeling I get from being out in the waves … it's nice."

He nods. "It's peaceful out there."

I smile. "This your first year?"

He nods.

"How'd you hear about it?"

"I'm from San Mar originally and I moved back, for work, about a year ago. I heard the program was looking for some corporate funding."

"And you think your company might donate?"

He nods.

"And your job is to check out possible charities to sponsor?"

"Something like that."

"Well, this is definitely a worthwhile cause. But I'm sure you saw that today."

He nods. "How did you get involved?"

The sincere interest in his blue eyes makes me offer more than my standard vague answer. "I benefitted from it myself, as a kid."

"Oh yeah?" No change in tone or expression. Not the reaction I usually get.

"Mm-hmm." My wetsuit is already half unzipped and folded down at my waist. I reach down to peel it down my legs as well but then I hesitate. *You don't have to do this.* I waver but then I convince myself that if I'm going to scare him off, I may as well do it quick. After all, I'm standing here talking to a nice, cute guy with the most interesting blue eyes I've ever seen, but even if he's interested in me, I just promised Grandpa Edwin I wouldn't date anyone. *Curse these stupid rules. Why do I always agree?*

I bend and peel the wetsuit down all the way, and rotate so he can see my left leg. "I needed a lot of physical therapy as a kid. Learning to surf helped."

He takes note of my leg and nods. "That's great that you're giving back. It says a lot about the program." His expression is neutral and sincere. "And about you, too," he adds, finishing off with a smile that knocks me off kilter.

Did he not register the zigzagging scar that craters deep into the muscle and runs down the side of my entire leg? I have a handful of explanations at the ready, depending on what mood I'm in: shark bite, rabid squirrel attack, trapeze accident, to name just a few.

He scrunches one eye in the late afternoon sun. "Can I ask you something?"

Here it comes: how did I get the injury, does it limit my abilities, how sad, I'm so sorry, blah blah blah ... nothing unkind, just typical. I nod. "Sure."

His eyes connect with mine before he speaks. "Would you like to get something to eat?" He runs his hand through his tousled blonde hair, displaying a touch of nervousness. Does he not realize how good looking he is?

I'm standing here with my wetsuit rolled down to my ankles, dramatically showing off my disfigured leg and he has no reaction or questions, he's just asking me out. A strong gust of wind off the ocean right now could knock me over.

"We wouldn't even have to leave the beach," he continues quickly. "We could go up to the Bliss Inn." He points in the direction of the beachside hotel, steps away. "And we could eat on the terrace."

I look at him for a beat, trying to figure him out. "Are you trying to reassure me that we'll be out in the open so I won't think you're a serial killer?"

He laughs. "Is it working?"

I smile. "Maybe."

"Does that mean you'd like to eat?"

"Yes." I blurt it out with a broad smile before I remind myself of the promise I made only this morning. I war with myself for a moment over whether it would be an actual "date." Couldn't we just be striking up a friendship? But when I look in his eyes I know I can't get around this with semantics. I made a promise—only hours ago—and nothing good ever came from bending the rules. Grandpa Edwin's edicts may not always make sense, but I'm the one who signed up to this and I need to follow through. Blue-eyed Charlie definitely counts as a possible new distraction.

"No," I say. "I mean, I thought I could, but I can't."

He looks confused. "Is right now not good? We could go later."

I shake my head. "No, I'm sorry." I want to tell him that if "later" means in about half a year, then great, put it on the calendar. But the thought of trying to explain to him that my grandfather asked me to follow a "no dating until my birthday" rule (and I—*a grown woman*—agreed) is a bridge too far. Attempting to explain will only make me look crazy or, at best, it'll sound like an insultingly wacky made-up excuse.

"Okay …" The expression in his eyes is about what you'd expect from a guy who thinks he's been shot down, and my heart lurches in my chest. *Should I try to explain?* "Uh … okay … well, it was nice meeting you, Mira. I had fun with you today."

As he makes tracks away from me on the sand, I consider calling him back several times, but what would I say? I remind myself that the whole point of this rule is to stay focused. For what? I have no idea, but the thought of figuring out whatever it is that remains tantalizingly out of reach in my mind is too important to let go of at the first sign of a cute guy.

I turn to look out over the water. It's fairly deserted now after the day's hubbub. You'd think I'd be tired from being in the ocean most of the day but the waves are calling to me—stronger, even, than they usually do. And where am I more focused than when I'm out in the waves?

I pull my wetsuit back up and decide to heed the call. I grab my board and head back in.

Chapter Six
Dany

In a strange sort of retail-induced trance, I get entirely kitted out at the bike shop. I purchase not only a powder blue beach cruiser, but a cute basket for the front, a storage rack for the back, a chain lock, a side surfboard rack, and a bike rack to affix the entire rig onto my Prius. All told, I'm pretty sure I've been taken over by aliens who think I have money to burn.

With directions given to me by my friendly bike salesman, I stop about a half mile down at a surf shop to rent a wetsuit and board and then, continuing my scavenger-hunt-like odyssey, I follow the surf shop guy's directions to the beach.

I can't explain it and I know it's corny, but the ocean is calling to me. As if the answers to the questions that have been roiling in my mind the past few weeks are waiting there. Questions like: "Where am I going?" "What the heck am I doing?" and "Have I gone completely nuts?"

It's a sunny, beautiful vista when I reach the cliffs above the beach. It's late in the day, but that's good because it's not crowded. There's only one lone surfer, far out in the waves. As I look out over the ocean, I take a hearty, soul-filling breath. I can't remember breathing this deep in a long time. I exhale and carefully make my way down the cliff side, board in hand.

When I reach the bottom I remove the booties that came with the rental suit. I scrunch my feet, drawing up the rough sand between my toes, and it feels good to connect with the earth in such a warm, visceral way. As I walk toward the water I relish the grainy massage my soles sustain with every footfall. At the water's edge I pause to look out over the vast blue waves, shielding my eyes from the late afternoon sun and letting the icy foam lap up to my ankles. I'm a little sweaty in my wetsuit at this point, and the brisk water feels good. For a long time, I stand and watch the surfer in the distance catch wave after wave. I can do that, right? I've been watching surfers all up and down the coast ever since I got to California.

Of course I haven't felt compelled to try it myself until now, but maybe that's because I've finally tipped into insanity, evidenced by me buying up a bike shop's inventory on a whim.

At least I *rented* the board and the wetsuit ... so maybe I'm not a total nutcase yet.

I slowly wade my way into the water and lie down on the board and start paddling.

Okay, Jameson, this could go slightly well or terribly unwell.

"Are you really a goofy foot?"

"Huh?" My ears are plugged with water. I turn in the direction of the shout and peer through the long strands of hair stuck to my face after my last epic wipeout, and I see the surfer I was watching earlier in the distance.

"Is that on purpose?"

I think those are the words I hear as the wet-suited silhouette paddles closer.

I've just surfaced after doing what felt like barrel rolls and I'm having a hard time hearing, seeing, or even knowing what day it is. "Falling? No, it's not on purpose," I say as I peel the hair from my eyes and get splashed in the face again. "I'm trying to surf."

The response is a loud laugh. The surfer paddles closer and it's clear now that the figure in the hooded wetsuit is a girl. She's smiling good-naturedly and I can't help but chuckle, too. The day I can't laugh at myself is the day I may as well pack it in.

"Left foot forward is regular," she explains, paddling even closer. "Right foot forward is 'goofy foot.' Either way is fine, it just depends on what feels best. But have you tried regular?"

I listen intently. Advice from a fellow surfer is highly welcome ('fellow surfer' being an overly generous term, considering my first-timer status and bumbling display). "I hadn't even thought about it, honestly."

"If it feels natural, what you're doing is probably best, but it can't hurt to try regular."

"None of this feels natural."

"Everyone starts as a beginner," she says with a smile. "The ones who get better are the ones who keep going. It's as simple as that. But you've got the hardest part down."

I raise an eyebrow. "If wiping out's the hardest part, then, yup, I've definitely got that down."

She laughs. "Actually, catching a wave is the hardest part—even harder than riding it."

I raise another dubious eyebrow.

"It's true," she insists. "When to paddle, how fast to go, and knowing where it'll break; getting into the right position and sensing the movement of the waves—that's the toughest part."

"Well I have no clue about any of that."

She shakes her head. "I've been watching you. You've got that part."

"You mean I'm actually doing something *right*?"

She laughs. "Do you ever watch the waves?"

"I guess." I shrug.

"Some people watch from shore for hours, learning wave dynamics."

"I like to watch but I wasn't studying them … clinically, anyway."

"Do you watch surfers?"

"Of course."

"Maybe you've been mind-surfing," she says. "You absorbed it without realizing it. You're a natural."

I snort out loud at the idea.

"I'm telling you," she insists, "it's much easier to teach someone how to ride a wave than to catch one."

"So you're saying there's hope for me yet?"

She smiles. "My nan always says there's hope for everyone. And when you're out here," she says as she gestures to the open sea, "there's always another wave coming, and that means another chance."

A rush ripples through me at her words. Another chance sounds good: a new start.

"I'm Dany, by the way," I say as I reach out my hand across the water. "Dany Jameson."

She flashes a bright smile that reaches her striking green eyes and moves to accept it, but our clasp is broken by a sudden large swell that bobs us apart. In the brief instant that our hands touched I felt a curious sensation: a strong pull, but also a push ... like a warning. *Strange.*

She laughs as she maneuvers back closer and grips my hand tight this time. "Let's try this again," she says with a smile. "I'm Mira. Mira Ronin."

Chapter Seven

Dany

"Have you taught many people?" I ask as we're trudging out of the ocean holding our boards. After all that paddling, my arms feel like overcooked noodles. I'm also starving, which is probably why I'm imagining my arms as spaghetti.

She shrugs. "Not formally. But I give tips if someone asks."

"Or if they look like a disaster who needs help, as in my case."

She smiles. "I remember how it was when I was learning for the first time."

"Who taught you?" Now that we're on even sand I can see that she's almost a head taller than me (then again, at five foot one, who *isn't* taller than me?).

"My first time was when I was five at a charity event that's held once a year. It was today, actually—I was here all day, volunteering. Anyway, I fell in love with surfing and I managed to convince my Grandpa Mark to keep teaching me—begged him to. My nan wasn't exactly thrilled, though."

"Why?"

"She worries ... understandably." She glances down for a moment. "But once she watched me out there a few times, she came around."

"Because you were a natural?"

"God, no," she says with a laugh. "But I was determined." She meets my eyes intently. "And by the way, if you stay with this and keep at it, you should know that in the busy spots, most surfers are polite, but some guys don't wait their turn. You just learn to claim it. Always remember that you have just as much right to be here as anyone else."

I nod. I like this girl.

We reach our towels and begin to remove our wetsuits. When she shakes off her hood, a long wave of golden hair emerges and as she peels off the suit from her limbs I can't help but notice a deep, jagged scar running the length of her left leg. From the way she handled herself surfing, though, it doesn't seem to slow her down any.

I also notice that her green eyes are even more striking up close on land. They're radiant and full of shiny … *kindness* is the only way I can put it—almost luminous, as if they're lit from within.

Or maybe I'm just hallucinating at this point, after the humbling beatdown I just took from the waves.

"Is this your favorite spot?" I ask. "To surf?"

"Hmm." She tilts her head to one side and then the other as she towels out her ears. "I have a few, all for different reasons. This is a good beginner's spot. But for me, as long as I'm anywhere out in the ocean, I'm happy." She finishes toweling and lifts her head up, facing out to the water. "I feel like when I'm out there, that's where the answers are."

I go still at her words, which are so similar to the thoughts I had earlier. "What answers are you looking for?"

"I don't know … plans … life …" She looks over and smiles. "The best tacos."

I chuckle. "I could actually go for a taco right now. Or two … or ten."

"Or *twenty*." She laughs. "There's a taco truck parked by the Bliss Inn. You up for some?"

"Definitely." If stomachs could cheer, that's what mine is doing right now.

When we reach the bright yellow food truck with "Rico's" written on the side in large script, I notice the peace I feel in this moment—the same peaceful "rightness" I felt intermittently out on the ocean (even after some spectacular wipe-outs). The brief warning from earlier feels distant now, or maybe it was never there.

I toy with the idea that this is the answer. Maybe this is what I've been driving towards. It's the first place I've been—maybe ever—where I don't feel compelled to move on.

Am I fooling myself to think all the answers I've been searching for could be here in a little beach town in Northern California?

As I ponder these thoughts (along with what kind of taco to order and how many), I notice a man, off to the side, who seems to be staring at us. He's in a crowd of people, and I don't know that I would have singled him out except that I think I've seen this dark-haired man before.

He was also in the parking lot outside the bike shop.

Chapter Eight
Dany

"Wow," Mira says as we sit on our towels on a ledge above the sand, devouring our tacos.

For some reason I just spilled my guts to this girl I hardly know. She has an openness about her that begs you to divulge. I blurted out everything in one long, cathartic purge. I even included the whole "the ocean is calling to me" business. TMI? Maybe. She probably thinks I'm a kook.

"So you just up and left when you got back to Boston?" she asks.

"Yep." I pop the "p" and then brandish a weak smile. Warring factions in my head are squabbling over whether I acted quickly and decisively or rashly and ridiculously. The latter is currently winning out. *Did I just blast my life apart in a fit of pique?* After recounting the whole story to a stranger, I have to admit it sounds a little nutty. I fan myself with a napkin.

"You didn't take *any* of your stuff?" she asks again.

"Just what I could fit in my car."

I swallow hard. I don't mention that I actually didn't *have* that much stuff to begin with. But the fact that I've always been a bit of a nomad and yet I managed to stay in one place for more than two years because all I ever did was work seems far too pathetic to add to the story at this point.

Yes, I left some baggage back in Boston—some literal, but mostly figurative.

I don't miss any of it though ... except maybe I miss my couch. It was a nice couch—stylish but comfy.

I'm reassured to see that Mira doesn't seem alarmed by any of my disclosures. "You must have sensed that was the best way to break free. And now, like you said, you feel like you're in the right place."

"I don't know. My intuition obviously wasn't firing on all cylinders before, so how can I trust it now? And how will I know the next guy I meet isn't another lying schmuckface?"

She laughs. "Because I think you're tuned into your DS now."

"My what?"

"Your deep sight. My Grandpa Edwin always says most thoughts are noise but if you tune in and really listen, you hear what's important. You had a feeling and you paid attention. That was your DS."

I shake my head. "You mean catching Jared? That was pure chance, not intuition."

"It's more than intuition. And you may think it was pure chance, but maybe it wasn't."

I take a deep breath in and consider her suggestion. Did I know? On some level? One thing I'll admit is that I always felt something was missing with Jared—that extra 'zing' you always read about in stories of true love. But does that even exist? We talked about our future and he even mentioned marriage. It made me nervous and I thought I was just scared about settling down, but maybe I knew, deep inside, that something was off? I ponder that possibility for a long moment but come to the conclusion that despite any doubts I may have had about whether Jared was "the one," I didn't suspect he was cheating—with Becca, of all people. I feel like a colossal fool again just thinking about it.

"I didn't suspect," I insist.

She shrugs. "It's not always a conscious thing."

The only "conscious" things I remember feeling before I walked in on them were exhaustion, hunger, and aching feet ... but I have to admit that it *was* unlike me to blow off going back to the booth right away to relieve Angus. I may be a nomad but I'm dependable as hell.

As I continue to mull over my levels of willful obliviousness, Mira turns to look out over the ocean.

"I sort of have the opposite problem," she says, breaking the stretch of silence.

"What do you mean?"

"I kind of have this thing where right away I know what people are all about."

"How?"

She shrugs. "I shake their hand or look into their eyes or whatever and I just know."

"*Really?* Always?"

She nods. "As far back as I can remember. When I was little, my Grandpa Edwin even had a rule that I wasn't supposed to shake hands with anyone."

"Why?"

"I think because the feelings were so strong."

"So he made it a *rule*?"

"One of the rules. There were others."

"And you followed them?"

She nods. "That's why I admire your story—you just took off on a whim and traveled across the country by yourself. I could never do that."

"Of course you could."

She shakes her head. "Maybe if my DS urged me to … but that's just it—it doesn't. I've always felt the rules are good ones. Besides, everyone has always wanted me to stay close to home. I even went to college and grad school locally."

"So you just follow all these rules?"

"It sounds nuttier than it is," she says with a laugh as she looks up at me. "But, yeah, I follow them. The one time I didn't …" Her voice trails off and she glances down. "Let's just say I never had the urge to do it again."

I'm wildly curious and want to ask more, but it's clear she doesn't want to talk about it and something in me senses that I shouldn't go there.

Her demeanor is brighter when she looks back up. "So now you think I'm crazy, right?"

I laugh. "Not really. I'm just wondering how you managed it if someone tried to shake your hand."

"Fist bump," she says with a smile. "When you're a little kid, people think it's cute."

I laugh. "You shook my hand today, though, out on the water."

She nods. "It's not a rule I follow anymore. As I got older, I could control it better."

"So you just shake someone's hand and you *know* about people, straight off?"

She nods. "I don't always get a clear read, but usually. I used to think everyone had it, but I found out pretty quick that other kids thought I was nuts when I said something. That's when my Grandpa Edwin told me about DS. He said everyone actually *does* have it, they just don't realize it because they don't know how to listen. For whatever reason I guess I tune into it more easily."

"But how do you know the impressions you get are right?"

"I've tested it and it's never been wrong, as far as I know."

"How do you test something like that?"

She shrugs. "As a kid, it was easy. I'd just watch. The kids I had good or bad feelings about always revealed themselves eventually. Adults are harder. They're better at masking things. And sometimes it's not that I have a straight-up good or bad feeling about a person, it's more that I just don't feel a tug to make a connection. Like I'll meet a guy and he'll seem nice but I'll just know it won't go anywhere. I've tested that a few times—dated someone long past when I normally would stop—and I've always been right. I think of it as knowing what's fated in advance."

"God, if that's true, that's fantastic. I wish I had that."

"It's good most of the time," she agrees with a nod, but then she takes a long breath in and lets it out with a sigh. "On the flipside, though, the longest romantic relationship

I've ever had has been about two months. Sometimes I wonder if the guy I'm waiting for even exists."

I nod. "I hear you."

We're both silent for a moment of sisterly commiseration, but then her eyes brighten. "I met a nice guy today, though."

"Really? Did you see your fate with him?"

She laughs. "Not exactly, but I saw something in his eyes. Potential, maybe."

"Did you set up a date?"

She shakes her head. "I don't even know his last name. And, anyway, I can't date until …" She holds up her wrist and pretends to study an imaginary watch. "Almost six months from now anyway."

"*What?* Why?"

She scrunches her face. "You're going think this is nuts, but that's the latest rule: no dating until March 20th, my twenty-fifth birthday."

My jaw goes slack. "You're joking."

"I know. It sounds wacky. But my grandfather said this is an important time of discovery—and that actually kind of rang true for me. And he said I should focus on myself until then and I should–"

"No, I mean, yes, that *is* nutty, but is March 20th really your birthday?"

"Yes. Why?"

"That's *my* twenty-fifth birthday."

Her eyes widen. "You're joking."

I shake my head. "I swear."

She smiles. "See? Fate. I knew there was a reason I wanted to talk to you when I saw you out there in the water."

"Or maybe you just saw someone flailing around so atrociously that you felt the need to intervene."

She laughs, and as we finish our tacos and watch the sun go down, I marvel at the fact that I may have stopped here on a lark, but I think I just made a real friend here in San Mar.

Maybe I'll stay a while.

Chapter Nine
Mira

"Oh my God, not the eyes thing again," Gemma says comically as we're eating lunch on our break in the hospital cafeteria.

I laugh. "I'm serious. I've never seen eyes like that. They were so blue … and I could see into them deep, the way I like."

"Okay, then help me understand again why you turned him down—because of your *grandpa*?"

"I know. That part's crazy."

She shrugs. "It's not like it matters, though, because you basically say *nope* to everyone after the first date anyway. Does your grandpa realize you've been unintentionally following his 'no dating' rule your entire life?"

"Very funny."

"Maybe he should have assigned this rule a long time ago because it's only now, after you know it's off limits, that you finally found a guy you're truly interested in."

"I know, I know. But I'm telling you, it was more than that."

She puts up her hands. "Hey, I'm not arguing. In fact, I want to find this Miracle Mystery Man before you change your mind. But since the only information you have is his first name and his devastatingly blue eyes, it may be outside the range of my formidable detective skills. I don't know if

I can track this guy down and put him in front of you again."

I laugh. "You're not tracking anyone down."

"Believe me, I would if I could. But if you're finally open to giving a guy a chance, how about going out with Dr. McStudly over there?" She gestures with her eyes to Dr. Vince Wilder, sitting at a table a few feet away with some other doctors. "I don't understand how you can keep saying no to a perfect male specimen like that."

I glance over at him. "He's too ... *much*."

"Too much what? Too much tall, dark and handsome? Too much brains? Too much nice butt and forearms?"

I laugh. Vince Wilder is a swoon-worthy guy, I'll grant her that.

"His eyes aren't deep enough," I say finally. "And they're inconsistent—I don't always get the same feeling."

"Oh my God, not with the eyes again."

"He's also a player. Probably."

"You can't prejudge a man just because he's good looking. How about we find out? Just one date. And then report back. I'm an old, boring married lady. I need to live vicariously through you."

I look at her sideways. "You're only two years older than me."

She scrunches her face. "I'm old in spirit. All Ramon and I ever do now is stay home and watch Netflix."

"You honeymooned in Greece last year and he just surprised you with tickets to Aruba."

"All right." She throws her hands up. "We're not boring. But you still need to get out there more."

I shake my head. "You know I've been out there."

"But you can't know about a person instantly. You need to give more guys a chance."

"Like Dusty? The guy who kept asking about my foot size?"

She laughs. "Okay, not him. But others."

"But why waste time with guys who I know aren't right for me? I'm tired of dating apps and blind dates, and I don't want to date anyone from work—it's too messy. I think it'll be good to just take dating off the table for a while and focus on me."

"I can't argue with that," she says with a shrug. "But I'll still be waiting to hear about your date with Dr. McWildly-Handsome after your birthday."

I laugh. "You're going to be waiting a lot longer than that." I raise my sandwich and take a large bite and, as I'm chewing, my eyes focus past Gemma's shoulder out to the atrium. "Oh my God," I mumble through my mouthful of ciabatta roll and chicken.

Gemma turns and looks behind her and then turns back. "What is it?"

"ar-ey," I mumble as I try to finish chewing, motioning with my eyes behind her.

She looks again and turns back. "Are we?"

I shake my head. "ar-ey," I try again as I attempt to swallow.

"Tar weed?" she asks. "What's tar weed?"

I laugh, inhaling, and that's when the trouble starts. I cough. Twice.

"Mira, are you okay?"

My eyes go wide as I realize I'm not. I shake my head and point to my throat. I can't breathe.

"Oh my God, Mira, I'll help you," she cries out. She swiftly stands and her chair falls over with a clang, but before she makes it to my side of the table, Dr. Wilder appears in front of me. "Mira, are you choking?" he asks with calm, professional urgency as he evaluates the situation. Panicking, I motion with my hands to my throat but I can't make a sound. He nods and shifts into position behind me and delivers a swift Heimlich thrust, followed by another and another, and finally, after one more thrust, a lump of roasted chicken sails out of my mouth. I suck in air in a loud, panicked gasp.

And that's when I lock eyes with Charlie, standing in front of me, as vividly blue-eyed as ever, and whose name was the source of my failed attempt to alert Gemma that my dream guy was here, in our hospital. He's stopped in his tracks only a foot away from me now.

"Are you okay?" Gemma and Charlie ask in unison as Vince shifts from behind me to my side to make his own assessment.

I feel a dizzy wave rolling within my gut and before I realize what's happening I heave forward and empty the rest of my stomach.

The last image branded in my memory—as Gemma spirits me away to the bathroom—is Charlie staring down at his shoes, which are now covered in my upchucked chicken sandwich.

Chapter Ten

Dany

"Crushed it," I shout jokingly as I paddle back towards Mira. I just wiped out in spectacular fashion: ass over teakettle—or however that saying goes, which, by the way, where does that even come from and what the heck does it mean?

She's still laughing when I reach her. "It's only been a few weeks. You'll get there."

"Ever the optimist."

"You're better than when we started," she offers feebly.

"That is a very sad and very low bar to crest."

She laughs. "Who cares, really?" She spreads her arms with a broad smile. "We're out here."

I take a deep breath and tune into the sounds of the ocean all around us and I have to admit I agree.

"How was your interview on Monday at the *Sentinel*?" she asks.

"Good ... great, actually. I got the job."

"No kidding? Just like that?"

I nod. "They told me one of their reporters met some girl and just up and moved to Colorado with no notice, so they needed someone quickly."

"Here's to whirlwind romances," Mira says with a laugh.

"I know, right? I start next week."

"It's official then," she says with a broad smile, "you're staying in San Mar."

I nod. It already felt official—financially, anyway—when I signed the lease on my shoebox apartment and coughed up first and last month's rent plus a deposit. I pray the stock options I demanded Synsa let me keep are worth more than "hope on paper" one day.

"My new boss is nice," I say. "It turns out she went to school with an old boss of mine."

"Jared?"

"God, no. Before I took the job at Synsa I worked for a newspaper. That's what I got my degree in—journalism. I even worked for the small newspaper in my hometown when I was growing up."

"So you're getting back to your roots."

"Yep, and getting back to being paid a pittance," I say with a laugh. "But it's not as if journalists sit through zoning hearings or study public school financing formulas because we want to get rich."

She nods. "My grandpa Mark always says that people who do jobs that are part of the community and help to make it better—like school teachers and all the other jobs that don't pay nearly as much as they should—get their riches in the next life."

I laugh. "I still think we should all be paid fairly in *this* life, but I'm obviously not in it for the money. I like journalism and I like contributing to a community. And I like San Mar."

She smiles. "What's not to like? Except when you throw up on your possible dream man's shoes."

I laugh. "Was it really as bad as you said?"

"Worse."

"And you haven't heard from him since?"

She shakes her head. "Why would I? So far, I've nailed him with a penny, turned him down for a date, and now I threw up on him. I think he got the message."

I laugh. "Well, in case he's a glutton for punishment, at least he knows where you work now. That's good."

"I think the only good thing was that if I had to choke on a chicken sandwich, at least it was in a hospital surrounded by doctors."

"Actually," I say, waving my hand in the air, "not to toot my own horn, but I could have saved you no matter where you were. I saved my sister from choking when we were little."

"Seriously?"

I nod. "We were home alone and Karin was hogging a box of Twinkies, scarfing them all down before I could have one. She started choking and it was probably the only time she was truly thrilled to have me around."

"You gave her the Heimlich?"

"Yep—a big chunk of Twinkie came flying out."

Mira chuckles. "Did she barf on you afterwards?"

"No, she actually thanked me—sincerely—which was nice."

"Well, I'm sincerely thankful to Dr. Wilder … but not enough to say yes to a date, which I think shocked him."

"What did he say?"

"After Gemma helped me clean up, he came by and asked if I wanted him to make a house call later, to make sure I was okay."

"Smooth."

She laughs. "Too smooth. He joked that if saving my life didn't warrant a date then maybe he should give up. I honestly don't even know why he'd be thinking about dates after watching me hurl."

"He's tenacious, I'll give him that."

"And kind of funny, but even if I was dating right now, he's too perfect."

"And perfect is bad?"

She shrugs. "I don't know … he's just so perfectly suave and slick. Give me a nice humble guy over that any day. It's not that I get a bad feeling about Vince—although I have gotten an odd sense from him once or twice—it's mostly that I just don't get a strong feeling from him one way or the other."

"I say, follow your instincts. Maybe Charlie will circle back around."

She shakes her head. "I think when you barf all over someone it's a good bet they're not circling back for more."

We both laugh and she signals me to get into position for the next wave. Mira rides it into shore easily. I manage to stand for about three seconds, wipe out, get tumbled around, and then paddle into shore, dazed as usual. I deem it progress.

Ten minutes later, we're trudging up the steps to the parking lot, surfboards in hand. We usually ride bikes to the beach—the surfboard rack I bought for my cruiser has come in handy—but sometimes Mira drives her classic white Jeep Wagoneer, like today. I stop to admire it. It's a cool surfer car with wood siding and, although I never knew I had a thing for old cars, every time I see it I feel warm inside. She opens the back and we slide our surfboards in and then climb into the front.

Mira lets out a groan when she hops up into the driver's seat.

"You okay?" I ask.

She grimaces. "It's just my leg. Gets tight sometimes." She massages her leg along the jagged scar running the length of it.

"Anything I can do?"

"Nah, it'll be fine." She keeps massaging and then looks over. "You've never asked me how I got this." Her tone is curious, not accusing.

I shrug. "I assumed if you wanted to talk about it, you would."

She nods slowly and is quiet for a moment. "When you have an injury—in my experience, anyway—the people who usually talk about it have a *before* and an *after*. But I don't have a *before*. I've always been like this, so it almost feels as if when people ask what's wrong, they're asking what's wrong with *me*, not with my leg." She meets my eyes. "And I don't think there's anything wrong with me—this is just the way I am. Does that make sense?"

I nod.

"The worst was when I was a kid. All the stares—which I still get, but I'm used to now. And the teasing was hard."

"Kids can be mean," I say as my heart goes out to her.

She nods. "But sometimes adults can be even worse. I remember seeing a doctor once when I was thirteen and he commented to a nurse that it was a shame about my leg because otherwise I'd be a pretty girl. He didn't even bother to get out of earshot."

My heart tightens in my chest. I know she doesn't believe that about herself, but I also know words can wound no matter how strong we are inside. Especially when you're a girl in the throes of puberty. I feel like going back in time and socking that doctor in the face. Mira hides it well but I hear the hurt in her voice and it makes me hurt, too. "I'm so sorry, Mira, that people can be so ignorant and awful."

She nods and shrugs it off. "It's all right ... honestly. In the big scheme of things, it's nothing. Less than nothing. I know that. And I'm not the pity-partying type."

She looks up at me and smiles and I nod. I admire her stance, and I try to live by it myself, but I think we both know it still hurts.

"Sometimes I make up stories," she says.

"Stories?"

"About what happened to my leg."

"What kinds of stories?"

She shrugs. "Whatever amuses me that day."

"Why?"

"I guess because the truth is crazier than any story I can think of. I got tired of people not believing me, or the horrified reactions of those who did, and that's when I realized I don't have to share the whole truth with random acquaintances or strangers. I don't have to take that on—I can just make stuff up. Or say nothing at all."

"Makes sense. And I understand if you don't want to talk about it."

She shakes her head. "With friends I always tell the truth."

She pauses for a long moment and when she finally speaks it's obvious from the tone of her voice that she's not telling me a made-up story. "I was still in the womb when it happened," she says quietly. "My mom was hit by lightning and it traveled through her body and seared my leg down to the muscle. I was born a month early."

I'm stunned and not sure what to say.

"My dad was there and he was hit, too," she continues. "It was a freak accident and they both died. The doctors said it was a miracle I survived."

The news hits me with a sorrowful ache in my stomach.

"That's my full name, by the way: Miracle," she says with a wan smile. "Miracle Jane Alexandra Ronin. I thought my nan named me Miracle because of what happened, but she told me my mom already had the name picked out for me—as if she knew."

"I'm so sorry, Mira, about your parents."

She flashes a soft smile. "It's okay. I mean, I feel sad that I never knew them, but my nan and Grandpa Mark are my parents. Plus I have my Grandpa Edwin and Aunt Liz and Uncle Finn. You'll meet them sometime. There were days when I felt I had too many parents, to be honest." She lets out a laugh. "They're all pretty overprotective."

"It must be nice to have so many people looking out for you."

She rotates slightly to show me the length of the scar. "It kind of looks like a lightning bolt, doesn't it? And you want to know the weirdest part? It was dry lightning, which makes me wonder if I'm a phenomenally bad luck charm."

"What? Why?"

"Because I attracted this one-in-a-million lightning bolt that killed both my parents and it wasn't even raining. I never say this to my family because it makes them all sad to talk about it, but how unlikely—and *unlucky*—is that? I think that's why they're always trying to safeguard me all the time ... because they know I draw bad luck."

"Do you really believe that?"

She shrugs. "Sometimes."

"What does your DS tell you?"

She looks at me sideways. "You're using something I taught you against me?"

I smile. "Well, what does it tell you?"

"Unclear. Maybe it was fate."

"You believe the lightning strike was *meant* to happen?"

"Well, if it was going to happen no matter what, then it wasn't my fault."

"Mira, fate or no fate, it wasn't your fault."

"You don't believe that things happen the way they're meant to?"

I meet her eyes. "I don't know. Definitely not terrible things, or random, awful things. I guess I believe that we all make choices that nudge things along in different directions. But we have the power to make our own destiny. No one is inherently unlucky. We can't just leave things all up to fate."

"Or maybe all the little decisions people make lead to the same place in the end."

"That's kind of bleak."

"Or comforting. It's either that or I'm bad luck."

"It's not an either/or. If you truly draw bad luck—or think you draw bad luck—you wouldn't have gone to work in a hospital, would you have? And yet you work there, helping people. "

"Maybe I'm drawn to people who also have bad luck, or else they wouldn't be in the hospital in the first place."

She looks at me and the corners of our mouths quirk up into smiles.

"You don't believe that."

She shakes her head. "No. I don't. But the randomness of it gets me sometimes. Patients who get hurt through no fault of their own, in accidents or worse—the kids, especially. We've even had kids who came here for treatment after getting injured in war zones in other countries."

I nod at the sadness and senselessness of it all and she pauses before continuing.

"Caregivers usually rotate in and out of covering the pediatric burn unit, because it's rough, emotionally, but I don't rotate out. I know what it feels like to have an injury like that and be in pain, and not be able to do what you want to do and move the way you want to. I had a lot of surgeries as a kid and a lot of physical therapy. I want to help people the same way my physical therapist helped me."

"Which you couldn't do if you were constantly drawing bad luck."

She nods slowly. "Maybe you're right," she says quietly before she goes silent and stares out the windshield with an absent look on her face.

"This is my dad's old car," she says finally, breaking the silence as she grazes her hand across the faded dashboard. "I only use it for surfing. He and my mom were both surfers and I picture them riding in it with their boards in the back. Sometimes I wonder if any of the grains of sand in here are left over from when they used to come to the beach." She glances over at me. "It just doesn't seem right that their lives ended right when mine began. They were just getting started. My nan says they were 'magically happy' and deeply in love. I don't know if she's exaggerating, but my Aunt Liz always jokes that they were so in love it was almost enough to make you sick, so maybe it's true." She laughs and I feel a tingle go down my spine.

"People always ask if I miss them," she continues, "but how can you miss someone you never knew?" She looks over with a thoughtful expression in her eyes. "The one thing I wish is that I could know them in person—just for a day, even—instead of just from pictures and stories. Everyone always shares all the great stuff about people who died, but I want to know the imperfect stuff, too—like times when my mom felt unsure, or maybe when my dad made a mistake that he regretted. Stupid stuff like that ... so I could feel like I really know them, all the way around."

My heart feels unbearably tight and I reach over and hold Mira's hand as tears well up within me.

"Dany," she says when she sees my eyes, "I'm okay. Really." She squeezes my hand back. "I have great parents.

When my nan and grandpa get back from their trip, you'll see. I'm one of the lucky ones."

I nod, trying to hold back tears. "I'm sorry I'm getting so emotional. I think these are happy tears because of how you always talk about your family and how close you all are. In my family, everyone fits together like puzzle pieces but I've always felt like a piece from another puzzle entirely."

Her brows knit together. "Really?"

I nod. "I picture them all as a golden landscape and I'm a piece of blue ocean."

She smiles softly. "My Aunt Liz always says it's a mystery how we all get dropped on the planet, but eventually we manage to find our peeps."

We both laugh and I reach under the seat to where we hid our purses so Mira can extract her keys and we can go to lunch.

As Mira starts the engine, I turn to look out the side window and I'm startled to note that the man I've seen several times before is there once again, staring up in our direction from the beach below. Dark hair, leather jacket, and jeans—it has to be him. This can't be a coincidence, can it? His focused demeanor makes me feel he can only be looking at us.

I point my finger against the glass and turn to Mira. "Do you know that guy with the dark hair?" I ask. "I keep seeing him everywhere we go."

She leans over to my side and peers out the window. "What guy?"

I look again but I don't see him. *Did I imagine it?* "He's gone."

She shrugs. "Must have been a ghost," she says with a smile as she puts the jeep in gear and we pull out of the lot.

Chapter Eleven

Dany

"Wake up, slacker."

The voice breaks through my sleepy haze and I groan and pull the pillow over my head and that's when the poking starts.

"Get up," Mira repeats as she nudges me in the side repeatedly.

"Howdyougetinhere? I mumble into my pillow.

"Your fake rock Hide-a-Key. You need to get rid of that thing. It isn't fooling anybody."

Whyrryouhere?" I groan.

"Bootcamp. I've been calling you and knocking on your door."

I pull the pillow tighter. "Itsover," I mumble into the mattress.

"No, it's not."

Huh? I roll over to face her perched on the bed beside me. "Six weeks. Over." I roll back to bury my face in the pillow again.

"Sergei sent out a group text—I know you got it, so don't try to tell me you didn't—and he offered a bonus day."

I roll back to face her again. "It's not a bonus when you can't bend low enough to sit on the toilet for a month."

She laughs.

"I couldn't bend my legs, Mira. I peed on my sneakers in that port-a-potty."

Now she's laughing so hard it's shaking the bed. "I thought you liked the hill sprints," she says.

My eyes meet hers, deadpan.

"What?" she says with a laugh. "You're always smiling when we're doing them."

"That's not smiling, it's rictus. It's what happens when you lose control of the muscles in your face."

"Stop," she pleads, as she laughs harder. "I'm going to pee."

I shake my head. "I'm done. Sergei can light someone else's quads on fire."

"Everyone else is going: Peter, Bruce, Maeve, Javier, Sharri-"

"They're masochists. And Sharri's only going because she's in love with Sergei. She *wants* him messing with her quads."

Mira laughs. "Too bad he only has eyes for Bruce."

"Go tell her, then," I mumble. "Let her down easy."

"You go tell her. You're awake now anyway."

I grumble but she has a point.

"Suck it up," she says finally. "C'mon, it'll be hard, but you won't die from it."

I roll over to face her. "I won't *die* from it? Have you considered writing that one down? It's super motivational."

She laughs. "Get up."

"Fine," I grumble as I sit up and swing my legs over the side of the bed. "How'd you get in here anyway?" I ask as I rub my eyes.

"You asked me that already. Are you sleepwalking right now?"

"If I am, don't wake me up." I stand and head to the bathroom.

"Bring clothes to change into," she calls out as I squeeze a bead of blue gel toothpaste onto my toothbrush. I look up and startle myself by the degree of crinkled sleep-face and bedhead going on in my frightening reflection.

"We'll get breakfast after and then there's an art show downtown," she continues cheerily.

I shake my head. How can she be so damn peppy at 5:45 a.m. on a Saturday?

My legs are wobbly as we stretch after our boot camp-slash-torture session. Mira signed us up for it with a Groupon and I have to admit it's been fun—in a masochistic sort of way—getting up early every day with the same ragtag group of exercisers. Some are hardcore, some are grannies, and some, like me, are in between. Mira's co-worker Gemma started out doing it with us, too, but she refused to come back after the first day, which was funny … and smart.

Mira's a funny one, too. She's so cautious in a lot of ways—with all of her rules and whatnot—but within the parameters she allows herself to roam, she pushes herself with a determination that never falters. She told me when she was younger her left leg was much weaker and she had a limp. She had to do a ton of work to get where she is today and now you'd hardly notice anything if you didn't see the scar. Her attitude drives me to work harder and save most of my kvetching for later—in private—at home. I suppose she's motivational after all, in spite of her abysmal pep talks.

We took Sharri aside earlier to gently explain what was obvious to everyone but her, and now I see her looking with sad doe-eyes as Sergei and Bruce stretch together. I groan involuntarily as I switch legs and watch as Mira rifles through my gym bag on the ground. "Inside pocket," I say.

She stands up, victorious, with a bottle of water in her hand. She's also holding the envelope I shoved in there yesterday. "What's this?"

"My pen pal's coming to San Francisco next week for a conference. He wants to meet for dinner."

"The Australian guy?"

I lean into my stretch with a groan. "Yep."

"My Grandpa's from Australia. So was my dad."

"Really?"

She nods. "How long did your family live there?"

"Three years. We left right after I turned ten. Actually, he turned ten, too. His birthday's the day after mine … and yours. We used to have our parties together." I smile, remembering.

"And you haven't seen him since you left?"

I shake my head.

"All you've done is write letters?"

"Yep. And the past few years, hardly even that—maybe one or two letters a year. But I think neither one of us wants to let it go completely."

She smiles. "It's kind of romantic, in an old-fashioned way."

"We were ten," I say with a laugh.

"But you're not ten now," she says with a smile before she twists the top off the bottle in her hand and takes a swig. Her expression turns to surprise as her focus goes past my shoulder and she coughs up a spray of water which lands on her seafoam green tank top, leaving a wet spill mark on her chest.

"What is it?" I turn and try to follow her eye line but there are a lot of people around and I don't know what she's focused on.

"Oh my God, that's Charlie," she whispers. "On the pull-up bar."

My eyes follow her mesmerized gaze to a tall, fit, blonde guy doing pullups at the next parcourse station along the track. Even from this distance I can see his muscles flex and strain as he pulls himself up, over and over, above the bar.

I turn to look at her. "*Charlie* Charlie?"

She nods vigorously. "Yes, oh my God, don't let him see me," she murmurs in hushed tones as she crouches down.

I look back to see if he noticed. "Too late," I say under my breath. "I think he's headed over."

When he reaches us, he smiles. "Mira," he says with surprise. "I *thought* that was you." His smile is genuine and it reaches his eyes and I can't help but notice the blue brilliance that Mira's been talking about. "How are you doing?" he asks.

She rises up from her crouched position, faking (badly) coming out of a stretch, and she faces him.

"Mostly recovered," she replies with a weak smile. "How are your shoes?"

He laughs. "Mostly recovered."

She winces comically. "I wanted to get in touch with you to pay your cleaning bill but I didn't know how to find you."

He looks confused. "Dr. Wilder didn't give you my card?"

"Huh?"

"After your friend took you away, I gave my card to the doctor who saved you. I asked him to give it to you so you could call, if you wanted, to let me know how you were doing. I would have stayed but I was late for a meeting that I couldn't miss."

"You went to a meeting with my lunch on your shoes?"

He smiles. "I improvised."

Mira stares up into his eyes for such a long time I almost reach over and nudge her to see if she needs a reboot. "I never got your card from Dr. Wilder," she says finally. "I'm sorry."

His eyes meet hers. "I am, too."

There's so much restrained feeling behind both of their eyes that I almost want to clear the area to give them some privacy.

"Or I would have reimbursed you for new shoes," she adds.

He shakes his head. "I just wanted to make sure you were okay. When you didn't call, I thought about tracking you down later at the hospital, but I ... I don't know, I didn't want to–"

"Seem like a stalker?"

He laughs and shrugs his shoulders. "You already wondered if I was a serial killer. I didn't want to make it worse."

I have no idea what he's talking about being a serial killer, but I watch Mira laugh and as she stares into his eyes I realize, oh my God, this girl has got it *bad*. I can't say I don't approve: he's nice and funny and cute ... and hopefully not a mass murderer.

"This is my friend, Dany," Mira says, gesturing to me. I'm shocked she still remembers I'm here.

"Nice to meet you," Charlie says with a smile. We shake hands and I definitely get a supremely good vibe but it's hard to trust my feelings anymore after falling for schmuckface Jared. I wish I could muster the certitude Mira gleans from a simple handshake.

"Dany Jameson," I say, pointedly emphasizing my last name. "And you are Charlieee ... " I draw out the last syllable questioningly. I'm not letting this guy leave without getting his full name, rank, and cell number for Mira.

He smiles and looks down and pats the sides of his Nike gym shorts. "I'm sorry I don't have a card on me. I'm Charlie Bing." He turns to Mira. "My older sister Molly is on the board at San Mar Good Samaritan. I was visiting her the day I saw you in the cafeteria."

It slowly dawns on me who he is. "Are you Charlie Bing who started CDS?"

He nods.

"CDS?" Mira asks questioningly.

"Candle Data Systems," he answers.

"The CDS software we use at the hospital?" Mira asks.

He nods.

I can't help cutting in. "This is really weird that I'm standing here talking to you," I say to Charlie. "I've been trying to get an interview with you for weeks. I'm a reporter for the *San Mar Sentinel.* After you moved CDS headquarters here last year, it's now the largest tech company in San Mar."

He nods. "People said it was a mistake not to be centered directly in the valley with everyone else, but I grew up here and I wanted to be on the coast. I knew there was a lot of talent in town and I knew more would come if the jobs were here."

"That's exactly the sort of thing I'd like to talk with you about. Your PR team says you're booked solid, but I was just hoping to get on the schedule." *Be persistent, Jameson, and don't leave without the promise of an interview.*

"If you call them again on Monday, I'll make sure you're put through this time and we'll set something up."

"Great," I answer. *Can it be that easy?*

Mira is still staring at him oddly. "So when you said you were looking at sponsoring Healing Waves the day we met …." She leaves the end of her sentence dangling.

Charlie nods. "I was looking at it for CDS."

"But you didn't say it was *your* company."

"Would it have convinced you to go out with me if I had?"

She blushes and smiles. "No."

He nods his head slowly. "You're a hard one to figure out," he says with a wry smile. "An *enigma*." He over-enunciates the word jokingly and Mira laughs.

I want to shout out that they should just date each other already but I know Mira would kill me. She takes her rules seriously.

"Who's your friend?" Sharri asks cheerily as she pushes her way between Mira and me and sticks out her hand. "I'm Sharri," she says with an eager smile, apparently recovered from her crush on Sergei.

As Charlie and Sharri introduce themselves, Mira glances over and gives me the eye. "We have to go now," she says to Charlie, "but it was nice seeing you."

Charlie looks befuddled as Sharri keeps talking. "Nice seeing you, too," he says quickly as we move to leave, "and nice meeting you, Dany. I look forward to talking with you soon."

"Me, too," I say as I grab my gym bag. I almost feel sorry for him as we walk away. I glance back and notice him watching after Mira out of the corner of his eye as Sharri peppers him with questions.

When we're out of earshot, I speak. "Why'd you say we have to go?"

"Because I like him and I don't want to waver."

"Well, I hate to say it but I like him, too. For you."

"Why do you hate to say it?"

"Because you're stubborn and you won't date him. Until your birthday, anyway. Even though you clearly want to."

Mira glances back at him and Sharri. "I kind of put him out of my mind until I saw him again today. But when I looked into his eyes, that feeling I get, it's still there."

"Is that why you were staring at him like that?"

"Like what?"

"Like you were trying to read the fine print on his corneas."

Her eyes go wide. "Oh my God, did I look crazy?"

"Not at all. Everyone loves prolonged, unblinking eye contact."

She pushes my arm. "I was trying to see how deep his eyes go."

"What?"

"Some people, their eyes are all surface, or they don't let you in. Other people, their eyes are windows and you can see into them and see who they really are. And sometimes you can see really far. Those are the best eyes: old souls. I think I'm getting better at seeing into them lately."

"How are his eyes?"

She smiles. "Perfect."

I laugh and shake my head. "Do you realize how bad you've got it for him?"

She pushes my arm again. "You just said I stared at him like a mental patient. I'm sure that scared him off."

"He still wants to date you after you threw up on him—I don't think he scares easily."

She laughs and we both glance back as we're walking. He's still enmeshed with Sharri on the parcourse.

"He's nice, isn't he?" she says. "And funny."

"And he knows how to improvise, apparently, and go to a meeting without any shoes."

She laughs. "Do you think that's what he did?"

I shrug. "I doubt anyone would blink an eye at a barefoot executive in San Mar—or in tech in general, for that matter. They'd probably just think he's eccentric."

"He's cute," she says.

"He is. And not that it matters, but do you realize he's worth like a bajillion dollars?"

She rolls her eyes. "Some of the richest people in the world are terrible human beings."

"True. But you saw into his eyes."

"I did," she says with a dreamy smile.

"I can't believe Charlie Bing is your Charlie."

"He's not *my* Charlie."

"Maybe he will be, in the future."

She glances back at him again when we reach the parking lot. "Or maybe he'll be with Sharri, or someone else, and it's not meant to be."

"So why not just tell him you like him? Or just go ahead and date him?"

She shakes her head.

"Are you worried about breaking a rule?"

"More like cautious. But that's not really what this is about. I'm trying to figure things out for myself. Until then, I think it's good to focus and not get distracted."

"Which I commend, but are you sure that's all it is?"

She groans. "Maybe there's a part of me that wonders if Charlie will be available when I'm ready … and if that means it was meant to be."

"So you're leaving it up to fate?"

"Or maybe I'm just chicken, and I'm scared that whatever connection I'm feeling won't last once I get to know him better." She looks at me. "It hasn't with anyone else."

"But you said his eyes are different."

"It *does* feel different with him."

"Well, maybe he's the guy you've been waiting for all this time—the one that you wondered if he even existed. I think you need to take the bull by the horns on this one."

"I've always thought that saying sounded wildly dangerous."

I laugh. "I mean it. You need to jump in, make decisions. You can't leave it up to fate."

"But I *am* making decisions. I'm making the decision to wait. And maybe all the decisions I'm making are the exact right ones for it all to work out the way it's supposed to."

"Or maybe sometimes fate needs a little nudge in the right direction," I counter. "The way you're going, it's almost like you're pushing fate away and seeing if it'll push back."

She sighs and glances back in Charlie's direction once more. "Maybe. But for now, I want to follow the rules and not upset the applecart—see how it all plays out." She pops the trunk on her car and tosses her gym bag in.

"Fair enough," I say as I toss mine in, too. Then I turn to look at her. "Can I ask you something?"

"Of course."

"What do you see when you look in *my* eyes?"

She closes the trunk and faces me. "Honestly? A puzzle."

My shoulders sink.

"That's a good thing," she says.

"How is that a good thing?"

"It means there's a lot going on. Your eyes are deep."

"So I'm an old soul?"

"You're an old soul wrapped in a riddle and tied with an enigma."

I smile. "Very funny. You're the enigma, according to Charlie."

"I'm serious." She places her hands on my shoulders, facing me square on, and searches my eyes for a long moment. "Definitely an old soul," she murmurs, "and something more …" Her voice fades and she lowers her hands to her sides. "Someday I'll figure you out and then I'll let you know."

"Great. Good luck with that. I haven't managed to figure myself out in almost twenty-five years."

"Join the club," she says with a laugh as we walk to our respective sides of the car and get in. She starts the engine and as we pull out of the parking lot, she glances over. "So when are you meeting up with your pen pal guy?"

"Thursday. Every day it gets closer I get a little more nervous."

"Why?"

I shrug. "I honestly don't know. I think I'm worried if we meet in person we'll find out we have no connection anymore." I look over at her. "And then it would be over. And I like having him as a pen pal. And I like our memories as kids."

"Well, you'll always have your memories. And it takes two to keep up with the letters, so the connection is still there."

I glance over as she drives. I hope she's right, but when I think about seeing Xander again, the thought of it not going well floods me with a level of worry that is, frankly, unjustifiable for simply reuniting with a childhood friend. What's going on with me?

Maybe I shouldn't go?

Chapter Twelve

Dany

"Tonight's the night." Mira's voice fills the car speakers as I drive to work.

For the past few days I've tried to push it to the back of my mind but now it's finally here: I'm meeting Xander for dinner and drinks tonight after work.

"Have you decided what you're going to wear?" she asks.

"I was just planning on wearing what I have on for work." I don't tell her that treating this like any other workday is one of my strategies to tamp down the mounting anxiousness I feel inside.

"Oh."

"Mira, it's not a date."

"I know. But it could turn into one. What do you have on?"

I glance down at myself as I drive. "Blue dress, tan wedges."

"The navy one with the cap sleeves?"

I laugh. "Yes."

"Good. Did you still want to meet for yoga at lunchtime?"

"Definitely, to relax. I need it."

"Great, see you downtown at 1:00 then. I have to go now, I have a patient."

We hang up and my Pandora station fills the car for the final minutes to work. It's not until hours later when I'm at my desk and getting ready to meet Mira that I realize my mistake. "Awww, no," I groan aloud.

"What's the problem now, Jameson?" Dante asks from his desk next to mine. He's the sportswriter for the paper and also my favorite co-worker because he never fails to make me laugh. His wife, Jana, is a busy school principal but somehow she finds the time to bring in homemade cookies for all of us at least once a month.

"I just realized I left my gym bag with my workout clothes in it by the front door at home and I'm supposed to meet my friend Mira for a yoga class in ten minutes."

"What do you need?"

I consider his question. "Shorts and a t-shirt would do," I say with a shrug.

"Would bike shorts work?"

Ten minutes later, when I walk up to meet Mira outside the yoga studio, she laughs.

"Don't say it. I forgot my gym bag. I cobbled this together." I'm wearing Dante's spare bike shorts and a t-shirt he got in last year's white elephant gift exchange that he had stuffed in his file drawer.

She smiles as she surveys my get-up. I lift the hem of the t-shirt to show her the navy bike shorts underneath. They're a little big, and they feel weird with the padding in the butt area, but they'll do the job. The t-shirt is white, wildly oversized, and it has a giant, smiling green pickle giving a thumbs-up on the front with the words "I'M KIND OF A

BIG DILL." I know I look ridiculous, but I'm feeling nervous about tonight and I need the yoga class to relax, so what choice do I have? It was this or coming naked.

"I like the shirt," she says with a wry smile. "And the shoes."

I laugh. The shoes are Birkenstocks that another co-worker, Clara, lent me that are two sizes too big. "I'm just grateful to be here."

"Hold onto that good attitude," she says, "because I've got some good news and some bad news."

My face falls. "The class is canceled?"

"No. That's the good news: there's a yoga class. The bad news is they switched the schedule around. It's not the Vinyasa Flow class we usually take."

"What is it?"

"Hot yoga."

"Where they heat the room to a zillion degrees?"

She scrunches her face and nods. "Want to try it?"

I sigh. "Maybe it'll be relaxing?"

She shrugs. "How bad can it be?"

The answer, it turns out, is pretty bad.

Exactly 60 minutes later, Mira and I are standing in front of the studio again looking like boiled tomatoes. We're trying to decide if we have time to grab a smoothie before heading back to work. I think I might actually *need* a smoothie, medically, to bring down my internal temperature from its current 5000 degrees. Mira can shower when she gets back to the hospital but I realize now I'm going to have to run home before I can return to work. I could probably wring out a gallon of sweat from my t-shirt and shorts. Even if I stuck my whole head under the bathroom faucet at the office, I'd still stink. There's no way I can just put my regular clothes back on without a full-on shower first.

"Dany?" The sound of the familiar voice freezes me in place.

"Dany?" The voice calls out again, and the person attached to the voice circles around to my front and makes eye contact. "It *is* you."

"Jared," I manage to croak out. I sense Mira stiffen beside me when I say his name.

"How are you?" he asks. His hazel brown eyes—which I used to think were honest and kind—sweep over me from head to toe and he looks confused as he takes in the large cartoon pickle on my giant t-shirt. "What are you doing here?"

"Livin' the dream," I say as I lift my arms out to the side and drop them back.

He chuckles. "I forgot how funny you are."

That's funny, I haven't forgotten what a schmuckface you are.

It's then that I notice the blonde he's holding hands with: the one I hadn't noticed until this very moment due to an acute onset of tunnel vision. "Hi Dany," she says meekly.

"Becca," I reply. I feel sick.

There's a long moment of awkward silence and I'm frozen in place like a stunned possum.

"What are you doing out here?" Jared asks. "This is so weird running into you. Are you in California now?"

I don't answer but he keeps talking.

"Becca and I are on vacation. We're celebrating. We got the next round of funding."

I still don't answer but he keeps talking.

"Listen, Dany, we're both sorry about how … well, you know … how it all went down. I got rid of your stuff like you asked. Well, most of it, anyway. Becca likes your couch so we decided to keep it. Did you need me to pay you for that or–?

"We need to get back to work," Mira interrupts loudly. "Dany's getting an important award today so we can't be late."

She grasps my arm by the elbow and guides me away like a newly ambulatory patient. I manage to keep up but I have to concentrate hard to lift each foot and set it down in turn, which was already hard anyway because my shoes are so big.

"That was *him*?" Mira asks when we make it around the corner a safe distance away.

I nod, still a little shell-shocked.

"You okay?" she asks. She places her other hand on my arm and we slow to a stop.

"Yes," I say quietly.

"His beard looks mangy."

I cough out a laugh and look up at her. "Thank you for that."

She smiles. "You're welcome."

"They're still together," I say with some sadness.

"Of course they are. Who else would have them?"

My eyes meet hers and we both smile.

It's been almost half a year now but seeing Jared brought everything back—the shock, the hurt and humiliation, and the feeling of utter betrayal. What if I hadn't found them together and I'd ended up marrying that two-timing sack of flaming garbage? *You never would have married him and you know it.* Okay, but what if I was still an oblivious idiot and I still thought Becca was my friend? I stare out over the crowd of people walking up and down the sidewalk, but it's all a blur.

"You okay?" Mira asks gently, bringing me back to the present.

I nod. "I just wasn't expecting it. I kind of had this idea in mind, if I ever saw him again, how I wanted it to be."

"You mean you didn't want it to be in a giant pickle t-shirt?"

A snort erupts from my chest and I meet her eyes with another half-laugh, half snort as I wipe under my nose with the corner of my shirt. "Or with a tomato face … and looking like I dunked my head in a bucket of sweat."

"I like tomatoes."

I laugh again and that's when I catch a glimpse of my red face in the shop window behind her. "Jesus, I look like I'm about to have a stroke."

She places her hands on my shoulders and turns me to look at her. "You're beautiful," she says. "And he's not. He's a horrible monster. With mange."

I meet her eyes and we both let out a laugh. "He *is* a monster."

"And an unhappy one, did you sense that? All is not rosy with those two."

I nod. "I don't really miss either of them. I think I'm just upset for being such a fool."

"But you know *he's* the fool, right?"

I look up at her. "Did you hear that fool ask if he should pay me for my couch?"

She laughs. "That's when I couldn't take it anymore."

"Did you say something about an award? I think I blacked out."

She laughs harder. "I didn't want to give him any information about you, but I wanted whatever I said to leave him wondering."

"So now he thinks I have a mysterious job that I'm getting an award for?"

"An *important* award," she adds, and we both laugh. "The truth is, you deserve an award for surviving that fool. So we're making time for smoothies. Come on."

She tugs my arm and as we walk to the juice shop, my thoughts turn inward again. "I think it makes me *more* sad, actually, if they aren't happy."

"Why?" she asks.

"Because why would they betray me so heinously if they're not even in love?"

"Did you change clothes?' Mira asks over the phone. It's a quarter to seven and I finally left work about ten minutes ago. I'm in the car, driving.

"Nope, still in the pickle shirt and bike shorts."

She laughs. "What time are you meeting him?"

"Around 8:30 but he said he'd be at the bar before 8:00 if I get there early."

"Got your tomato face on?"

I laugh. "I think it's back to a color that won't raise medical alarm."

She chuckles. "Hair up or down?"

"What? Down. What does that matter?"

"It doesn't, I'm just trying to distract you."

"From what?"

"Your nerves … and the crappy day you had today."

"Ugh. It got even more crappy, if you can believe it. When I got back to my car after our hellish yoga session the rear bumper was smashed in on the side."

"What? Are you kidding me? Did they leave a note?"

"No."

"What kind of dirtbag does that?"

"My thoughts exactly."

"Well, don't think about it for now. I want you to have fun tonight. And not be nervous. And not turn back."

"How'd you know I was thinking of turning back?"

"Oh my God, you were?"

I laugh. "I won't. I *want* to. Partly. But I won't." I let out a long groan. "Ugh. Why did I have to agree to meet up with Xander tonight?"

"You mean because of everything that happened today? Or are you still just worried about how it will go?"

"I don't know. I feel a mixture of emotions: anxious … excited … and unsure."

"Pretty much the way I greet each day."

I laugh.

"Remember, he's the same guy who's written you sweet, old-fashioned letters for years."

"His letters *are* funny."

"I'm sure you'll have plenty to talk about. But text me later if you need an extraction."

"And what will do you? Call and tell me I'm urgently needed to accept an award?"

She laughs. "It was all I could think of in the moment!"

When we hang up I'm still chuckling. I merge onto Highway 280 and as I press down on the accelerator, I take a deep breath.

I can't help wondering if I'll be renewing a happy chapter from my past tonight or closing that book forever.

Chapter Thirteen

Dany

I had a crummy day, yes.

But if that gorgeous guy sitting at the bar at Rubicon and staring at me right now is Xander River then perhaps things are looking up for little ol' Dany Jameson.

My heart is in my throat as the man smiles and I walk over to him at the bar.

"Dany?" he asks when I get closer.

"*Thank you, universe,*" I whisper silently inside. "Xander?" I ask and his smile goes wide.

He stands and gives me a warm, embracing hug and I can feel his muscled frame beneath his slate gray suit. "The moment you smiled I knew it was you."

"Me, too," I reply. His eyes meet mine and as I stare into their familiar green depths all ambient sound falls away: no more steady din of conversation around us; no more ice tumbling in the cocktail shaker as the bartender makes a drink; no more distant chatter and pots and pans clanging from the kitchen as the waiters move in and out. A waft of rum and lime brings me back to awareness that other people still exist outside of this moment.

Eventually I realize Xander's been talking.

"I'm sorry, what?" I manage to croak out. His voice is pleasantly deep and it makes me realize how much I miss Australian accents.

"A drink? Can I get you one?"

I nod and he motions for the bartender.

"This is weird, right?" he says after we order. "Seeing each other after all this time?"

"*Yes*," I sigh with relief. I'm not the only one.

His eyes trace over my face intently. "I'm glad we didn't exchange pictures. I wanted to see if we'd recognize each other. Your smile is just as I remembered."

We gaze at each other for a long beat and I can't stop staring into his eyes. They have a soulful quality I forgot about from when we were kids.

"And I remember your eyes," he says, as if he's reading my mind. "Sea blue."

I smile and reach up to tuck my hair behind my ear.

"And I remember that, too," he says with a chuckle, "the way you tuck your hair behind your ear when you're concentrating … or nervous."

I stop, mid-tuck, feeling self-conscious. "You think I'm nervous?" I complete the tuck against all effort not to. *Damn you, OCD.*

He smiles. "I drank two shots trying to calm myself before you arrived. If you aren't nervous to meet again after all these years, good on you."

I laugh. The genuineness of his reply touches me.

"I remember the way your eyes look when you smile," I say. "Your voice is different though—much deeper."

He laughs. "It would be alarming if it wasn't."

"And I remember your laugh."

He nods. "We laughed a lot. I missed that. After you left."

"Me, too," I say as our eyes meet again. And like a gentle tug on a string between us, I feel that same connection we had when we were kids. It's as if no time has passed, except for one heady difference: an adult, electric charge that now fills the air.

Is it just me or does he feel it, too?

As we continue to talk, I survey the line of his jaw and his genuine smile and the smoothness of the way he brings his drink to his lips, so confidently and sexy. Not to mention his deep laugh or those green eyes that search mine and make me feel like I'm the only person in the world.

There's a pause in the conversation and we both smile and a long beat goes by as the voltage between us builds and I'm not sure what to do. I take another sip of my drink and swallow hard.

"This is–"

"How's the conference going?" I ask at the same time he begins to speak. "Sorry, what were you saying?"

He shakes his head. "Nothing. The conference is going well," he says. "So well, in fact, I have some news. I may be moving here."

"Here? As in San Francisco?"

"Actually, San Mar."

I nearly choke on the sip I just took. "Really?"

"I have a job offer. Alvarado & Brass. Do you know it?"

I nod. Alvarado & Brass is a well-known architectural firm in San Mar.

"I met John Alvarado at the conference this week and we got on. Really well. His firm is one of the top ten firms in sustainable architecture."

"Your focus," I say, remembering his letters.

He nods. "And he and his partner are surfers."

"Another one of your focuses ... or foci? Is that a word?"

He laughs. "That's why they're in San Mar. John told me he and his partner Wade believe in balance—in design and in life. They decided if they were going to start a firm, they'd focus on good design and, hopefully, clients would seek them out wherever they were. Their goal was to be able to surf whenever they want to and also do the job they love."

I shrug. "It must have worked. They have a great building downtown. Not too far from where I work at the paper."

"I'm taking the job offer as a sign."

"Of what?"

"That I should consider it. I'd be working for a firm doing what I studied and it happens to be located in San Mar—the same town you sent me a change of address for months ago. Wouldn't you see that as a sign?"

"You're asking someone who literally saw a sign and stopped driving and now lives in San Mar. I may not be the best one to comment on snap decisions."

He laughs. "Maybe we both know when to follow our intuition."

I meet his eyes. "Maybe."

"So you think I should consider the job?"

The electricity between us fills the air and I search his eyes but I can't be sure if he's feeling it too. I decide to play it safe. "I think that anyone who can take basic sandcastle-building skills and parlay them into a career as an architect must be doing something right."

He smiles. "*Basic* skills?"

"Some of them were pretty good," I say with a laugh.

"I managed to get that arch to hold up the day we met."

"You remember that?"

"Of course. I had just moved to the neighborhood and you waved me over and asked for my help. A blue-eyed damsel in distress."

"I didn't ask for your help. You offered."

"You say that like it's a bad thing?"

I smile. "It was a good thing. Once you got the arch to hold up I started to believe you knew what you were doing."

He raises an eyebrow comically. "I'm offended you ever doubted I knew what I was doing. I had a plan and it worked."

"You and your plans," I say with a shake of my head.

He laughs. "I wasn't sure about the plan for tonight, though."

"What do you mean?"

He hesitates for a moment and peers down at his drink before he looks back up again. "Was there any part of you that didn't want to come tonight?"

I hold his gaze, surprised. "Yes … but I knew I had to."

"Because you felt compelled to? Or because you wanted to?"

"Both."

He nods. "Me, too."

We're both silent for a long beat.

"We've had this thing," he says finally, "all our lives, with the letters."

"And you worried this might spell the end of it?"

His eyes hold on mine and he nods.

"Me, too," I say quietly.

"I don't even know why we kept up with the letters, to be honest, but–"

"I didn't want to let it go," we say in unison.

Our surprised chuckles fade into another stretch of silence—comfortable silence of the kind you feel with only an intimate few.

"I have good memories of us," I say. "And I was worried it wouldn't be like it was."

"But it is," he says as he meets my eyes. "At least for me it is."

I smile. "It is." I'd almost forgotten how good it always felt between us. Only now the feeling is suffused with a powerful current of anticipation. I feel warm all of a sudden and I shift on the bar stool. God, he's good looking. Maybe Mira was right when she said this could turn into a date. *Please, Mira, please be right about that.*

"John invited me to stay on another week and meet more people at the firm and explore San Mar and see if it's a good fit. I'm set to go down on Friday. I just need to change my return flight to Sydney."

I nod.

"I could use a guide while I'm there, to get to know the town, if you know anyone available?" He says the last part with a sly glint in his crinkling green eyes that makes my heart skip a beat.

I summon my inner drill sergeant to restrain me from thrusting my hand in the air like a schoolgirl and yelling out, *"Yes! Me! I'll do it!"* Instead I manage to answer calmly, "Of course, just let me know when you get to San Mar."

"San Mar?" The dismayed voice comes from behind me. "You're not still thinking about taking that job, are you?" I turn to see long legs in black jeans and heels striding past. As my gaze shifts up I see a sleeveless white silk blouse and light blonde hair in a stylish bob. Tan arms encircle Xander's neck and glossy red lips place a pronounced kiss on his mouth, the effect of which lands like a medicine ball to my gut.

Oof.

Then the head of this beautiful creature turns toward me, revealing a friendly smile, and extends a well-manicured hand to shake.

"I'm Alora, Xander's fiancée," she says with a cute Australian accent.

Chapter Fourteen

Dany

I fight valiantly to look neutral. *"Suck it up, Jameson,"* commands my inner drill sergeant. I convince myself it was good to get a cold splash of ice water in the face because my imagination was flying off into nutso land: as if Xander and I would meet up after all this time and fall in love and blah blah blah ... *yeah, right.*

"I'm Dany," I say with genuine warmth mustered from my depths. I accept Alora's hand with a smile and out of the corner of my eye I notice Xander eyeing her oddly.

"So you're the American he knew when you were in nappies," she says.

My eyebrows go up, amused. "Actually, I was out of diapers by the time we met." I glance at Xander sideways. "Can't speak for him, though."

He laughs. "Had that sorted as a young lad."

We both share a chuckle but Alora looks confused so I explain. "We met when we were seven. I was potty trained for at least a week by then."

Xander laughs but Alora stares without a flicker.

"Just joking," I add.

"Oh," she replies with a forced chuckle. "Funny."

God this is awkward.

"So you're getting married," I say with extra cheer to fill the silence. "That's big news. Congratulations."

She immediately becomes animated. "Thank you," she says with a smile as she slides her arm through Xander's and pulls up tight against him. "It's time."

"When's the big day?" I ask.

"We–"

"We're still getting that sorted," Alora says, speaking over Xander. "It takes time to plan the kind of wedding I'd like." She goes in for another kiss and my eyes instinctively shift away and take my mind with them. *Was I ever like that with Jared? So possessive? How did I ever fall for that schmuckface anyway? How did I–*

"… show me around." When I come back to the present, Xander is finishing a sentence.

"Hmm?" I ask.

"I was just telling Alora that you offered to show me around San Mar."

I nod and turn to Alora. "I'm happy to show you both around. It's a great vacation spot as well as a nice place to live."

Alora shakes her head. "My holiday's over. I'm going back to Sydney tomorrow and I expected Xander was going with me." She looks pointedly in his direction. "I thought we agreed."

He flicks his eyes in my direction and then back to her. His expression is neutral, but he's obviously signaling her that they have an audience. "We can speak more about it later."

Alora seems visibly perturbed and I can't help feeling as though I'm intruding. I make it a point to pull out my phone and look at the time. "Wow, I didn't realize how late it is. I should probably get going."

Xander's face falls. "I thought we'd all have dinner." He gestures to the dining room. "I've been told this is one of the best new restaurants in the city."

I wait a beat to see if Alora chimes in to encourage me to stay, but she very conspicuously doesn't. I take that as my cue to leave them alone to spend their final night together in San Francisco. "I've enjoyed the drinks. It's been so nice seeing you after all this time and I hope you'll forgive me, but I should probably get going before I'm too tired to drive home. I had a long day and I have an early start tomorrow."

"Of course," Alora agrees quickly.

I smile at her. "It was nice meeting you, Alora." I stand and grab my purse off the bar. "Congratulations, again. You'll make a beautiful bride."

Her face softens and I have to admit she has a lovely smile when it's genuine. "Thanks, Dany. Nice meeting you, too."

"Thanks for coming tonight," Xander says as his eyes hold mine in a way I can't interpret. "It was great seeing you after all these years."

When I exit the restaurant I pause on the sidewalk and take a deep, steadying breath. Okay, there'll be no romance, but the connection is still there and we'll always be friends. That's "not nothin'" as my middle school math teacher used to say. All in all, it's a good outcome.

Except for the fact that I can't get his green eyes out of my mind.

I shake away the thought and head up the hill in the direction of my car, thankful that I only had one glass of wine. Halfway up, I hear quick steps behind me and turn to see Xander striding up the sidewalk.

"I wanted to walk you to the car park," he says when he catches up to me.

"Oh. Um, sure … thanks. That's nice. But I'm just up the next block. Parked on the street." I point to the top of the hill.

He shrugs. "It'll be a short walk."

I smile and we start making our way up the hill together.

"So, I'll text you when I get to San Mar," he says.

"You're staying?"

"Yes."

"Okay." I don't ask how Alora feels about that decision.

"It's uncertain when I'll be free. Part of the time I'll be spending at the firm, and John invited me to surf with him and Wade—to show me some good breaks."

I nod. "On weekdays I'll be working, so I won't be available until evening anyway. Or maybe lunch."

"Plan for the evenings then?" he asks with a smile.

"Sure." *Every evening?* Before I can ponder that thought further, we reach our destination. "Here we are," I say.

He nods.

"I mean this is my car." I tap twice on the hood of my dusty blue Prius.

"Yes." He makes no move to leave.

"Made it here safely," I say. "Thanks for walking with me, though."

He chuckles. "Yes, I realize we're here. I plan to stay until you drive away safely."

"Oh. I didn't realize you had a *plan*."

He laughs and meets my eyes and we both smile, enjoying the easy moment. "I forgot what it was like with you," he says after a beat.

"Me, too."

His eyes drift to the side of my car. "What happened there?" he asks, gesturing to my dented bumper.

I shrug. "Don't ask. Just happened today actually. After seeing my old boyf-" I stop myself from mentioning Jared. Why ruin this nice moment? "Suffice it to say I had kind of a crummy day today."

His brow furrows with genuine sympathy. "Until tonight?"

I smile. "Until tonight."

"Well, I'm glad your crummy day has turned around." His smile reaches his warm green eyes and his gaze holds on mine. After a moment, he lets out a laugh and rakes a hand through his dark chocolate-colored hair. "Have I told you that you make me feel like I'm ten again?"

I flush. *Is that a good thing?* I smile as I open the car door and he holds it while I climb into the driver's seat. After he closes the door he knocks on the window and I roll it down.

"I'm glad we didn't cancel tonight," he says. "You?"

I nod and he smiles.

As I pull away from the curb I watch him wave to me in the rearview mirror and I lift my hand in return.

Yep, I feel ten again, too.

Chapter Fifteen
Mira

I brace myself with both hands on the side of the sink in the tiny bathroom at Krispy Kreme Donuts. The rush I just felt is similar to the one I had last week and just dismissed as standing up too fast. I look up into the mirror and my face is flushed. I stare into my green eyes in the reflection. Maybe I should see a doctor. But I do a mental and physical survey of my body and I have to admit that I don't feel as though anything's wrong. I feel strong, and the rosy color looks healthy. I splash some water on my face and fix my ponytail before taking a deep breath and exiting the restroom.

"You okay?" Dany asks when I reach her outside waiting by her car.

"Think I just had a wild sugar rush."

"Told you we shouldn't have split that third glazed," she says and we both laugh.

When we get into the car and Dany pulls out of the parking lot, I turn to her for what seems like the hundredth time. "I still can't believe he's engaged."

She looks over at me and smiles. "I think you're more bummed about it than I am."

"How come he didn't ever talk about it in his letters?"

She shrugs. "We didn't write about it. We always wrote about stuff like with school or work, or observations on life, or memories, or I don't know … all kinds of stuff, but we never wrote about our relationships or anything like that."

"And he's not on social media?"

"Neither of us are."

"I don't know," I mutter. "It just doesn't seem right somehow. Like that's not how it was meant to go."

"Well, I don't know if I subscribe to your idea about fate, but I'm not going to lie and say I didn't let my imagination run wild, flush in the moment of seeing him again." She looks over at me after we roll to a stop at a red light. "I'm starting to wonder if life may just be a big crapshoot."

"Calling anything a crapshoot makes it sound awful."

She laughs and gives me a shrug. "Well, if I focus on the good news, it's that the chemistry Xander and I had is still there. So I'm pretty certain now we'll stay friends for life. And I'm happy about that."

I stare at Dany quizzically. I can't figure out if she's an optimist masquerading as a realist or a realist with bouts of relentless optimism.

"At any rate," she continues, "I'm busy at work right now and I don't need distractions, which I know you can relate to. I'm working on my story on the hospital, and next week I'm interviewing your future boyfriend."

"Very funny."

"I'm not kidding. I called his PR team and he personally called me back within minutes. I highly doubt I would have gotten that kind of treatment if I wasn't a friend of yours."

"Or maybe he just wants some good PR for CDS in the *Sentinel*," I offer.

Dany glances over at me with a knowing look. "I think we both know who he wants good PR with."

I laugh. "Maybe."

When we reach Sea Cliff Beach for the annual beach cleanup, the good news is a ton of people showed up. The bad news, if you can call it that, is that so many people turned out that the pickings are slim. After walking far and wide to search for an untouched area, we've resorted to sifting the sand for hidden trash and cigarette butts. After a few hours we sit down to rest on the big rocks along the cliffs and Dany looks down into the crevices between the rocks and then looks up and smiles.

"What is it?"

She reaches in between two rocks and carefully pulls out a brown beer bottle. "I think we found all the trash."

I peek into the crevices around me and carefully pull out another bottle. As we keep searching all long the cliffs we realize we've hit pay dirt. Apparently a sizable portion of the beach population has been treating the holes between the rocks as nature's garbage cans. Soon we've collected so many bottles and cans that we're lugging stuffed lawn-size trash bags through the sand behind us, clinking and clanking with every step.

As we walk on the shifting sand I can't help noticing that my leg isn't bothering me today. When I was a kid I not only had a pronounced limp, but it was painful much of the time. When I look at how far I've come, after all the therapy and muscle work, I can hardly complain that it still hurts every once in a while, but it's nice that it hasn't been hurting lately. Not for weeks, actually, when I think about it.

"Wow, look at that view," Dany says as we pause to take a breather and look out over the ocean. It's one of those crisp, clear days where you can see for miles, with the sun up high in the blue sky and the glistening blue ocean below, and the sound of the rhythmic waves lapping at the shore. We pause to fill our lungs and that's when I get a funny feeling and turn to my right. My eyes focus on a tall figure walking along the shoreline in the distance. "Is that Charlie?" I ask, disbelievingly.

Dany follows my eye line to the blonde man in a t-shirt and board shorts striding towards us. "No. Way," she says, deadpan. "He just keeps turning up. I told you—he's so into you that there's no way you scared him off."

I nudge her arm. "Shh, he's almost here."

"I *thought* that was you," Charlie says as he reaches us. His blonde hair is mussed from the wind, and when he flips his sunglasses up onto his head he reveals his blue eyes that I can't get enough of. They're deep and interesting and they draw me in every time I see him. He's holding a large trash bag over his shoulder with one hand, causing the muscles of his arm to flex as he sets the brimming bag down in the sand. "It seems I'm destined to keep running into you two."

Dany greets him and I say, "Yeah," slightly disconcerted. It does seem odd that we keep seeing him. And it's odd that he's been at the hospital a lot lately, too. "What are you doing here?" I ask.

"Cleaning up the beach," he replies with a smile.

"But why?" I ask.

Charlie's eyes flicker to Dany and then back to me as if he's not sure of the question. "To respect the planet and–"

"Are you following me?" I ask.

"What?" I hear the shock in his voice and all of a sudden I feel foolish.

"It's a community cleanup," he says evenly. "We all live in the same community."

He's right. I'm acting like a paranoid psycho—and a rude one, to boot. *What's wrong with me?*

"Mira," he says, searching my eyes, "If you're trying to send me a message, I get it: You're not interested. That's okay. I hoped we could be friends at least, but if that's not something you're open to, that's okay, too." He glances over at Dany standing next to me, but when I look over at her she's turned slightly away and pretending to be wholly absorbed in tracing shapes in the sand with the toe of her Vans.

When Charlie speaks again, his voice is low and earnest. "I happened to be here, I saw you, and I was glad to see you—and that's all this is. I'm sorry you'd think otherwise."

His blue eyes meet mine and I can feel the sincerity of his words. The fact that he would pour his heart out in earnest like that—in front of my friend no less—makes me like him all the more. I want to explain to him that it's not that I'm not interested. I'm just not interested *now*. "Charlie, I–"

"Charlie! There you are," calls out a silky voice to my right. I turn to see a very pretty, very fit brunette stride up and place her hand, territorially, on Charlie's bicep. She lets the gesture linger for a moment before letting go and she stands close to him. "I'm Carly," she says with a bounce in her step as she sticks out her hand for me to shake.

"I'm Mira," I say as I accept it. She delivers an unexpected bone-crushing squeeze but I manage to hold my own.

She shakes Dany's hand next. I watch Dany's face to see if she also gets the crusher treatment and I see her eyes go wide for a microsecond but then just as quickly revert to unfazed.

"Shall we go to lunch now?" Carly asks, looking directly at Charlie. "My bag's full and so is yours." She lifts up her bag as proof and shows off a nicely toned bicep of her own. "I don't think we can pick up anymore trash." Her eyes flicker briefly to Dany and me as she says it, and I don't know whether to laugh at the sheer unsubtlety or to be offended. I glance over at Dany and when our eyes meet I have to look away before I burst out laughing at the stupefied expression on her face.

Charlie hesitates for a moment before answering. He looks like he's not sure what to do. "Sure," he answers finally. Then he turns back to us. "It was nice running into you both. *Accidentally*."

I smile at the emphasis he places on the word and I'm gratified to see him smile back before he turns to walk away. Maybe I didn't offend him irreparably.

Dany and I watch in silence as they grow distant. I see Carly grip Charlie's arm again and throw her head back and laugh out loud as they talk about whatever the heck he's saying that could possibly make a person laugh so dramatically.

"Fake laugh," Dany says, as if on cue, and I turn to her and we both laugh genuinely.

"You think that's his girlfriend?" I ask.

"Crusher Carly?"

"She got you, too?"

She dangles her limp hand in front of me. "It's like a sack full of Skittles now."

I laugh. "You didn't flinch."

"And show her the pain she was raining down? No way. With girls like that you have to hold your own."

I smile because it's exactly what I was thinking.

"I did feel a little sorry for Charlie, though," Dany adds, "when she asked him to lunch."

"Why? He was with Sharri before and now Carly. He has a new girl every time we see him."

"First of all," Dany says, "we're the ones who left him with Sharri at the parcourse. And second of all, you not only haven't told him you're interested, you accused the poor guy of being a stalker, so you can't fault him for dating other girls."

"But even you said that it was weird that he keeps popping up."

"Yeah, but it's more like *nice* weird, or *interesting* weird, not 'get-a-restraining-order' weird. I gotta tell you, I don't get a stalker-ish vibe from him."

I nod. "I don't either—I feel like my instincts are going haywire lately. I can't believe I said that."

"I wish you'd just tell him you like him."

I take a deep breath. "I was actually getting ready to say something when Carly showed up, which is probably for the best, now that I think about it."

"Are you talking fate again? Because they didn't look fated to me. When Carly showed up he looked like a lost little boy. I almost wanted to hug the poor guy and assure him it would be all right."

I look over at her. "A lost little boy?"

She smiles a little and shrugs. "Or maybe I have heatstroke from lugging these bags around."

"Or maybe you've got a ten-year-old Australian boy on the brain."

"That sounds creepy," she cries out with a laugh. "We're both adults now, thank you."

"Wasn't he supposed to come to San Mar yesterday? Did he text you?"

She shakes her head. "He probably decided to go back to Australia with his fiancée after all." She leans over to gather the ends of her bag together so we can begin to drag them along the sand again.

As I watch her, and then I glance after Charlie in the distance, I'm starting to doubt whether fate is moving in the right direction for either one of us.

Chapter Sixteen

Dany

"Dany. Hi. Short notice, but I'm wondering if you're available tonight? I meant to call yesterday but I had dinner with the partners until late. Hope to see you. This is Xander." He chuckles. "Obviously."

The voicemail ends with his pleasant low rumble of a chuckle—the chuckle that I've now listened to about 30 times as I keep replaying his deep, accented voice. I just arrived home after doing the beach cleanup and then having lunch with Mira and finally got a chance to plug in my phone to recharge.

I decide to text him back because I've been known to leave rambling voicemails. Worse, if I call back and catch him live, who knows what I might blather on about in the pressure of the moment. With a text I can keep it short, breezy and cool. Like the friends—*just* friends—that we are and will forever remain.

> Got your vm. I can meet
> tonight. 7? What are you
> mooching for?

I immediately see the mistake after hitting send. Stupid autocorrect! I retype quickly and hit send again.

u in the mood?

Ah God, did I make it worse? Now it sounds like a weird come-on.

Brilliant. Anything's fine.
Mexican?

I breathe a sigh of relief. I type carefully this time and proofread before hitting send.

Sure. There's a great hole-in-the-wall place with the best food. Or a nicer restaurant that's also good. Your choice?

Hole-in-the-wall. Full stop.

I laugh. Man after my own heart.

I text him the address for Rico's—a San Mar staple— and we decide to meet there. Dinner and then what? I guess we can play it by ear depending on what he wants to do and see. I begin to feel nervous again but I tell myself all the reasons I shouldn't be. For one thing, we've met now as adults and any worry about us not staying friends is gone.

And secondly, he has a fiancée so this isn't going anywhere in a romantic direction.

So why is my heart pounding at the thought of seeing him again?

Chapter Seventeen

Dany

When I pull into the parking lot at Rico's, Xander is already waiting. He's leaning casually against a support beam for the overhang at the strip mall in a t-shirt and jeans. With his tan, muscled arms and his hands halfway in his pockets pushing his jeans low on his hips, I imagine him posing for a calendar titled, "Sexy Aussie Gods." I let out an involuntary sigh.

He smiles when he sees me and, as I walk up to him, he points to his faded, vintage-style t-shirt with *San Mar, California* written in script across the front. "Do I look like a local?"

I laugh. "Hardly."

"Should have suspected that when the shop I bought it in was called 'Goods for Idiot Tourists.'"

I laugh again. "If you're determined, after dinner we can get you a proper local's t-shirt."

He smiles. "I'm determined." The look in his eyes, and the low timbre of his voice when he says it, makes my knees go weak, and he's just talking about t-shirts, for Christ's sake. "*Focus, Jameson!*" shouts my inner drill sergeant. I haven't had thoughts like this about anybody since Jared. That's progress, right? Next step: find someone to feel this attracted to who *doesn't* already have a girlfriend.

Inside, we order at the counter and then find an open table and start munching on the warm chips and salsa in front of us.

"So what have you been doing since I last saw you?" I ask.

I endeavor to keep my tone strictly friendly and not sound at all like I'm wondering how my childhood best friend grew up to be a hot male model.

"These are really good," he says with surprise, as he holds up a chip before he scoops up some salsa and devours it.

"I know, right? Glad you chose the hole-in-the-wall option." *And thank God you're oblivious to my inner thoughts.*

He smiles. "To answer your question, I saw Alora off Friday and then I had dinner with the Alvarado & Brass partners, John and Wade. This morning I met with them again and we went surfing."

"You like them both?"

"Aye." He nods. "They're a lot alike. On Monday I'll spend the day meeting with people in the office. They're all working on projects of the sort I want to specialize in. It seems like it'd be a fantastic place to work."

"So you think you might accept their offer?"

"I think I'm *going* to accept their offer. Provided, that is, that the rest of the employees I meet on Monday aren't wankers."

I laugh. "Really? So you'd be moving here?"

He nods and then stays silent. I suspect I know what he's thinking.

"Will that sit well with your fiancée?"

He looks up and meets my eyes. "There have only been two times in my life when I knew for certain what I wanted and this is one of them."

I feel for him because what's left unsaid is that asking Alora to marry him is the other one. "You must feel torn," I say with genuine empathy. How can he know what to do when his two greatest impulses lead him in two different directions? "Would Alora consider moving here?"

He takes a deep breath. "We'll get it sorted."

I nod. He obviously doesn't want to discuss it, so it's time to change the subject. "What do you want to do after we eat?"

His demeanor lightens. "Well, one of the things I remember I always liked about you was you always had fun ideas for what to do."

I smile.

"Three ideas and a wildcard."

"Oh my God," I say with a laugh. "I forgot about that."

"You made the wildcard sound extra thrilling but it was really just you choosing the one you wanted to do the most."

I laugh. "You fell for it every time."

"I knew what you were doing," he says with a sly smile. "I just wanted to make you happy."

"As if you didn't enjoy what we did."

He smiles. "I didn't say it wasn't what I wanted to do, too."

"Although you mostly wanted to search for frogs."

"Sure, when it was my turn to toss out ideas. But you always went along."

"Because I wanted to make you happy."

He smiles. "You mean we had a little *Gift of the Magi* thing going on there?"

"Not quite," I say with a laugh. "You said you liked doing what I suggested. Where's the sacrifice?"

"You didn't like looking for frogs?"

"It was fun," I admit. "And I liked hearing about your frogs in your letters."

"That's good to hear, because it was probably 90 percent of what I wrote about the first year after you left."

I burst out laughing. "I remember you had a whole family at one point named Dany and Andy and their kids Wizz and Tinkle."

"I think I had a theme going there." He laughs as he scrubs his hand down his face. "I can't believe you remember that."

"I liked that you named one after me. I kept all your letters, you know."

"Me, too," he says, meeting my eyes.

The connection between us hangs in the air, unacknowledged, but the fierce undercurrent of attraction makes my heart beat faster. I do my best to ignore it and keep talking.

"One of the things I remember liking about *you*," I say, "is you were always prepared. Like the time we found that waterfall."

He nods. "I went back there recently. It's tiny."

"Aww, don't tell me that. I remember it being big. And wonderful."

"That's how all things look when you're ten."

I laugh. "And then we stayed too long and couldn't find the trail back, but you assured me we weren't lost and that you just wanted to take the long way around. You even brought food so we could stop and take a break on the way home."

He nods. "Fairy bread and Weet-Bix, as I recall."

"Oh my God, that's right! I was amazed when you pulled it all out of your backpack. Along with juice boxes. I was starving and worried, but you'd planned for it all along."

"I hate to tell you this, but we actually *were* lost."

"Are you kidding?"

He shakes his head.

I burst out laughing. "No wonder it took us so long to get back!"

"I didn't want to worry you."

I stare at him, incredulous. "I'm rethinking everything about you now."

"Then I probably shouldn't also tell you that my mum packed the rations."

"You didn't even make the food?"

He shakes his head, laughing. "My mum knew you loved fairy bread."

I toss a chip at him from across the table. "Fraud."

"At least I'm coming clean now."

"Fifteen years later?"

He laughs. "Better late than never for the truth to come out."

"Next you're going to tell me you had a ghost-writer for your letters."

He shakes his head. "No ghost. I take my letter writing very seriously."

"What about all your plans? Were they scams, too?"

"I take my planning even more seriously than my letters," he says with mock gravity. "In fact, I looked at all the brochures in the hotel lobby and I have plans for us tomorrow afternoon, if you're free."

"What plans?"

"First you have to say if you're free."

I raise an eyebrow. "Do you think I won't want to go once you tell me?"

"I don't know. Are you free?"

"Yes," I say with my lips pursed in a smile.

"Brilliant. You'll find out tomorrow."

"You're not going to tell me?"

"Do you really want to know?"

I shrug. "No."

He smiles. "You haven't changed."

"You haven't either. Except for the sneaky liar stuff."

"Sneaky liar? Don't you think that's a little harsh for a ten-year-old boy who just wanted to impress you?"

I laugh. "By pretending you knew what you were doing?"

He tilts his head to the side and flashes a lopsided smile. "I always know what I'm doing." His voice is low and the way he's looking at me with those green eyes of his makes me exhale with relief when our name gets called to pick up our food.

I need every available distraction to break whatever spell I'm under.

"Have you decided what you want to do next?" I ask Alexander when he joins me at the door after clearing our table. I gave him three options over dinner, plus a wildcard for old times' sake.

"You know I'm going to say wildcard."

I smile. "Predictable."

He smiles crookedly as if he's struggling not to say something.

"What?" I ask.

"You have a little," he points to the corner of his mouth, "a little … looks like red sauce."

I feel my face heat. "Here?" I rub at the side of my mouth.

"Other side," he says with a smile.

I rub again.

"Still there," he confesses, looking highly amused. "Can I?" he asks, scrunching his face comically.

I nod and he reaches out, cups his hand under my chin, and uses his thumb to wipe the right side of my lips. His thumb lingers in place a moment and his green eyes stay on mine. The heat between us is indescribable.

"Thanks," I manage to croak out. "Be right back." I walk unsteadily for the bathroom. Whoa, what is going on with me? *He has a fiancée, Jameson.* I want to shout at my inner drill sergeant that I know that fact very well and that what I could use right now are some helpful tips about how to suppress my overwhelming attraction. I can't have my knees going out every time Xander looks at me, for Christ's sake.

When I enter the bathroom I head straight for the mirror. *Nice.* A red ghost halo from where the sauce was smeared in the corner of my mouth is still there. *Couldn't resist taking that final bite of enchilada as you were clearing the table, could you, Jameson?* Or was it there for the entire dinner? I don't allow myself to contemplate that level of humiliation. I wash off the last remnants and then I check my teeth about eighty times to make sure I don't have anything else lurking. All I need now is to go back out there and smile wide with a big piece of cilantro stuck to my tooth.

"Thanks," I say when I find him waiting for me outside the front of the restaurant, "for saying something … about the red sauce."

He smiles. "In cases like that, you have a two minute window to say something. If you wait too long, they think you're an arse for not saying something sooner. And if you say nothing, when the person finally looks in the mirror later they'll never want to see you again."

I'm struck by his words. "That's my philosophy exactly," I say with amazement.

"I know," he says with a laugh. "You wrote it to me in a letter once."

"I did?"

"When you were at uni and you let that nasty professor know she had a bit of beetroot in her teeth when she started her lecture."

I look up at him. "I used the word *beetroot*?"

He laughs. "It may have been something else. No matter, I still loved the story."

"Why?"

"Because you could have let it go. But you interrupted her lecture and somehow you made her step outside the room. And she was very resistant."

I laugh, remembering. "She was."

"But you were very persistent, as you always were, and somehow you convinced her to follow you out the door. And that's where you told her. Quietly, in private."

I laugh. "I'm sure the whole class thought I was nuts. She was kind of scary."

"You were brave."

"I was scared."

"But being scared has never stopped you from doing the right thing," he says quietly, meeting my eyes. "That's what makes you brave."

I glance down. "I don't know about that."

"Do you remember defending Denny Barto when he wet his trousers in year three?"

I look up at him. "I haven't thought of that in years."

"All the kids were laughing at him and you shouted that they were all a bunch of buffoons."

I laugh. "As I remember, Denny wasn't very happy for my help, though."

"That's because he was a bully. And a chauvinist. But you stuck up for that tosser anyway."

I laugh. "Whatever happened to him?"

"Believe it or not he owns a chain of dry cleaners."

"Are you serious?"

He smiles. "Completely."

We both laugh and our laughs fade to smiles and then eventually we go silent as that electric feeling starts to build again between us. *Think of something else, Jameson. Anything.* I clear my throat. "We'd better get going."

"Where are we going?"

"You really want to know?"

He smiles. "I want to know what your wildcard is."

"San Mar Boardwalk. The Big Dipper."

He looks at me questioningly. "Is that ice cream?"

"It's a roller coaster."

"Brilliant."

I smile. What I don't say is that every minute with him has felt like I'm on a roller coaster already.

Chapter Eighteen

Dany

"You're showing him around again tomorrow?" Mira asks over FaceTime. She called while I was brushing my teeth.

I nod. "Mm-hmm." I spit in the sink and then pick up the phone as I carry it with me into the bedroom. "Actually, he's making the plans this time for where we go."

Mira scrunches her face. "And this is just friends?"

"Of course."

"But you kind of like him."

"Whatever it is I'm feeling—or imagining—I've stuffed it down deep where it'll never see the light of day, trust me. He has a girlfriend and we're strictly friends. In fact, I was going to ask if you want to come with us tomorrow?"

"I would, but I'm having lunch with my Aunt Liz and Uncle Finn and then I'm babysitting their son Niko while they go to a fundraiser for the bio-tech research center at the university. My Uncle Finn's getting an award."

"Wow, that's great. For what?"

"Some DNA thing. He told me, but I don't think I could explain it if I tried."

I laugh. "How old is their son Niko?"

"Five. He's so cute. You'll have to meet him."

"I'd love to. I love little kids. But I'm still hoping you can meet Xander sometime this week so you can give him the ol' Mira Ronin Handshake Test and see how deep his eyes go."

She laughs. "I don't know if my DS has been working right lately, but I'm free Wednesday and I can give it a go then. Although, if you like him, I'm sure he's great and he'll pass the test."

After we hang up I climb into bed and can't stop thinking about what she said. Yes, Xander is great and of course he'll pass the handshake test. He's amazing and funny and handsome and I feel so electrically alive every time I'm with him that I literally get weak in the knees.

And that's exactly why you should be avoiding him as much as possible.

I consider the idea and then decide to advise my inner drill sergeant to mind her own business for once and that I've got it under control.

For now, anyway.

Chapter Nineteen

Dany

"Mystery Point?" I ask with a laugh as we round the corner in Xander's rental car and see the sign among the large trees.

He smiles. "I thought you'd like it. You were obsessed with trying to work out that Magnetic Hill thing we read about when we were kids."

I look over at him. "It's all optical illusion. It plays on perspective."

"So you don't want to go?"

"No, I *definitely* want to go. It's the one place in the world where I can be taller than you for once."

He laughs. "The most dramatic perspective tricks on earth couldn't make up for that height differential."

"Very funny."

We get our tickets and we're placed in a large group mostly made up of international tourists who don't speak much English, which is too bad, because our tour guide, Rahul, is a guy working his way through college and he's pretty hilarious. He's obviously making the most of what could be a monotonous job by perfecting his spiel and inserting what I suspect are plenty of original jokes of his own. All in all, it's more fun than I expected to see golf balls roll "uphill" and watch people "shrink" and "grow." I make sure we get a picture of when I'm standing on the "grow" side, opposite Xander.

"Didn't quite make it," Xander says, pointing to our photo on his phone. We left Mystery Point back in the mountains an hour ago and now we're close to Xander's hotel, having dinner at a seafood restaurant on the wharf that he wanted to try.

I lean over and study the photo again. He's right. We're both standing about six feet apart, facing each other. The "trick" is that whoever stands on the left side looks super tall and the one on the right looks short. But even in this photo with me on the left and Xander on the right, no slanted background illusions can make up for the fact that I'm a foot shorter than him. "It's close," I say. As I look at the picture once more, I feel strange for a moment. The image shifts to two people I don't recognize. "Wait a minute, that's not us." Instinctively, I push the phone back to his hands.

He looks at the photo again. "Who else would it be? That's us, Dany." He looks at me strangely—the way you'd look at someone who just bonked their head and is now spouting nonsense.

I'm almost afraid to take the phone from him again, but when I do, I breathe a sigh of relief. It *is* us in the photo.

I look up at him. "I don't know. For a second there, I just … saw something different."

"You're not used to seeing yourself so tall."

I nod. "Must be."

For the rest of dinner we reminisce and talk about my job, living in San Mar, his current job, and his potential *new* job at Alvarado & Brass. As usual, the conversation is easy and the undercurrent between us is as strong as ever—at least on my side of the table. Who knows what he's thinking? I remind myself to get used to dealing with it if we're going to be seeing each other regularly as friends.

After dinner we walk down the boardwalk and get shaved ice: blueberry for me and grape for Xander, and we sit down on a bench facing the ocean to eat it. After I finish, I stand to throw away the cup and walk back over to the bench where Xander is still sitting, watching the waves. I feel so drawn to him that I don't dare sit back down. He looks up at me and his mouth widens into a smile. "Your lips remind me of our birthday party when we were eight. You had blue cupcake frosting all over your mouth and you refused to let your mum wipe it off because you said you were saving it for later."

I laugh. "That was on purpose! I was trying to make it look like blue lipstick."

"Well, your eight-year-old self would be mightily impressed with your look today."

"And yours," I point out. "Your lips are purple right now. And if you remember that party, you'll remember you smeared frosting all over your mouth, too."

He smiles. "I would have done anything you asked me to." His eyes meet mine and the connection between us simmers.

I clear my throat. "Maybe we should take a picture of you for Alora," I say hurriedly, "with your purple lips." I tear my eyes away from his to search through my purse for my phone.

Xander exhales and slides his palms down his thighs to his knees. "Dany, can I tell you something?"

I stop rummaging in my purse and look up at him. "Of course."

He motions for me to sit down. "When I tell you," he says as I sit down on the bench next to him, "it's going to make Alora sound … I don't know, a little mental. And I don't want you to think poorly of her."

I meet his eyes and take a moment to ponder what the heck he's going to say and then I answer sincerely. "I hardly know her, Xander, and I'll take your word on anyone."

He nods. "Good. Because she's not crazy."

I nod.

"But she's not my fiancée either."

I sit in stunned silence and a tiny flicker of promise begins to build within me.

"We're together," he explains. "We're just not engaged."

The tiny flicker disappears in a poof.

"We've been dating nearly a year and she's been hinting about marriage but we haven't had any discussions."

I nod.

"After you left the restaurant, I asked her why she introduced herself that way. She said she wanted to see what it felt like to say it and she thought once I heard it I'd see that it was right for us. She thought it was the push I needed."

I don't know what to say, so I just nod, dumbfounded.

"I would have corrected her in the moment but, firstly, I was shocked; and, secondly, I didn't want to embarrass her. I didn't know why she did it and I wanted to speak with her privately and work out her thinking."

I nod. That explains the odd look he had on his face that night. "You're a good boyfriend."

He takes a deep breath and slides his palms down to his knees again. "I don't know. I realize now she had a different idea about the trip than I did. She joined last minute and I think she imagined I would propose. The whole thing has put into stark relief how far apart we are."

"Because you want to move here?"

"Partly. But even if I stay in Sydney, I'm realizing now that we may not want the same things."

I don't know how to respond, so I just keep listening.

"She's a great person, really," he continues. "She can be witty and she's smart and fun and we used to get on well."

"Used to?"

"Things changed over the last few months. And then this job came along and she doesn't want me to take it. And when she left on Friday she said if I didn't leave with her, it was over."

"Wow," I say softly. "I'm sorry."

"She called and left a message yesterday telling me if I want to keep her in my life I need to propose when I get back."

I'm silent for a moment, taking it all in. "So she'd consider moving here if you propose?"

"I don't think she has it sorted, even in her own mind."

"How do you feel about it all?"

He takes a deep breath. "I feel that she's right."

My stomach tightens, but I nod. "So you should propose."

"No, I mean she's right that we're not meant to stay together," he continues, "long term. It's clear now. Has been for months, but I didn't want to see it."

The flicker of hope in my chest, which has no business being there, starts to stir again.

He looks up. "She never brought it up in a straightforward way so we could have a chat and see what page we're on. And she doesn't know me at all if she thought blindly pushing me into it was the way to go."

"That wasn't your plan?"

He chuckles. "She didn't even give me a warning. Or at least three choices and a wildcard option."

I laugh, but I quickly revert to sincerity. I feel for him as he tries to figure this all out. "Well, I'm sorry, Xander, that you're going through this."

"Thanks." He takes a deep breath and plants his hands on his knees in a way that seems to signal the end of the conversation. "So now that I've told you, I guess that's a longwinded way of saying that maybe it's not a good idea to send Alora a picture of me with purple lips tonight."

I smile. "Noted. Have you spoken with her at all since she left?"

He shakes his head. "I thought we could both use time to think. I plan to tell her in person when I'm back in Sydney."

That's Xander. Always with a plan.

Chapter Twenty
Dany

"Wait a minute, you found out he's actually single and yet you told him you can't see him tomorrow night? Please explain the Dany logic behind that," Mira says, animatedly, from inside my phone screen. She made me promise to FaceTime her when I got home but I would have called her anyway. I'm sitting on my bed and she's sitting on the couch at her Aunt and Uncle's house, babysitting.

"First of all, he's not single," I say.

"*You* said that *he* said that *she* said that if he didn't leave with her it's over. He's still here. Ergo, it's over."

I smile at her convoluted-sounding, but accurate, argument. "But then she called and said he needed to propose to her when he gets back. So I don't think they're officially broken up until he goes back and they talk in person."

"Hmm," Mira hums. "It's murky, I'll grant you that."

"And he could always change his mind. He could go back, see Alora in person, she could jump into his arms and who knows what could happen?"

Mira shakes her head. "Like in the movies? At the airport? Is *that* why you told him you have plans tomorrow? Because you're imagining some fantasy reconciliation from a rom-com?"

I shrug. "Even if they're broken up, he'll need time. I know I did."

She nods. "That's reasonable."

"And, besides, I don't even know if the way I feel around him is mutual. He may be looking at me solely as a friend to lean on. I think a short break is good, if only so I don't make a fool of myself. I don't know how to describe it, Mira, but being with Xander just feels *right*. I forgot how strong the connection was between us when we were kids. I don't know what it is … it just makes me smile when I'm with him."

"Really? He makes you smile? I never would have guessed."

I laugh and throw a balled-up sock at her that bounces off the screen. "Do I look dopey right now? Please tell me I didn't have this dopey smile on my face with him all night."

"You look sweet, not like a dope."

"Mira, can I have some water?" A little boy with big eyes and wavy brown, mussed-up hair comes into the frame behind Mira as we're talking.

She turns to face him. "Of course, sweetie. What are you doing up?"

He rubs his eyes, sleepily. "I had a dream I was thirsty."

"So you woke yourself up to get some water?"

He nods.

"Awww." She turns to look back at me as if to say "Isn't he adorable?" And she's right—he truly is. "Niko, look at the phone, this is my friend Dany. You'll meet her soon."

He smiles and waves to me. "Hi, Dany."

"Hi, Niko," I say. "I can't wait to meet you in person."

Mira gets back into the frame. "Gotta go. I think you should tell Xander your plans were canceled and you're free. That's the last I'll say on it."

I laugh. "Bye, Mira. Good night, Niko," I call out to him in the background.

I hear his sweet little boy voice wishing me good night before we hang up.

I watch some shows on my iPad until I get sleepy and then I set it down next to my phone on the nightstand. I'm beginning to drift off when I hear the ding of an incoming text message. I pick up my phone, sleepily, expecting it to be from Mira, prodding me one more time to tell Xander I'm free, but instead I'm shocked into wakefulness because it's a message from Xander himself.

You up?

I dither over whether to ignore it but the curiosity is killing me. What the heck, I can't help myself, I reply.

Yes.

I see the typing indicator appear immediately and then his reply pops up.

Can I ask you a
question?

Tentatively I type in my response.

Sure.

The typing indicator displays for a while and then disappears and reappears several times before his next text pops up.

Did you say you have
plans tomorrow
because of everything I
told you tonight? It was
too much?

I take a moment to think about how to answer.

It wasn't too much.
We're friends. I
want to hear about
your life. I'm glad
you told me.

It takes a few seconds but then I see the bubble appear to show he's typing.

We haven't talked
about relationships in
the past. In our letters.

Before I can answer, another text pops up.

Why is that?

I ponder his text for a moment and then start typing the first thing that comes to my mind.

I don't know. Maybe because ~~we knew~~

Before I complete the thought, I start backspacing to delete the second sentence but I only manage to delete half of it before I accidentally hit send. His reply pops up immediately.

Maybe because why?

I swallow.

I don't know. I was texting the first thing that popped into my head. I don't even know what I was going to say. I didn't mean to send it.

I'd like to know what
popped into your head.

I type out a reply.

Why?

Because your thoughts
are always interesting.

I smile.

Thanks.

A minute goes by and then he types a response.

You're not going to tell
me?

I think for a moment before replying.

Ask me again in a
month.

? Why a month?

Because you'll
forget by then.

Laughing.

Seconds tick by and then the bubble appears again to
show he's typing.

Can I ask if your plans
tomorrow are with a
boyfriend?

I smile as I reply.

No.

I can't ask or they
aren't?

My plans aren't
with a boyfriend.

A few seconds go by and then he replies.

Significant other?

I smile again.

No.

Tinder date?

I'm laughing as I reply.

LOL. No.

Smiley face.

Smiley face?

I don't like emojis.
I spell them out.

You're funny.

I've been told that.

Why are you texting
me so late?

It's early in Sydney.

But we're in California.

Does it matter?

Smiley face.

You don't like emojis either?

No, I don't share your strange aversion to tiny images.

Funny.

I don't respond right away and I see the typing indicator appear and then disappear several times before another message pops up.

It's been fun hanging out
with you the past two days.

I smile as I reply.

Ditto.

Do you have plans for
Tuesday? I'm leaving
Wednesday.

? I thought you were
staying until Friday.

I have enough info to
make my decision.

What info?

Explored the town, looked at
housing possibilities, and I'm
interviewing with everyone I
need to at the firm tomorrow.

I stare at his text. I had planned in my mind that the next
time we'd see each other would be Wednesday night, with
Mira. One of my co-workers, Clara, is going on maternity
leave and we're having a get-together for her after work
Tuesday and I don't want to miss it. So that means if I don't
see him tomorrow I won't see him at all before he goes back
to Sydney. I mull over the dilemma and decide Mira's right
– I should just tell him I'm free tomorrow. I have to go to
the hospital in the morning to interview some board
members and then I have my interview with Charlie Bing in
the afternoon, but I could swing meeting Xander for dinner.

I have plans Tuesday. But I
can be free tomorrow.

I see the typing indicator pop-up for a lengthy stretch
and then disappear and then re-appear again before his
response arrives.

So you're free now
Monday night?

Yes.

Pick you up at 5?

How about I pick you up
at 6?

Big smiley face.

Laughing.

G'night.

I set the phone down and fall asleep with a grin on my
face.

Chapter Twenty-One
Dany

"How's your story coming?" Mira asks as I take another sip of my coffee and glance around the crowded cafeteria at San Mar Good Samaritan Hospital. I interviewed the hospital CEO last week and I have interviews with board members this morning, but right now I'm having an early coffee with Mira before both of us dive into work.

"Great. I like your CEO—she's tough and friendly and she knows her stuff." My eyes widen as I focus past Mira, over her shoulder, to the atrium. "In fact, there she is. With Charlie."

"Tell me you're joking." Mira turns to look behind her.

Charlie Bing, looking casually handsome in jeans and a blue button-down shirt, is walking with Heda Flourant, the hospital CEO, and they seem to be in a serious conversation.

She turns back. "He's been here so much lately. Do you think he's trying to get Heda on board with his sister's plan to sell the hospital?"

I narrow my eyes to get a better look. My story for the *San Mar Sentinel* concerns the hospital's upcoming decision over whether or not to sell to PBH, a large for-profit conglomerate. PBH stands for Perry Brannon Health, but it's better known by the moniker assigned to it by many former patients: "Profits Before Health." It's been a controversial lightning rod for the town because Good Samaritan has been a non-profit ever since it was formed decades ago by two church congregations with a mission to serve everyone in the community. For many people who live here, the idea of adding a profit motive to something as fundamental as health care has ignited fears it will lead the hospital away from its founding values, and limit services and raise costs. In my interview last week with Heda—a pleasant and supremely competent woman with four advanced degrees—she stressed that no decisions have been made yet. In her mind, the founding mission and values for the hospital are paramount in terms of guidance and priorities as the board debates all options.

"His sister's the one leading the charge for this whole sale idea," Mira continues. "What if that's what he's doing here? He agrees with her?"

I watch as Charlie and Heda shake hands and part ways. I'm interviewing his sister this morning and I have my interview with Charlie this afternoon, so maybe I'll find out.

My first interview after coffee with Mira is with Brian Ramirez, a board member who happens to be a brain surgeon with an MBA. He made a data-backed case for why the hospital can and should remain a non-profit entity rather than being beholden to shareholders demanding maximum short-term profits, and his concerns gibe with those raised by many in the community.

To get an opposing perspective, my next interview is with the woman Mira warned me about: Charlie's sister. Only she's late. Thirty minutes now. I called and I've been checking messages on my phone and drumming my fingers on the table in the conference room. I have plenty of time until I have to interview Charlie this afternoon but, still, I'm starting to feel anxious. I go over my notes again and double-check the batteries in my recorder and after another ten minutes, she strides in, no apologies.

She's beautiful with even features, long legs, flowing blonde hair, and flawless, unlined skin. So flawless that it's a little unnatural looking, to be honest. Are foreheads supposed to be that tight? She has blue eyes like her brother's, but they're different somehow—they don't draw you in, but rather keep you at a distance. She must be in her mid-forties—at least a decade older or more than Charlie—but she could pass for mid-thirties if you don't look too close. I wonder what Mira would say if she was here, but I suspect she'd tell me Molly's eyes aren't "deep" like her brother's.

"*San Mar Sentinel*?" she asks without waiting for an answer. "Molly Bing Beaumont." She sits down and begins talking without even giving me a chance to tell her my name. I quickly turn on the recorder in the middle of the table between us to start the interview. "I know Heda and Brian must have made their case, as wrong-headed as it is. But we're not running a charity here. Healthcare is a business and it has to be run like one. And sometimes that means making tough but necessary decisions."

"Can you share some examples? There have been rumors of cuts being planned—in terms of services and also jobs. What kinds of tough decisions are being planned by PBH?"

She surveys my face in silence for a beat. "You're young," she says, almost accusingly, "and I'm guessing you haven't run a business or you'd know that's a naive question. They won't know exactly where to cut until they run the hospital firsthand."

I hold her gaze, unblinking. Her statement doesn't hold water and, on top of that, she's insulting me. Hasn't anyone ever told her that ad hominem attacks are the lowest form of argument?

"Actually," I say, "I have a background in business. I helped run a start-up for two years." *Take that, Mrs. Condescending Smarty Pants.* "And since you mentioned running it like a business, in independent ratings across the country, hospitals PBH has purchased have subsequently been rated lower in quality and satisfaction by their communi–"

She puts up her hand. "That's not true. PBH has their own data to prove it."

"Doesn't it serve the board's interests to use independent, unbiased data?"

"The bias is your opinion."

I'm tempted to tell her she's entitled to her own opinions but not her own facts, but I remind myself of my objective and decide to call a reset. From the moment this woman stepped into the room she's been condescending and defensive. Mira told me she inherited her spot on the board after her husband passed away last year—maybe she feels insecure and she's overcompensating? Regardless, I've been told that the board is split on the decision, and I have to get her out of personal attack mode so that I can gather the information I need for a fully-informed article.

I stand up and hold out my hand. "You know, I just realized we started right in and didn't even get a chance to introduce ourselves properly. I'm Dany Jameson, by the way."

She leans forward slightly to take my hand and replies with a practiced veneer, "Molly Bing Beaumont. And I'm confident, Dany, that before we're done here, you're going to see things my way."

Her declaration comes across as more of a threat than a promise.

Chapter Twenty-Two
Dany

"Hi, I'm Dany Jameson with the *San Mar Sentinel*, here to see Charlie Bing," I say to the receptionist in the light-filled atrium at Candle Data Systems, located in the new tech hub downtown. She makes a call and, soon after, a friendly assistant retrieves me and escorts me up to the top floor of the seven-story building, where I'm now seated on a couch in a large, open area. It's light and bright and functionally designed. Long tables in rows serve as workstations for the 50 or so people working on their laptops and mobile devices. Sunlight spills through the tall windows, greenery is artfully displayed at pleasing intervals, and quiet cross-chatter fills the room.

Soon I see Charlie walking down the middle of the rows in my direction. He has a shadow of dark blonde stubble to match his dark blonde hair today and he looks cute, as usual, in jeans and a blue button-down shirt that matches the blue of his eyes—the same clothes I saw him wearing earlier at the hospital. "Hi, Dany," he says with a smile when he gets closer and extends his hand out. "Nice to see you again."

I shake his hand. "Thanks for fitting me in."

"Happy to do it. Anything for a friend of Mira's."

I smile. The difference in demeanor and personality—and whole aura, really—between Charlie and his sister, whom I finished meeting with only hours ago, is striking. Charlie is like a warm puppy, drawing you closer, and

Molly is like a glass of beautifully clear but painfully icy glacier water. I follow him through the halls and we make friendly chitchat as he leads me to a quiet area of small, glass-walled offices with sliding glass doors to enter, each with a window to the tree-filled courtyard below. Every office has a desk workstation with a whiteboard on the wall behind it and two visitor's chairs in front. As we pass, they're all revealed to be populated with men and women working diligently until we get to the end of the hallway and find one empty. My amiable escort slides the door open and motions for me to take one of the visitor's chairs.

"This is your office?" I ask.

"These are all drop-in offices for when people need a quiet space to work. We reserve whichever one is open. A lot of people choose to work from home at least a few days a week and others travel. I'm not big on status and, more importantly, space is at a premium because we're growing so fast. It doesn't make sense to have large, empty offices sitting around unused half the time. Although some people who work in the office every day claim spaces permanently as their own, and that's perfectly fine, too—whatever works. We're all different."

I nod as he sits down behind his desk and I take a seat in the visitor's chair.

"Would you like anything before we get started?" he asks. "Coffee, tea, water?" He holds up the glass bottle on his desk filled with green liquid and smiles. "Green juice?"

"I'm good," I say.

He laughs. "I've become one of those guys everyone hates who tries to get you to try their green protein shakes."

I smile. He's so open and earnest. It's hard not to like him.

"It honestly tastes good but I have to close my eyes when I drink it or I can't get it down."

I laugh again.

"You sure you don't want to try one?"

I assure him I'm good and we get started, first covering the background of how he started CDS and then more about coming to San Mar. When we're nearing the end of the interview, I don't know why but I ask a simple throwaway question I already know the answer to: "Where did the name Candle Data Systems come from?"

He looks up and meets my eyes. "I tell everyone it's a metaphor for shedding light on data, which it is. But it also has personal meaning for me." He sits back in his chair after he says it, seemingly surprised. "I haven't ever told anyone that part before."

"Really? Can you share the meaning?"

"Something from my childhood," he says noncommittally. "It actually came up today, with my sister, in a roundabout way." He looks distracted after he says it and he glances away, out the window.

"Can you be more specific?"

He shakes his head. "It's private and wouldn't mean anything to your readers."

I nod. Charlie Bing is getting more interesting.

"I understand your sister helped you get your foot in the door to use Good Samaritan as a beta site way back when. Was that crucial for you?"

He nods. "I'm grateful to her for that."

"So grateful that you'd speak to board members, on her behalf, regarding the hospital's sale to PBH?"

His brow furrows. "Are you suggesting a quid pro quo arrangement?"

"Or maybe you simply agree with your sister's viewpoint?"

"I rarely agree with my sister on anything," he blurts out and then stops himself. "That's off the record."

"So you do or don't agree with your sister regarding the hospital sale?"

"I'm not at liberty to discuss it."

"Why?"

"Because I have some business before the hospital board."

"What business?"

"I'd rather not say."

"Can you be less opaque?"

"I've already told you more than I've revealed to anyone."

I look up. "But you're not giving me anything."

He meets my eyes. "Can I say something weird? I feel like I know you."

I don't tell him that I also have a sense of odd familiarity. "Maybe we met before at a tech conference. I used to work for a company called Synsa."

He shakes his head. "It's more than that. I feel like I can trust you."

"Well, maybe that's because I'm a trustworthy sort."

He laughs. "Is that right?"

I smile. "I don't think anyone could say otherwise."

"Can we end the interview and talk off the record then?"

"Of course." I reach over to my recorder and press stop.

"First off," he begins, "I want you to know that although I'm grateful to my sister for helping me secure the beta test at the hospital for our software, I don't feel indebted to her. If anything, it's the other way around. She's twelve years older than me and we didn't even have what you might consider a decent relationship until a few years ago."

"Because of your age difference?"

He shakes his head. "No," he scoffs, "I *wish* it was as benign as that. It's because she dealt me never-ending shit growing up. When I was a kid, starting in elementary school, I was overweight. I got a lot of grief for it but what was worse than getting teased at school was the treatment I got at home. I don't know if all the belittling comments my sister made—and even careless things my mom said—were what made me overeat in the first place, or if I was already overeating because of something sad that happened when I was in first grade ..." He pauses for a moment and his eyes drift to look out the window and into the courtyard below. "But what I *do* know is: the only good thing about my sister back then was that she wasn't around all the time."

He pauses again and meets my eyes. "I'm only telling you this because I was on track to get CDS off the ground with or without her help. The healthcare market was a good start and it's an important vertical for us, but we've branched out far beyond that. I love Molly, because she's family, but like I said before, we rarely agree on anything and she and I have only just started having any sort of relationship in the last few years. So make of that what you will."

I nod. My heart hurts for him as I think about his story. I'm not surprised what a piece of work his sister is, but, Jeez, even my sister Karin on her worst day would never needle me where it hurts the most. And Molly did it to him when he was a *little kid*.

"And now," he continues, "still off the record, I'll tell you why I've been meeting with Heda Flourant and the hospital board."

And he does. And it's illuminating. But unfortunately I can't print any of it, or even mention it to anyone. For now, anyway.

When we're finished and I'm packing up my things to go, he hands me his business card and writes his personal cell number on the back and offers to answer any follow-up questions for my story if I need it. He jokingly offers me a green drink again but I demur because I want to get back to the office and get some things done before I meet with Xander later.

"Can I ask you one last thing?" he posits as I stuff my recorder in my bag.

I nod. "Shoot."

"It's personal, not business."

"Okay, go ahead."

"You don't have to answer if you think it's unprofessional."

"Okay."

He rakes a hand through his golden hair nervously. "Christ, I'm 31 but I feel like I'm still in middle school." He meets my eyes and we both smile. He may be older than me but I really like Charlie in a kid-brother sort of way.

"I'm just going to say it," he says finally. "I like your friend Mira."

I laugh. "I know."

"You do?"

"It's obvious. Plus, you basically said it at the beach cleanup."

"Is she interested? Because I get wildly conflicting signals every time I see her."

I consider what Mira would want me to say—she's so attached to those rules of hers—and since I don't know for sure, I answer noncommittally. "You should ask her."

"Fair enough," he says, glancing down at his desk, "fair enough." Then he looks back up. "Can you at least tell me if she's dating anyone?"

I shake my head. "No."

"No, you won't tell me, or no, she's not dating anyone?"

"No, she's not dating anyone."

His eyes brighten. "Good to know. I won't ask you anything else."

I laugh and we go back to chatting about the story as he walks me out. I hope Mira will approve of what I've done because although she wants to leave everything up to fate, I think sometimes fate needs a little nudge in the right direction.

Chapter Twenty-Three
Dany

"How'd the interview go?" Mira asks over the phone. She caught me in my car on the way over to Xander's hotel.

"With which Bing?"

She laughs. "Both."

"Awful with Molly. Great with Charlie … thanks to you."'

"Thanks to me?"

"I would never have gotten on his schedule this fast if he wasn't hopelessly in love with you."

"Very funny."

"Do you need proof? When I got to his office and thanked him for making the time, he said, and I quote: *Anything for a friend of Mira's*, unquote. And if that's not enough, after the interview he told me, straight up, that he liked you and he asked if you were dating anyone."

"What?" Mira squeaks. "Are you serious?"

"Yes."

"What'd you say?"

"I told him you weren't dating anyone."

Silence.

"Was that okay?" I ask, tentatively.

"Yes."

"Why didn't you answer right away? Should I not have said that?"

"I didn't answer because I was smiling."

I exhale with relief amid a smile of my own. "Good. By the way, he also asked me if you were interested in him, but I wouldn't answer that. I told him to ask you himself."

"Is he dating anyone?"

"I didn't ask."

"*What?* What kind of reporter are you?"

I laugh. "The kind who tries to maintain a semblance of professionalism. But I'm happy to do a deep-dive investigation into his romantic life as soon as you say the word."

"You'd have to get in line behind Gemma."

We laugh and say our goodbyes as I reach the hotel parking lot. I'm relieved that Mira's okay with what I said to Charlie—maybe things could end up working out for them after all.

I park and walk into the hotel lobby and make my way to the elevators to head up to Xander's floor, where I make an effort to relax before I knock at his room.

"Hi," he says with an easy smile that reaches his green eyes when he opens the door. He's wearing faded jeans that sit just right on his hips to draw attention to his flat abs and a heather gray t-shirt that skims his hard body in a way that makes me feel the need to steady myself with a hand on the doorjamb.

His eyes trail over me. "Good, you're casual, too."

I peer down at my light-blue crew-neck tee, jeans, and sandals. I was trying to signal "friends hanging out" rather than "I desperately want to date you and rip your clothes off." I pat myself on the back for succeeding.

"Do you have plans for us?" he asks. "Wildcard ideas?"

I smile. "I always have ideas, but is there something you'd like to do that you haven't yet?"

"Actually, a few people mentioned a sandwich place on Surf Street that's said to be incredible. It's still nice out. We could walk to it from here, get takeaway and go eat on the beach."

"Sounds great to me. I think that place is new and I've wanted to try it."

He smiles and walks over to the closet and grabs a blanket from off the shelf and turns around. "Picnic blanket."

"Always prepared," I say with a chuckle.

As we walk down the hall, our hands accidentally brush against each other and I do my best to ignore the electric charge that runs through me at his touch. I put more space between us but it does no good—the charge continues to build. In the close quarters of the elevator it's as if a magnetic force is filling the space around us, and just when I think I can't take it a moment longer, the doors open and I manage to step away.

As we walk through the spacious lobby to the open air outside, I'm careful to maintain a healthy distance to try to break the spell I'm under. I didn't dare make eye contact with Xander while we were in the elevator but now that we're outside and a safe distance apart, I glance over at him as we walk and chat on our way to the sandwich shop. I'm trying to glean if perhaps he feels any of what I'm feeling when we're together, but he's smiling and laughing as usual and I can't begin to decipher his inner thoughts.

When we reach the restaurant, one of the straps on my sandal snaps loose and I sit down at an empty table outside to try to fix it. Xander offers to help but I tell him to go on in and surprise me with whatever he wants to order while I futz with it. After several minutes I think I've managed to get the strap to hold and I glance through the tall glass windows to see if Xander is still in line.

At the counter inside I see a pretty girl with chestnut hair waiting on him attentively with wide eyes, extra smiles, and a very swoony-looking expression, and I smile to myself and shake my head. I can't blame her. He looks like a Greek god and he's got an Australian accent. *Get in line, sister.*

He emerges with two large bags and a lidded cup with a straw just as I finish taking a few steps to test the strap.

"Fixed?" he asks, and he smiles when I nod. "Iced tea," he says as he hands the drink to me. "Unsweetened, with lemon."

The fact that he remembered what I like to drink is not lost on me. "Thanks."

We cross the street to the beach where Xander spreads out the blanket on the sand and we sit down.

"This is nice," I say as we take a moment to look out over the waves. "Eating on the beach was a perfect idea."

He smiles. "I'm glad you think so. Do you want to know what I ordered for you?"

"I pretty much like all food, so you can't go wrong."

He laughs. "Hope you still like fairy bread then."

"Very funny."

"I'm serious. They had it on the menu."

"They did not …"

He lets out a deep-throated chuckle that warms me from the inside out. "You have no idea how much I wish it was in here," he says with a laugh as he gestures to the bags sitting on the blanket. "But I do have two of Sea View Café's supposedly best sandwiches and some crisps. And I convinced them to sell me a bottle of wine. How's that sound?"

I meet his green eyes, twinkling with amusement, and I'm still trying to process that this is, in fact, my childhood friend Xander, all grown up. And he's here with me now in California, on what feels almost like a date. Even in the beginning with Jared, during the rosiest honeymoon stage when everything was idyllic, it never felt like this.

"Good?" Xander asks, and I realize I never answered him.

"Great," I say with a wide smile.

He opens the bag and hands me one of the wrapped sandwiches. "It's their signature sandwich. The concierge at the hotel raved about it."

I unwrap the sandwich and take a large bite. "Mmmm," I mumble with eyes wide as he watches me. It's not what I was expecting.

He unwraps his own and takes a bite. A surprised look falls over his face. "What kind of sandwich did you get?" he asks. His brow is furrowed.

I pull open the corner of my sandwich and peek inside. "Looks like cheese and … mustard."

"That's it?"

I nod.

He peeks inside his sandwich. "Mine, too." He picks up the bag and turns it around. "Save for Mikey," he reads aloud. The words are written on the side in black marker.

He looks back at me and we both burst out laughing.

"She gave me the wrong bag," he says.

I nod. "Somewhere out there is a very unhappy kid named Mikey without his cheese and mustard." What I don't say is that the girl behind the counter was probably struck dumb by Xander's Aussie Awesomeness and I can't blame her for mixing up the orders. We're lucky we got food at all—if I'd been in her place I might have put a shoe in the bag.

He looks at me and laughs.

"What?"

"You said, 'Mmm,' with those wide eyes of yours when it was clearly terrible."

I chuckle. "I didn't want to seem ungrateful. The picnic is nice."

He nods. "I'll take these back," he says as he starts wrapping his up.

"Don't do it on my account. I'm fine with Mikey's Cheese Special."

"You are?"

I shrug. "You'll miss the sunset if you go back now. Besides, we used to eat fairy bread, which is basically prison food when you think about it."

He laughs. "You think they put hundreds and thousands on prisoners' bread and butter?"

"Maybe they add the sprinkles on their birthdays."

He searches my eyes. "You really don't want me to go back?"

"If you want to get the real sandwiches, that's fine, but I'm perfectly content right now."

He nods. "I'm perfectly content, too." He looks out over the ocean for a long moment and then looks back at me. "You're very easy."

"You mean easygoing, I hope."

He laughs. "I mean it's easy ... being with you. It always was."

I smile and as his eyes meet mine the air crackles again with anticipation. My eyes trail to the sensual curve of his lips and all I can think about is how much I'd like him to lean over and kiss me right now ... and how it would feel to have his lips on mine and ... *Stop!* I shouldn't be thinking any of these thoughts. He still has a girlfriend.

Sort of.

Technically.

I drag every bit of willpower I still have—kicking and screaming—to the surface and I smile and raise up my sandwich as if to say "cheers" and then I take another bite. You can't think about kissing someone when you've got a mouthful of cheese and mustard.

Xander smiles back, raises his own sandwich in return, and as we eat and drink together and look out over the ocean, I can't help but marvel at just how perfect everything feels in this moment—as if I'm soaring in a state of sublime equilibrium.

"This is so *nice*," I say as we finish off the bottle of wine and watch the sun make its last dip below the horizon. *Nice* seems wholly inadequate as a description but I don't think words exist that could convey how pleasant this feels, honestly. Striking pink and orange hues crisscross the sky in candied warmth and I don't ever want this evening to end.

"I could get used to this," he says as he glances over. My heart skips a beat when our eyes meet and it takes every bit of strength left inside me to look away. *Remember, he has a girlfriend. And he may decide to stay in Sydney.*

"Yep," I say, looking down.

"Did I say something wrong?" he asks.

"No," I answer as I shake my head to clear it. "Not at all. It's been perfect." I meet his eyes and smile casually. "Shall we pack everything up now?"

He eyes me strangely. "You want to leave?"

"I have an early day tomorrow."

"Oh, of course." He starts gathering wrappers and stuffing everything in the bags.

We finish packing everything away and when we stand up he lifts the blanket and shakes it out.

"Are you getting cold?" he asks. "Is that another reason you want to go?"

"A little." It seems like a decent excuse.

He steps closer, his eyes never leaving mine, and he lifts the blanket and wraps it around my shoulders like a shawl. "That better?" he asks. He's holding the two ends of the blanket in his hands and it would take the slightest of tugs to bring us together. I don't trust myself to speak, so I just nod.

He smiles and releases the blanket and then he takes the bags from my hands. "I'll take these to the bins," he says before he walks across the sand to the garbage cans by the stairs to throw them away. I follow and step up to a stair above the sand, holding my sandals, so I can put them back on before we walk back to the hotel. I have one sandal in place and I'm on that foot trying to slip the other back on when the strap comes loose again and I lose my balance and tip forward.

"Whoa," Xander exclaims as he catches me in his arms.

The electricity that runs through my body as we touch is indescribable. The hard plane of his chest is pressed tight against me and my face is tucked in his neck. I inhale a heady mixture of soap and his natural scent that makes me want to stay in his arms forever. As I slowly pull back, his lips are so close I feel dizzy—and not just from the wine.

"Whoa," I manage to utter softly. "Two glasses of wine and I'm out of control."

He meets my eyes. "Sometimes it's good to lose control." His voice is low and with only the slightest of movements his lips could be on mine. The thought sends a wanton thrill through me and, as the charge between us builds, my last ounce of willpower weakens. *He has to feel this, too.* I shift in his arms and that's when Xander pulls away. Actually, that's not even a strong enough word for what he does. He *jumps* away—the way you'd leap back from a hot pan.

I watch as he closes his eyes and presses the tips of his fingers against them, shaking his head as if to say, "no."

Oh, what did you do, Dany? He's either not interested or not ready. I chastise myself for not exerting more self-control.

He looks up and the expression on his face is confused. Or maybe worried. Whatever it is, it's scaring me. "Are you okay?" I ask.

He scrunches his eyes closed and then opens them again. Then he rubs his eyes once more.

"Xander, are you okay?" I ask with alarm.

He nods. "Aye," he says finally. "I think you're right, though, we should call it a night."

"Are you okay to walk? I can call us a ride." I pull out my phone.

He shakes his head. "I think it must be jet lag. I'm fine."

"If you're sure." I say the words with hesitation and watch him closely as we start walking. The trip back to the hotel is short and quiet. He walks me to my car in the parking lot and then he turns to face me. "Thanks, Dany," he says with a finality in his voice that makes my heart sink. "For everything."

"Are you sure you're okay?" I remove the blanket from my shoulders and hand it to him.

"I think I just need some sleep," he says as he holds the door for me while I get in.

I nod and he closes the door and I resist the urge to lower the window and say something more. I wave to him as I pull out, and on the drive home I can't help running over and over the entire evening in my mind.

The more I think about what just happened, the more I'm confused. And embarrassed.

And I have a sinking feeling I may never see him again.

Chapter Twenty-Four
Dany

"It *is* odd that he left the next day," Mira says. We're in her car after she picked me up from the body shop where I dropped off my Prius to have the rear fender fixed.

I nod. We've had this discussion many times before.

"He texted and said he decided to go back another day early? Nothing else?"

I nod again. "Couldn't leave fast enough, which is not a good sign for him ever wanting to return."

"And he hasn't called or texted at all in the past two weeks?" Mira glances over as she drives. We're headed to her grandparents' house for dinner. They finally returned from their around-the-world trip and she wants me to meet them.

I shake my head. "I haven't tried to get in touch because I think I should give him space." I lean down to reach into my purse on the floor of the car by my feet. "This came yesterday, though." I pull out a folded-up envelope and hold it up to show her.

"*What?* You got a letter?? Why didn't you say so? What does it say?"

I glance over at her as she drives. "I don't know. I'm afraid to open it."

"What? Why?"

"Because it was awkward when he left and I feel foolish. I read all the signs wrong. He probably decided to stay in Australia and marry Alora, and I just don't want to read that. Not yet."

"I thought you said he accepted the job before he left?"

I shrug. "He could have changed his mind."

"Didn't he also say he may have found an apartment?"

"That was all before I fell into his arms and basically tried to kiss him."

Mira glances at me sidewise. "You think he changed his plans and fled the country to avoid kissing you?"

I laugh. "Maybe. I don't know how else to see it." I press my fingers to my forehead, trying to erase the humiliating memory from my mind.

"It couldn't have been that bad."

"He *jumped*, Mira." I look over and meet her eyes. "*Jumped*. Like he stepped on a snake."

"Stepped on a snake? Was that a common thing you've seen, growing up?" She says it with a laugh and I can't help but smile back.

"Very funny."

"Well, whatever happened, I'm sure it wasn't enough of a reason to not accept the job. You said yourself that he wants to move to the States and he wants to work for this kind of firm."

"That was before he went back to break the news to his girlfriend. She may have convinced him to stay."

"Well there's only one way to find out." She nods to the letter in my hand, urging me on. "Open it!" She laughs and nudges my hand. "I don't know how you've resisted this long!"

"Okay, okay," I mutter as I unfold the envelope I creased so tightly yesterday. I slide my finger under the flap and my hands shake. I pause when I've torn it open halfway.

"Keep those fingers moving," she warns as she watches me out of the corner of her eye.

I look over at her and we both laugh.

"Go on," she urges again, and I resume, and when I release the flap all the way I slide out the sheet of notepaper inside. I slowly unfold it to see Xander's familiar handwriting.

I take a deep breath and begin to read to myself.

Dear Dany,

I thought I'd continue with our letter-writing tradition. Somehow it feels right. That said, I've written and rewritten this a hundred times because my thoughts are ... I don't know what my thoughts are ... and I don't know what to say, honestly.

I have all these memories I'm trying to sort and place. Memories of us as kids but also dreams. Dreams that feel like memories that couldn't have happened. But I know that doesn't make any sense.

The moment I saw you in the bar at Rubicon, when I looked in your eyes, I knew it was you.

Do you believe in fate?

I know this sounds disjointed.

My mates think I've gone mad.

The thing is, Dany, I always have a plan. But right now I'm flying blind.

The only thing I'm certain of is that I'll be back on the 7th and I want to see you again.

Xander

P.S. Listen to the song "Buy a Dog" by Luce.

"What's it say?" asks Mira.

I glance over and meet her eyes. "He wants me to listen to a song about a dog."

Her face flashes confusion and then she bursts out laughing. "You're making that up."

I chuckle and shake my head. "Not kidding."

"What'd he say about his girlfriend?"

"Nothing. But he says he's coming back on the 7th."

"So he took the job?"

I shrug. "I don't know."

"Read it to me."

I read her the full text of the letter.

"Wow," she responds with eyebrows lifted when I finish. "That is ... hard to understand."

"Right?"

She nods. "But he obviously likes you. More than a friend."

"Where'd you get that?"

"Read between the lines. And he said it outright, he wants to see you."

"Yes, but for what reason? Maybe to tell me his feelings are platonic."

She shakes her head. "That didn't read 'platonic' to me."

I reread it again. "I don't know, Mira. The letter doesn't really say anything."

"Play the song. Do you know it?"

I shake my head. "Never heard of it. Or the band."

"Look it up. Now," she orders, and I laugh at her militant demands.

I type "Luce, Buy a Dog" into my phone and when I find it, I stream it through Mira's car speakers and we both listen in rapt silence.

The moment it ends coincides with when we're pulling into the driveway of Mira's grandparent's house. She shuts off the engine and turns to face me. "Not platonic," she says with flat comic affect.

I meet her eyes and we both laugh.

"It's a good song," I say.

"It's a *great* song. He pictures you and him."

"And a dog, which I would love, but my landlord doesn't allow them."

She shakes her head. "You're way too literal," she says with a laugh.

As we exit the car and I walk up the steps to meet her grandparents for the first time, I'm still confused by the letter but now I'm smiling wide.

Chapter Twenty-Five

Dany

Mira knocks once and opens the door and calls out, "Nan? Grandpa?" as we step into the foyer.

A handsome man who looks to be in his late sixties appears from around the corner and enters the hallway. "Mira!" he cries out joyfully as he walks towards us with open arms. He folds Mira into a hug and she hugs him back and kisses his cheek. "Grandpa," she says, gesturing to me as they end their embrace, "this is my friend Dany. Dany, my grandpa, Mark Stephens, the former San Mar Chief of Police and newly retired."

I hold out my hand. "Nice to meet you, Mr. Stephens." He shakes it heartily with a genuine smile on his face. "Call me Mark. It's always a pleasure to meet one of Mira's friends. We've heard great things about you."

"Likewise," I say with a smile. "And congratulations on your retirement."

"Is that Mira?" a woman's voice sounds from upstairs. The owner of the voice appears at the top of the staircase and descends quickly. "Mira!" she says with her arms outstretched as she enfolds Mira in a long, tightly held embrace. When they draw back, she kisses Mira on the cheeks with gusto. "We missed you."

"Me, too," Mira says with a laugh. "I can't believe it's been three months since you left."

"Longest trip we've ever been on. We had such a nice time, we kept extending it." She looks over at her husband with a shrug and a laugh, and when he smiles back at her the love between them is visible.

"It was perfect," he responds.

She nods. "It was heavenly. But we're glad to be home, too."

Mira smiles and turns to me. "Dany, this is my nan, Judy Jane."

Judy welcomes me with a genuine smile that radiates from within. She's trim and fit, like her husband, and looks to be the same age, with a naturally pretty face that resembles Mira's. Her blue eyes, although a different color than Mira's, share the same remarkable kindness that Mira's hold within their depths.

As I focus on her eyes, her gaze meets mine and I feel something like a jolt, deep in my heart. She hugs me hello and a whispery sound emerges from my lips, unbidden. "*Mom?*"

We draw back from the hug. "What, dear?" she asks.

I shake my head to clear it. *What am I doing?* "Mrs. Jane," I say, clearing my throat, "it's nice to meet you."

She smiles and tells me to please call her Judy and what a pleasure it is to meet me and, as I listen to her voice and look into her eyes, images race through my mind in flashes of a millisecond. Images that feel like memories … *of me?* … but not me … and this woman … only she's much younger. I start to feel dizzy and I put my hand on the wall to stay upright.

"Are you okay, dear?" she asks with concern. She looks at Mira and then back to me. "Let's go sit down in the kitchen and get you a glass of water."

"Actually, can I use your bathroom?" I ask.

"Of course, dear," Judy says and I start walking quickly toward the bathroom as she calls out, "It's around the corner on the right."

But I already knew that. *How did I know that?*

I reach the bathroom and close the door behind me and sit down on the closed toilet and lower my head between my knees. "Don't pass out, don't pass out," I whisper to myself over and over. "You'll be okay, you'll be okay, you'll be okay, you'll be okay." I keep repeating it, like a mantra, but I don't believe it.

I rub my temples and take deep breaths in and out, over and over, slow, slow, slow. *What's happening to me?* After several long minutes, I feel steady enough to stand, and I gaze into the mirror over the sink.

Who am I? The thought pops into my head out of nowhere and, for a terrifying millisecond, I'm not sure how to answer. I splash water on my face and stare again into the mirror for a long time. The pressure to get my head on straight and join everyone else is acute. What kind of person meets her friend's family for less than a minute, calls them mom, and then escapes to the bathroom for God knows how long I've been in here? When I feel marginally normal again, I exit the bathroom and locate Mira and her grandparents in the kitchen. They're with three other adults and a cute little boy I recognize as Niko. Everyone is seated on stools around the large island.

"You okay?" asks Mira as she slides a glass of ice water in front of me.

I nod, unsure. "Thanks," I say, as I take a sip.

"This is my Grandpa Edwin," Mira says, introducing the elderly gentleman on her left.

He has a kind face and smile. I take his outstretched hand and shake it and he meets my eyes in a most curious way. "Delighted to meet you, Dany," he says as he adds his other hand to the grip, enfolding my hand in both of his. I immediately feel a sense of calm wash over me. He holds tight for a long beat and then lets my hand go abruptly. Maybe it's his demeanor or his soothing Australian accent, but whatever it is, I'm hugely relieved to feel normal again.

"And this is my Aunt Liz and Uncle Finn," she says proudly, as she introduces a woman and man who look to be in their forties. The woman has dark hair with bangs in a sleek, stylish bob. The man has a boyish face and artfully mussed brown hair. They make a cute couple and it's obvious from their body language that they adore each other. "Call us Liz and Finn. Always nice to meet our favorite niece's friends," Liz says.

Finn looks at her. "Mira is our *only* niece."

Liz returns his gaze. "Even if we had a thousand nieces, Mira would still be our favorite."

"That premise is impossible."

Everyone chuckles and Liz turns her attention back to me. "It's nice to meet you, Dany." I shake her hand and then Finn's, and I start to feel a little strange again but it quickly fades, thankfully.

"And this, as you know, is Niko," Mira says as she walks over and gives the little boy sitting on the stool next to Finn a hug and a kiss. Mira looks over at Liz. "Niko met Dany over the phone already," she explains. "We FaceTimed when I was at your house."

"Hi Niko, it's nice to meet you in person." I walk over and extend my hand for a shake and he smiles wide.

"Not everyone shakes kids' hands when they meet them," he says in his sweet little boy voice as we clasp hands. "But they should, because kids are people too, only smaller. And that's just temporary."

I laugh. "I agree." What a cutie. And smart, too.

I turn back to Finn. "When I met Niko, Mira mentioned she was babysitting because you were getting an award."

"For cancer research," Liz interjects. "Finn runs a bio-engineering lab up at the university."

"We focus on immunotherapy," Finn explains, "by altering the DNA of T-cells to recognize and attack cancer cells. But we're looking to broaden it to correct genetic mutations."

"The award was for a process Finn helped develop that makes the alterations more precise," Liz says. "It's really amazing."

I nod. "It sounds like it. Congratulations."

"Grandpa Edwin works at UCSM, too," Mira chimes in. "He's a Professor Emeritus in the Space Sciences program."

"With no hint of ever slowing down," Judy adds as she turns to look at Edwin. "Or aging. He still looks great year after year."

Edwin chuckles. "More gray hair." He runs his hand over his full head of silver hair absent-mindedly.

"Do you work at the university, too?" I ask Liz.

She shakes her head. "DA's office."

"Never lost a case," Finn proclaims proudly.

Liz smiles at him. "He loves that I help put criminals away," she says. "It's orderly."

For the rest of the evening we talk, laugh, and eat and I get to know Mira's family. They're funny and welcoming and I feel like I *fit* with this tribe.

All the more reason it's strange that a persistent undercurrent of worry is coursing through me.

Why do I have an uneasy feeling that I'm somehow bringing danger to their door?

Chapter Twenty-Six
Mira

My first early patient of the day is Greta, a cantankerous 70-year-old recovering from a knee replacement. After we finish in the gym, I make a pit stop in the cafeteria to grab two coffees before I head to my office on the third floor. I push the button to call the elevators and turn to admire the new art on the walls as I wait. The hospital features different local artists regularly and the photography displayed this month is interesting—a host of local landmarks captured from uncommon angles. When I hear the ding of the elevator car's arrival behind me, I spin around and step forward directly into the path of the man exiting.

"Ah," he cries out as I stop short and watch in what feels like slow motion as my hot coffee flies forward onto his chest.

"Oh my God, I'm so sorry." I look up, horrified, and that's when our eyes meet. "Charlie?"

He tugs his wet shirt away from his skin. "Mira?"

"Are you okay?"

He nods. "Are you?"

"I think you took the brunt of it," I say as I survey the damage. His light gray t-shirt is soaked down the front, revealing the outlines of his chest underneath. When he tugs the wet part away from his chest again, the bottom hem gets pulled up, revealing what I can't help noticing are very defined abs. He pushes the waistband of his jeans down as he tries to dab at the drips of coffee running down his chest before the liquid makes it into his pants. I realize I'm staring and I force my gaze back up higher.

Once he manages to contain the damage, he looks up at me again with his brilliant blue eyes and reaches for the cups in my hands. "Let me take those."

"To keep me from spilling the rest on you?"

He laughs. "No, so you can dry your hands."

"Thanks," I say as I shake my hands out to get the drips off.

"Feel free to use any dry part left on my shirt."

I laugh.

"I'm serious," he insists.

"I can't use you as a napkin."

"Suit yourself, but I just did it, and a little more coffee on here won't make a difference now."

I shrug and assess the dry parts of his shirt, which happen to be down low and off center, which makes me feel like I'm putting my hands on his hips, which feels acutely intimate. I wipe my hands, feeling his hard musculature underneath, and then I look up at him and smile sheepishly. "This seems like adding insult to injury."

"I just thank God the coffee here is lukewarm."

I laugh. "I'm so sorry," I say as I take the cups back from him. "Every time I see you it's a disaster."

"What do you mean?"

"First your shoes and now your shirt."

He smiles. "If I didn't know better, I'd think you were trying to get my clothes off."

I chuckle. "Starting with your shoes?"

"Can't take your pants off when your shoes are still on."

I feel my face flush. "You think that was my long-term plan? Shoes first, shirt second, then pants?"

He laughs. "Like I said, if I didn't know you weren't interested."

"I never said I wasn't interested."

Did I really just say that? The look of surprise on his face tells me I did.

"Are we talking in a pants-less way?" he asks wryly. "Because you turned me down for dinner and even accused me of being a stalker."

I smile. "I'm sorry about that last part."

"But not about the first part?"

"I had to turn you down."

"Why?"

"Because I'm not dating right now. Or then."

He nods, silent for a beat. "Does that mean at some point you *will* be dating?"

I smile. "Yes."

"May I ask when?"

"March 21st."

He laughs. "That's oddly specific."

"It's a long story."

He nods, silent again for a moment. "Would it be a date if we sat down, right now, over there, and drank what's left of those lukewarm coffees in your hands?"

I glance at the table he's pointing to as I mull over his offer.

"It might make up for the fact that you ruined this very important t-shirt," he adds as he tugs the wet cloth away from his skin again.

"Very important?"

"Vitally," he says with mock seriousness.

I nod, suppressing a smile. "I suppose it's the least I could do for destroying a vital shirt."

"The least you could do," he agrees with a nod, and his rueful smile makes me laugh.

"I only have 15 minutes. That wouldn't be a date."

He shakes his head. "Not at all. Dates require two hours, minimum."

"Who says?"

"It's in the handbook," he answers with a glint in his blue eyes, and I can't help but smile.

"But I feel compelled to tell you," he continues, "that if we do this, I'm not taking my pants off. So don't try to throw the rest of that coffee on me, because it won't work. I don't do that on a first date. Or first non-date."

I laugh and press one of the coffee cups into his hands as we walk over to the table.

"I really am sorry about your shirt," I say after we sit down.

"Don't be. I'm having it bronzed and framed."

"Because it's so vitally important?"

"No, because it somehow got you to have coffee with me."

I smile. "But it's not a date."

"Can I ask what's behind this no-dating thing?"

"The short version is, right before I met you I decided to stop dating until I turn twenty-five."

"And you turn twenty-five on March 21st?"

"March 20th."

His blue eyes search mine. "That's the reason you turned me down?"

I nod. "I wanted to have dinner with you—that's why I said yes at first. But then I remembered I couldn't."

"Why didn't you just tell me that?"

I shrug. "You were already walking away. And then the next time I saw you I threw up on your shoes, and then there was Sharri, and then the Bone Crusher, and-"

"The who?"

"That girl, Carly, at the beach clean-up. She practically broke Dany's hand when she shook it."

"I hope you're kidding."

"Why? Is she your girlfriend?"

"Carly? I just met her that day. After you accused me of following you, I thought I may as well go to lunch with her but that was it. She's not my type."

"What about Sharri?"

"The Sharri you left me with at the parcourse?"

"Are there other Sharris?"

He smiles. "No. And she wasn't my type either."

"So you're not dating anyone?"

He takes a deep breath and exhales. "I'm not going to lie and say I've been a monk, but no one I've dated has been what I'm looking for."

"What are you looking for?"

"You really want to know?"

"Yes."

He meets my eyes and holds my gaze for a long, meaningful beat. Finally, he shakes his head with almost a laugh and says, "This seems nuts, but I think I might actually tell you."

I smile. "Please do."

He smiles and searches my eyes again for a long beat.

"I'm looking for a girl I met at the beach," he says slowly, breaking the silence. "She has a warm smile and radiant green eyes that I can't stop thinking about. She's smart and witty and she has cute freckles across her nose and she likes being in the ocean and helping people. She's a girl I've been pining after for months, not realizing that she was turning me down only because it wasn't her birthday yet."

I smile, besotted. "That's oddly specific."

He nods. "Hard to find that on Tinder." We both laugh and my eyes trace the curve of his jaw and his smile, and then I find my gaze drawn back to his blue eyes again, which keep drawing me in.

"That was a pretty bold move," I say quietly.

"Under the right circumstances I have fleeting moments of boldness."

"The right circumstances?"

"When I see potential for something," he says as he meets my eyes. "Like in the early days, with my company—it's what kept me pushing forward. Or when I'm negotiating a deal ... or with you."

I smile. "And that's what made you boldly ask if I was interested in you in a *pants-less way*?"

He scrubs his hand down his face and looks at me crookedly. "I'm sorry. Was that awful? It just came out. I wanted to make sure you weren't interested only as a friend. I have a history of that with women I like."

"I find that hard to believe. Every time I see you there's another woman after you, clearly not as friends."

He raises an eyebrow. "That's how you see me? Because it hasn't always been that way. About five years ago I started working out and watching what I eat. I was the same guy as before but suddenly everyone looked at me differently. Believe it or not, I was overweight since I was a kid in elementary school, which wasn't easy."

"Were you teased?"

"I'll put it this way: most people will tell you—for one reason or another—that growing up wasn't a picnic, and that definitely includes me."

I meet his eyes and I see the sincerity there, with a touch of sadness. "Maybe that's why your eyes are so kind. That was what I first noticed about you when I met you that day—your blue eyes. I liked them."

He smiles. "If you're saying that getting called Chubby Charlie as a kid, relentlessly, led you to like my eyes years later, then maybe it was all worth it."

I laugh. "I'm saying that people who have been on the receiving end of stuff like that are usually more empathetic."

"Would you know that firsthand?"

"I got teased as a kid, too. About my leg."

He looks genuinely pained by my admission. "Kids are rotten bastards," he growls with a mixture of honesty and humor that makes me chuckle. "But maybe that's why I like your green eyes so much. They're the kindest eyes I've ever seen."

"Must be from all the teasing."

We both smile and there's a stretch of comfortable silence before he replies, "Maybe ... and maybe those rotten kids made us who we are, which led us to have coffee today, and, if that's the case, I'm not complaining."

I laugh and our eyes meet again and I realize how much I'm falling for this guy already. In the back of my mind, I wonder if this is what Grandpa Edwin warned me about—losing focus. Not calling this a date is semantics and it doesn't change the fact that I only have a few weeks to go and here I am, distracting myself with a cute guy with amazing eyes.

But then again, if I haven't figured anything out in all these months so far, will I ever?

"I found out recently we have a connection," Charlie says. "A positive one."

"What is it?"

"I mentioned something to my sister about you when I was at the hospital—the day your friend Dany interviewed me, actually—and when I told Molly your last name she told me who you are. I didn't recognize the name Ronin, but I knew your mom, Declan Jane."

His mention of my mom's name is so unexpected it's jarring. "You did?"

"Until I was six. She was my favorite babysitter. My favorite *person*, to be honest."

"She was?"

He nods. "My sister actually went to school with both of your parents. Full disclosure, she wasn't a fan, but that just means they were supremely nice people."

I laugh. "Are you kidding?"

"I wish I was," he says as he shakes his head.

"You really remember her?"

He nods. "I not only remember her, I remember really, *really* missing her when she was gone." His eyes fill with emotion as he speaks and it makes my eyes well up.

"A lot of people feel that way," I say quietly.

He reaches across the table and places his hand over mine. "Mira, I'm sorry. Maybe I shouldn't have brought this up. I wasn't thinking."

I shake my head. "No, I'm glad you did. I like hearing nice things about my mom."

I look up at him and we both smile and as our gazes hold, I can't help but wonder: is this why I'm drawn to him?

"She was a uniquely kind person, Mira. She made an impression on me."

I nod, touched by his words. We talk some more, and after he leaves I consider whether all of this is fate or if my interest in Charlie is taking me off course. The last time I had breakfast with Grandpa Edwin he reiterated that these last few weeks are the most important. What that means in terms of day-to-day practice, I have no idea. It all still seems a little crazy, but for now I think I should stay the course and follow the rules if I have any hope of working out whatever the universe is trying to tell me.

When I reach my office area on the third floor, I hand one of the two new coffees I procured to Gemma in the low-walled cube next to mine.

"Oh thank God," she says dramatically. "Just what I needed. *Bless you.*"

I tilt my head at her. "I bring you coffee every day."

"That doesn't make it any less momentous," she says with a laugh.

She slides both hands around the cup on her desk, bends forward to inhale deeply, and then sips from it like it's a treasured chalice. When she looks up from her coffee-induced reverie she narrows her eyes at me. "Why do you look like that?" she asks suspiciously.

"Like what?"

"Extra smiley."

I laugh. "Because I just had coffee with someone."

"Who?"

"Charlie."

"Are you messing with me?"

I shake my head.

She plants her cup down hard on her desk and it nearly spills out of the white plastic top. "Tell me everything. Start to finish."

I laugh and tell her the story.

"What was he doing here at the hospital?"

I shrug. "I forgot to ask."

She laughs. "Just like you 'forgot' you weren't dating."

"It wasn't a *date*. Just coffee."

"Right," she says with heavy sarcasm. "Maybe you can non-date him again for dinner tomorrow."

I toss a wadded up napkin at her and she laughs and throws it back.

I sit down at my desk and I'm still smiling as I click on the CDS logo—Charlie's logo, which is how I think of it now—to open the patient files database and type up a summary of my morning session with Greta.

"Are those notes about Grumpy?" Gemma asks as she peers over the cube wall. "I heard her call you a demon from hell at least four times during your last inpatient session. Did you put that in there?"

I laugh. "That's just the pain talking. She's a tough nut. I like her."

"You would," she says before she goes back to typing up her own patient notes. She pokes her head back over less than a minute later. "Stop thinking about Charlie."

I laugh. "I wasn't."

"Yes, you were."

I smile because she's right.

I was.

Chapter Twenty-Seven
Dany

We're standing next to a vibrant, beautifully azure pool of water and Xander extends his hand to me. I smile into his green eyes and my eyes trail downward, admiring the hard lines of his broad shoulders and bare chest, down to his sculpted abs and the "v" of his hips and leading lower ... until I become aware, gradually, that I'm naked, too. I glance down at the curve of my breasts and my hips, but I'm not embarrassed—Xander's gaze makes me feel beautiful, and natural. I reach out and take his hand and he smiles, and when he speaks his voice is low and filled with promise. "I'm going to make love to you under that waterfall."

My eyes follow his gaze to a tall, gorgeous waterfall in the distance and he takes my hand and leads me into the water. It's warm and inviting, and when we emerge, we're behind the descending cascade in our own private cove.

It's there that he kisses me, against the red rock cliffs, and it's celestial and seductive and when his tongue strokes mine, teasingly, the level of erotic pleasure that rolls through me is euphoric. I press my body into his and he groans, deep in his throat. "I want you, Dany, so much." He kisses along my neck like it's an art form and I breathe out in a sigh, and he groans again and lifts me up, pressed against the wall. I wrap my legs around him and his eyes are smoldering as he kisses me, hard and wanting. When I feel him pressing against my entry, I'm aching for him so intensely I don't think I can bear it a moment longer. We pause and stare into each other's eyes as he enters me, deliciously slow, and the sensual fullness causes me to breathe out his name in sheer rapture. He groans in return and slowly rocks into me again and the satisfaction is nearly overwhelming. "You feel so good," he rasps, his eyes dark with desire. We move together, slowly and rhythmically, until a powerful wave of pleasure begins to build within my core, climbing higher and higher until I know there'll be no holding back. Our breathing gets ragged and his lips are on mine and the tension intensifies and concentrates, building stronger and stronger, until–

I wake up.

It takes a few moments to realize where I am and that it was just a dream, but when I do, I quickly go from ecstasy to dismay.

Oh, Dany, you'd better rein this in quick. Xander could be coming back engaged, for all you know.

My heart literally aches at the thought of it.

Chapter Twenty-Eight

Dany

"Xander's back. I'm seeing him today." I try to sound breezy as I inform Mira of the news but I'm full of butterflies at the thought of seeing him again. It's Saturday morning and we're out on the water, as usual, sitting on our surfboards and rocking with the motion of the waves.

"What? Really? It's only the 6th. He's a day early."

"I know. I'm as surprised as you are. He texted and asked me if I could help him go furniture shopping for his apartment."

"*Furniture shopping?*"

I shrug. "Yep."

"He didn't say anything else?"

I shake my head. The whole thing has left me with a lump in my throat. "It's weird, I know. I'm meeting him at noon. It all feels very … practical. And platonic."

She looks at me, deadpan. "It's not platonic."

I try to smile. "So you keep saying."

"You haven't spoken with him since he sent you the letter?"

"I thought I should wait until we see each other in person. I keep rereading it but I still don't understand it."

"The message was in the song. Not the letter."

I smile genuinely, thinking about the lyrics. I've listened to it at least a hundred times.

"It's romantic," she adds.

I'm so anxious wondering about what everything might mean that I honestly have to distract myself or I'll go crazy—I decide to change the subject. "Not as romantic as that soliloquy Charlie gave you about what he's looking for in a date."

She smiles. "We've been texting a little but I told him we can't meet again until after my birthday."

"You've got amazing discipline, I'll give you that."

She shrugs. "I just feel like there's something I need to figure out and this is the only way I can do it."

I nod. "Any more insights?"

"Not really. But I feel like I'm on the cusp of something, if that makes sense."

"It does, actually." I think back to the feeling I had at her house when I met her family. That felt like I was on the cusp of something, too, only I still haven't figured it out yet. I think about how nice it all was, but also strange and confusing, as I stare out over the water and sway with the gentle swells, waiting for the next wave set.

"How nervous are you to see Xander today?" Mira asks, breaking the silence.

I look over at her. "Scale of one to ten? Eleven." I take a deep breath and let out all the worries rushing through my head. "I have no idea what he's going to say. And when I think about the fact that we hadn't seen each other in almost fifteen years and then right away there was that connection again ... but we only spent a few days together. I worry that

I've manufactured the whole thing in my head, or at least built it up beyond reality. And even if it *is* real, who knows if it can last? Logically."

"Don't think logic. Think fate."

"The way you see it with Charlie? Just letting the chips fall where they may?"

"I honestly don't know what to think anymore. I just know I like him."

I smile. "Two more weeks to go and you can have a real date with him on your birthday. Then you can make things happen—give fate a little nudge."

"*Our* birthday," she says with a smile. "You're turning twenty-five, too."

"Maybe your Grandpa's right and twenty-five will be a transformative year."

"I guess we'll find out." She gestures to the wave coming our way. "This one's yours."

I smile and get into position. Sometimes I think of waves as feelings: some thrilling highs; some toss-you-around lows; and some days where the ocean is as still and as placid as a lake. If the feeling within me right now is a wave—the feeling of potential, and nervous excitement, and hope for the future—I plan to hold onto it and ride it as long as I can.

Because I've learned that once you catch the wave, it doesn't always go the way you want.

Chapter Twenty-Nine

Dany

I convince myself on the drive over to Xander's apartment that if he's into me, I need to control my impulses and take this one step at a time. In retrospect, I think I fell too fast for Jared. I took everything at face value and maybe that was part of the problem. I don't want to make that mistake again.

Of course, I never had the chemistry with Jared that I feel when I'm with Xander. In fact, I don't even know if chemistry is a strong enough word. It's an electric pull from the earth's core: magnetic and irresistible and so powerful it could bring down cities.

Okay … maybe I've elevated it in my mind. It could bring down *one* city.

I chuckle to myself. A *big* one.

But it may not even feel the same way as before. It's been weeks since Xander was here and who knows how we'll feel when he's around full time? Either way, I need to take a step back from getting too close or going too fast. For all I know, I interpreted his letter completely wrong and Alora's moving here, too. It's not like I haven't been mistaken about people's intentions before.

I pull into the tidy Sea View Condos complex and park in one of the visitor spaces. When I get out of the car, I smooth my navy skirt and straighten the strap on one of my wedge sandals. I stroll through the nicely landscaped paths until I locate his address overlooking the swimming pool in the interior courtyard.

I feel nervous excitement as I walk up to his door. I try to hold onto the feeling of anticipation, but I also know that I can't hold onto it forever. I have to move forward and see what happens—however it ends up going.

I remind myself that we're simply meeting for a mundane activity. I can do that. *Be cool, Jameson, you're only going furniture shopping, for Christ's sake.*

I chuckle to myself and then I take a deep breath and knock on the door.

Chapter Thirty

Dany

A smile spreads over Xander's face when he sees me. "Dany." The way his green eyes crinkle when he says it washes away most of my nervous energy.

"Hi," I say, smiling back. He's dressed in jeans and a white button-down shirt with the sleeves rolled up to reveal strong, tanned forearms. He has a hint of shadowy stubble on his face and looks like maybe he hasn't slept, but that just makes him look all that much sexier. As I take it all in I'm starting to feel a little wobbly in the knees. *"Get ahold of yourself, Jameson,"* chides my inner drill sergeant and I steady myself on the wall next to me.

He opens the door wide. "Come in."

I walk into the living room and step to the side against the wall to survey the room for furniture needs. Immediately I'm perplexed.

"You already have furniture," I say, looking up at him.

"It's what they call an Executive Condo. Fully furnished."

"Then why did you ask me to help you go furniture shopping?"

He scrubs his hand down his face. "Can I be honest with you?" He looks at me nervously. "I haven't been thinking straight."

"You forgot you had furniture?"

189

He laughs. "I'm not completely off my nut."

He doesn't say anything more and as we stand in silence, looking into each other's eyes, I'm starting to wonder if he's at least partway off his nut.

"I wanted to spend the day with you," he blurts out.

"And you couldn't just ask me?"

"I didn't want to scare you off."

"Scare me off?"

"I showed that letter I sent you to my mate, Liam, and he thought I sounded mental."

My eyes are full of confusion as he continues. "I expected that if I asked you to spend the day with me you might decline."

"Why would I decline?"

"Because on paper I'm a mess: I left in a hurry, I sent you that garbled letter, and the last time you saw me I had a girlfriend who claimed she was my fiancée."

"So you thought you'd ask me to go furniture shopping?"

He lets out a laugh but his eyes look hopelessly lost. "It sounds ridiculous now, but I knew you'd say yes to a favor, if you were able."

I take a beat to contemplate what he just told me.

"So you tricked me?"

He rakes his hand through his hair. "Agh, Dany, that's an awful way of putting it. It wasn't meant to trick you. I haven't been thinking straight. I wanted to spend some time with you and I thought if I came on too strong ... I've been having these images of us, and I … agh, hell, I'm making it worse. Do you want to leave now? I wouldn't blame you." His eyes meet mine and I search them for a long moment and find only sincerity.

"No," I say softly. "I don't want to leave."

He registers surprise.

"And you don't have to make up excuses to spend time with me," I continue.

He smiles. "I don't?"

I shake my head slowly and, as he holds my gaze, I feel that magnetic connection begin to build between us that tugs every molecule in my body closer to his. I take in his green eyes, the classic lines of his face, and his sensual lips and all I can think about is how much I want him to kiss me.

Right now.

Resist, Dany, Resist.

"What's your status?" I ask.

"My status?"

"With your girlfriend."

He shakes his head. "There is none. It's over."

"Completely?"

"Completely. We're not right for each other. Alora knew it, too. It was over a long time ago, but I was certain of it after I was here."

"Because you wanted to move here?"

"That's part of it."

"But not all of it?"

He shakes his head. "No." Our eyes lock and he takes a step closer. "Dany, I-"

"Yes?" I breathe out, heart pounding.

"I can't stop thinking about you."

I search his eyes, desperate to discern what he means. "As friends?"

He shakes his head slowly.

Silence stretches between us for aching seconds and when he continues, his voice is low. "I can't stop thinking about you … and what I'd like to do with you."

I swallow hard. I think I may combust if he tells me but I don't care. "Like what?" I manage to whisper.

The corner of his mouth quirks up in a smile and there's a sly glint in his eyes when he answers. "I want to kiss you here," he says huskily, touching his finger gently to the corner of my brow. "And here," he says, gliding a little lower. "And along here," he says as he slowly trails his finger down to just under my jaw and over to my ear. "But more than anything I want to kiss you here," he says, drawing a slow line to my lips and holding for a beat.

I stare up into his eyes and the heat of his gaze is making me press against the wall to remain standing.

"Would you like that?" he asks. His voice is low and rough and it resonates deep, causing my stomach to clench. I nod, hardly breathing.

With a sexy smile and smoldering eyes, he leans in slowly and kisses my brow. The feeling is exquisite from the moment his lips make contact, and my whole body tingles with anticipation. He moves lower, taking his time, until he's just under my jaw, leaving a trail of soft, expert kisses that ends with the heat of his breath on my ear. I sigh softly and he lets out a low groan, deep in his throat. "I love how you sigh," he says huskily, and then, just as in my dreams, he takes me in his arms and his lips find mine.

So much for resisting.

Chapter Thirty-One
Dany

The kiss starts off soft and sensual and gradually becomes harder and wanting. Xander lifts me up, pressed against the wall, and I wrap my legs around him as he pulls me closer, devouring me, and carries me to the couch, our mouths never losing contact.

We lie back and he deepens the kiss and I sigh softly when I feel his hard body pressing into mine. His lips are soft and his tongue strokes and teases, sending me into another realm of erotic sensation. This feels so *good* ... and so *true*. The way he's taking his time, looking into my eyes and savoring every moment—even in my altered state I know it's the most amazing kiss I've ever had.

"Dany," he groans, deep in his throat, as he kisses along my neck.

"Xander," I breathe as the heat of his breath on my skin sends another rolling wave of pleasure through me. When he finds my mouth again, I begin to forget everything else except this moment, right now—the rest of the world no longer exists.

Slowly, slowly, as his tongue teases mine, I remember how sublime it feels to be in his arms again, the way it always was.

The way it always was?

"Alexander," I moan as he kisses me and pulls me closer.

"Declan," he groans as I hold tight to his hard, muscular frame.

We both stop.

"*Declan?*" he says as he looks into my eyes.

"*Alexander?*"

Chapter Thirty-Two
Declan

We both sit up. Alexander cups my face in his hands, searching my eyes as I look deep into his with the same disbelief and burgeoning joy.

"Is this really happening?" I ask.

Tears well up in both of our eyes as we realize the magnitude of what we're experiencing.

"Declan," Alexander chokes out with emotion. "I thought I'd never see you again."

"Is it really you?" The elation blossoming within my heart is almost too much to bear.

I place my hands on his cheeks as he holds mine and we search each other's eyes with wonder as we re-discover the souls we recognize, deep within.

Tears spill onto my cheeks as we whisper each other's names, over and over again, with disbelief and utter, incomprehensible joy.

"How?" I ask. "How can this be?"

He shakes his head and smiles, transfixed. "I always knew when your heart was involved, you could do anything."

I smile back and a flood of emotion and memories overcome me. "I remember seeing my mom at the hospital, from above," I say as hazy memories fill my brain, "and then letting go…. And I saw my dad. It was peaceful. All white light and …*love* is the best way I can describe it. He told me I had a choice. I could become a guardian or I could go back and start over."

"Why would you ever choose to go back?"

I look up and meet his eyes. "I wanted a chance to see you again. I thought if you were ever able to come back, you'd be starting over, too."

He squeezes my hands, his eyes filled with emotion. "I remember nothingness. Not black or dark, just *absence.* And I was fighting, Declan—fighting like hell—to come back. I was billions of atoms, racing apart at light speed, and I knew I had to hold onto what I was and find them all and piece them back together if I wanted a chance to come back to you."

"But how?"

He smiles and shakes his head, still awestruck. "All I know is, nothing was going to stop me from seeing you again."

I kiss him, softly, and the bliss that spreads through me is overwhelming. A thought occurs to me and I stop and look at him. "Is that why your birthday is one day after mine? Because it took you an extra day to come back?"

He tilts his head, surveying me with a crooked smile. "I just told you I had to piece a billion atoms back together and then tear my way through space and time."

"Took you long enough," I say wryly.

He laughs out loud in that genuine, hearty way he always did, and it fills me and warms me like the sun. God, how I love his laugh.

"However we did it, we're here," he says with wonder in his eyes.

"You always said souls with a connection like ours have a way of finding each other across space and time."

"Did you doubt me?"

I smile. "Never."

We gaze at each other for long minutes, soaking in the miracle that we're both here and alive, and together. Looking into his green eyes again, and the way they crinkle when he smiles, my heart bursts with the joy and madness of it all.

"You look different," I say as I trace my hand over his face, studying it in fine detail.

"So do you. But your eyes are still the same: sea-blue and beautiful."

I smile. "Yours, too. I always loved your eyes. I'm glad they haven't changed."

"What about the rest of me?"

I look him over. "You're still as tall, dark and knee-weakeningly handsome as ever."

"Knee-weakeningly? Is that a word?"

I laugh. "Maybe not, but it's true."

"So you still fancy me?" There's a glint in his eyes as he waits for my answer.

"I've been kissing you almost since the moment I walked in the door. What do you think?"

He laughs.

"You're still you," I say, looking deep into his eyes, "just different."

"You're different, too," he says as his eyes slowly trace my features and he brushes his fingers over my cheek. "Same eyes, same golden hair, and still beautiful, but in a different, kindred way. I like this different."

"But I'm still short. What's up with that?"

He laughs and then, as he traces my face again with his eyes, his demeanor shifts to utter sincerity. "I love your size, but I'd take you in any shell, anytime, anywhere. I'm still trying to process if this is just a dream."

"Me, too," I say, as my eyes well up anew. "Kiss me again before we wake up."

He cups my face in his hands and gazes at me soulfully, and then, very slowly, my green-eyed Alexander—who has somehow found his way back to me through space and time—does just that.

Chapter Thirty-Three
Declan

"Mira," I say. "Miracle." We're still sitting on the couch immersed in the awe and wonder of finding each other again, but the ramifications of what we've discovered are flooding in, too.

Alexander nods. "I know what happened with Avestan. And Alenna. After I was gone."

"You do?"

"I held onto this plane as long as I could."

"I did my best," I say quietly as tears well up and I cast my eyes down.

He gently cups my chin in his hand. "You saved her."

"But we were gone—her *parents*. And now I know her. In this life."

"You've met our daughter?"

I nod and smile. Tears escape down my cheeks and I wipe them away. "We're friends," I say. "Good friends … *best* friends." The words spill out in a poignant stew of marvel and melancholy. As I tell him about our daughter, my thoughts of Mira take on a new dimension and color. Everything I thought I knew pivots now that I'm seeing her through the lens of a parent, and not just as my smart, funny friend. The emotions rushing through me are almost too much to absorb all at once.

When I finish my portrayal, Alexander is smiling. "She sounds wonderful."

I burst into tears.

"Isn't that a good thing?" he asks with alarm. "We have a wonderful daughter."

I shake my head. "Yes ... but, *no*." I look up at him. "Twenty-five years, Alexander. It's been almost *twenty-five years*. We missed everything. We missed her growing up."

He folds me in his arms. "I know," he says quietly, "I know." Sadness infuses every word as he strokes my hair and I rest my head on his chest.

I hold onto him tightly as everything continues to sink in. After a long while I lift my head up and look into his eyes. "The song. I get it now."

Alexander smiles. "I didn't get it myself. I just heard it and it fit what I was feeling. I kept seeing all these images or dreams about us. I couldn't work it out."

"When did the images start?"

"When you lost your balance on the stairs at the beach and I caught you."

"Is that why you pulled away?"

He nods. "I wanted to kiss you ... and it was electric. Images raced through my mind of us and the way we were. I thought I was going mad."

"I thought it was because you weren't interested in me romantically."

He tilts his head to the side. "You must have felt, on some level, that couldn't possibly be true. In this or any other lifetime."

I smile. "You did have a girlfriend at the time."

He shakes his head. "That was over. This is what was meant to be."

"But when we were eating at Rico's you said there were only two times in your life you were certain about what you wanted: one was moving here and the other, I assumed at the time, was marrying Alora."

"Which is why people should never assume," he says with a wry smile. "What I was certain about was you—that I wanted to never lose contact with you. All I knew was that I was drawn to you."

I smile.

"I'm impressed with us," he remarks, "that we found each other as kids."

"But then we lost each other again."

"But we kept up the letters."

I nod. "I didn't want to let go."

"Our souls knew."

I smile softly, gazing into his eyes, but before long thoughts of the outside world rush in again. The implications of everything keep hitting me in waves.

"My mom ... and Liz, and Finn ... I saw them. Oh my God, Alexander. I saw them. They're all older now. And I had flashbacks, like you did. I *knew*." I look up at him. "When she hugged me, I knew—I called her *mom*." I take a deep breath. "And oh my God, I saw Molly Bing, too. I interviewed her for a story and she gave me such a hard time. Can you believe that? She's still insulting me to this day and she doesn't even know who I am."

He meets my eyes and we both let out a laugh. "Some things never change," he says with a smile.

"And I saw Charlie Bing, too. Sweet little Charlie! But he's grown up now. He's actually *older* than us, by six years. And he likes Mira. Oh my God, Alexander, I can't believe any of this. It's too much. I feel dizzy." I bend over and put my head between my knees.

"It's okay, just breathe," he says as he rubs my back. "In and out, nice and deep and slow. Just breathe. It'll be okay."

I do as he says and after a few minutes, when I think I'm all right to sit up again I face him on the couch. "My mom." I meet his eyes. "I *left* her." The words are almost too painful to voice aloud. "After she already lost my dad." I choke out the words with a sob. "It's too much … it's too much that she had to bear that. I'm sorry that I did that to her … and I'm *angry* … I *hate* the dark guardians. I hate what they did to us! Twenty-five years, Alexander! All gone." The fury in my heart erupts into heaving sobs and he holds me tight against his chest as I cry for all of our pain and loss.

For a long time we sit this way—holding each other as my tears wet his shoulder. Eventually I feel spent, and my tears dissipate and my breathing becomes even, and I tune into the warmth of Alexander's arms around me and the steady metronome of his heartbeat. Memories of holding each other like this many times before course through me and, as we sit in silent thought and I listen to the life-affirming rhythm, it soothes me the way it always did.

"We can't do anything about the past," he says quietly. "As much as I wish to." The low timbre of his voice resonates deep within his chest and I sense the slow burn underneath, being restrained. He takes a long, deep breath and lets it out. "But we can move forward and do our best with what we've been given."

I peer up to meet his eyes.

"A second chance, Declan. Do you realize what this means? We've been given a second chance. For us."

The pure love in his expression swells my heart. He's right. Why am I focusing on what we lost? What we have is remarkable and wonderful and amazing—and it fills me with hope again. *I'm here, with Alexander.*

"You're right. You made it back to me," I say as tears spill over once more. "I don't know how it's possible, but we did it."

He smiles softly. "It's possible," he says as he kisses away my tears, "because a love like ours bends the universe."

Chapter Thirty-Four
Declan

"We need to find Edwin," Alexander says. "Sooner rather than later."

"Why?"

"Because we were drawn here—to San Mar—for a reason. We need to find out what it is."

"Couldn't it just be that we wanted to see everyone?"

He shifts his glance away. "Possibly, but I'd like to find out from Edwin what the ramifications have been. You said Mira's safe and healthy, which is heartening."

"Ramifications of what?"

"Her birth."

"But her birth was supposed to tip the balance to good forever. Are you saying you think she might be in danger?"

He doesn't answer.

I force him to look me in the eyes. "What are you not telling me?"

"I don't know anything. I just know it can't be a coincidence that we're both here ... now. Edwin can tell us more."

"That's it?"

"That's it." He looks directly into my eyes when he says it and I believe him.

"Did you carry over any sprite powers?" he asks. He stretches his arms and flexes his fingers. "Because I feel purely mortal now. I don't feel the balance the way I used to."

"So you don't have a specific reason to think Mira's in any danger?"

"No."

"You're just being an overprotective dad?"

He smiles. "Maybe."

"Well, I think we're both stuck being mortals this time around." I stretch my hands out and try to summon something to my fingers but I can tell the effort will be fruitless. "And I saw Edwin. He's still here, in your old house. Mira lives in the cottage in the back."

He looks surprised. "She does? That's brilliant. She found her way to the house we would have lived in."

I nod. "She was going to get an apartment but Edwin convinced her to move into the cottage. She said he's always been overprotective. Everyone has, actually."

"Good. As they should be."

I smile. "Spoken like a true dad. What are you going to say to Edwin?"

"Whatever we need to, to get this sorted."

"How will we explain who we are?"

"If I know Edwin, he'll know when he sees us."

"What if he doesn't? Maybe we should think through what to say first."

He shakes his head. "Edwin will know us." Then he looks over at me. "I'd be willing to wait an hour or two, though."

"For what?"

The glint in his eyes tells me.

I laugh. "Are you kidding?"

He shakes his head and mouths 'no' and I chuckle again.

"I can't say I don't like the idea. I've missed you."

"You have no idea how much I've missed you," he says with a smile.

"You're not going to sell me on the wonders of waiting and anticipation?"

His response is a slow shake of his head. "It's been twenty-five years. I think we've built up enough anticipation."

"That's funny, actually, because my sole plan when I came here today was to resist you."

His eyebrow quirks up. "What a terrible plan," he says, and I laugh. "But we both know you never could resist me," he adds with a sly glint in his eyes.

I push his arm. "I think it was the other way around. But I'm glad I gave in, because it was the kiss that made us see who we are."

"I thank the universe for your lack of self-control."

"Very funny."

He smiles, gazing into my eyes. "I missed you, Miss Jane."

"It's Miss Jameson now."

"That'll take some getting used to. What would you like me to call you? Declan? Dany?"

"I feel like Declan ... but I'm also Dany." I look up at him. "How come you got lucky and your name hasn't changed?"

"No one calls me Alexander."

"Well I do, starting now. Would it be weird if you called me Dany?"

He shakes his head. "I've known you by both names. And a rose by any other name ..."

I smile. "In public, for now at least, you'd better call me Dany."

"Done," he says with a smile.

"And as for the other thing ... I think maybe we should wait."

"You want to?"

I shrug my shoulders. "As you always said, we only get one first time ... *again*."

He smiles. "True." He takes my hands in his. "We'll wait as long as you like."

"But that doesn't mean we can't enjoy ourselves in the meantime."

He laughs. "In that case, come here, Dany Declan, so I can show you how much I missed you."

He pulls me into his arms again and my heart is overflowing when he shows me, slowly and tenderly, exactly what he means.

Chapter Thirty-Five
Declan

"What do we say when he opens it?" I ask. We're standing outside Edwin's door, which Alexander just knocked upon.

He shrugs. "Long time, no see?"

I laugh and push his arm. "Be serious. What if he doesn't know who we are?"

"He'll know."

Edwin opens the door and appears startled to see us. His eyes track from Alexander to me and back again. Finally, after a lengthy stretch of silence, he speaks. "I've been waiting for you two."

Alexander turns to me with a satisfied smile on his face.

I shake my head at him. "Always so cocksure," I mutter, and he laughs.

Edwin closes the door behind us. He plants his hands firmly on Alexander's shoulders and peers into his eyes. "It's really you," he says, his voice filled with emotion. They hug, long and hard, and then Edwin turns to me and takes my hands in his. "I knew it was you the moment I looked in your eyes. You and Mira were drawn together, as I knew you would be. It's so good to see you again, Declan." The emotion in his eyes makes mine well up, too. "You, too, Edwin," I say, tears spilling over, as we hug.

He nods. "I knew you'd make it here in time."

"In time?" Alexander asks.

Edwin looks at both of us. "We have something to tell you," he says as he motions us toward the kitchen.

We?

In the kitchen I see a face that stops me in my tracks. "You?" The tall man with the dark hair that I've noticed everywhere, watching, for months, is sitting at Edwin's kitchen table. "You're a guardian? Is that why you've been following me?"

"I prefer to phrase it as watching out for you ... and Mira. I'm Soren." He has a deep, comforting voice and a plainspoken American accent and now that I'm up close, what seemed ominous from afar—his laser focus and serious demeanor—is recast as protective and paternal.

"We can fill you in on Soren's role later," Edwin interjects. "Right now we should discuss the matter at hand." He turns to Alexander. "You must know how grateful I am that you're here. What you did is meant to be impossible, and I don't know how you managed it, but, as we all know, there are rules governing the universe." He pauses. "And when you act against them your actions create consequences."

Consequences?

Alexander looks stricken. "What consequences?"

Dread crawls up my throat as I wait for Edwin to answer.

"You'd better sit down." he says gravely as he motions us to the table.

Chapter Thirty-Six
Declan

We sit down across from Edwin and Soren.

"What consequences?" I ask again, holding back the panic surging within me.

Edwin peers down at his hands. "When Alexander managed to return, he tore an opening in the fabric of the universe." He's silent for a moment and then he looks back up. "Unfortunately, Malentus found that opening, too."

"I led him back?" Alexander's voice is hoarse as he utters the words.

Edwin nods almost imperceptibly.

"All of them? Avestan, too?" I ask with mounting horror.

Edwin shakes his head. "Avestan and Alenna transformed fully." He looks up at us. "I'd like to believe it's because she saw the folly of her betrayal in the end and she did it to save Mira. Regardless, Alenna's actions caused their transformation, and Avestan and Alenna no longer exist as they once did."

I nod, silent. I'm not sure why I feel a pang of sadness for them, but I do. I glance over at Alexander. He's also silent regarding the news of his brother. My eyes stray to his temple which no longer bears the scar that he kept to remind him of Avestan. In my heart I hope it's because he left that pain behind in his last life and he's not as haunted as he once was by his brother's betrayal and fall to the dark guardians.

"Where is he?" Alexander asks, breaking the silence. "I need to put it right." His voice is sober and stern.

"Malentus?" Edwin replies. "That's the problem. We don't know."

"How do you know he's back?" I ask.

"There's been talk," Edwin says. "And signs that can't be explained otherwise—tremors, if you will, in the force of darkness."

"So he's been in touch with his brothers?" Alexander asks.

"Yes," Edwin replies. "But the disdain they hold for one another runs deep, as you know."

Alexander nods.

"What does this mean for Mira?" I ask. "Is she in danger?"

"That's what we need to discuss. I've been doing some reading," Edwin says. He glances at Soren next to him. "In fact, that's how Soren and I came to cross paths. He shares my affinity for ancient texts."

Soren nods. "When Edwin and I met, we discussed Mira and it called to mind an obscure fable I once read about the fruit of two guardians."

"And you think that's Mira?" I ask. "But she's the daughter of a guardian and a sprite."

"Some fables reflect forgotten history," Edwin replies. "Others have proven to be prophecies. And they're not always exact."

"In the story," Soren continues, "this unique and impossible fruit they manage to grow requires a quarter century to ripen fully."

"And?" I ask.

"Mira is turning twenty-five in two weeks." Edwin says soberly.

"But a lot of people are turning twenty-five this year. It doesn't necessarily mean anything."

"Would you deem it a coincidence that you and Alexander both found your way to San Mar now, and worked out who you really are, only two weeks before she turns twenty-five?"

I have to admit Edwin has a point. I was bouncing around from place to place for years prior to six months ago and Alexander was firmly rooted in Australia until he came here last month. The fact that we'd both find our way to a small beach town in Northern California in the final months before Mira's twenty-fifth birthday lends credence to Edwin's theory.

"So what are you saying? What's going to happen?" I ask.

"We believe that when Mira turns twenty-five, her energy will mature." Edwin says grimly.

"And?" I ask.

Soren looks at me. "Power of that magnitude makes Mira a target. *The* target."

I look at him, horror stricken. "But why would we be drawn here if we can't do anything? Alexander and I are only mortals now."

"Your role isn't clear as yet," Edwin answers. "I believe you may be here simply to help surround Mira with those who love her most and want to protect her."

I lower my head into my hands. "I don't understand why she's in danger. I thought when Mira was born the balance was shifted forever." I lift my head up and meet Edwin's eyes. "That's what I felt, in my heart, when I let go."

He reaches over and puts his hands over mine. "What you endured wasn't in vain, Declan. The day you and Alexander sacrificed yourselves to remove Avestan and Malentus from this plane and ensure Mira entered the world safely, you contributed mightily to the forces for good. Mira's birth was just the beginning, and now it's coming into full fruition."

"Then why aren't the dark angels all just *gone*? Why don't they just leave us all alone for once? Why do we have to worry about them coming after Mira at all? I thought her birth would just make them all disappear." I pause in my emotional rant to see Edwin's eyes looking at me with compassion. "Declan," he says softly, "with light there will always be some darkness."

"But why does she have to be in danger?"

Edwin looks down. "There are natural rules that govern the universe. And when those rules are broken, it can have a cascading effect. Malentus is here now, and able to join forces with his brothers again."

"All because I came back." Alexander's voice is filled with pain. I reach over to take his hand but he doesn't look at me.

Edwin shakes his head. "Don't go there, Alexander. Your return is a good thing—a necessary thing. The fact that you were drawn to San Mar and you realized who you are prior to Mira's birthday is a sign. This is how it was meant to happen."

Alexander shakes his head. "If I hadn't come back, Declan's vision would have come true: Mira's birth would have cemented the balance on our side forever. Malentus's return is what makes rebuilding the Triumvirate possible."

"The Triumvirate?" I glance at Alexander.

"Three brothers," he answers grimly. "Stolvos, Mortegur, and Malentus."

"They call themselves blood brothers." Edwin explains. "Not because they share a bloodline or any shred of brotherly love, but because they rule the dark realm. They each hold court over their domains. They despise one another, and yet, for all their bitter competition over followers and power, they also need one another. And that only makes their enmity cut deeper."

"Why do they need one another?" I ask.

Edwin glances down at his folded hands on the table. "Because dark energy is volatile," he says before he looks up again and meets my eyes. "And connected, like all energy is."

"They're part of Malentus's line, then?"

Edwin shakes his head. "No, not of the same line, but part of the same entity. If you imagine dark energy as balancing on a three-legged stool, the Triumvirate is formed with each leg representing one brother's domain. If you remove a leg," Edwin says as he mimics snapping a leg off a stool, "as Alexander did when he transformed with Malentus, the stool becomes unstable. Malentus's absence struck a hobbling blow to the strength of dark forces."

I glance at Alexander and squeeze his hand. "That's good," I say firmly.

"Yes," Edwin acknowledges. "And Mira's birth cemented the balance in our favor further, by preventing the remaining members of the Triumvirate from replacing the leg."

I nod.

"But they want that power back," Soren interjects.

Edwin nods. "And no brother is strong enough to attempt it alone. For years we heard rumors that Malentus had returned and we expected the Triumvirate would join together again, but there have been no attempts to take Mira. Not even a whisper. We couldn't understand it until Soren found the reference in the fable. They must be waiting until she turns twenty-five. It's the only reason that makes sense."

"But we can't let our guard down beforehand," Soren interjects. "They could also make an attempt before she turns twenty-five, so she won't be at full strength. Once her power matures and she learns how to use it fully, the chances of the Triumvirate being able to take Mira's energy—let alone control it—go down dramatically each day, even if they do all work together."

"But nothing is certain." The sober expression on Edwin's face dampens any burgeoning sense of optimism within me that Mira will be safe once she turns twenty-five. "There's a fine line between striking before her strength is more than they can handle, and striking when they can seize the most energy possible. Unfortunately, we don't know where that line is. We've heard Malentus is weakened and at severe disadvantage but we don't know in what way—or if it's even true. No one has seen him."

Soren must see the dejection in my eyes because he proffers a hollow notion. "There's always a chance they hate each other so deeply that they'll never agree to work together."

Edwin tilts his head with seeming consideration. "The hate they harbor runs deep, and it's a surety that Stolvos and Mortegur are enraged that Malentus made himself vulnerable to transformation and left them in this position. They won't have welcomed him back into the fold easily."

Soren nods in agreement. "They've been marinating in their resentment for twenty-five years and struggling to rebuild their power in the aftermath of his actions."

Alexander shakes his head. "That's just it. Twenty-five years of struggling can bend even the bitterest of minds. Of course they won't want to reward Malentus—even if it would help them in the process—but the temptation to gain a power like Mira's and tip the balance again in their favor would be too great. We all know they'll join forces. They have the potential to wield power far greater than any single brother could ever attain alone. They'll do it—even with any unpredictable risks that an attempt to take Mira's power poses."

"I have to agree," Edwin says. "They may be bitter competitors rather than collaborators, but above all they have a thirst for power. Which means the only reason they haven't made an attempt on Mira yet is because they're lying in wait until they can gain the greatest power possible."

I look at them, confused. "I still don't understand why twenty-five is such an important year."

"Even beyond the symbolism in the fable," Edwin replies, "there are natural cycles in the universe. There are flowers that bloom every 100 years, cicadas that surface every seventeen, and phases of the stars in the sky. The twenty-fifth year represents transformation and the inception of achieving true potential. It all fits."

Alexander looks up. "Is it possible Stolvos and Mortegur may not be aware of who or where Mira is? I find it hard to believe they wouldn't pursue her on their own out of arrogance. If Malentus is weakened, as you say, maybe that's what he's holding over them. He won't tell them until he has to."

"Yes, we've considered that," Edwin states with a nod.

"And we've also considered that as Mira's energy grows stronger, her aura will shine brighter and she'll be easier to discover." Soren adds soberly. "But I haven't noticed a change. And Mira hasn't said anything to Edwin about gaining any new—and potentially alarming—abilities, which is good, but it's also odd."

"Why is that odd?" I ask.

"Because perhaps her power isn't maturing in the ways we expect."

The idea that neither Edwin nor Soren are one hundred percent sure about anything leaves me with a sick feeling in my stomach. "What will they do if they come after her?"

Soren is the one who answers. "They'll take her to Nusquam where they'll destroy all the good in her and feed off of her energy, keeping her trapped and out of our reach for eternity."

I feel the blood drain from my body. Memories of that hopeless, suffocating netherworld are imprinted on me forever. "But only if they join forces?"

"They're each not strong enough alone," Edwin confirms.

"Well, how have you been keeping her safe? Mira knows when she's around dark energy. She told me so, not in so many words, but I get it now. And I'm sure when you told her about Nusquam she understands what the dangers are and how to avoid them."

Edwin eyes me evenly. "We've been doing everything possible to keep her safe. And, no, Mira doesn't know, consciously, what the dangers are."

I stare at him, dumbfounded. "You haven't told her?"

"Of course not."

"*What?* Not anything? Why not? You have to tell her!"

Edwin shakes his head. "Absolutely not. It will only put her in more danger."

"How?"

"Guardians can't reveal themselves—"

"I know all that," I say, waving Soren's interruption away with my hand. "But she deserves the truth. How could knowing what she's up against possibly make things more dangerous for her than they already are?"

"It would do nothing more than cause undue stress," Edwin answers. "She'll be focused on her power, which will make her shine brighter and create greater risk that she'll be found. That's why I didn't tell her in the past. And now, while her energy is building, it would only be more of a calamity to tell her presently. We need only look to what happened to you and Alexander to witness the folly of sharing the existence of guardians with mortals," Edwin states forcefully as his voice rises.

My eyes go wide. "First of all, I wasn't a mortal, I was a sprite. Second of all, Mira isn't a mortal either. She's a ... a ... *earth guardian*. You don't even have a name for it, that's how special and unique she is. And third of all, the danger comes from *not* telling. Do you realize she knows she has some sort of power but she doesn't understand it? And now that it's growing more powerful, who knows what she'll be experiencing? She's searching for answers and no one's pointing her in any direction. How could you let her go through her whole life that way? How could you let her struggle to understand things she can't possibly hope to ever comprehend on her own?"

"We make decisions at times that are profoundly difficult, but are for the best," Edwin says quietly. "You experienced that firsthand: you made a similarly difficult decision once for Alexander."

His words land like a fist to my gut. "You're comparing my decision to do what I thought was necessary to save Alexander's life to you not telling Mira who she really is? Keeping secrets was the problem, Edwin," I say as my voice rises. "Sharing information was the solution. Can't you see that?"

"What would have happened if you'd never been told of the guardians' existence, Declan? Have you ever considered that? Once?"

I'm shocked by his words and take a moment before answering. "I think it would have turned out worse," I answer quietly. "I *know* it would have."

"I don't know that I agree. What I *do* know is that I'm trying to save Mira's life. I've looked after her and kept her safe since birth, and with only two weeks to go I'm not going to change what's been working for more than twenty-four years." He slaps his palm on the table when he speaks the last word, but when he begins again his voice is quieter. "I'm protecting her every way I can, Declan. The way I couldn't protect you and Alexander." His voice strains on the last part, and when I meet his eyes I see the searing anguish held there.

"You blame yourself?" I whisper. "For what happened?"

He stares at his hands on the table. "The responsibility for what happened rests with me," he says quietly, "and the weight is … *considerable*." He looks up and the torment in his eyes is acute. "I should have been there. I should have seen ... but I wasn't. I've accepted my mistakes. But don't you ever doubt how much I love Mira. I've done everything in my power to protect that little girl as she's grown up, and I'll continue to protect her the best way I can until I exist no longer." His words are forceful and determined and they gain sparking energy as he speaks.

I reach across the table and place my hands over his. "Edwin, what happened wasn't your fault," I say softly. "We were all fighting with everything we had and it worked: we saved Mira. And now Alexander and I are back, just in time, like you said, and that's what matters."

He looks up and meets my eyes but I can tell I haven't relieved his burden. I won't let his regrets stop me, however, from what I have to say next. "But, Edwin," I say, my voice firm and sure, "I know in my heart that telling Mira is the right thing to do. And I may be only a mere mortal this time around, but I'm Mira's mother and that means I'll do whatever I think is necessary to protect her. And that includes telling her everything about who she is and the danger she's in. And there's nothing anyone can say or do to stop me."

Chapter Thirty-Seven

Nusquam

"I'm trapped here like a ghost of the damned," Malentus seethes.

Stolvos peers down at his brother with acrid disdain. Only Malentus—the one he always considered to be the weakest link in the Triumvirate—could be felled by his own arrogance and manage to crawl his way back but only make it halfway. He spits a dark fluid on the ground next to Malentus's shimmering, slithering visage.

"Stuck in Nusquam without a shell or any power worth pissing on is more than you warrant," hisses Mortegur.

Stolvos spits another stream of black fluid on the ground, this time near Mortegur. "We all know who the true leader of the Triumvirate is," he rasps.

"Arrogance of that order is what led us here, having to listen to this vacuous carcass." Mortegur kicks at Malentus dully with his pointed black boot.

Malentus bites back the maledictions he's straining to withhold. "I thank you, brothers, for finally agreeing to consider my proposal. As I said, when the time is ripe, I'll bring the girl here. Then I'll send for you both and we can get started doing what we do best."

"Your best has always been marginal," Stolvos spits out with derision.

"It's unfortunate then," Malentus retorts with a quiet reserve that belies the level of enmity rising within him, "that you need me."

Mortegur looks directly at him. "How do you expect to lead the girl here when you're trapped here yourself with no shell?"

"Perhaps I'm not as trapped as you think." The barely suppressed rage in Malentus's voice emerges as a forceful hiss.

Stolvos discharges another long ejection of dark liquid on the sand. "My patience is wearing thin, Malentus."

"As I spelled out, several times, the most desirable time to act is just prior to her power maturing. She'll be at peak strength for us to harness her energy but at the lowest ebb of knowing how to wield it in defense. If we act then, together, we can control it for ourselves. I don't have the power to start the process, but once you both begin, I can join in and we can reign once more."

"Why not tell us where she is," Stolvos demands, "so we can bring her here now and begin to repair the damage you wrought twenty-five years ago."

"And risk you attempting to take her power without me?" Malentus's eyes track from Stolvos to Mortegur. "Lest you forget, gentlemen, it's called a Triumvirate for a reason—it takes all three to control a power of that magnitude. I'm giving you the chance to restore the Triumvirate's standing and gain a more formidable source of energy than we've ever held."

"You're giving *us* the chance?" Mortegur's voice is quiet and menacing. "That's rich, since we wouldn't be in this position, save for your incompetence."

"We *all* stand to benefit," Malentus hisses, unfurling the words with a sharpened edge of barely restrained tension.

"Although one of us—who holds no power at all at the present time—stands to benefit the most." Stolvos delivers his screed as his eyes bore into Malentus with contempt. "We'll allow you to reclaim your lowly position among us. But that's all." He spits another ejection of thick, black fluid onto the ground before he leaves.

Malentus watches as they disappear, seething in silence because he knows he can't exit with them. His sole consolation is a fact he chose not to share: he isn't completely at their mercy. He swipes a portal open and searches for a vulnerable prospect for his spirit to enter. His record so far is fifteen minutes out of his trapped, miserable existence and into a host in the surface world.

Perhaps he can remain within the chosen mortal longer this time.

Chapter Thirty-Eight
Declan

"He just wants 48 hours," Alexander says after he closes the door and we're back in his apartment.

"And you think that's reasonable?"

He shrugs. "He wanted two weeks but you convinced him to settle for two days."

"But do you agree with him?" I ask. "Not telling her? Not telling anyone?"

Alexander hesitates. "I agree that we should at least conceive a plan before we go off half-cocked and tell everyone information that will upturn their lives and change the way they think about everything they thought they knew … forever. There's no going back once that box is opened."

"But do you agree with Edwin and Soren about not telling, ever?"

He takes a deep breath. "Edwin has a point. Knowing could put Mira in more danger."

I shake my head. "I can't believe you don't see it. It's so clear to me."

"Guardians aren't meant to reveal themselves," Alexander reminds me. "And, as you know, it's not easy explaining all this to mortals. It's a lot for them to take in." He sits me down on the couch and meets my eyes. "There's even a chance they won't believe you or they'll think you're crazy."

He says the last bit with a glint in his eyes, which coaxes a lopsided smile from me. He's not wrong. When he first tried to tell me he and Edwin were guardians I thought he was a lunatic.

He takes my hands, facing me. "And the other question is, how much to tell? If Edwin tells Mira about guardians, should we be there? Do we also tell her we're her parents? Or is that too much to toss on her all at once? And if she knows who we really are, should we also tell your mum? You know Mira will want her to know. And if we're going to tell Judy, that most likely means telling her husband Mark, and are you suggesting that we tell Liz and Finn as well?" He looks at me questioningly. "And that's not all. If you tell Judy who you are, will you also tell her that your dad, Frank, was a fallen guardian? And that his law partner betrayed him and killed him?"

His endless questions are making me dizzy. I press my fingers to my temples. "I don't know what the answers are. I just know that having information is better than being kept in the dark."

"Well, there are secrets within secrets within secrets here, and it's hard to know where to stop."

I look up at him. "Then we don't stop. We tell Mira everything. And we tell my mom and Mark, and Liz and Finn, too. I want them to know who I am. Who I *really* am. And that I'm back. And I missed them." Tears are welling up now and Alexander takes my hands again and eyes me with compassion. "You mean all at once?" he asks. "You're honestly suggesting we gather them all together so we can tell them that guardians exist and that we're Declan and Alexander, back again? Do you realize how that will sound? What they'll think?"

"Yes," I say, knowing full well he's right. "But Mira's in danger and we need to do everything possible to help her."

"What if *helping* her in this way ends up causing more harm than good?"

"I can't think like that. I only know that she deserves to hear the truth."

I deliver the words with confidence, but on the inside worry is gripping my heart.

Tightly.

Chapter Thirty-Nine
Declan

I hear the ping of an incoming text and I lift my phone off the nightstand next to me. We're sitting on Alexander's bed while we continue to ponder everything we've been talking about for hours. We literally haven't stopped talking since we figured out who we are. There's so much to wrap our minds around ... and worry about.

I look over at him when I see who it's from. "It's Mira. She wants to know how our furniture shopping went."

"What are you going to say?"

I pretend to tap out a response. "How about: 'It went great, and by the way, I'm actually your mom, and your dad and I are back from the dead, and you're in danger of having your soul sucked out by three homicidal dark angels who want to rule the universe.'"

The corners of Alexander's mouth quirk up in a smile. "That wouldn't sound at all alarming."

I let out a laugh. "What am I supposed to do? Ignore her?"

His expression morphs to compassion. "I understand how hard this is. I'm torn, too. And I want to meet Mira more than you can imagine. But we agreed to consider Edwin's viewpoint before we do anything rash."

"But there's only two weeks until her birthday. And Edwin said she's getting stronger every day. We need to protect her."

"You're right. But doing anything without a plan could make things worse. Let's take solace in the fact that we know Mira's safe right now. In this moment."

"Is she? Truly?"

"I believe Edwin and Soren when they say she's protected. They've looked after her all these years that we've been gone."

"I just feel so powerless." I hold up my hands. "I can't even do the laser thing with my fingers anymore."

"I agree we're at a disadvantage being mortals, but that doesn't mean we're powerless. We obviously sense things. You and I found each other. And you connected with Mira months ago."

I nod. "That's true."

"I'm not saying I don't agree with you on any of this. But let's honor our promise to Edwin for now and work out all the angles."

"You mean who to tell and how much to say?"

"Among other things."

"It makes my head hurt just thinking about it."

He takes a deep breath. "It's well late now, and it's a lot to get sorted. Let's allow things to settle some more until we work out next steps. The answers may come when we allow everything to sink in and process."

I nod. He's right. And Edwin's right. I can't go off with a half-baked plan without seriously considering what's best first. This is life-changing information I'd be sharing. Heck, I'm still reeling from it myself. I'm basically two people now. How do you explain that?

I pinch myself for the hundredth time just to make sure I'm not dreaming before I pick up my phone again and stare at the text message from Mira still waiting for my reply.

After a few minutes, I type a response. Otherwise she'll worry.

I'll fill you in later.

I stare at the words I wrote. At least it's honest. I turn off my phone and place it back down on the nightstand and glance back at Alexander. "I can't talk to her right now. And I can't see her anytime soon, either ... because if I see her I won't be able to act natural. She'll sense something's up. Knowing who I am changes everything—the way I look at her, the way I think about her ..."

He nods. "We have a daughter," he says softly with a smile. "A *grown daughter*." The look of wonder in his eyes as he says the words makes me smile, too.

But as we continue to absorb the miraculous nature of it all, I can't quiet the nagging worry in my chest that Edwin may convince us the best way forward is to never tell our daughter who we really are.

Chapter Forty

Declan

I wake up to see light streaming through the blinds. My head is still on Alexander's chest and I peer up at him to see if he's awake. He groans and stretches. "Morning," he says with a sleepy smile.

"Morning."

"Our first night back together and all we did was sleep in our clothes," he says lazily.

I slide myself up higher to lay beside him, face-to-face. "Are you complaining?"

He shakes his head. "Not at all. On the one hand, with all of our worries about Mira hanging over our heads, I can't see us having the … um, *focus* that I'd like until that's sorted."

I smile. "Focus, huh?"

He nods his head slowly. "I want to take my time with you. To rediscover you, slowly."

His voice is low and the way he says the words makes my stomach clench. "Plus there's the anticipation," I say softly.

He takes a deep breath and exhales. "Yes, there's definitely that."

"And on the other hand?" I ask. "You said 'on the one hand.'"

"The other hand wants to ravage you wildly and not waste another moment."

I laugh. "Is that the right hand or the left hand?"

He smiles. "Not sure." He slides his right hand over my hip and under the hem of my blouse until I feel the warmth of his palm on my bare skin. He continues to slide his hand up, slowly, as we hold eye contact and when he reaches my breast he kneads it gently and skims the nipple with his thumb. When he does it again I close my eyes and he tugs me closer before his mouth finds mine.

As we kiss, I find myself falling back in time and it all feels so natural and so *good* and I surrender myself to the intensity. All worries fade to the background as our hands explore and we kiss, slow and sensual, as a swell of pleasure builds within me. My hands move to undo the waist of his jeans and he groans, deep within his throat, but then he stops me.

"I know you want to wait, so I think we need to halt this here. My right hand has obviously gone rogue and I apologize for that."

I laugh. "I'm pretty sure your left hand was involved, too, but at least now we know which one is the ringleader."

He chuckles. "I think we should get out of here and go somewhere."

"I'll go anywhere with you."

"You don't even know where we're going."

"Maybe I do."

He smiles. "You always know."

"I know I need to be distracted today or I'll never make it through the full 48 hours."

He nods. "We need time to think—away from everything and everyone."

As Alexander drives through the familiar curves and turns to the back of Redwood Park, I feel as if no time has passed. The ranger access road; the sign; the gravel lot— they're all still here, if not older and more weather-beaten.

When Alexander parks and we get out of the car, flashbacks to when I last saw him here, his body crumpled on the ground, cause my body to stiffen.

"I know," he says, putting his arms around me. "I remember, too. But this was ours before all that happened. Let's not allow them to take our place and our memories away from us."

I tighten my arms around him and take a moment to stare up into his soulful green eyes. "You're right. Let's just get past this part."

He shifts his position and sweeps me up into his arms.

"What are you doing?"

"Carrying you," he says as he moves forward.

"But you're not a guardian anymore."

"You're still as light as a woodland fairy."

I smile. "Woodland fairy? First of all, I'm addicted to chips and guacamole, so I know that's not true. But even if it was, you can't carry me the whole way. It's too far."

He raises an eyebrow. "Are you implying I'm not strong enough?"

"I'm implying that when you were a guardian you could fly and lift cars and do all sorts of things that you can't do now."

"Lift cars?"

"I'm just spitballing."

He smiles. "Spitballing?"

"Are you saying you couldn't have lifted a car? You built a house on a mountain, for Christ's sake."

He laughs. "I'm just saying you never saw me lift one."

"Well I'm saying that if you try to carry me all the way there, you're going to get tired and sweaty."

"What's wrong with getting a little sweaty?"

The look in his eyes and the way he lowers his voice when he says it makes me perspire a little myself. I force myself to focus. "Look, we're both dressed for hiking. We knew we had to do this the old-fashioned way. Let's walk together, like the sad, lowly mortals we are."

He chuckles and sets me down. "Fair enough. If that's what you want," he says as we start to walk. "I think it's farther than I remember, anyway."

I laugh. "See?"

"As long as you know I could still do it if I needed to."

I shake my head. "Still 'chucking your brass about,' as you used to say."

He laughs. "Still just trying to impress my girlfriend. Is it working?"

I look up at him. "Even as a mere mortal, you never fail to impress."

"Ditto." He looks around at the overgrown trail we're on. "You may remember that you asked me to kiss you once, in this very spot."

"And I also remember, clearly, that you declined."

He laughs. "Because we hadn't had a proper first kiss yet."

"But we've had one now."

"Many."

"So you're not saying no anymore?"

He shakes his head. "I'm seizing every moment with you in this life. I won't take even a second for granted."

His words, and their delivery, touch my heart. "Then I want you to kiss me like you wanted to that day," I say softly.

He smiles and pulls me to him gently, fingers entwined in my hair, and his lips meet mine. The kiss is soft at first, and then it deepens, with more longing, and I'm transported to a state of utter, sensual bliss. As his tongue teases mine, the trees, the sky, and the earth below disappear until all that's left is the two of us and our ardent desire for one another. When we finally pause, he searches my eyes.

"I still can't believe it's you."

I smile.

"I can see your aura right now," he says as his eyes trace a path around my face.

"You can?"

"In my mind, I can. It's as beautiful as ever. You're so beautiful, Declan." His voice trails off to a whisper.

I smile, besotted.

"This." I motion with my hand back and forth between us. "It feels the same with you. Just like before. As if we're on the same frequency."

He nods. "The essentials haven't changed."

"Do you think everything will be the same? When we … you know."

"Make love?" A slow smile spreads over his face. "I *know* it will be."

The look in his eyes makes my belly stir way, way down. "How do you know?" I whisper.

"Because of how this feels." His voice is husky and raw as he pulls me close and kisses me once more.

"Is this it?" I sense that we've finally reached the spot we're looking for, but everything is so fiercely overgrown it's hard to tell.

"I think it's just through that entry there," Alexander says as he points to some thick overgrowth off to the side. "This was a much longer trek than I remember."

I look up at him. "Does it suck being a mortal now and having to walk around with the strength and stamina of a regular human man?"

He laughs. "*Regular?* I hope you'd say 'exceptional' or 'above average' at minimum."

"Your kissing is definitely exceptional."

"Is that why it took us four hours to get here?"

I laugh. "That was all you. And I think you're being a tad hyperbolic."

"That was both of us. And I forgot how much I missed your entertaining vocabulary."

We both grin.

"What if it's not there?" I ask as we glance toward the overgrown entry.

"It'll be there. It won't have gone away."

"Even though we went away," I say quietly.

He meets my eyes and we're silent for a long beat.

"You ready?" he asks as he takes a step forward.

I nod and he tugs and pulls at the overgrowth to create an opening. But when we step through and emerge on the other side, the image that greets us is so unexpected I raise my hand to my lips and let out a gasp.

Chapter Forty-One
Declan

We step into the fairy ring, holding hands, and in many ways it's just as before: a ring of stately redwood trees towering up to the sky, formed when the enormous parent tree in the center—over a thousand years old—died long ago, sending sprouts around the perimeter to form a new generation.

Dappled sunlight fills the center of the ring, lighting the space where Alexander once burned our initials into the petrified tree remains. Only now, there's something else there: two smaller redwood trees, each barely five or six feet tall, stand together within the center of the ring.

They're striking for their placement—beside each other, behind our initials, with their branches and needles touching—but mostly because of their appearance: ghostly white.

The stark, poignant beauty they represent coaxes a wave of sadness from within me. Alexander puts his arm around my shoulders gently and pulls me close.

"Ghosts of the Forest." His voice is quiet, breaking the silence as we both stare at the immaculate sight before us.

I look up at him.

"That's what they're called." He glances at me and then his eyes are drawn back to the trees. "White redwoods are the *Ghosts of the Forest*."

"Why do they look like that?" I ask as I stare at the delicate ivory figures.

"They're unlike the other trees. They don't have chlorophyll."

"Will they grow taller?"

He shakes his head. "They're stunted. It's said they draw and store pollution away that could harm the other trees."

"They sacrifice themselves?"

"In a way."

I stare at the two ghostly figures, guarding our initials, and a tear spills over and trails down my cheek.

He takes my hand. "We're not ghosts, Declan. We're here."

"Are we? If we can't tell anyone who we are, then are we really here?"

He doesn't answer as he tugs my hand and leads me over to the phantom-like trees. I reach out and touch one of the branches, rubbing the alabaster needles between my fingers. Alexander kneels down in front of the trees and clears away debris with his hands until he reveals our initials, frozen in time, underneath. He looks up at me. "Still here," he says with a poignant smile.

I nod and as I stare at the heart with our initials, "D.J. loves A.R. Always," written within, memories flood back to me: how hard I practiced so that I could write the initials in the air for Alexander on our first Valentine's Day; how I wished I could make them last; and how Alexander told me he had an idea and brought me here, to burn them into the petrified remains of this giant redwood tree for all eternity. When I think about how we were to be married here, and how it never happened, another wave of sadness overwhelms me.

"We never got married," I say quietly.

"Yes we did," Alexander replies as he stands.

I look up at him. "You mean when we practiced the night before?"

"You have to admit, we made up pretty good vows: jaffles and peanut butter and strawberry jam."

I smile, remembering. "Am I still the tomato soup to your jaffle?"

"As long as I'm still your jam."

I laugh. "You're definitely my jam. But practicing vows doesn't count."

"Who says? We're more in love than any two people in the universe. How would a formal contract add anything more to that?"

I consider his words. "We *did* manage to find each other again, in the next life."

"Against all odds."

I nod. "Alright, I'll go along with your argument that we were married."

"And we did it again, in this life."

I scrunch my face skeptically.

"You can't have forgotten. It was at your insistence."

"You're counting *that*?" I peer up at him sheepishly.

He laughs. "Ten years old. At our favorite place by the river."

"I'm surprised you went along with it."

"If you haven't worked it out by now, I was under your spell from the first time you were snarky to me about my sandcastle-building skills."

I laugh. "I wasn't snarky."

He raises an eyebrow. "We can agree to disagree."

"I wanted to seal our friendship before I moved away," I say. "Pretending to get married felt like it would make it last."

"Or, knowing what we know now... "

I meet his eyes. "I must have known, on some level."

"Regardless, our kiss held an exalted place in my memory after you left."

I smile. "It was just a silly peck."

"I don't know about you, but it was my first kiss."

"What do you mean, you don't know about me? I was ten. Who else do you think I was kissing?"

He laughs. "I don't know how many other boys you may have been beguiling."

"First of all, you weren't beguiled. We were just best friends playing around."

He shrugs. "I don't think you realize how consequential your kiss was for me—it ruined me for other girls for a long time after."

I push his arm. "I highly doubt that."

"But you admit we've been married twice now."

I glance up at him. "Where are you going with this? Are you trying to get out of marrying me again? Legally?"

He laughs. "No, I'm trying to say that you and I are meant to be. We'll always find each other—in any life, any age, any shell." He meets my eyes. "You transfix me, over and over."

The shift in his expression to utter sincerity catches me by surprise and goes straight to my heart. "You transfix me, too." I smile up at him. "And I wasn't beguiling anyone else, you know."

"That you know of," he says with a grin. "Teddy Heath always liked you. That's indisputable."

I push his arm. "I accept your marriage proposal—if that's what all that was about."

"That wasn't a formal proposal. I can do better than that. And I will."

"Because you have a plan?"

He laughs. "I'm always planning something."

I look out to the ring of trees, peaceful and eternal. "I cherish this place, but I don't think I could get married here. Not after what happened."

He nods and we're both quiet for another long moment.

"I'm glad this is still here, though," he says with a gesture to our inscription.

"D.J. and A.R." I read the initials out loud. "Dany Jameson and Alexander River. Our initials are still the same."

"One more thing we carried over with us."

I turn to meet his eyes. "This is still a special place."

He nods. "It's quiet. And beautiful."

"Hauntingly beautiful," I agree softly.

He pulls me tight against him as we stare at our declaration of love, watched over by two ghostly guardians in a fairy ring of sentries rising up to the sky.

After long minutes spent in silence, I turn to him. "I think we need to reclaim it before we go."

"How?"

"Create a new *last* memory of being here."

"What would you like to do?"

"Kiss me again like you did when we had our first kiss."

He smiles and pulls me into his arms and begins to sway with me to silent music. "Like this?"

I look up at him and smile. "At last."

"At last I get to kiss you all over again." His voice is low and he gazes into my eyes before he pulls me closer and parts my lips with his. The sensation of his lips on mine takes me back in time to the exquisite ecstasy of our first kiss and the joy I felt as we were finally able to show our love for each other without restriction.

The kiss deepens and the emotions welling within me are almost too much to bear. I pull back and look into Alexander's eyes.

"Why are you crying?" he asks as he tenderly wipes away my tears with his thumbs.

"Because I'm so happy to be with you again."

He smiles as we stare into each other's eyes.

"What if this is all a dream?" I ask.

He shakes his head. "We're here," he whispers as he kisses me softly. "It's real."

I nod and a fresh wave of tears overflows.

"It's okay," he says gently as he kisses away another tear.

I shake my head. "What if it's not?" I look into his eyes with the turmoil I'm feeling inside. "Because if we're really here, then—right or wrong—I know what we have to do."

And, although I'm following my heart, I'm far from certain that it won't bring more danger to everyone we love.

Chapter Forty-Two
Declan

Now that everyone is gathered, I'm having second thoughts. I never did manage to convince Edwin and Alexander fully, without reservation. I waited the requisite 48 hours, as promised, and then I told them I was doing what I felt was right, with or without them.

But, oh, how grateful I am that they agreed to be here, because the chances of me coming off as a nutjob are pretty much close to 100 percent. I tried to convince Edwin to show off some of his guardian powers to prove I'm not completely insane, but he said he won't be compelled to "perform like a sideshow act," and that everyone will have to decide for themselves on the merits of what I have to say.

Great.

So that's where we are.

Mira, Liz, Finn, Judy Jane, and Mark Stephens are here: otherwise known as my daughter, my two best friends, my mom, and the chief of police who married my mom, and therefore became my "stepdad after-the-fact," I suppose. Also in attendance are me (of course), Edwin, and Alexander. Edwin tried to convince me to keep the circle of reveals as small as possible (a circle of exactly "zero" being his ideal), but I just couldn't imagine keeping any of the people here in the dark. I agreed Soren need not be here, however. Why reveal a guardian who isn't part of the immediate family?

We're all gathered at the house I grew up in a lifetime ago. Literally. They think we're here for some sort of surprise. I asked Mira to set it up.

"Well?" Mira says excitedly. "When are you going to tell us what this is all about?"

"I must admit it's been quite intriguing," chimes in my mom with her usual sunny disposition. "Mira told us you have something you want to tell us?" She looks at me and then to Mira, but Mira shakes her head. "I swear I don't know, nan," she insists with a smile.

Then everyone looks at me again.

I swallow. I'm sweating and I begin to feel faint. I gaze around the living room at everyone seated before me. I've gone over this in my mind a thousand times but I still haven't come up with a non-psychotic-sounding way to say that, essentially, I'm back from the dead. Where do you even start when you have information like that to impart? What's my opening line? I decide to rely on simple honesty.

I clear my throat and begin.

"Thank you all for being here. I know this must seem strange that I asked Mira to gather you all together. But I thought it would be best to tell you all at once. For anyone who hasn't met him already, this is Alexander, by the way, my friend."

I gesture to Alexander and he smiles. "I introduced myself when I came in," he says. "It's nice to see all of you."

He glances back at me in the ensuing silence and I freeze. Oh God, maybe Edwin's right. There's still time to back out. I'll seem a little nutty, but not as crazy as if I go through with it. Alexander's eyes urge me on. I know he's torn about what the best thing to do is, but he supports me always. One more reason I love him.

I clear my throat again before starting. "First of all, I just have to tell you that what I'm about to say is going to sound completely bonkers. And you're not going to believe it at first. But I hope you'll hear me out until the end." I fan myself, nervously, with my hand. "I'm not sure how to start."

My mom's expression changes. "What is it, dear?" she asks with concern.

I glance at Mira and she looks utterly confused. She mouths the words, "Are you okay?" and I nod and push forward.

"I'm not who you think I am. I mean, I am. I'm Dany Jameson, but I'm also someone else." I glance around the room. Now I've managed to make everyone look confused … and worried. They're probably wondering if they should call the authorities.

As if on cue, Mark speaks first. "Are you in the witness protection program?"

I shake my head. "No, nothing like that."

"What is it, then?" asks Liz, looking concerned.

"I'm going to tell you some things. Things that I wouldn't know … unless I was a certain person."

"Okay, now you have me worried," Mira says with an uncomfortable laugh. "What are you trying to say?"

"Are you in trouble with the law, dear?" asks my mom.

Oh God, this is going all wrong. I'm winging it when I should have practiced and planned out every word. I take a deep breath and press forward. "For instance, I know that

Finn doesn't like jelly on his peanut butter sandwiches. And he likes lemonade, but he doesn't eat fruit." I look over at Finn. "Unless you do now?"

He shakes his head, bewildered. "Did Liz tell you that?"

"And, Liz, I know that you met Finn in sixth grade when you called Molly Bing 'Malibu' and told her to go someplace else to sit when she tried to kick you off her table during lunch."

Liz, confused, looks over at Mira. "Did you tell her that story?"

"And Judy," I say, looking at my mom, "I know that you used to have a cat named Willow and you and your husband Frank used to say she was 'the cat who thought she was a dog,' because she was the sweetest cat in the world and she followed everyone around and came when she was called. Your daughter, Declan, made a sign that said 'The king of love and rainbows is a cat named Willow,' and you laminated it and hung it over Willow's food bowl."

"How would you know that?" Judy asks, looking disconcerted and increasingly alarmed.

"I know these things, because—this is the part that's going to sound crazy—but I know these things because I'm the one who made that sign. I'm Declan." I turn and gesture to Alexander. "And this is Alexander. We came back. I know we look different, but our souls are in here."

Complete silence falls over the room.

Liz is the first to speak and she stands up, angrily. "I don't know if this is some kind of sick joke or what, but it has to be the cruelest thing that anyone could ever do. If you only knew the pain we all went through, losing Mira's mom and dad." She looks over at Mira and then back to me. "For

you to say such a thing. You have no idea. *No* idea. Finn
didn't talk for months after Declan died!" She places her
hand on Finn's shoulder. "We were all just barely hanging
on, and for you to come here and dredge it all up again and
say something so cruel. It's just ... it's just ... *inhumane*. I
don't know what game you're playing, but this is sick. Just
sick!"

Her words make my heart sink and I worry that I've
made a terrible mistake. But I also know that I can't stop
now—I have to do better. I have to convince them. "Liz, I
know it sounds cruel, but I swear it's true. Ask me anything
and I'll tell you. Remember how we used to hang out at the
river as kids? And that picture I gave you and Finn for your
seven month anniversary? The one with my thumb in the
corner?"

Liz looks at Mira, the color drained from her face. "Did
you tell her these things?"

Mira shakes her head.

Finn looks frozen in place, staring at me.

I press on, sharing memories in a hurried stream of
consciousness. "And Finn, remember when I told you Liz
liked you and you gave her that pink rose and asked her to
the dance? And how we found Zeno when he was a puppy?
With his head stuck in that six-pack box? Or when you told
me to drink barbecue sauce so I could stop thinking about
Alexander?"

He shakes his head vigorously. "What you're saying is
impossible. We could have told Mira any of those things
and she must have told you."

"Did you tell her you used to hold my hand when I had panic attacks? Or how Molly Bing mowed down that fence when we took Driver's Ed with Mr. Guilford?"

Mira shakes her head and looks at Finn and Liz. "I couldn't have told her. I didn't know half of that stuff."

"You must have told her and you don't remember," Liz replies resolutely.

I look at my mom. "We used to go to the beach every year and send balloon messages to dad. And the last year before I died we sent up paper lanterns instead. I want you to know, mom, that I saw dad, and he's fine. And you were right when you thought you heard him talking to you after he died. He said 'it's okay,' and you knew he meant that it was okay to move forward with Mark. And you were right. He wants you to be happy. He spoke to me, too, and he saved my life once. And I saw him after I died. You'll see him again one day, too." I look over at Mark. "And Mark, I remember your wife. She was so kind when we were kids and I used to play with your sons, Jake and Zach. I want you to know that you'll have a chance to see her again, too."

They're both shaking their heads with a mixture of shock and, in Mark's case, it looks like burgeoning anger. I can tell I've overstepped my bounds. I press on before they throw me out of the house.

"I can prove it." I look at my mom. "Every year on my birthday you'd tell me the story about the day I was born: how I came out right on my due date but I waited until you and dad had a good night's sleep."

She's still shaking her head, so I press on, panicking with anything I can remember. "Do you remember when I was five and I fell when I was roller skating, barefoot, with those strap-on skates? I got that weird triangle-shaped cut on the top of my foot. When I came through this time I still had that scar. It carried over from when I was Declan." I start to take off my shoe to show her.

"That's it!" Liz says, standing up. "I don't know what this is, but it's mean and it's sick and it's making me so damn sad I can't stand it anymore. If you only knew what Declan meant to me—what she meant to all of us here—you wouldn't do this. You wouldn't say these things." She has tears in her eyes as she reaches for Finn's hand. "Finn, let's go."

"It's true, Liz," I plead, "I swear."

"Liz, it's me," Alexander says quietly. "I spoke to you my first day at San Mar High and asked you about your friend with the sea-blue eyes that I sat next to in Mr. Brody's homeroom period."

She stops, appearing stricken, and looks at him.

"You had an Avett Brothers t-shirt on," he continues, "and I talked to you and Finn at lunch. You told me all about the ins and outs of school and who and what to avoid."

Liz remains silent and I take the opportunity to press forward. "I'm not trying to hurt anyone, Liz. It really is me. I miss you guys so much. I missed the last twenty-five years. It's hurting me, too." I look over at my mom, desperately reaching for memories that might convince her. "You told me once that dad used to call you his 'little ray of sunshine.' What you didn't know is that it's because he saw your aura and it's bright and beautiful and-"

"Stop," my mom cries out, and I immediately go silent.

"How would you know all those things?" she asks in a pained whisper.

Her face is still contorted when she turns to Liz, Finn, Mark, and Mira, in turn. "How?" she asks again. "It's not possible."

Slowly, she stands up and walks across the room and takes my hands, drawing me up from my seat. When we're both standing, she raises her hands to cup my cheeks and looks deep into my eyes—searching, seeking, and studying. I stare back and all the love I feel for my mom swells within me as I return her gaze, looking deep into the eyes of the woman I know so well … and missed so much.

"Declan?" she whispers as her blue eyes well up with tears.

"It's me, mom," I croak out with tears of my own.

Chapter Forty-Three
Declan

The ensuing hours are a jumble. Convincing them that Alexander and I are who we say we are was just the first step. Then we had to reveal the existence of guardians and go back and fill in all the details of what truly happened to us twenty-five years ago. I even told my mom what really happened to my dad, with Burt Fields and the law firm. I decided I'm through with secrets and I don't want to hold anything back. For good or ill, they deserve to know the truth, the whole truth, and nothing but the truth. *But please, oh please let it be for good and not for ill.*

Suffice it to say that many hours later we're all exhausted from the sheer enormity and cascading emotions of it all. Liz and Finn had to call their babysitter twice to see if she could stay longer with Niko.

"I still don't understand why you didn't tell me," my mom repeats ruefully. She directs the comment to Edwin and me but the answers we give will never be enough because, the truth is, no good answer exists. Edwin has tried to explain, as have I, about the danger involved, but it sounds like a weak plea. And perhaps it is. The certainty I felt in my heart for gathering everyone here today and upsetting their lives forever—in defiance of Edwin's warning—was because I believe strongly that knowledge is power. Secrets are weak. Maybe if I had come to that conclusion a lifetime ago it would have made the outcome different. But if it would have been better or worse, I'm not sure.

"Well, I don't know about anyone else," my mom says, bleary eyed, "but I'm exhausted. I think I need some time to digest all of this—at least overnight—and try to make sense of it. But in the meantime, is Mira in imminent danger? Is that what you're saying?"

Edwin's voice is reassuring when he answers. "She's safe. We're keeping her safe. But Declan felt it was important to tell you everything because she feels that the benefits of disclosing outweigh the dangers." He glances over at me. Clearly he still doesn't agree.

"How long have you known?" Mira looks at me and asks.

"Since Saturday," I say, swallowing hard.

"And you didn't tell me right away?" she asks.

"We spoke with Edwin and agreed to wait 48 hours to consider the ramifications before disrupting everyone's lives," Alexander answers.

"So there was a possibility you never would have told me at *all*?" Her expression is incredulous as she looks from Alexander to me and then settles her accusing gaze on Edwin.

Edwin's eyes are cast down. "It was to protect you."

"Protect me from figuring out who I am? And what I can do?" She asks with wide-eyed affront. "You're saying I have powers? Why wouldn't you tell me that? What are they?"

"They're yours to discover," Edwin answers.

"But how could I discover them if you never told me they existed? And all these rules you told me to follow and never explained?" The hurt in Mira's eyes as she speaks is agonizing. "All my life I've been asking you these questions and you didn't say anything? I don't care what your reasoning was, it was *cruel*. I honestly don't know what to believe about any of this, but I need some time to think before I want to talk to you, or anyone, frankly."

I feel a twinge of hurt, but I can't say I don't sympathize. I look up at everyone. "What we told you tonight is hard to believe, and I understand that ... and I understand you'll need some time to absorb it, and think about what it all means."

"That's the first thing you've said tonight that I can get on board with 100 percent," Liz says. She looks over at Finn. "We need some time, too. To think. I can't even believe we're considering any of this as true." Finn nods and mutters, for what must be the hundredth time, "None of this is possible."

I look at my two friends, in their forties now, and here I am not quite twenty-five and claiming to be their long, lost best friend from childhood. I hardly believe it myself.

"Edwin, help me understand. Why is it more dangerous for us to know rather than not know?" my mom asks, still obviously mulling things over in her mind.

"Because the energy shifts," he says plainly. "I already feel it happening now. The energy shifts when you know what's around you."

"But isn't it good to be aware and on the lookout?" she asks.

"What you focus on, you can draw to you," he replies. "So we need to ensure we all focus on the right things."

"What are the right things?" she asks.

Edwin takes a deep breath before answering. "If you can, try not to focus on Mira and how her power will manifest ... and your worries about what might happen when it does." He glances down. "Although I realize that's a little like closing the barn door after the horse has already left." His words strike my heart like a dagger. "Rest assured, the other guardians and I have been protecting Mira since she was born, and we're protecting her now more than ever. And we're protecting all of you, too. We haven't forgotten that the dark guardians have targeted loved ones in the past." He looks directly at my mom and, for the first time ever, Edwin looks fragile to me. "Judy," he says quietly, "I pledge and promise you that we'll do everything in our power to keep Mira safe and make certain we won't have an outcome that will break your heart again. Nor mine."

Tears well up in my eyes as I see the expression of shared pain between them. It's in that moment that I notice Mira seeing it, too.

"If what you're all saying is true," Mira says unevenly with tears in her eyes, "then Declan and Alexander sacrificed their lives to save me ... and ruined everyone else's lives in the process." She looks over at me. "And it was *my fault*. And now everyone's in danger again, and that's because of me, too. And no one told me." Her voice cracks as she looks at each of us. "My whole life, no one told me ... and you almost didn't tell me tonight."

She stands up as a tear escapes down her cheek. "I don't want to see anyone for a while," she says quietly and then she walks out the door.

Chapter Forty-Four
Mira

Nan ran up to me in the driveway after I left the house, and I assured her I just needed some time alone. I asked if I could stay in my old room for a while because I don't want to go back to the cottage behind Grandpa Edwin's house and risk running into him. She agreed, but then she tried to defend Grandpa Edwin by assuring me that whatever decisions he made, she knows he made out of love. All I could think was "Et tu, nan?"

I honestly don't want to see her or anyone now. I'm so angry. And confused. And sad. And overwhelmed.

When she asked me where I was going I told her, "What does it matter?" According to Grandpa Edwin, there's a bajillion guardians following me everywhere I go at all times.

I still haven't decided if that thought is more creepy than comforting.

In the end, I didn't tell her where I was going because I didn't know.

Until now, anyway. I just pulled into the parking lot of the San Mar Bar & Grill, open 24 hours. It's half past midnight when I walk inside and take a seat at an empty barstool and order my first drink. I look around at all the other patrons and wonder if any of them are guardians looking out for me. By my second drink I'm wondering if half of them are dark guardians hell bent on killing me—or whatever it is they plan to do with me. When I was listening in stunned silence earlier in nan and grandpa's living room, I remember hearing something about suffering somewhere cold and hopeless forever. *Nice.*

By my third drink, I'm on my way to not thinking about any of it. Isn't that what Grandpa Edwin said to do? Not focus on my power? But that doesn't make any sense because earlier he told me this whole year was about focusing on myself, which is the whole stupid reason I haven't gone out with Charlie. So which is it? Apparently he wants me to focus when I don't know what the heck I'm focusing on, but now that I know I've got homicidal dark angels after me, he wants me to forget all about it?

And what if everything they said tonight is wrong? What if I'm not this mythical being with miraculous power that they think I have? It's only T-minus eleven days until doomsday, apparently, on my birthday and I don't feel a thing. And, besides, if I was really that powerful, why would I need protection? Couldn't I just protect myself?

By my fourth drink, I'm starting to think it's all a crock. *Screw the rules.* I pick up my phone and text Charlie. I'm going to finally date the man I've been drawn to and resisting for months.

I wait and have another drink and when I see Charlie come in, I sing out his name. "Hi, Charlie." I wave my whole arm so he can see me at the bar, but there aren't many people here now, so I think he spots me. He walks straight over.

"You want a drink?" I ask. "Sally," I call out to the bartender, who's actually more like a friend now. "Can you get my friend a drink?"

Charlie waves her off. "Thanks, Sally, I'm good."

"How'd you know I was here?" I ask him.

He tilts his head and gives me a funny smile. "Your texts and phone calls gave me a clue."

"You sure you don't want a drink?"

He shakes his head. "You look like you're finished with that one. How about we go home now? My car's outside."

I try to focus on his blue eyes as I consider his suggestion. "Okay," I sing out as I hop off the bar stool and land a little unsteadily on my stacked heel boots.

Charlie puts his arm around me for support and leads me out to his car.

"Is this a Tesla?" I ask as I look around the interior when we're seated inside.

"Yes," he answers.

"It's nice." I look over at him and he smiles.

"Thanks, Mira."

"No sweat."

He laughs. "Where are we going?" he asks.

I look at him strangely. "You don't know where you live?"

He laughs again. "I know where *I* live. But I don't know where *you* live. Can you give me your address?"

I shake my head. "Just take me to your place."

He smiles. "Mira, I think I should take you home."

"I don't want to go home. In fact, I'm texting my nan right now to tell her I'm staying over." I pull out my phone and very slowly and deliberately type in the words, "Staying with a friend tonight. No worry. See you tomorrow," and I hit send. I look up at Charlie and smile. "Done."

He smiles back. "You live with your nan?"

"For the time being."

"What's your nan's address?"

I start to formulate the answer in my mind and then I look at him knowingly. "I know what you're doing, Charlie, and it's not gonna work."

He laughs. "All right, Mira, you win."

Chapter Forty-Five
Mira

I start kissing Charlie before we're even all the way in his front door.

"Whoa, whoa, whoa, Mira," he says as he takes a step back and holds me at arms' length by the shoulders.

"You don't want to kiss me?" I ask.

"Oh, I *definitely* want to kiss you," he states with an amused glint in his eyes.

I brandish a relaxed smile and step closer, but, confusingly, he steps back. "Then why won't you?"

"Because you've had a lot to drink."

"I think I know my own mind, Charlie. And I want to date you. Tonight."

He laughs. "I hope you'll want to date me tomorrow, too. When you're sober."

"Charlie?" I look up at him.

"Yes?"

"Does this house have a bathroom?"

He smiles. "It has several. If you let me take you to the guest room I can show you one."

"Good, and then I think you better strip yourself naked and get out of there."

He laughs. "Why would I do that?"

"Because I think I'm gonna be sick, Charlie, and I don't want to demolish anymore of your clothes."

The next thing I remember is Charlie racing down the hallway with me in his arms and then holding my long hair back as I barf up five Moscow Mules in his tidy guest room toilet.

Chapter Forty-Six
Mira: T-minus 10 days

When I wake up, the room is gloriously bright.

Glorious if you don't have a raging hangover, that is.

I glance over at the nightstand and see a tall glass of water next to a bottle of ibuprofen, which sits atop a notepad. I lean over and squeeze my eyes closed, twice, so I can focus enough to read the handwriting on the notepad.

Good Morning, hope you're feeling okay. Towels and everything else you need are in the bathroom. Come out and have breakfast when you're ready.

Charlie

Hmm, very neutral sounding, which is amazingly restrained considering what I put him through last night. I cringe at the memories and push them away for now as I take in my surroundings.

The clock on the nightstand says 7:06 a.m. The room is large with a high, wood-beamed ceiling, and the wall opposite the bed is composed entirely of windows that provide an unobstructed view of the ocean. The décor is understated coastal chic—light gray hardwood and muted colors that are stylish and relaxing in a way that enhances rather than competes with the view. On the corner of the bed, I see a t-shirt and sweatpants, neatly folded. I vaguely remember Charlie telling me I could change into them and I must have passed out before I had a chance.

I get up and pad my way over to the bathroom where I'm delighted anew. The gray tile floor is heated (heavenly) and there's a large shower with a glass wall and door that connects it to its other half: another mirror-image shower enclosed outdoors. There's also a long, oval, freestanding tub that is decidedly modern and sitting in a picture-perfect nook surrounded by windows with views to the ocean. It's all a surprise to me, which is surprising in itself, since I know very well I was in this beautiful bathroom last night puking my guts out.

It's also surprising because, although I knew Charlie was rich, I hadn't ever considered all the accoutrements that go along with that condition. I take off my rumpled clothes and have a shower and I almost feel like myself again after I brush my teeth with the brand new toothbrush and tube of toothpaste left on the counter for me. I redress myself in the t-shirt and jeans I wore last night. I don't put my sweater back on in case it has any residual throw-up on it. The thought sends a wave of nauseated humiliation through me, and that gives me a headache, so I fill up the glass of water again and drink the whole thing down.

I sit on the edge of the bed and check my phone and am relieved to discover no urgent messages. I half expected a text from Grandpa Edwin asking me what the hell I'm doing—he must have gotten a report from the guardians following me that I went straight to a bar, got drunk, and spent the night at a guy's house whom I (kind of) hardly know. I'm glad to see that guardians aren't judgmental—or at least if they are, they're keeping it to themselves.

I realize as I'm thinking all of this that I came to Charlie's to forget about all this craziness, so why am I hashing over it now? I push it out of my mind and stand up. I need to force myself to face the music after my embarrassing display last night.

It isn't hard to follow the smell of eggs to the kitchen. I find Charlie standing in front of a professional-grade eight-burner cooktop, making what appears to be an omelet. The kitchen and the living room (which I remember getting a vague glimpse of last night) are all part of one massive great room with a wall of windows and more postcard-ready ocean views. The tall, exposed ceilings feature weathered-grey beams and the effect of the décor and the view and the sight of Charlie cooking omelets behind white marble countertops makes me want to take a picture in my mind and soak up the laid-back normalcy and perfection of it all.

"Morning," Charlie says with a dimpled smile and blue eyes that, surprisingly, don't look at all tired—or ticked off. Other than the fact that he's sporting a day's worth of stubble—which honestly makes him look more handsome than ever—he looks as fresh as daisies and he obviously just got out of the shower, judging by his hair, which isn't fully dry yet.

"Morning," I answer, a little abashedly.

His eyes meet mine and there's a moment of silence before he clears his throat and speaks. "Did you sleep well?"

I nod. My brow furrows because I want to apologize to him for my behavior last night but I'm not sure how to begin.

He looks at me curiously. "Were you upset to wake up here?"

I realize when he asks that he may think that *he's* the one that needs to apologize and I quickly work to relieve his mind. "Charlie, if you're afraid I think you brought me here against my will, please don't worry. I know I insisted on coming to your house, I attacked you before we even got in the door, I demanded you kiss me, and then I ordered you to take off all your clothes and I threw up in your bathroom. If anyone was taken advantage of here, it was you. You might even have a good case for assault if you called the cops."

He laughs. "So you *do* remember."

"Unfortunately ... and I'm mortified. I seriously considered slipping out the back door and never seeing you again. But I know that, in life, it's always better to just face things head on and get on with it, even if you have to suffer through excruciating embarrassment to get there."

He laughs. "You have nothing to be embarrassed about. I *wanted* to be taken advantage of by you. Very badly."

I laugh and then scrunch up my face. "I don't usually drink like that."

"Never would have guessed." He smiles and turns his attention back to the omelet. "I hope you like mushrooms and you have time for breakfast."

I don't want to turn down his hospitality but I'm still feeling a little queasy. "I'm not sure my stomach is accepting food yet, but I could use some of that coffee." I point to the pot brewing on the counter.

He pours me a cup and slides it over and I take a deep breath in. It smells heavenly.

"You have a nice view," I say as we sit at the breakfast bar and look out on the ocean's blue expanse. The sea melds with the sky at the horizon line and I could stare at it forever. I glance over at him. "I don't know if I told you last night, but I've been kind of trying to avoid my family lately so I appreciate you letting me stay here for the night."

His eyes show concern. "I'm sorry you have something going on with your family."

I nod.

"Do you want to talk about it?"

I shake my head. Even if I wanted to talk about it, he'd be on the phone to the loony bin before I even finished. "I just need a few days—or weeks—away. To think about some things." All those "things" start to push their way to the forefront of my mind again and I forcefully push them back. I'm still not ready to try to make sense of any of it.

He sets his fork down and looks at me. "In that case, can I make you an offer?"

"What kind of offer?"

"An offer to stay here while you're working things out." Before I can answer he speaks again. "And there's no agenda, by the way—I'm talking about you staying in the guest room."

I cough out a laugh. "I don't doubt that. I'm sure you want me and my puking ways as far away from you as possible."

"Actually—strangely—I've come to like you and your puking ways."

I look over at him and smile. "Which makes me wonder about you."

He smiles back. "Well, the offer's there, if you want it."

"Thanks. I want it."

His eyes register surprise and I have to admit I'm a little surprised by my answer, too.

"But you have to answer one question," I tell him.

He looks intrigued. "What?"

"Do you still want a date?"

Now he looks confused. "Does your offer from last night to go out still hold?"

I shake my head.

"No?"

"I'd rather just stay in tonight. With you. Here."

He smiles. "Have I mentioned how confusing you are?"

I smile back. "You don't know the half of it, Charlie."

When I get to work, for the first time in my life, I go through the motions with my patients. I'm not really focusing or being in the moment, right up until I get an unexpected break when my 11:00 a.m. appointment is canceled. I sit at my desk and, with nothing else to distract me, I start thinking about everything Dany (or should I say *Declan*?) told us last night.

To say it's all hard to absorb is an understatement. Apparently I have ten days until "doomsday," on my birthday.

I considered calling in sick to work today, but what would be the point? So I could sit at my nan and grandpa's house or Charlie's place all day and ruminate? Plus, if what Dany said is to be believed, I'm some kind of special being, right? With super powers? The least I should be able to do is show up for work after learning that my mom and dad are back from the dead and my grandfather has been hiding everything true and important from me for my entire freaking life.

I feel so angry with him still. When I think about all the rules Grandpa Edwin had me follow—for reasons he knew but wouldn't explain—it leaves me incredulous. All those questions I've had swirling in my mind about what I'm supposed to *do* and what my *plan* is. He knew it all! He knew how it was eating me up inside and yet he never said a word. The thought crushes me because I don't know if I can trust him anymore.

And now I'm supposed to believe there's a bunch of dark guardians desperate to destroy me and my energy? And what energy are they even talking about? Other than the way I've always been able to sense things about people when I meet them, I haven't discovered any additional "powers" lurking inside me. Although, maybe I *would* have if Grandpa Edwin had told me what's going on. Maybe I could have been trying to summon whatever powers I'm supposed to wield, and I could have been practicing all along, and training—and I could have been some kind of amazing freaking wizard by now.

Instead, lately, all I've felt is that I'm malfunctioning because my sense about people has been surging all over the place—warning me one minute and relaxed the next. I even got a weird feeling when I spoke with Dr. Wilder this morning and I've known him a long time. So now I'm paranoid *and* malfunctioning. Maybe the joke here is on the guardians, because their supposed "earth angel" energy source is out of order. Because that's how I feel. I've always been "in order"—following the rules, doing what

I'm supposed to. The thought of everything they told me being true is terrifying, but it's also freeing. Sure, it turns out that my "plan" I've been wondering about all these years involves vanquishing dark angels and saving the world, but at least now I know what I'm headed towards. *Even if it is completely insane.*

Gemma pops her head above the wall of my cubicle. "What's with the funny look?"

I glance up at her. "Hmm, what?"

"The look on your face."

I shake my head. "It's nothing."

"It didn't look like nothing. It looked like you were deep in thought."

I decide to distract her. "I agreed to a date with Charlie tonight. A real one."

"Seriously?"

I tell her the story about getting tipsy last night and ending up at his house. I don't tell her why I was at the bar getting drunk in the first place, but I think she's engrossed enough with the story of my antics at Charlie's that she's not even thinking about what led to it.

Her eyes are wide when I finish. "Wow. That is *not* what I was expecting to hear from you this morning. But a guy who'll hold your hair back while you barf is a guy I like."

I laugh and she shakes her head with mock seriousness. "And, *wow* … Mira Ronin shamelessly flirting and breaking the rules. I think I like this turn you've taken. It's about time you stopped being a perfect angel for once."

I toss a wadded up piece of paper at her and she laughs.

Inside I can't help thinking *if you only knew.*

Gemma asked me to go to lunch but I told her I couldn't because I'm meeting with Uncle Finn today. He texted me this morning and asked if I would to come into his office and give him a DNA sample. He said he collected them from everyone and apparently they all complied. He's obviously trying to work things out the only way he knows how—with science. I don't know how much good it will do, but I agreed to give him the sample because: number one, I don't have a beef with Uncle Finn; and, number two, it's an actual tangible step I can take—unlike simply trying to "avoid dark angels" or cower in a closet somewhere and cry. Uncle Finn's request is based in reality, which is something I'm wrapping my arms around tightly right now after all the crazy claims Dany tossed out last night.

Who knows? Maybe his analysis will determine I'm part dolphin since I love the ocean so much, which would actually be kind of cool.

Or maybe now I've obviously gone crazy, too, along with everyone else.

After work, when I hear the knock on the door as I'm gathering my things at the cottage, I know it's Grandpa Edwin. I tried to sneak in to pack a few weeks' worth of clothes, but he must have seen me or noticed my car out in front of his house on the street.

"I don't want to talk to you right now," I call out through the door.

"Mira, please, just hear me out."

I open the door and I'm surprised to see he's not alone. There's a man standing next to him with dark hair, a solid physique, and what I'd label as "experienced eyes." He looks at least ten years older than me but his exact age range is hard to pinpoint.

"Mira, this is Soren. I want you to know that I'm breaking protocol here, but Soren has agreed to be known to you as a guardian. He'll be protecting you. Many guardians will, of course, but Soren will be guiding them and watching over you as I would, in my stead." He pauses and clears his throat. "Since you're upset with me at present. I hope you'll allow this."

I look from Grandpa Edwin to Soren. I don't know what to say. "I've seen you before," I say finally. I realize now he was one of the patrons at the San Mar Bar & Grill when I was there drinking myself silly. It's nice to know (or perhaps concerning?) that guardians don't intervene when you're acting completely stupid.

Soren nods.

"You've been watching me?"

"Many have."

I'm not sure if I should feel uneasy or grateful. "Nice to meet you, I guess."

Soren smiles. "My pleasure."

"So you'll agree to this?" Edwin asks.

"What am I agreeing to?"

"You're agreeing to—and embracing—your protection," Grandpa Edwin answers. "Soren will always be close by. Only now you'll know who he is and what he's doing." I wonder if perhaps he thinks the reason I went to Charlie's was to try to give my guardians the slip. If so, he'll be surprised when I end up there again tonight.

Soren reassures me. "It won't be obvious to anyone but you. It'll be just as it has been. We just wanted you to know so you wouldn't worry if you see me often, and you'd know you were being protected."

I look at Grandpa Edwin. He's obviously trying to throw me a bone by revealing Soren to me when he didn't have to. "If everything you've all said is true, a personal bodyguard would be nice I guess."

Soren smiles. "We prefer guardian over *bodyguard*."

I smile back. At least my new bodyguard has a sense of humor.

"Good," Edwin says. "That's settled. Mira, I want you to know I understand why you're upset and—"

"*Upset*? Do you understand how it feels to know that you've kept this secret from me my whole life? When you talked to me about my birthday and I was talking about figuring out my plan and all you said was not to date and to stay '*vigilant*'? When I think of all the vague directions and rules you've put around me my whole life … and I listened to you without question. But you knew I was in danger. And you knew a million other things and you didn't trust me enough to tell me a *single one of them* … even after I grew up. And please don't say you were 'protecting' me, because I think truly protecting someone means telling them the truth about things." I look up at him with pain in my eyes.

"Grandpa, I love you, but I don't understand how you could ever think that was the right thing to do?"

He's silent for a moment and I can see pain in his eyes, too, when he answers. "I love you, too, Mira—more than you could ever know—and I assure you that every step I've ever taken has been made with your best interests foremost in my mind."

I stare deep into his kind, world-weary mahogany eyes and I try to put myself in his position but it's difficult because I feel so betrayed. "I don't see it that way," I say sadly. "I need time to process everything before I want to talk with you about it anymore."

Grandpa Edwin nods.

I turn my attention to Soren. "I'm just gathering my things in here. I'm headed to my nan's next and then I'm going out." I don't mention where I'm going. I'm a grown woman and I can do what I want.

Soren nods. "We've got your back, Mira."

I still don't know if I believe any of this stuff, but it's hard not to smile inside when someone says they've got your back.

As I'm getting dressed for my date in my old bedroom, my nan knocks and I call out for her to come in.

"I'm so glad you're here, sweetie," she says when she enters. "How are you doing?"

"Okay."

"You really don't want to talk about things?" She texted me numerous times and I told her I'm not ready to talk about any of it yet.

"It's barely been 24 hours, nan. Give me a little time for it to sink in. And it's not like I'm the only one affected—you must be feeling shell-shocked, too, not to mention Grandpa Mark. Aunt Liz texted me and said she's running background checks on Dany and Alexander ... and even Grandpa Edwin. And I saw Uncle Finn today and he was pacing around his lab in circles, muttering that none of this is possible. Did everyone really give him DNA samples?"

She nods. "We're all trying to make sense of it in our own way." Her voice is quiet and we're both silent for a long moment.

"Are you sure it's really them, nan?"

She meets my eyes. "Yes."

The simplicity of her answer—with no qualifiers or equivocation—makes me sit down on the edge of the bed. She sits down beside me and puts her arm around me. "Mira, I know how you feel about seeing the truth of a person in their eyes, and I can tell you that I see the truth in Declan's eyes. It's her." Her voice starts to crack. "A mother knows her own child."

When I see her eyes well up, mine well up in return. "I saw something, too," I whisper. "But I didn't know what it was."

She hugs me closer. "Mira, I know you don't want to talk about it but I'm worried about you—this is so much for you to take in."

"As if it's not a lot for you?"

"It's a lot for all of us, but you especially."

275

"I just can't get over the fact that Grandpa Edwin knew the whole time and he didn't tell me. Or you, or anyone."

"Whatever we may think about his actions, he did it out of love and what he thought—right or wrong—was the best way to protect you."

I shake my head. "I still can't believe you're defending him and what he did."

"It's just that I know in my heart your Grandpa Edwin is a good man. And I'm just trying to understand … and make sense of the indefensible."

When she says "indefensible," the wall that I was feeling between us starts to come down. She *does* understand. After all, Grandpa Edwin kept her in the dark, too.

I meet her eyes and she smiles the way she always does when she's making the best of things, which is her nature. "Are you going somewhere?" she asks as she takes in my appearance. "You look nice."

I'm glad to focus on something else. "Thanks," I say as I look down at the fine gauge cotton sweater dress I put on. It's slouchy and sexy-casual, and the dark green color looks good with my tall brown suede boots. "I need to wear tights if I wear this, though, and I forgot to pack them. And I think they're in the wash anyway."

"Why do you need tights?"

I stare at her. "My leg."

"Your leg is beautiful. It's the mark of a warrior."

"I was an infant," I scoff. "I wasn't a warrior fighting anyone."

She takes my hands in hers. "You survived," she says as she looks into my eyes. "Your scar is your shield. And now that we know what really happened, we know what an even greater miracle it is that you're here. Your light and goodness won out against evil."

I shake my head. "I don't know how much of a miracle it is if everyone else died."

She looks at me for a long moment. "You know that isn't your fault."

I nod. "I just wish I had my tights," I whisper as I pinch my eyes closed and push back at all the feelings swimming for the surface that I'm not ready to deal with yet.

She puts her arms around me again and holds me tight, rocking us gently as I lay my head on her shoulder. After a few minutes I lift my head and wipe under my eyes. "I'm okay," I say quietly.

She nods and smiles—the same smile that has comforted me through trials and tribulations my whole life—and the expression in her eyes tells me she gets it. She glances over at my brown boots on the floor by the bed. "Are you wearing those boots?"

"I was planning to."

"What about boot cuffs? Or boot toppers or whatever they're called? I have a pair of knit cream-colored ones that would look great with those boots and the dress you have on."

I consider her suggestion. It's actually not a bad idea. "That would help, but you'd still be able to see a little of the side of my leg below the hem of the dress."

"Does it matter, honey?" She adjusts her position until she's facing me and she takes my hands in hers. "You're beautiful, Mira. And strong. You were always so brave that it honestly broke my heart—your Grandpa and I were more scared about your surgeries when you were a kid than you were. And all the physical therapy exercises you had to do were so painful but you always pushed through it. When you were born, the doctors weren't even sure you'd walk, let alone walk without a limp, but you overcame every hurdle, through sheer determination. So, wear that scar as a badge of honor that proves you can persevere against anything and anyone. Even dark angels."

Her words coax a smile from me. "Despite what Grandpa Edwin says, I don't think I have superpowers, nan. I haven't felt anything."

"We all have superpowers, sweetie. We just have to believe and tap into them." She smiles. "Now, who are you going out with tonight? Gemma?"

I shake my head. "It's a date."

"A date with someone new? *Now?*"

"Don't worry, Grandpa Edwin apparently has me surrounded. And, besides, you know the guy … sort of. He's Charlie Bing."

It takes her a beat or two but then she registers surprise. "Little Charlie Bing? Who your mom used to babysit? Charlene's son? Oh my goodness, I haven't heard that name in years."

"He's a grown man now, nan."

She smiles. "He was a very cute little boy. Your mom loved him."

"I'm actually going to stay at his place for a few days. He offered me his guest room."

"What? Why?"

"I think I need a little time away from everything, if that's okay."

She meets my eyes, skeptical. "Are you sure, sweetie? Do you know him well?"

"He's a good guy, nan. I met him six months ago. I like him a lot. I trust him."

"Okay, well …" She pauses and takes a deep breath. "Okay … I trust your instincts. But if you know him so well, then why are you worried about wearing tights?"

"I don't know—force of habit I guess. He's already seen my leg, actually."

She squeezes my hands. "Mira, if a man is even close to being worthy of you, then seeing your scars—physical or otherwise—will only draw him closer. If we're not vulnerable and honest in our relationships then it's not real, and who wants that?"

I nod and she squeezes my hands once more and stands up. "I'll go get the boot cuffs."

While she's gone I stand before the mirror on the back of my closet door and straighten my dress and peer at the deep, jagged scar running down my leg. I have to admit that I'll never look at it the same way again. Having it reframed in my mind as a battle scar from a fight to the death with dark angels is admittedly intriguing. Maybe it *is* my shield. One thing for certain is that that's one crazy explanation even *I* never came up with.

"So you decided to scrap the 'no dating until your birthday' idea," my nan says as she comes back into the room and hands me the boot cuffs.

"Yep." I sit down on the edge of my bed and slide them on and then slide on the boots. I stretch my legs out straight for a better look. They look nice. "Thanks, nan."

"I thought that dating rule was ridiculous anyway," she comments.

"You did? And you're not upset that I'm going out?"

She shakes her head. "I'll admit that I'd like to wrap you in bubble wrap and keep you at home." She pauses. "And I'm anxious for your safety—certainly—after everything Edwin told us, but I've always known you to have good instincts. And I never understood most of Edwin's rules, to be honest."

"Really? You never said anything."

"Well, I understand them *now*," she says, "since he told us. But I went along with them through the years because we all deal with trauma differently. After everything that happened with Declan and Alexander, I thought Edwin was just being overprotective of his granddaughter in his own quirky, but harmless way." She meets my eyes. "Just as I've been guilty of being overprotective with you in my own way, too. And I'm sorry about that."

I can see the pain in her eyes. I still don't understand why she isn't as angry with Grandpa Edwin as I am, but I have to accept that we're all dealing with the news differently. For my part, I just feel like I need space and time away from everyone to think.

I take a deep breath and stand up. "I'd better go. I'm meeting Charlie at seven."

She gives me a hug. "Mira, I—"

"Don't worry, there's a fleet of bodyguards tailing me at all times, which means I've pretty much been wrapped in bubble wrap my entire life and I just didn't know it."

She hugs me tight again and I leave, and, as I'm driving to meet Charlie, I try to make sense of the conflicted thoughts in my mind. I know part of me has been acting immaturely and I may be taking out my shock and frustration in the wrong way on the wrong people, but I feel so jumbled inside that I don't want to think about any of it. I don't want to think about danger lurking; or some dark guardian triumvirate being after me; or everyone keeping secrets; or my parents coming back after they sacrificed themselves and left everyone unspeakably sad (all because of me); or the fate of the world being on my shoulders; or anything, basically, of that ilk.

I just want to go out on a date like a normal human girl and have a good time and forget about everything else.

For a while at least.

When I get to Charlie's and he opens the door, he smiles, and it's one of those genuine smiles—with his blue eyes fully involved—that makes me feel warm and tingly inside. I was worried he may have spent the day regretting his offer to have me stay, but his smile reassures me.

"Come on in." When I step inside, he hands me a key. "I just want to get this out of the way up front: this is so you can come and go as you please. I can't always promise we'll keep the same hours and work schedules."

"You're giving me a key to the house?"

"Should I not?"

"No, it's just nice that you're so trusting."

"Well, to be fair, you may have noticed that the guest room has a private entrance through the back yard. This key opens that door. Although I suppose, of course, you could come in through the guest room and then roam the rest of the house and murder me in my sleep, so maybe I am being a little too trusting."

I laugh. "So now *I'm* the serial killer?"

He chuckles. "I'm counting on being wrong."

We walk into the kitchen and there's a large box from Surf Pizza on the counter and a bottle of wine next to it. "That looks great," I comment.

"You said you wanted a low-key night, so I thought we could have pizza and watch a movie."

I smile. "Sounds perfect."

"Good. And the wine is optional. I have plenty of other drink options in the fridge."

I laugh. "I'm sure you do, after my performance last night."

His expression is amused and empathetic. "How are you feeling?"

"Much better than I deserve to."

He chuckles. "I'll get the pizza ready and you can grab yourself whatever you'd like to drink."

I nod and open his refrigerator. There's a wide array of drinks to choose from but I decide on bottled water. Charlie calls out to me to grab one for him, too.

We settle onto the couch with our plates of pizza on the coffee table in front of us and then, as we're checking out movie options, Charlie looks over at me. "Can I ask you something?"

I nod.

"Why now?"

"Why now, what?"

"Why did you call me last night and ask me out?

I shrug. "Because I like you."

"So you were just toying with me before, about having to wait until your birthday?"

I shake my head.

"But you never told me what the reason was behind your choice to stop dating."

"Well, for one thing, I wasn't meeting a lot of gems."

He chuckles. "I look forward to hopefully changing that assessment."

I smile. "You are." I'm not sure what else to say.

"So that was the reason?" he asks. "Some terrible dates? And you decided your birthday would be a reset?"

I shrug. "You know what? It was stupid. It was a stupid rule that I set up for myself and I finally realized I don't need stupid, arbitrary rules anymore. I decided to say screw it and just do what I wanted."

He smiles as his blue eyes search mine. "Is that a serious answer?"

I nod. "Believe it or not, it is."

He chuckles. His questions are verging into territory that I came here to forget and, although I don't want to lie to him, I'd like to veer off this topic somehow. I consider my options and decide to say something honest that will jump ahead to what I've wanted to do since the moment I walked in the door.

"Charlie?" I ask.

"Yes."

"Would you like to kiss me?"

He smiles, amused. "Is that a trick question?"

I shake my head. "No."

He stares into my eyes before he sets his bottled water down. Then he slides his arm behind me on the couch as he leans in and kisses me softly. I like the way his lips feel and as I kiss him back and he parts my lips with his, I can't help smiling inside because I really, really like the way he kisses—slow and sweet and with attention and passion, and not at all sloppy like some of the guys I've dated. I was worried that the chemistry I feel when I look in his eyes couldn't possibly hold up to the reality of a physical connection, but I feel almost drunk with what a great kisser he is. And I tell him so, out loud, without meaning to.

He chuckles as we're embraced and I feel it reverberate against my chest. "You're a great kisser, too," he says and, as we kiss some more, we start to lie back on the couch and I enjoy the feeling of his body pressing into mine.

I maneuver my legs under him to push off my boots and boot cuffs with my feet. "More comfortable," I mumble as we continue making out, and he accommodates me and grunts in approval.

Our hands move everywhere and when I slide his t-shirt up he reaches behind his neck and yanks it off over his head. I catch only a brief glimpse of his hard, sculpted chest before his lips find mine again, and I'm lost in how good it feels to kiss him and forget about everything else except the way our bodies feel as we touch.

When his hand runs up the outside of my leg, I stiffen.

He pauses and meets my eyes. "This okay?" he asks. "We can stop."

"It's just my scar."

"Does it hurt when I touch it? I'm sorry, Mira, I was lost in the moment—I wasn't thinking at all."

"It doesn't hurt. And I don't want you to stop." I slide up the bottom of my dress a little more and arch against him.

He smiles and we go back to kissing, but when his hand brushes over my scar again, I feel the need to ask him about it. "You don't mind it?"

"Mind what?" he murmurs in between kisses.

"My scar."

He pauses kissing along my jaw and looks at me. "Why would I mind it?" He peers down at my leg. "I love your legs," he mumbles before kissing me again. "Long and sexy," he adds in a low voice with an easy smile before he begins trailing kisses along my neck.

"It's pretty ugly looking, though."

He stops and looks at me. "Mira," he says, training his blue eyes on mine in such a sincerely pained way that it pierces my heart, "there's nothing ugly about you. You're the most beautiful girl I've ever seen. Inside and out."

A smile spreads across my face and he commences kissing down my body, slowly, until he reaches my hip and then my leg, and, very gently, he kisses along my scar. As his lips trace a path and his eyes are on mine, peering down at him, the level of intimacy between us is profound. I smile and tug his head back up to mine so I can kiss his lips again. "Should we forget about the movie?" I murmur against him.

He groans and I can feel his answer pressing into me as our bodies entwine. "What movie?" he chuckles as he kisses down my throat again.

I smile and start to pull up my dress but he gently moves his hand to stop me. "But maybe we shouldn't," he says as our eyes meet.

"Why not?"

He takes a deep breath. "Because, I have to be honest, the rational guy in me thinks we should take this slow."

"Why?"

"Because we're building up to something … something good, I think."

My eyes meet his and settle there for a long beat, considering what he's saying. "The rational guy in me thinks you're probably right."

He smiles. "You have a rational guy, too?"

"My 'guy' is gender neutral."

He laughs. "I hate rational guy."

I nod. "Always wrecking everyone's fun."

"I'd like to punch his lights out sometimes."

I laugh. "I never pictured you as the violent type."

"You're right: I'm a lover, not a fighter. And rational guy knows it."

"You're also a comedian."

"So are you."

We smile at each other for a long beat. "So it's a movie, then?" he asks finally.

I nod and we sit up and I snuggle next to him with his arm around me as we scan for Netflix options with the remote. I can't believe how comfortable it feels to be with him.

In the back of my mind, as we talk and eat and kiss in between pretending to watch the movie, I wonder if this is what Grandpa Edwin warned me about. Shouldn't I be focusing on everything I just learned and trying to figure out my powers and watching for dark guardians, rather than going out on dates?

But it feels good to forget about all of that for a while and just break free and be with the man I've been drawn to and resisting for months.

I don't know whether it's my swoony infatuation with Charlie, or me not wanting to think about Grandpa Edwin's lies by omission, or if I simply don't want to talk to anyone that will make me face the truth about the danger I'm in, but I want to hold onto this moment and keep the rest of the world at bay a while longer.

And I'm grateful, and excited, that Charlie wants me here, too.

Chapter Forty-Seven
Declan: T-minus 9 days

"Did we do the right thing?" I ask Alexander as we're lying in bed together in his apartment. I lift my head off his chest to look up and meet his eyes. "Did *I* do the right thing?"

His kind green eyes reassure me. "It came from your heart. All of it. So it can't be wrong."

"But you didn't really agree with me telling them, did you?"

"There's one thing I know: despite all my decisions and plans, things went awry last time."

"But we saved Mira."

He nods. "We did. The most important thing, we got right."

We're silent for a long beat.

"I wasn't thinking about the aftermath," I say. "How everyone would process it. I can only imagine how they all must be feeling. It's been two days and–"

"We need to give them time." He takes a deep breath. "It's a lot to take in."

"You think?" I pretend to hold a phone to my ear. "Hi there, we're Declan and Alexander, back from the dead. And by the way, guardian angels exist. Bad ones killed us and now they're after you, too."

"Happy birthday," Alexander adds, and we both burst out laughing.

After our laughter dies down, I meet his eyes. "I keep joking because it's scary and I feel helpless."

He nods.

"I need to come up with a better way of describing it other than we're *back from the dead*. That sounds gruesome."

"Not to mention, it's not true."

"Because energy never dies?"

He nods. "It's our souls that live on."

"We're lucky they didn't have us carted away when I told them."

"If it wasn't for Edwin, I think they might have."

"Right. Two random strangers spouting nonsense is one thing, but they've known Edwin for years. They could say you and I are delusional, but they can't dismiss it as a folie à deux when it's three people. How do you say three in French?"

"Trois."

"It'd be hard to make a case for a folie à trois."

"But I'm sure they're considering it, and wondering if Edwin has gone spontaneously insane."

Our chuckles die down and I lay my head on his chest again, listening to his heartbeat.

"Do you think Edwin's right?" I ask. "That we're courting extra danger by telling them?"

"Possibly. But Edwin's not infallible. None of us are."

I look up and meet his eyes again. "I feel helpless. I want to be able to do something to help protect Mira."

He nods. "It's not easy feeling powerless."

"I finally understand that quote, viscerally, that says having a child is 'like having your heart go walking around outside your body.'"

He smiles poignantly. "Welcome to the world of being a mortal parent."

"Or any kind of parent—Edwin obviously feels that way, too."

He nods and we fall into a comfortable silence again, focused on our thoughts.

As I go over everything in my mind again, I think about what Edwin said and I lift my head up to look at him. "Edwin and Soren both said it was critical that we were drawn here. That must mean we have some purpose. We need to figure out what it is before Mira's birthday."

"I agree that it's telling that we came here now."

"With hardly any time left."

He nods. "Two weeks prior is cutting it fine. But have you considered that maybe our purpose is to do what we did?"

"What do you mean?"

"If you and I hadn't come to San Mar and found each other again, we wouldn't have discovered who we are. And if it wasn't for you, the issue wouldn't have been forced and we wouldn't have told your mum and Mira and everyone else the truth. Whatever the outcome, you started a ball rolling."

I feel a little sick inside. "But what if I shouldn't have? What if it's rolling in the wrong direction?"

Alexander takes a deep breath. "I believe we should trust our instincts."

"But your instincts didn't fully agree with me. There has to be more that we can do."

"Maybe." He lets out a deep breath. "But we need time to think just as much as everyone else. We're mere mortals now and I don't know about you, but I'm knackered. We need our sleep."

"We always needed sleep."

He grins. "But I feel it more now."

I look up at him. "Are you planning something?"

His eyebrow rises. "I'm always planning something."

"About how to save Mira?"

"I'm not going to pretend I've worked out how to put that right. I'm thinking about all sorts of things … but tonight my only plan is to fall asleep with you next to me."

I smile and lay my head back down on his chest. "I like your plan, Mr. Ronin … for tonight."

"I like everything about you, Miss Jane." He strokes my hair and the soft rumble of his voice, along with his steady heartbeat, calms my worries and lulls me to sleep, as it always has.

Chapter Forty-Eight
Declan: T-minus 8 days

I knock on the door and wait.

I'm nervous. When I got the call from my mom about coming over I was excited that she was ready to talk finally, but now the overwhelming feeling is nervousness about what she'll say and how it will be between us. Alexander is meeting with Edwin and I wanted to see my mom alone.

It feels weird to be knocking on the door of my own house. My *old* house.

Although it's not mine anymore…

But the memories are still mine.

When my mom opens the door, more of those memories come flooding back. She's older now but she still has the same eyes, the same mannerisms, and, remarkably, she still welcomes me with a loving hug. "Oh, Declan," she says as she hugs me. She pulls back, cradling my face in her hands and looks into my eyes with a fierce intensity. "I still can't believe it's truly you."

"I called you *mom* the day I met you. I didn't understand what was happening, but that was when I started to remember. When I saw you and you hugged me, it brought memories flooding back."

She smiles. "The strength of a mother's love."

"But you didn't sense anything?"

"How could I? How could I have known, or even imagined?"

I nod. She's right. How could she? It still seems so fantastical that I'm surprised Mark didn't call his old buddies at the police department and have me arrested.

She takes my hand and we make our way to the living room and sit down on the couch. The same place we used to sit to watch movies together.

"You got a new couch," I remark as I run my hand over the fabric.

She laughs. "I hope so. It's been twenty-five years."

"A long time," I agree and, as our eyes meet, the joy of seeing my mom again is overshadowed by what was lost.

"Twenty-five years," she whispers painfully as she takes my hands in hers and squeezes. Her eyes well up, and mine quickly follow.

"But you're here now," she continues after a long beat. "And that's what we should focus on." She forces a smile and wipes away an escaped tear.

That's Judy Jane: always focused on the glass half full. My emotions are so close to the surface I'm having a hard time speaking, so I let her continue to take the lead.

"I've had a lot to absorb over the past few days." She meets my eyes and we both smile and break into a laugh.

"I'll say."

"There are so many layers to this, Declan," she says, getting serious again. "I mean, about your father, for one. Why didn't he ever tell me he was a guardian? And all that he sacrificed to be with me?" The anguish in her eyes is

293

acute. "And why didn't *you* tell me? Not just about that, but about everything? Or *anything*?"

"I thought I was keeping you out of danger. But I question that now, and I'm sorry."

She meets my eyes and nods slowly. "I've spoken with Edwin about it. I was angry with him at first but he's profoundly remorseful and, while I can't say I agree with his keeping secrets, I understand his perspective. He's a good man." She pauses and then chuffs out a laugh. "Of course he's a good man—he's a guardian angel, for Pete's sake. And that explains why he's barely aged! I thought I was just getting old myself and losing my mind." She laughs again at the absurdity of it all.

"Guardians don't usually stay in one place long enough for anyone to notice. But Edwin stayed in San Mar to be close to Mira."

She nods. "I know. He loves Mira as fiercely as we all do."

"I'm glad she has all of you. I know this must be incredibly strange for her ... and everyone ... Alexander and I, reentering your lives and–"

"Declan," she says, stopping me as her eyes well up. "Having you back..." she pauses and places her hand over her heart, "it's like warm sunlight on my soul." Her words come out hoarse and she's visibly choked up as she continues. "After you were gone, I was lost. I don't know what I would have done without Mark. Or Mira. Taking care of that beautiful little girl—a new life—is what saved me." She meets my eyes and we're both teary. "Now, having you back, and knowing that your dad is out there, too, and he's okay... and he spoke to me ... and I *heard* him ..." She chokes up again and pauses for a long minute. "I don't know how to describe it, but it's like my heart is *at peace* ... and whole again."

I smile and we hug and she holds me tight and I spill tears onto her shoulder. "Mine, too, mom. Mine, too."

"So tell me about your family," my mom says after we've covered practically every other topic under the sun. "The one you grew up with. How does that work, with you being both Dany and Declan?"

I shrug. "One person with two life memories is I guess how you'd explain it. But I just didn't remember both of them until now."

"What about your mom and dad?" Her expression is strained. "They were good to you?"

I touch her arm to reassure her. "They're good people, mom. I love them. My sister, too. But I never felt like I *fit*, if that makes sense. Other than our love of animals, we don't have a lot in common. But at least now I have an explanation."

"Your sister is older?"

I nod. "Three years. I feel bad for her in a way, because I'm sure she has an idea in her mind about the kind of sister she'd love to have, and I just don't meet the specs. I love her, and I know she loves me, deep down, but we've never agreed on much or been interested in the same things."

"But were you happy?" she asks. "Growing up?"

"As happy as most, I suppose. Even when I felt like an outsider, I knew I was lucky to have a family that loved me."

"Do you see them often?"

"I visit. But we've discovered it's best to love each other from afar. We don't see eye-to-eye on a lot of things."

My mom looks pained.

"It's okay," I say, taking her hand. "My family knows I love them and I know they love me. It's good."

"How do you reconcile that? Two moms? Two families? Two sets of memories?"

"I don't know," I say with a shrug. "It's all a part of me and there's more than enough love to go around."

She smiles. "Spoken like the Declan Jane I know and love and missed so very, very dearly," she says as she squeezes me tight for another long hug.

Chapter Forty-Nine
Declan: T-minus 7 days

"You need to come over."

"I do?"

"Now," Liz adds.

I hang up the phone and then realize I have to call her back.

"I don't know where you live."

I hear her chuckle. She gives me the address.

I park in front of a tidy house about a mile away from where Liz's parents used to live (perhaps still do?). I press the doorbell and wait. I feel nervous.

Liz opens the door. She stares at me, squinting, but doesn't say anything at first. "Let me just say this: I'm pissed at you ... if it's really you."

"It's really me."

"I should also let you know that Judy wanted to see you the day after you told us who you are, but I made her wait a few days until one of our investigators at the DA's office could run background checks."

"You ran background checks?"

"Had to make sure you weren't scammers or nutjobs."

I smile. "I kind of expected Mark to do something like that, actually."

"He would have but we both decided I could do it more discreetly."

"What did you find out?"

"That you've led a pretty boring life."

I let out a laugh.

"And that's surprising," she adds.

"Why? You were expecting a life of crime?"

"No, but if I came back from the dead and knew we get multiple rounds, I'd be jumping out of planes or something."

"It doesn't work that way. And, besides, I didn't even know who I was until last week."

"Good point."

"Can I make a request that we don't refer to it as being 'back from the dead?' It's more like my soul came back."

She steps closer and scrutinizes my eyes. "If your soul is really in there, I'd like to ask it a few questions."

"I'm really in here, so go for it—ask me anything."

She stares at me intently for a long beat and then fires off her first question as if she's cross-examining a hostile witness. "Who were the two boys that liked us in high school, but we weren't interested in?"

"Scott Griffin liked you, and Ryan Dell liked me."

I see a flicker of surprise in her eyes before she bullets another question at me. "Name the craziest entertainment my mom ever arranged for one of my birthday parties."

"That's a tough one. The contortionist?"

She smiles a little. "What did Finn get me as a present for our first wedding anniversary?"

"How would I know that? You got married after I was gone."

"The Declan I knew could guess." She folds her arms.

I take a deep breath and roll it over in my mind. "Well, the first anniversary is paper … and Finn would have looked that up, so I'm sure he followed that rule."

I can see from her expression that I'm on the right track.

"And, if I'm thinking of Finn, I'll bet he gave you money. Because that's how your relationship started. His girlfriend Serena broke up with him for giving her a twenty dollar bill for Valentine's Day, and you said you'd be fine with what he did."

Her eyes register surprise again.

"And, I'll bet that's what he gave you. A twenty dollar bill. In a card. And probably took you out to dinner. Like he did for your first Valentine's Day as a couple, at my suggestion."

She squints and purses her lips to the side. "It was a hundred dollar bill," she says, correcting me. "Inflation," she adds with a tiny shrug of her shoulder and a chuckle. "But you're basically right, on all counts." She pauses for a moment, looks me in the eyes again, and then she bends forward dramatically and plants her palms on her knees and blows out air in a long exhale.

"Are you okay?" I ask with alarm.

She nods and waves me off as she keeps breathing deeply. "It's like it's just finally sinking in—this craziness is true." She takes a few more minutes, breathing in and out, and then she stands back up and searches my eyes. "Your eyes are the same." She looks up to the sky. "I can't believe I'm falling for this! I'm a freaking lawyer. I'm hardwired to screen out bullshit." She meets my eyes again, surveying them closely. "I may be temporarily insane, but I think it's you. I don't understand it, but I really think it is. There's no other way to explain it."

"We worked at Jack's Burger Shack and you used to 'forget' to wear the red Hula Burger t-shirts all the time." I form air quotes with my fingers when I say the word "forget."

She holds up her hand. "You can stop now. You actually had me at contortionist." She tugs my arm and pulls me inside and shuts the door. "Jack and Al sold Jack's Burgers about ten years ago, by the way. They retired to Hawaii."

"They did? Back to where Jack grew up?"

She nods. "The burgers are still good, but it's not the same." She looks at me again. "I still can't believe you're here again. I'm torn between wanting to hug you or yell at you for leaving us." She steps back and meets my eyes, searching them again.

"I did it for Mira," I say.

"I know why you did it. What I'll never understand is why you didn't tell us."

"I didn't want to put you in danger."

"That pisses me off the most. We could have protected you. I mean, Jesus, Declan, we're smart people. Finn and I could have helped you figure something out."

"Where *is* Finn?" I ask.

"I didn't tell him you were coming. He's still upset."

"With me?"

"With everything. He doesn't know what to think. You don't realize what losing you did to him."

I nod. My heart aches in my chest at the thought of it.

"I mean, all of us were hurting. Your mom, of course, especially. Thankfully, she had Mark, and Mira to focus on, which turned out to be a blessing. I was so angry at the unfairness of it all, and Finn just turned inward. I wasn't exaggerating when I said he didn't speak for months."

I meet Liz's eyes and the pain I see in them rips at my heart.

"I didn't want to leave," I say quietly.

"I know," she answers.

"I missed you guys."

She nods, tears in her eyes. "We missed you, too." She pulls me in for a hug and we shed silent tears onto each other's shoulders, holding tightly. When we finally separate, we wipe our cheeks and she looks into my eyes once more. "I know I keep saying this but I can't believe it's really you."

I nod. "It feels really good to see you, Liz. So good that it hurts."

She smiles and squeezes my hand. "If you think it hurts now, just wait," she says. "Do you realize how much I have to catch you up on? Twenty-five years. I mean, holy *shite*, your ears are going to be on fire when we finish. I'm older now than our parents were back then."

We both laugh as she tugs me toward the kitchen and we sit down and catch up, just like old times.

"So you and Finn have been married for ten years?"

Liz nods. "I always said I wouldn't get married before thirty and I was serious. But we've been together the whole time since you've been gone. Except for one unfortunate six-month period right after law school."

I meet her eyes, questioningly and she waves her hand in the air with clear annoyance. "Oh, I'm over it now, but it pissed me off royally at the time."

"What happened?"

She shakes her head. "Finn and his statistics are what happened. I had just passed the bar and Finn was working on his PhD and he said we were obviously heading toward marriage and that the average number of boyfriends or girlfriends a person should have before marriage was 6.3 or some stupid number he read somewhere. He thought we should break up so that we could make sure we had the right number of other relationships, so we would know that we should stay together forever."

"What?"

"I know. By his convoluted logic, it was romantic: we'd date other people, confirm we were the best fit for each other, and we'd get back together in the end. Or not. Win, win, either way."

I laugh. "He did not say 'win-win.'"

"No. But that's basically what he was saying."

"So what'd you do?"

"Well, first I told him *sayonara* and good luck with his next 4.3 other girlfriends."

I laugh.

"But then I thought about it. And he was right. We'd both had other relationships, but not significant ones. Before we settled down for the rest of our lives, it made sense, in a pragmatic way, to make sure we were right for each other."

"That's quite an objective and sensible perspective."

She glances at me sideways. "It took me a while to get there."

"So what happened?"

"I dated some other guys—had fun. But no one fits with me like Finn does."

"What about Finn?"

"He lasted thirty days. Missed me so much he told me he 'didn't need any more data' to know that I was the one person in a world of eight billion people he wanted to be with."

I smile. "Awww, Finn."

She nods. "I took him back. Eventually."

"He's a romantic at heart."

"But he hides it well sometimes. You know what he got me for our tenth wedding anniversary? A roll of aluminum foil."

I laugh. "What?"

"He looked it up – just like you said he would. That's what the tenth anniversary is: aluminum. So he handed me a roll of Reynolds Wrap."

"You're kidding."

"But you know what he'd done? He made a list of all the things he loves about me and he unrolled the foil and wrote them all down with a Sharpie and then rolled it back up and sealed it. So that's what he gave me. Basically a love poem on a roll of tin foil."

I smile and my heart melts thinking about him conceiving of the gift and pouring his heart out on a roll of foil. "That's Finn. No one has a bigger heart."

She nods. "I think of him as the perfect guy, stealthily hiding in plain sight."

"I always knew you two were a perfect match."

She smiles. "And I have you to thank for being a buttinsky and getting us together."

"What's this about Finn working on cancer research? I thought he was set on studying Space Sciences?"

Her expression turns sober. "About a year after you were gone, Finn's mom got cancer."

I raise my hand to cover my mouth and she nods at the look in my eyes. "Late stage. It didn't look good, but immunotherapy trials were just starting and they tried an experimental treatment and it saved her. She's still alive today."

"Oh, I'm so glad." I exhale with relief and my hand instinctively slides down to rest over my heart. "I loved Mrs. Cooper."

"It was like a miracle. And Finn was always interested in biotech—that was what he was doing in that research lab at Stanford, remember? But then he decided to focus on space instead. But after he almost lost his mom, he changed his mind and said he wanted to work on things with more immediate benefits in his lifetime. And to tell you the truth, I think what happened to you and Alexander also contributed—it took the wind out of his sails. He told me that nothing made sense to him anymore and he wanted to stop looking outward, at the unknown, and focus on things that were closer—that he could control. He hasn't lost his interest in space, though. And now, with what you revealed to us, I'm sure his discussions with Edwin are going to be even more focused than before. He wants to understand what you told us, from a science perspective. We all do."

"So now he runs a research lab?"

She nods. "He has a partner to manage the people aspect of running the lab—which he found out quickly wasn't something he enjoyed. But he directs the research and he's been working on mapping the functional genomic characteristics of different cancers and modifying T-cells to recognize and destroy cancer cells without affecting healthy ones."

"Wow, that's really amazing."

She nods. "I know. He loves it."

"Can't say I'm surprised to hear Finn's curing cancer."

She smiles. "We always used to joke about that, right? It's not a consistent cure yet, but he's helping."

"And you're an attorney."

She nods. "Prosecutor. Took my debate skills and put them somewhere that I can do some good. I love the DA's office. I work with a lot of great people … in fact, oh my God, you know what? One of them is someone you know—Justin."

"Justin?"

"Justin Wright."

"Justin? From UCSM? I can't believe he decided to become a lawyer after that disastrous summer we spent scanning documents at Fields and Morris."

"Yeah, well, I know you said he doesn't remember all of what happened, but he does know about the corruption part—maybe it made him want to join the ranks of all the good lawyers out there."

I nod. "He was a good guy." The memory of Justin's offer to me when I was pregnant and fighting with Alexander warms my heart.

"Still is. He's married now, by the way—very happy—with two kids and a wife that I like a lot."

"It doesn't surprise me that he married someone nice." The thought of Justin, happy and healthy with two kids, makes me smile. "And Niko?" I ask. "I can't believe you have a son! He's so cute."

She nods. "Just turned five. We put off having kids while we focused on our careers and then we finally decided to go for it. And I have to tell you, having Niko changed me. I swear I'm a nicer person now, if you can believe it," she says with a laugh. "I just love that kid so damn much." The emotion in her eyes says it all. "I felt like a mama bear from day one—I'd rip anyone's limbs off who tried to hurt him." She pauses. "I guess that doesn't make me sound like a nicer person, after all," she says with a laugh.

"He reminds me of a tiny Finn, but with your attitude."

"I know, right? He's fun. And Finn is such a good father."

"He was always so good with kids." I look up at her, a little misty-eyed, thinking of them as parents. "Thank you,"

I say, "for helping Mira all these years. I know how much she loves you guys."

She smiles. "We love her back. You have a beautiful daughter, Declan. The best." She reaches over and squeezes my hands. "We always said we'd help raise her. We just didn't know it would be without you." Her eyes well up as they meet mine.

"It hurts that I wasn't here. That I missed it." The words catch in my throat. "I missed her growing up. And I missed you guys."

"I know," she says quietly, as our tears begin to escape and fall. "I know."

The sound of the front door opening turns both our heads.

I wipe away the tears on my cheeks as Finn steps into the kitchen. He stops in his tracks and looks from Liz to me and back again.

Finally, his eyes settle on me and he speaks. "What are you doing here?"

I look up at him. "Do you believe that it's me, Finn?"

"I analyzed your DNA. It's not a familial match to your mom's."

"I don't think it works that way."

He glances at Liz and then back to me. "But it doesn't make sense. And I don't understand it."

"But do you believe it's me?"

He pauses before answering. "If it's not you … then it's the cruelest trick anyone could ever do to another person."

The hurt in his eyes strangles my heart. He still has the same boyish face, even in his forties. When I look at him I see the Finn I remember—young and vulnerable. "I swear it's not a trick, Finn. Ask me anything."

"Anything I ask, I might have told Mira over the years, and she might have told you. And now that you've obviously been talking to Liz, who knows what she might have shared inadvertently."

"Ask me about something that you know you never told anyone else."

He's silent for a long time—so long that I'm not sure that he heard me. I wait a few more minutes and then I speak. "Finn?"

He looks up. "When I was five, I gave blood."

"That's the question?"

"That's all I'm giving you," he says with finality.

I know what he's referring to, and I look up and meet his eyes. "When you were five, your mom told you they needed to take your blood, for a test. But you refused—kicking and screaming—because you thought they meant *all* of your blood. Your mom didn't realize you took it literally, and she pleaded with you. She told you she wanted you to do it—for her—and you loved her so much you gave in." I remember how much my heart hurt when he told me, and I still feel the same way again just thinking about it.

Liz's mouth is open. "Is that true?" she asks Finn.

He nods.

"How come you never told me that story?"

"I was ashamed," he says as he meets her eyes.

"Ashamed of what?"

"I should have understood phlebotomy by that age."

Liz lets out a disbelieving laugh. "Oh my God, Finn! I swear I love you so much it hurts sometimes." She puts her arms around him and he smiles and she kisses him. Seeing them that way—so loving and happy together—warms my heart inside.

Finn turns to look at me again. He steps closer and studies my eyes for a long stretch. "I don't understand it, but I think it's you, Declan."

"It's me, Finn. I promise."

"In that case, I missed you. A lot."

I nod. "Me, too."

"Is it okay if I hug you?" he asks.

"Of course," I say as I jump up off the stool I'm sitting on. I hug him as tightly as I can and my eyes get misty.

"You're still short," he says while we're still hugging.

I laugh. "Some things carried over."

He pulls back and takes one of my hands in his. "Do you still have panic attacks?"

I shake my head. "Just your garden variety anxiety that everyone on the planet has."

"So you don't have attacks?"

"No," I reassure him, "I don't, thankfully, but I appreciate how you were always there for me before, holding my hand, when I did." I squeeze his hand. "You really helped me, Finn—you carried me through a lot of rough days. More than you know."

I can see the emotion he's holding back when our eyes meet. "You were my best friend," he says quietly.

"You guys are going to make me cry again," Liz chimes in. I look over and see that her eyes are brimming with tears.

I laugh and wipe under my eyes with my fingers. "Let's talk about something happy," I say to Finn. "I can't believe you're a dad. Niko's so cute."

He smiles. "When Niko was born I had to remind myself that the instant love and protection I felt for him was natural, and necessary, from an evolutionary standpoint. It's nature's way of perpetuating the species. It felt overwhelming, but I understood it, and that was comforting."

I nod.

"But now, with you and Alexander back, I wonder how much I really understand at all." He looks into my eyes. "And that's unnerving."

"I know, Finn. I know."

"I need to understand. That's why I'm analyzing the DNA and testing how the cells interact."

I nod. "I get it. I just don't know if you'll find the kind of answers you're looking for. Or any answers at all."

Chapter Fifty
Mira: T-minus 7 days; morning

All morning at the hospital, my mind is on Charlie, which I'm pretty sure is exactly what was meant to be avoided by not dating anyone—but, ironically, it's exactly where I *want* my mind to be. I'm supposed to be focused on dark angels and whatever the heck powers I have, but every time I think about all that stuff it feels so ludicrous and scary and out of control that I want to go back to thinking about Charlie and how much fun we've been having and the way he kisses me. He is, undeniably, an expert kisser, and maybe that's just what I needed right now.

"You've got that dreamy look on your face again."

I rouse from my thoughts and notice Gemma staring at me from across the counter in the break room as I wait for my bagel to toast. "See what happens when you break the rules?" she adds.

I smile. "What happens?"

"You get to smile like that."

I laugh. "I know what you're thinking but all we've done is kiss."

"I don't care if all you've done is stare at each other all night like a couple of maniacs. You're nuts about him. That's what matters."

My phone pings and I peer down to see the latest text from Dany, which brings me back to thinking about dark angels and my imminent destruction.

Hi Mira, just checking in again.
Whenever you feel ready to talk,
I'm here.

I stare at it and then respond the same way I have been.

Still processing.

I miss Dany, as my friend. And I don't understand fully what I'm feeling inside because isn't this what I wanted? To meet my parents? Now I finally have a chance to, and yet I've been avoiding them. It's all been so overwhelming. I don't know what to think about anything and I'm not ready to figure it out. I feel a pang for Dany (I can't make the leap to calling her Declan) and Alexander. If they really are my parents, it must hurt that I'm not ready to see them and talk yet. But the Dany I know—and I'm hoping she's still in there—would understand.

As if on cue, she replies.

I understand. Take
your time.

A few moments later, another text appears.

I heard you've been staying with Charlie and I just want you to know that I loved him as a little boy and from all I've seen, he's just as sweet now as he was then.

And, by the way, he puked on me once, spectacularly, when I was babysitting him, so maybe it was fate that you threw up on him, too.

Now he's even with the Jane family.

She ends it with a winking emoji and I can't help but laugh. I don't understand where Dany leaves off and Declan begins or if they're one and the same, or just a mish mash, but I'm certain that the Dany I know—who makes me laugh—is still in there.

The phone rings in my hand, startling me. It's Uncle Finn. "I have some interesting data to show you," he says without preamble.

My heart quickens. "I'll be there after work."

Chapter Fifty-One
UCSM: Finn's office

"Is Mira coming in, too?" Edwin asks Finn when he enters.

"She's coming later, after work."

Edwin nods. "That's probably for the best. She's not speaking with me at the moment."

"I understand her thinking. It's not unreasonable."

The words rankle but Edwin knows it's just Finn being honest. "What's this finding that you want to tell me about? You said you had a question for me?"

"We have a large database of DNA, as you know, for research purposes," Finn says. "I was testing interactions and I found some peculiarities with the way Mira's cells react with some of them."

"In what way?"

"Is there a chance that some of the DNA in the database includes guardians, other than you and Mira?"

Edwin considers the query. "It's possible."

"Dark guardians, too?" Finn asks.

"Why do you ask?"

"Because I'm isolating environmental factors for gene expression, and I haven't found an explanation yet."

"For what?"

"In certain circumstances, Mira's cells lock onto others and destroy them," Finn explains. "Similar to the way T-cells can identify and isolate cancer cells for attack. It only occurs with a particular subset of samples. And even within that subset, it doesn't occur with all of them."

"And you're wondering what her cells are reacting to?"

Finn nods. "I'm wondering if Mira's cells react to dark guardians in the same way T-cells can be modified to recognize and overcome the blocks that cancer cells exhibit."

Edwin considers the idea as Finn continues talking.

"The right circumstances cause genes, which are otherwise dormant, to suddenly be expressed." Finn's voice becomes more animated as he suggests the implications. "What if she's the ultimate force when she's around dark energy? It's a hypothesis, and the data pool is small, but in *Sargon Four: Transcendent Darkness* they had a weapon that behaved in the same manner. A classic Trojan Horse."

Science fiction references notwithstanding, Edwin considers what Finn is suggesting.

"The next step is for you to confirm the samples are from dark guardians," Finn adds.

"You mean by looking at the DNA?" Edwin shakes his head. "It's not possible. I would need to meet the person the sample was taken from."

"Well, can you get me a DNA sample from a dark guardian then? Or better yet, many of them?"

Edwin shakes his head. "Unfortunately, even if I did and you replicated the results in your lab, we couldn't rely on it. Every guardian has different levels of power and ability. "

"That means I can't test it."

Edwin nods, distracted. Something Finn said rings familiar. "I'm sorry, Finn, this is good work but there's no way to rely on it, unfortunately. I have to go now. I don't recommend you share this with anyone. It can't be confirmed."

Hours later, as Edwin sits at his desk in his study, he pores over the ancient texts he has scoured many times before. There are multiple versions of every fable and many of the versions don't appear to be related until they're studied and compared closely. Still, he recognizes what he's looking for when he finds the title. Although the fable he and Soren referenced to Declan and Alexander was titled *Kindred Fruit*, this version—even more obscure—goes by another name: *The Destroyer*.

Edwin locates the words that triggered his memory: *ultimate force*. He places his finger on the phrase he was looking for and rereads it. "In the end, the ultimate unknown that an unfamiliar malevolent heart seeks may prove to be an ultimate force that consumes instead."

But who does it consume? Everyone?

Chapter Fifty-Two
Mira: T-minus 7 days; evening

I arrive early, and, when I reach the door to Uncle Finn's office at UCSM, I hear him talking and I recognize Aunt Liz's voice, too. I raise my hand to knock but when I hear Aunt Liz say my name, I pull my hand back and listen quietly instead.

"You can't share that theory with Mira yet," Aunt Liz warns.

"It's not a theory, it's a hypothesis," replies Uncle Finn.

"Exactly—it's not even a theory—which is why you can't tell her because she might try it, Finn. And if all this crazy stuff Edwin says is true, then she's in enough danger already."

"It would be foolish to try something that isn't reliable."

"Yes, so why tell her when it's not information she can use?"

"All information has some utility. I won't lie to her."

"Of course not. I'm all for telling the truth, but why not wait until you figure out what it means? When you're sure and you can tell her something useful? This is Mira we're talking about—the girl we love like our own daughter. We need to do everything we can to *help* her, not possibly make things worse."

"If I'm asked directly, I have to tell her."

"You think Mira's going to waltz in here and ask you about epigenetics?"

If Uncle Finn answers, I can't hear it.

"Did you already say something to her?" Aunt Liz asks.

"I called Mira and told her I found something interesting. That's all." Uncle Finn goes on to say something about environmental factors next and, as the conversation continues, they lose me in minutia. I quickly look up "epigenetics" on my phone: *The study of changes in organisms caused by modification of gene expression rather than alteration of the genetic code itself.* I click on another link: *"Certain circumstances in life can cause genes to be silenced or expressed over time. In other words, they can be turned off (becoming dormant) or turned on (becoming active)."* I reread the words several times. How does that relate to me?

I decide I'm through with eavesdropping. I knock on the door and call out "Uncle Finn?" and I walk in.

"Mira," Aunt Liz calls out with affection when she sees me. "How are you doing?" She enfolds me in one of her bear hugs, which always make me feel adored, and then she pulls back and looks into my eyes. "You holding up okay? With all of this?"

I nod. "Are you?"

She shrugs. "I still don't know what to believe, to be honest. When I'm with your mom I believe it, and when I'm not, I go back to being rational and I think it's all insane again."

"Nan told me you ran background checks."

"Had to make sure it added up. But I have to tell you, Mira, I cross-examined Declan and Alexander's butts off—

separately—and they knew everything. They passed every test."

"You cross-examined their *butts* off? Is that an official attorney tactic?"

She laughs. "Bottom line is, and I can't believe I'm saying this: I believe them. So does Finn … and that's saying something."

I turn my attention to Uncle Finn, sitting at his desk. "You said you found something interesting in my DNA?"

"It's not anything definitive yet," Aunt Liz interjects.

"But there are some interesting preliminary findings," Uncle Finn answers.

"That add up to a lot of questions and need to be proven," Aunt Liz says quickly, glancing at Finn. "I have to go pick up Niko now," she says as she turns back to me. "You're being careful, right?"

I nod and we hug again and before she leaves she makes me promise to meet her for lunch soon.

When the door closes behind her, I turn to Uncle Finn. "What are the interesting findings?"

He moves some papers around on his desk absent-mindedly and then folds his hands in front of him before answering. "You understand I collected samples from you, Edwin, Declan, Alexander—everyone in the family. I analyzed them and I also ran them against our database of DNA samples to see how they compared."

My heart is thumping in my chest. *Is he going to tell me I'm not human?*

"I also experimented with interactions."

"And?" I ask, swallowing hard.

"Have you ever heard of junk DNA?"

My heart deflates. *My DNA is junk?*

"Everyone has noncoding DNA sequences. It used to be termed junk because no one understood what it does. We all have it. The difference is, you and Edwin have more of it. Much more."

"More junk?"

He nods. "Only 2 percent of DNA in humans codes for proteins," he explains. "The rest is the non-protein-coding DNA that was considered repetitive junk. But over the years it's been found that it isn't junk. It's important—it interacts with the surrounding genomic environment and increases the ability to evolve."

"To *evolve*? How?"

"Partly by providing signals for turning on and off gene expression."

"I don't understand what that means, Uncle Finn. You're saying Grandpa Edwin and I have more junk …"

"And others do, too."

"Others?"

He nods. "I ran a search across the millions of DNA samples in our database. A small percentage have similar characteristics—the extra 'junk' that you and Edwin have."

"But what does that mean?"

"I can't prove it, but possibly it means that those sub-samples are all guardians."

"Good ones or bad ones?"

He shakes his head. "I can't answer that, but when I isolated cells from those samples with yours, sometimes they interacted in interesting ways. But not always. It wasn't predictable."

"What do you mean by *interact*?"

"Sometimes your cells locked onto theirs."

"I still don't understand."

Uncle Finn takes a deep breath. I know he's trying to dumb this down for me as a non-scientist. "The way immunotherapy works for cancer is, we modify T-cells—which are like soldiers—to recognize cancer cells. It's like two puzzle pieces recognizing and locking onto each other."

"Uncle Finn, I'm sorry, but I still don't understand what you're trying to say."

He looks nervous and I sense we're getting close to the part he doesn't want me to ask about.

"Epigenetics, Uncle Finn. Please tell me about epigenetics and what they have to do with whatever powers I supposedly have."

He's silent for a long moment, but I know the answer is coming because he's the one person I know who is congenitally unable to tell me anything but the full truth.

He clears his throat. "You can think of epigenetics as environmental factors that turn genes on and off."

I nod. "So you're saying my powers, or whatever, turn on and off? Based on what? When?"

He clears his throat again. "I'm saying that it's possible that when you connect with dark guardians, certain genes are expressed—they turn on, in other words—that enable your cells to recognize and lock onto theirs."

"Lock onto them? And do what?"

He swallows. "Destroy them."

"So I *do* have power? I can destroy the dark guardians?"

He shakes his head vigorously. "This is a hypothesis and there's no way to prove it or rely on it. It would be irrational to act on it in any way." He looks at me with concern. "Edwin said that dark guardians have different levels of power and abilities. It may only work with some of them … or none."

"Grandpa Edwin said that?"

He nods. "He was here this afternoon."

I nod. Uncle Finn would never lie—not even well-meaning lies meant to "protect" me—but I can't say the same about Grandpa Edwin. I wonder if what he told Uncle Finn is true. I honestly don't know what to believe about anything anymore.

The only thing I know for sure is that Uncle Finn will always tell me the truth. Whether it's dangerous for me to know or not.

And that, right now, is about as comforting as it gets.

Chapter Fifty-Three
Mira: T-minus 6 days

What Uncle Finn told me ran through my mind all night, and when I see Soren in the courtyard as I'm eating lunch at the hospital, I weigh my options and decide to approach him. "Can we talk?" I ask. I have to be careful what I say because I know he's probably reporting everything back to Grandpa Edwin.

He looks surprised at my request. "Of course."

We find a quiet table away from the crowd. "I need to know my options," I say quietly.

"Options?"

"If the dark guardians get to me, I need to know what I can do to shut it down … if it reaches that point."

"What point?" he asks guardedly.

"The point where I'm fighting back and nothing is working and I don't want my power to go to them—to the dark side of the equation."

Soren shakes his head. "You don't have to worry about that, Mira. We're protecting you."

I meet his eyes. "Soren, I've seen it in your eyes—I know how worried you all are. And if I understand correctly everything I've been told, we both know what's at stake."

He doesn't answer.

"I know they'd take me somewhere dark and cold and hopeless."

He nods. "Nusquam."

"And they'd keep me there?"

He meets my eyes and reluctantly nods.

"Forever?"

He meets my eyes but doesn't respond.

"Soren, you have to tell me what to do if I get there and there's no other option."

"There are always other options."

"But if there aren't." I meet his eyes in the ensuing silence and I don't allow him to look away this time. "Please, Soren, just tell me."

His eyes are uneasy. "Tell you what, exactly?"

"How to end things … if it comes to that."

He shakes his head. "Mira, I'm not going to tell you how to destroy yourself."

"Because it's not possible?"

"Because it's not going to happen—it won't ever be needed."

"But what if it is?" I hold my eyes on his, pleading. "What if it is, Soren? You also said the good guardians wouldn't be able to go to Nusquam to save me. So you need to tell me how to save myself—and everyone—from the ramifications of what could happen."

He shakes his head. "I can't, Mira."

"You'd let me languish there for eternity?"

He digs in his heels. "It won't come to that."

"But what if it does?" I plead. "Soren, I need you to tell me. Just in case. I know no one else will. It's for the good of all of us."

He glances down for a long time and when he looks back up again and meets my eyes, I can see he's made a decision. Reluctantly, and in a quiet, sobering voice, Soren tells me about what he terms the absolute last resort or "failsafe."

Which is really just a euphemism for how to destroy my energy—and myself—forever.

Chapter Fifty-Four
Mira: T-minus 5 days

I look over at the clock on the nightstand: 5:11 a.m. It's not too early to get up. "I think I need a shower," I whisper to Charlie as I roll away from him. We've been sleeping next to each other since my first night staying here but we've continued to take things slow. I've enjoyed falling asleep cuddled together and in his arms every night. I may be fooling myself, but it makes me feel safe against the world.

But the last two nights, after meeting with Uncle Finn and talking to Soren, I hardly slept.

"Are you okay?" Charlie asks as he stirs. He must sense my anxiety.

I nod. "I'm fine. Just can't sleep." What I don't say is that I want to shower, and then I want to go surfing, alone.

I haven't listened to the ocean in a while and I need it to tell me what to do.

Chapter Fifty-Five
Mira: T-minus 4 days

"Are you ready to talk yet about why you're avoiding your family?"

Charlie looks over at me, sitting on the couch next to him, as I take a sip from my glass of sparkling water and set it down on the coffee table. I consider all the different ways I could answer him but I certainly can't tell him the truth or he'd have me committed. "Not really. Sorry."

"You don't have to apologize, but I just want to make sure that you want to be here. It's not just convenient?"

I meet his eyes. "Of course I want to be here. In fact, over the past few days I haven't felt the need to keep avoiding my family like I was, but I stayed here anyway because I wanted to. I've been thinking that I'll start staying at my nan and grandpa's house after tomorrow night, though."

What I don't tell him is that I've been allowing more and more bits of worry to creep in about dark angels and possible annihilation, and I've decided that I should play it safe and stay close to family for the last two days until my birthday (otherwise known as doomsday). It can't be a bad idea to be surrounded by people who know what's going on.

He smiles. "I'll miss you but I'm glad to hear you've patched things up."

"Me, too."

Our eyes meet and as his blue eyes hold mine, I realize how close I feel to Charlie, after staying here only a week and a half.

He leans over and kisses me, just the way I like, and when we lie back on the couch I allow myself to forget about everything else for a while and just enjoy the feel of Charlie's lips and his hard body on mine. Our hands roam and I arch against him and when I reach down to start to undo his jeans, he groans into my mouth. We pause kissing and he looks into my eyes. "Mira, I like you."

"I like you, too."

"No, I mean, I like you *a lot*." He takes a deep breath. "And I want to be with you like this— more than anything I think I've ever wanted in my life."

"Me, too."

He smiles but then his brow furrows. "But you've been in a vulnerable position, in a rift with your family, and I can't believe I'm saying this but I still think we should wait. I don't want to ruin what's happening here." He meets my eyes.

"What's happening here?" I ask softly.

He doesn't answer.

"Tell me."

He searches my eyes. "I think you know."

I smile. "Tell me."

He stares into my eyes for a long beat. "You have the most beautiful eyes I've ever seen," he says quietly. "I think I've memorized every gold fleck and shade of green and I dream about how radiant they are." He says the words with a reverence that makes my heart swell. "And you make me laugh and you're smart, and kind, and all day long all I can think about is coming home and spending time with you again." As he speaks, he holds my gaze, and the intimacy between us is beyond words.

"And I know it's crazy—we haven't even known each other that long—but I feel like I've known you much longer and I want to tell you how I feel." He pauses. "Because there's something about you that makes me want to lay all my cards on the table. No games."

The look in his blue eyes makes me swallow as I wait for him to continue.

"I'm falling for you, Mira. Hard." The depth of sincerity in his eyes reaches me on a level I wasn't expecting. "And if you don't feel the same way—or think you could someday—I need to know now, before this goes too far. To protect myself."

As I stare into his eyes, it's as if I can see what's in his heart, and I can't find the words to respond right away.

His brow furrows with concern. "Have I said too much?"

I shake my head slowly back and forth. "You said just the right amount."

A smile forms on his lips and he kisses me again, slowly and sexily and oh-so-competently, and I feel myself melting against him.

"Charlie?" I say.

"Mm-hmm," he murmurs before he kisses me again.

"Are you sure you want to wait?"

He chuckles, deep in his throat, as he kisses along my neck. "No."

I laugh. "Maybe we should see how we feel after my birthday. It's only three days away."

He stops and looks at me. "Is that what you want?"

I nod. "Yes."

We both smile and he kisses me again and I allow myself to drift into the sensation and not think about anything else for a while except how good it feels to be with him.

For the rest of the night we talk and snuggle and kiss until we nod off together on the couch. Hours later I wake up in Charlie's arms and nearly roll to the floor as he flails in his sleep.

"No, don't take me there," he mumbles. His body jerks again. "It's dark, no. No. *Hurts*. No. it's cold. No no no no don't."

Concerned, I gently push against his arm. "Charlie."

"No no no," he mumbles again. "Don't leave me here–"

"Charlie," I say again, a little louder, as I gently rock his arm again.

"Not in the land of no light. No no no no no–"

"Charlie," I cry out much louder as I rock him harder.

His eyes fly open and the panic I see in them strangles my heart. He quickly takes in his surroundings and exhales with relief and when his eyes finally settle on me, he looks worried. "Was I talking in my sleep?"

"It sounded like a nightmare."

"What did I say?"

"Something about being in the dark. And being cold."

He's quiet. "I have that dream a lot. I'm sorry I woke you."

"Charlie, I don't care that you woke me. I'm worried about you. And about the dream. Did somebody do something to you?"

He shakes his head. "It's a recurring dream I've had since I was a kid. My mom told me I must have seen a scary movie and it just lodged in there for some reason."

I consider his theory, but the terror in his voice sounded like more than just a movie.

He stretches his neck and looks around the room in the twilight of the morning. "What are we still doing on this couch?"

I shrug. "We fell asleep."

He dislodges himself from his prone position and I do the same and after he stands he holds out his hand for me to take. "Let's get into a proper bed."

I follow him drowsily down the hall.

"I'll sleep in here so I won't wake you again," he says as we reach the door of the guest bedroom.

I yank his hand back to follow me to his bedroom at the end of the hall. "I like sleeping in your arms."

He smiles and pulls me in for a kiss. "I like having you there."

"Until you had a terrible nightmare."

He shakes his head. "That has nothing to do with you."

When we get into his bed he wraps his arms around me and we both mumble about being tired before we start to fall asleep again, together. Just before I drift off, I can't help thinking that I hope he's right. But what if the dream has something to do with what's building within me and what's about to happen to me—or all of us?

Hours later, I wake up in a cold sweat with my heart racing and feeling like I had a nightmare of my own.

But what's most frightening is not what I remember about the dream. The most disturbing thing is that I can't remember any part of it at all.

Chapter Fifty-Six
Mira: T-minus 2 days

Tonight will be the first night in almost two weeks that I don't sleep at Charlie's. It was two nights ago that we both had nightmares, but last night we managed to sleep peacefully and now I think it's time to stay with my nan and grandpa for a while. At least until "doomsday" is over.

I park in front of her house after work and glance down the street to Grandpa Edwin's house. I don't see his car in the driveway so I decide to make a quick walk over to the cottage to pack up some more of my clothes. He's the one family member I still haven't made peace with in my mind yet and I'm not ready to talk to him.

When I slip into the backyard, quietly, I hear voices coming through the kitchen window and I wonder if maybe Grandpa Edwin is home despite his car being gone. For all I know he could have flown here—what does an angel even need a car for, anyway? My curiosity gets the better of me and I tiptoe up to the window and peek inside.

There's an assortment of men and women seated around the table, each speaking over one another, immersed in a discussion. I don't see Grandpa Edwin among them, but I do see Soren seated at the head of the table. Some of the other people seem vaguely familiar—or maybe I'm just imagining it because I'm assuming they're all guardians who have been following me. I quickly pull away from the window and press myself against the back of the house and listen to what I can of the conversation.

"She's acting out."

"She's confused."

"She's also holding more power than any of us have ever encountered."

"Which has helped us maintain the balance."

"Or it could make us lose it for good."

"In some respects, it would almost be safer to take that kind of power off the table."

"You can't be serious."

"Have you heard what's been said? She's acting out. She's unpredictable … and that's dangerous. For everyone."

"That's dark thinking and it has no place here."

The last voice is stern and I recognize it as Soren's. I don't hear any more because inside I'm panicking. These are the *good* guardians? And they're talking about … what? Eliminating me? Uncle Finn said he told Grandpa Edwin about what he discovered in my DNA. Did that change the calculation? Do they think my power is too unreliable or dangerous to them now? Grandpa Edwin is the one who pulled this team together to supposedly protect me. Could he possibly know about this?

As upset as I am, I don't truly believe Grandpa Edwin would ever do anything to hurt me. But that doesn't mean another one of these guardians wouldn't. Might they do it for a higher good? Maybe that's why Soren was finally willing to tell me about the failsafe—so I would think about using it.

My world shrinks smaller around me as I realize I don't know what to believe or whom to trust.

I slip away as quietly as I arrived and when I get back to my nan's I get into my car and drive a meandering route as I try to figure out what to do. Eventually I decide to park at the mall, and when I go inside I do my best to get lost in the crowd. I exit at the opposite end of the mall and hop into a waiting Lyft driver's Toyota, and I watch in the side view mirror as we drive, to see that I'm not being followed.

I honestly don't know what to do, but I think I need to see Dany.

I knock on the door of Alexander's condo but it's Dany who opens it.

"I was surprised, and grateful, when I got your text," she says with a hopeful smile. "We can definitely help with what you're asking."

I was vague in my text—I'm still not sure what my plan is—but I asked for help activating or summoning (or whatever guardians call it) my power. I step inside and she closes the door and, compelled by curiosity, I search her eyes. I'm surprised to find they're no longer a puzzle—they're comforting and familiar. She smiles, "Hug?"

I nod and we hug and it feels good to hold each other tight. "Listen," I say as we let go of our embrace, "I haven't been mad at you, if that's what you've been thinking. Well, a little mad, actually, at everyone for defending Grandpa Edwin—but I know you insisted on revealing the truth."

She nods and motions to the couch in the living room. "I can only imagine how you've been feeling," she says as we walk over and sit down.

"I'm still working on processing the fact that you guys are my parents, but that's why I'm here."

She smiles and squeezes my hands. "Believe me, I understand. I'm still processing it all, too."

"I still want to call you Dany."

She nods. "Of course."

"But are you Dany or are you Declan?"

She shrugs. "I'm both."

"It feels like I became friends with Dany and now you're a different person. I'm just wondering if I still know you."

"I promise you, I'm still Dany. It's just that now I also know I'm Declan, too. But I'm the same person I always was."

I nod. It's strange, looking at her and knowing she's my mom, but my love for her as a friend hasn't changed. Staying away was my own doing but I missed her greatly these last two weeks.

"Alexander will be here any moment," she says, glancing at the door. "He's been pouring himself into his new job and working long hours—we both have, actually—because we feel so helpless. We don't have any power and Edwin keeps telling us we've already done our part by simply being here, but that doesn't feel like enough. We've been going crazy. That's why I was so glad when you reached out."

My head turns at the sound of the door opening and I see Alexander walk in. His eyes go from Dany to me and he walks over. "Mira," he says with a warm smile as he sits down in a chair across from us.

"Hi, Alexander." I realize as our eyes meet how strange this is. I've met him exactly once before and he's my age—and yet he's my dad. I decide to be honest. "Can I just tell you that this all feels very strange?"

He nods and it's as if he read my mind because he answers, "We hardly know each other yet. I understand."

I look into his eyes and see compassion and kindness, and I'm comforted because I also see familiarity—his eyes are the same eyes I've been looking into in the mirror my whole life. "I don't know if Dany told you, but I'm not ready to talk about everything yet and ask you guys all the questions that I know I'll have at some point."

He smiles. "She told me what you asked for and I know exactly why you're here. Shall we get started?"

I nod. The night Dany revealed everything to us in my nan's living room, she said that Alexander had taught her to use her power. She started from nothing and he helped her figure out how to fight back, so I'm hoping they can help me figure it out, too. Because I'm running out of time.

Alexander moves the coffee table and we all sit down on the floor, cross-legged. As I stare at them both, it still boggles my mind to believe these two are my parents. *My actual parents, here, alive.*

Dany's voice cuts into my thoughts. "As I mentioned before, when I was trying to control my panic attacks, Alexander taught me some things that ended up helping me discover the powers I had as a sprite."

"It's about focusing with intention," Alexander says. "But first you have to get to a place where you can focus from."

"Like getting quiet so you can listen to your deep sight," Dany says, and I nod.

"Exactly," Alexander agrees. "When I worked on this with Declan, I held her hands and I was using my power as a guardian to guide her. I don't have any power anymore, but maybe we should still all hold hands."

I nod and take his hand in my left and Dany's on my right.

"Focus on your core and nothing else. Imagine the power you hold as a ball of light in your center."

As I listen to Alexander's words, the thought that I'm sitting here holding hands with my mom and dad and that I'm supposedly some sort of angel meant to save the world is front and center in my mind. I keep trying to push it away but it pops back up. Finally I decide to go in the other direction and embrace the absurdity of it all, and my mind slowly quiets and I'm able to tune back into Alexander's words, following his directions.

"It's a bright ball of light and you have complete control. You can move it throughout your body and release it at will. It won't ever be depleted because it regenerates endlessly and effortlessly."

I listen to his soothing voice and try to imagine that I truly do have this power within me. I focus the way I have in the past when I'm trying hard to listen to my DS about a person or a decision and I find myself relaxing into the tranquility of the suggestions.

"As the light moves within you, you may even feel its warmth as it travels and grows."

"I used to imagine it as laser lights shooting out of my fingers at the dark guardians," Dany whispers as an aside. "I zapped Alexander once."

I open my eyes and look at her, surprised.

"It's true," Alexander says. "And I couldn't work it out. I didn't know yet that she was a sprite. I thought she was just some amazing mortal."

"I *was* an amazing mortal," Dany says.

"You still are." Alexander laughs and, in their eyes, I can see the love between them and it makes me feel warm inside. And safe.

We settle down to try again. I listen to Alexander's guidance and as I give myself over to this other state, I see things. I see my parents, not as they are now, but as they were. I see them laughing together and I see a string of light connecting them ... and I see them struggling ... and I see my mom fighting for her life, in pain, and she's dying and she's in a gray place and her energy's being stolen from her and she's saying "behind my heart," over and over as she rocks in pain. The image is unbearable and I cry out and pull my hands away.

When I open my eyes, Alexander and Dany are staring at me with concern. "What happened?"

"I saw you," I say to Dany, "I felt what you were feeling. You were in a dark place and you were rocking in pain and saying 'behind my heart.'"

She looks stricken. "That was Nusquam. When they were taking my power I imagined that I tore off a tiny piece of it and hid it behind my heart. I think it's what saved me. It's good for you to know that, but I'm sorry you had to feel what it was like to be there. Even for a second."

339

I nod, and shudder inside again at the memory, but I know I need to keep going and figure this out. I won't be able to tear off a piece of my power to save it if I can't locate it or activate it in the first place. "Can we try again?" I ask.

"Are you sure?" Dany asks.

I nod. "I need to do this."

"Focus on my voice," Alexander says as we all join hands again.

I listen to his words and let myself drift back into a calm state and attempt to conjure the power in my core. I try to draw it to my fingertips and imagine zapping dark angels as Dany described. I try everything, over and over, but nothing materializes. Hours go by and I'm feeling desperate and I'm losing focus. It's getting harder to hold onto the tranquil state I know I need to be in for this to work.

"It's not working," I say finally with frustration as I let go of their hands.

"What did you feel?" Alexander asks.

"I couldn't feel anything. That's the problem. Maybe a little warm, and relaxed, but that's it. I think Grandpa Edwin's got it all wrong. I'm not some all-powerful angel with accelerating powers."

"Or it could be that your power will manifest in some other way." Alexander is trying to be reassuring but I can see the worry exchanged in his looks with Dany.

"Well, I don't have time to figure it out. It's almost midnight and that means my birthday is basically 24 hours away now." I think of all the time in the past two weeks when I could have been more focused on all of this, but I was too blinded by my anger at Grandpa Edwin, and my feelings of being overwhelmed by everything, and, I'll admit it, my distraction with Charlie. Which is exactly what Grandpa Edwin warned me about—not focusing. Only now it's too late. There's no more time left.

I can tell that Dany sees the anguish on my face. "Let's go at this another way," she says as she places her hand on mine to calm me.

I look up at her. "How?"

"Remember when you told me the reason you follow the rules is because one time you didn't and you regretted it?"

I nod, and an icy shiver runs down my spine at the memory.

"Tell us what happened."

I swallow and steel myself to share a memory I've spent my whole life trying to suppress.

Alexander must see it on my face because he reaches over and takes my other hand. "It's okay."

I nod. Something in his demeanor—or maybe it's his eyes—calms me. He and Dany both make me feel safe. I clear my throat before I begin the story.

"I was five. There was a boy in my class named Graham. Grandpa Edwin had already told me not to shake hands with anyone at that point, but he also specifically told me to avoid certain people ... and one of those people was Graham's mom." I pause and take a breath before I continue. "But one day Graham's mom came to pick him up early and I was sitting next to him in class, and she walked over and she saw the picture I was drawing and she complimented it." I pause and look up and Dany must see the terror in my eyes because she squeezes my hand. "It's okay," she says, "go on."

I nod and it's as if I'm going back in time, remembering. "That week in school we were learning about people in the community who help us. I was drawing a firefighter and I remember being really proud of my picture because I thought the smile I drew on my firefighter made her look friendly but also strong." I pause for a moment, recalling the feeling and that day. "When Graham's mom saw the picture, she said that my firefighter looked friendly and fierce and I remember thinking, 'What a nice lady. Grandpa Edwin must be wrong about her.'"

I look up at Dany and take another deep breath before I can continue. "She put out her hand and said, 'I'm Graham's mom, Eleanor, and who might this talented artist be?' and I thought, what harm can it do to shake this nice lady's hand? And I accepted it. And that's when I saw it."

"Saw what?" Dany asks.

"When she shook my hand, for an instant, I didn't see her face anymore. In its place I saw thousands of tangled, angry snakes writhing and hissing as one demonic image. I couldn't pull away and when she finally released my hand, she scratched her long red nail down the inside of my wrist and blood dripped onto my picture. She looked at the droplets and said, 'That's a pretty red,' and then she walked away."

I look up at Dany with the same terror in my heart that I felt that day as a little girl. She holds my hand and I can see the pain reflected in her eyes, but when I look over at Alexander, his eyes are unmistakably registering fear.

"What is it?" I ask him.

"It was a woman?" he asks.

"Yes."

He releases my hand and tugs his phone out of his pocket. "I need to find out from Edwin which dark guardian she was."

I shake my head. "She couldn't have been a guardian. You said they don't age, right? Graham's mom got older. She was admitted to the hospital a few years ago. I kept my distance but I saw her. She lives in a nursing home now."

Alexander sets the phone down and, despite what I was expecting, the look on his face now shows even greater fear. "She's a *mortal*?"

"She has to be."

"That makes sense with what Edwin told us," Dany replies. "He kept you surrounded so no dark guardians could get near you. And he said that's what baffled him— that none have tried. Even now."

"Did you tell Edwin what you saw? At the time?" Alexander asks me.

I shake my head. "I was afraid to. I didn't want him to know I'd broken the rules."

"That's why he doesn't think the dark guardians have reached you."

"But she wasn't a dark guardian."

Alexander shakes his head. "In that moment, she was. Because that image you saw? That was Malentus—his true image, without a shell."

"What are you saying?" Dany asks.

"I'm saying that somehow Malentus must have gained the ability to enter vulnerable mortals."

"What makes them vulnerable?" I ask.

"It could be a connection to Malentus in some way," Alexander answers. "Or it could be the same things that influence mortals to listen to dark guardians time and again: willful ignorance, intolerance, lack of compassion, hate, arrogance, demonizing others—we all know the list. We're all the same and we're all connected, and when mortals choose to forget that, dark energy finds an opening."

"That means Malentus could be almost anywhere," Dany says with fear in her eyes.

"I don't know," Alexander answers. "Guardians have never been able to enter and control mortals in that way, but there's no other explanation. Edwin said he thought Malentus was weakened when he followed me back, but perhaps he lost some powers and gained others."

Dany looks at me. "Mira, can you think of any other time he may have contacted you?"

I shake my head. "I've never had another experience like that."

"It could be anything. I had a dream once, about Avestan, and he was killing me and mocking me with all my fears and insecurities—it was like he got into my head."

When Dany says the word "dream," the memory of waking up two nights ago at Charlie's in a cold panic flashes before me. Was it a dream? Why didn't I remember it? It feels more like an implanted scene, secreted into my consciousness, and then tucked away, hidden.

"I think I may have had something," I say hesitantly, "a nightmare. But when I woke up I couldn't remember anything."

Dany meets my eyes. "Can you remember anything now?"

I take a deep breath and try to recall the moments before I woke up, seized with terror. I close my eyes and then, slowly, the horror of it slithers over me in a slow, nauseating wave and I recount the memory to Dany and Alexander as if I'm watching myself on a screen: "I was at the hospital and Dr. Wilder was walking towards me in his scrubs. He told me Niko was in the ER. My heart plummeted and I asked him what happened and he said Niko fell at school and he needed surgery. I asked him if he would be the one operating and he answered, 'Yes, but I haven't decided yet.' I remember feeling confused about what he meant and I tried to move in the direction of the ER but my legs felt like they were stuck in deep, thick mud and I couldn't lift them. I asked him what he hadn't decided yet and he answered in a voice I've never heard before."

A creeping shiver runs up my spine at the memory and I swallow before I continue. "It was a hiss, and it sounded like pure evil. He said, 'I haven't decided if Niko will live or die.' I felt like I couldn't breathe but I managed to say, 'But you're a doctor—you save people. You saved me when I was choking.' He looked at me with this horrible, garish smile and he told me that he and I have something in common—we both share the power to decide who survives. The hallway began to close in on me and I slowly realized that his scrubs were blood red and the hallway we were standing in wasn't right. It was similar to the hallway outside my office, but it curved, making me dizzy, and it ended in darkness, out of reach. I asked him who he was and he asked me who I thought he was. Then I asked if Niko was safe and he said, 'The question is: Can anyone ever, truly, be safe?' I begged him to stop and he told me that I was the one putting Niko in danger. He said the only way to protect the ones I loved was to take his hand and join him."

I open my eyes in horror and look at Dany and Alexander. "Oh my God. Niko. We have to let the guardians know." I stand up in a panic and Alexander pulls out his phone and dials. "Edwin? Check on Niko, now," he demands with a studied calm that I wish I could conjure. Within seconds, his face relaxes and the grip on my heart eases. "Okay ... okay," he says. "And everyone else? Okay." He covers the phone with his hand and looks at us. "Everyone's accounted for, which makes sense, since Edwin assured us he's had a fortress surrounding everyone. He's taking no chances."

I breathe a sigh of relief and Dany squeezes my hand. "It's going to be okay," she says reassuringly, but I can see the grave worry in her eyes.

Alexander nods to us as he stands and continues talking on the phone. He walks toward the back of the condo and I hear him informing Grandpa Edwin about his theory of Malentus entering mortals.

"Why don't you stay here for tonight?" Dany suggests. "Alexander has a second bedroom. It's late now and you'll be safe."

I nod as I realize how utterly depleted I feel. "I think that's a good idea."

She shows me to the guest room and I'm so exhausted that I climb into bed with my clothes on.

"Can I get you anything?" Dany asks as she stands in the doorway.

I meet her eyes from where my head is resting on the pillow and I feel terribly vulnerable ... and scared. "Can you stay with me? Until I fall asleep?"

The warm gratitude in her eyes—and compassion—is evident as she walks over and lies down next to me. "It's going to be okay, Mira, I promise," she says as she turns on her side and puts her arm over me and holds my hand.

I don't know if she's hugging me as my mom or as my best friend, but I feel protected as I drift off to sleep.

Chapter Fifty-Seven
Mira: T-minus 1 day

I wake up with a start to the sound of a gasp in the morning. Dany is still here, only now she's sitting bolt upright beside me and the look on her face is sheer panic.

"What is it?' I ask. "What's wrong?"

"What if Edwin's not protecting the right child?" she says as she meets my eyes.

I stare at her, confused.

"We need to get over to Charlie's," she says with distress rising in her voice. "Now."

When we get to Charlie's house I can see the back of him through the kitchen window and I feel immense relief. He's here and he's safe. I turn to Dany and Alexander. "Wait out here a minute. I don't know what excuse I'd give to have you come in with me and I don't want to alarm him. I'll just go in and make sure everything's fine." They agree and I wait for them to move around the corner in front of the garage where they can't be seen, before I knock.

"Mira," Charlie says with a smile when he opens the door, "come on in." I step in and he closes the door. "I've been expecting you."

I follow him into the living room. "You've been expecting me? But I didn't say I was coming over."

He turns and that's when I see it. His eyes are still blue, but there's no light within. They're shallow, the way Dr. Wilder's were in my dream. "It's nearly your birthday, Mira, and whether you know it or not, you were compelled to come." His voice has changed and it's familiar, just as his eyes are from the dream, and it's starting to feel like two cold hands are slowly tightening on my throat.

"Malentus?" I whisper.

The sneering smile he delivers in return makes my skin crawl. It's not Charlie's face—it's a perversion, an image of Charlie stripped of all kindness and heart and being used for evil. For an instant, his face shimmers away to the same slithering visage I saw in my dream. "You recognize me."

"I've been told of you," I respond with disgust.

"Then you've also been told, no doubt, what I can do to this mortal if you don't agree to join me now."

I consider screaming for Dany and Alexander to come in but something makes me hold the urge in check. What could they do? Malentus has control of Charlie already— could he take control of them, too?

"I see you doing the calculus in your mind. Cry for help? Fight? But you know as well as I do what decision you're going to make. Charlie's life is at stake, Mira. Take his hand and follow me and perhaps you can save him."

"Leave Charlie out of it," I plead. I search Charlie's eyes to see if there's any part of the man I know still in there but all I see are shadows where light should be.

"I wish I could do that, Mira. You don't believe me, of course, but I truly wish I could present myself to you properly in this realm. Unfortunately, although I managed to follow your father and return, I didn't manage to emerge fully intact. I give you my word Charlie's shell will simply be used for transport."

"Use me instead."

"It has to be a mortal. And, as a former visitor to Nusquam as a child, Charlie is uniquely qualified to travel in and out. He survived the journey before and you'll have to trust that he has the stamina to survive it again. Charlie is simply a shell I'm using, Mira. A shell that I require at the moment. And, fortuitously for me, a shell you care about. Deeply."

"I won't allow you to put him in danger. Leave Charlie here. I'll agree to go with you but only if you leave him alone."

"I'll remind you that your mother was once in a similar bind, and one of my most hot-headed acolytes kept his word to her, or else Charlie wouldn't be here today. To my mind, using Charlie as the vessel completes the circle winningly. It's a tribute to Avestan's memory that I could repurpose his playbook and make it work properly this time. And none of you saw it coming."

I want to tell him that my mom saw it coming, and she's here, with my dad. But they no longer have any powers, and if I call to them I'll only add to the danger everyone is already in. I close my eyes, shutting out the image of Charlie's distorted face, and try to focus. I try to find the light within my core and make something happen. Grandpa Edwin assured me I have this energy within me and that the power is accelerating. But if that's true, then where is it? It's only hours now until I turn twenty-five and yet I can't seem to access anything.

As my mind freefalls into a spiral of panic, I frantically picture Charlie—and all the people I love and who I'm fighting to protect—and I manage to still my mind, and find a space of quiet, and I listen. And that's when my DS tells me what I need to do.

The same thing it told me to do when I went out on the ocean alone the other day, surfing in the early morning hours.

I take a deep breath, open my eyes, and extend my hand to Malentus in Charlie's form.

As I put my hand in his, Dany and Alexander burst through the door with Grandpa Edwin and Soren close behind. "No!" they all shout as I begin to be pulled away. They reach for me, but when I look down I can see that my arm is already gray.

The last thing I see as I leave the world of color behind is their faces filled with horror and disbelief and yelling, "Stop, Mira, don't do it!"

"But it's what I have to do," I whisper.

Then everything goes black.

Chapter Fifty-Eight
Mira: Nusquam

The heaviness is overwhelming. I feel the air being sucked from my lungs the moment we enter. Immediately, the description Dany gave me of this desperate, hopeless realm becomes clear. The despair is thick and heavy—relentless and inescapable. I can't see anyone surviving here for long. And yet I've been told the dark guardians' plan is to keep me here forever, feeding off my energy. Only a place this bleak could make death preferable.

Charlie is slumped on the ground next to me, silent and motionless. I try to reach him but it's as though I'm moving through thick water that's holding me back. All my senses are muted and I can't reach him. "Charlie?" I try to call out his name but it emerges no louder than a whisper. "Charlie!" I try again but it's like my dream—I'm stuck and trying to move but nothing works.

"He'll be out for a while." Malentus's deep hiss comes from behind me. I turn to see the demonic visage I glimpsed earlier, only now it's a permanent, shimmering mass of snakes and serpents writhing and hissing together in tangled, angry knots. "I've sent for my brothers and when they arrive, we'll get started." His forked tongue emerges as he speaks and the acrid stench coming forth from what serves as his mouth makes my eyes water.

"Let Charlie go!" I cry out. My throat feels like sand as I strain to speak.

"Until I gain my power back, the mortal will have to stay."

"But you said–"

"You approached this with a rational mind, Mira. Let's keep it that way. I've told you what I can do and I'll honor our agreement after my brothers arrive and I reclaim my power. I have a long history with your family, and rational actions haven't always been taken. Your father, Alexander, for instance, was willing to disappear for eternity as long as he took me with him ... but I've had twenty-five years to ponder my momentary lapse in guard, and I can assure you that won't happen again. And, although it's obvious, I'd like to point out that Alexander's valiant effort to save your mother was worthless in the end. Yes, they may have both returned, but they're powerless ... and a life without power isn't really a life, to my mind. This is *my* triumph now, and repaying your father by punishing you will be almost worth it. Because, as you're realizing firsthand," he says, as he gestures to Charlie lying slumped on the ground, "seeing others punished for your misdeeds can be worse than being punished yourself."

Malentus's gaze shifts to behind me. "My brothers," he states with an air of beastly welcome. I turn slowly, with extreme dread, to view the rest of the Triumvirate and am startled to see that they appear normal, in human shells. "Stolvos, Mortegur, this is the day we've been waiting for."

The man Malentus refers to as Stolvos is older—tall and fleshy with a barrel chest, vicious eyes, and yellowed hair that looks like spun candy. His exact age is hard to pin down but he looks hard and weathered and mean. As I watch, his thin lips form into a cold sneer, steeped in bile, and his image flickers and fades into a malevolent, writhing, shrieking heap of vermin.

Mortegur, on the other hand, is even more alarming, if only for the fact that he appears young and mundanely attractive. Tall, muscular, with dark hair and broad shoulders, his eyes are ink black, and the deadness behind their glare is jarring. His shell, too, begins to shift and fade into a shimmering visage of what looks and sounds like teeming insects, clicking and hissing and sparring for survival.

Fear crawls up my throat, thick and overwhelming. How did I ever think I could hold my own against such vile evil? *Did I do the wrong thing?*

"This?" shouts Stolvos. His voice is deep and booming and it hurts my ears.

"There'll be no second chances, brother, if she isn't as promised." Mortegur's words are quietly restrained and therefore more menacing, and the loathing he embeds in the word *brother* feels like fingers snapping bones.

"Look into her eyes," Malentus hisses.

Stolvos grips my jaw and jerks it to face him squarely. The feel of his nails pinching my skin imparts a dank cold that penetrates deep and sends a tremor of revulsion through me. Despite my intense fear and repulsion I force myself to stare back defiantly. Mortegur is beside him now and, as they both bore their dead eyes into mine, the cold I feel reaches deep, to my soul. Demonic smiles spread across their evil, shimmering visages and they turn to Malentus.

"She'll do me well," Stolvos rasps.

"She'll do *us* well," Malentus corrects with barely held restraint. "We're *all* here to restore dark energy to its rightful place and tip the balance in our favor forever. Once you both start the process, I can join in, and the Triumvirate can reign again."

The acrid animus emanating from the three entities before me feels as though it's seeping into every cell in my body. Hopelessness clings to me like a heavy cloak—damp and suffocating. I'm finding it hard to focus and I remember what Dany said about the pain. Have I made a terrible, irreparable mistake? The cockiness of my plan seems laughable now in the face of this scale of malevolence.

Stolvos and Mortegur stand over me, appraisingly, as if they're trying to decide where to cut first. I see in their eyes that I'm not a person to them ... or a guardian ... or anything, really, other than an object to exploit for their own ends.

When the first strike hits, from Stolvos, the sharpness steals my breath away. Mortegur hits next and the feeling can only be described as knives scraping bone and carving off pieces of my soul. The ironic part is that in this moment I finally feel the power in myself that everyone has been alluding to. Only, as I finally get a taste of it for the first time, I worry it's also the last, because it's being drained away even as it surges up within me. I see now that the chance I've taken is too reckless. Too irresponsible. In this instant, I also see the pettiness of my response to Grandpa Edwin—and everyone else—when I found out the truth. I'm ashamed and overwhelmingly sad. I know how much Grandpa Edwin loves me. I feel his love, and everyone else's, as my cells—and memories—leave my body. I surely won't get another chance to tell them.

Because it's only now that I see how misguided my plan was: submit and let them take my energy, hoping Uncle Finn was right and I'm a Trojan Horse; or, if that fails, destroy myself in a last-minute failsafe as Soren instructed.

Only I don't know how to tell if my power is working against them, and the pain is blinding and paralyzing and I can't find the means to focus on anything, let alone doing what it takes to trigger the failsafe option. And even if I could, I didn't factor in Charlie being here.

I've made a terrible mistake.

The two twisted, demonic visages standing over me writhe with the power they're stealing away and I begin to lose hope as the strength drains from within me. They're glowing with power and vitality—*my* power and vitality— and when they extend their arms to Malentus, I feel a searing, blazing heat down the length of my scar as my light begins to flow among all three.

As Malentus begins to glow, a flash of his human shell returns. His youth and unassuming good looks are a stark surprise, and more frightening than his true visage. Because you expect evil to come wrapped in the form of writhing serpents, not in the mundane, appealing smile of an everyman standing next to you in line at the local coffee shop. His eyes, though, remain as unequivocal windows to his real self—filled with pure, vile hate and nothingness.

"Are you feeling it yet?" Malentus shouts to his brothers triumphantly.

I look up and notice the glow around the two brothers is dimming as Malentus shines brighter.

"There's something wrong," Stolvos booms as he looks down at his hands.

"We need to stabilize the energy among us," Mortegur echoes with alarm.

"It's not stability that's the problem," Malentus remarks snidely. "It's you." He turns to look at Stolvos. "And you."

Stolvos and Mortegur are not only dimming now but starting to shrivel.

"I thank you for your help, *brothers*." Malentus emphasizes the last word with dripping derision. "There's one fact, however, that I neglected to tell you about this girl. Her father was a guardian and her mother was a sprite, as you know. But did I also mention that her grandmother was close to me at one time? Close may be too strong a word— she was a widget of mine. She was a widget in a plan that netted benefits beyond even what I hoped—benefits that continue to this day. She was here once, young Judy, in Nusquam, and her naiveté led to a guardian surrendering his power to me to save her. What he didn't know—and what Judy couldn't know—is that I planted a seed that day, long ago. My essence, placed within Judy's womb, so that when she and Frank conceived a child, it would be mine, too."

Malentus peers down at me, twisted in pain on the ground. "Your mother, Declan, refused to believe me when I informed her. She insisted Frank was her father, but she was only partially right. I'm in there, too. My blood runs within her veins. And that means it runs within *your* veins as well, Mira. You can add me to your list of grandfathers."

The shock I feel at his words registers through the pain. Could he be telling the truth? Or is it more lies, like Dany warned me about? "I don't believe anything you say," I grunt out with supreme effort. "You made a deal with my grandfather, Frank, but you killed him anyway."

"Indirectly, that's true. And Frank never saw it coming." His vicious smile and cackle coincides with a fresh wave of searing pain to my spine that splinters out in radiating lines in every direction.

Malentus returns his attention to Stolvos and Mortegur. "If you haven't put the pieces together, that's what you're feeling, gentlemen. I won't call you brothers anymore because we all know we're not true brothers. By the blood of others, yes, but not our own. And that's important, because the interesting thing about being stuck here for the last twenty-five years is you can do a lot of reading ... and planning ... for vengeance. And when I found an obscure story of the spawn of two guardians that wreaked havoc many years ago, I took a chance that perhaps the spawn of a guardian and a sprite could do the same. What I didn't tell you is that, in the story, the spawn becomes a destroyer of unfamiliar malevolent hearts. *Unfamiliar* ones. And I tested my theory, with Mira's blood, many years ago. And although I couldn't be certain until this moment, I think my gamble has borne fruit, gentlemen, based upon what you're experiencing."

He steps closer to each of them, and places his face inches from theirs. "Perhaps you could confirm: do you feel as though every individual cell is being surrounded and attacked? Death from a million cuts, as they say, is still death. You're dying from within, gentlemen. Victims of your desire for power above mine."

"Explain yourself!" Stolvos thunders.

"The spawn of divine beings have the unique ability to find and destroy dark energy. Her cells lock onto unlike cells—yours—and consume them. The yin destroys the yang, you could say."

"You'll be destroyed, too," Mortegur grunts in obvious distress.

"That's the beauty of it," Malentus hisses. "I won't. My cells, unlike yours, aren't seen as invaders. They're recognized as comrades. Collaborators. *Family*. Mira's cells *add* to mine, they don't destroy." He pauses, seemingly to savor the moment. "How much does it hurt, gentlemen? A great deal, I hope."

"Malentus," Stolvos growls, but his protestations are becoming visibly pained now.

"I can infuse my cells with yours to save you," Malentus offers, "but only if you pledge yourselves to serve under me."

"Never," Stolvos grunts out.

"*Never.*" Mortegur's voice seethes with fury.

"I'll remind you what's at stake," Malentus jeers. "Not only you, but your entire line—your domains, both of you—gone for eternity. Pledge to serve under me or you'll no longer *exist!*"

"I'll never bow to you, Malentus," Mortegur seethes once more, his voice growing fainter.

"I'm the true leader," Stolvos spits and rages, but his voice emerges as a last gasp, as he continues to shrivel and collapse into himself.

"You won't … do it," Mortegur rasps, shrinking. "You need us … to reclaim the balance."

"Without the Triumvirate," Stolvos whispers, "dark energy can never reign again."

"Then I'll reign alone!" Malentus roars as he raises his arms in the air, glowing with power.

Stolvos gasps. "You're crippling dark forces forever."

"Only a *fool* would threaten the reign of dark energy in this way …" Mortegur attempts to finish but his voice trails off.

"Then submit to me!" Malentus thunders, shaking the ground beneath us. "Submit to me! Or I'll watch as you're destroyed forever!"

"*Never.*" Their last words emit from withered lips as their bodies shrink and shrivel and begin to disappear before my eyes.

I watch in stunned silence as Malentus is surrounded by an ink black aura with white light escaping all around. His eyes appear crazed with power and hate. "*Fools!*" He rages. "Prideful fools!"

He trains his eyes on me and, in an instant of terror and clarity, I try desperately to recalibrate in the face of this new development.

Malentus now stands alone, focused on drawing the rest of my power.

While he was delighting in destroying his brothers, I should have been doing what Dany told me to—tucking a tiny bit of energy, hidden, behind my heart. But the pain was too great and I can't seem to focus and I'm not sure my heart even remains. The fire is searing through my body, scraping every molecule, and I feel it in my scar, like a familiar lightning bolt of pain. Is this what it felt like as a child? To be struck in my mother's womb? I remember what my nan said about my scar being a shield, protecting me, and it's there that I decide to imagine a pinpoint of my soul hanging on, in the tip of my lightning bolt scar, nearest to my heart.

As the waves of pain become overwhelming, I begin to lose focus and I know if I fail, there's no hope for rescue and the stakes extend far beyond my suffering alone.

"Save Charlie," I manage to gasp.

"I gave you my word," Malentus seethes. His twisted, demonic visage stands over me, writhing with the power he's stealing away.

At first I was fighting back, but now I'm simply hanging on.

As I feel my life force slipping away, I remember Uncle Finn's hypothesis—backed only by uncharacteristic conjecture and hope. It was an alluring fancy, and it almost worked, but we didn't realize Malentus had already factored it in. I'm afraid what may have looked promising turned out to be only as good as junk after all. As Malentus said, as far as DNA is concerned, we're comrades, not adversaries. If I wasn't already drowning in despair, the thought of having a connection to such evil, and facilitating it, strikes the final blow.

As darkness seeps in and consciousness fades to nothingness, I console myself with the fact that after I'm gone, the ones I love can no longer be used as targets and cudgels.

Because how can you threaten someone whose soul no longer exists?

Chapter Fifty-Nine
Mira

Pain rouses me. I roll over, cold and choking with desperation and, with a measure of agony, I manage to look around. To my surprise, Malentus is gone.

Two heaps of ashes remain where Stolvos and Mortegur once were, convincing me that my memory of watching them wither away to nothing wasn't a pain-induced delusion.

"Mira?" I hear the voice and as my eyes focus I remember how I came here.

"Charlie," I rasp when I see him crumpled on the ground. My throat feels as though I've swallowed knives. "Charlie." I repeat his name with groaning despair. Malentus promised to let him leave but he's still here. *What have I done?*

"Mira," he moans as he pushes himself upright. He looks around him. "Is this a dream?"

I try to shake my head but the pain is too much. "No, Charlie … I'm sorry." I'm so heartsick at seeing him that I choke on the words. "This is my fault."

He looks at me with confusion. "You brought us here?"

A tear rolls down my cheek. "Yes," I manage to whisper. I didn't think I had any tears left in me but perhaps that bit of soul I imagined hiding behind my scar survived.

"*Why?*"

I nearly break down again at the horror in his eyes. "I had a plan ... but it didn't work. I'm so sorry, Charlie. I'm so sorry." I repeat the apology over and over as my heart, already a shriveled mass, dies yet again.

"This is my dream," he says.

"No, it's not a dream, Charlie. I'm sorry, but this is real."

"No," he replies, shaking his head. "This is *my* dream. The one I've had since I was a kid."

"Your nightmare?"

He nods and looks at me strangely. "Your mother saved me from this place."

"You remember that?"

His expression is confused. "She saved me from the Land of No Light."

"This is the place from your dream?"

He nods again. "I remember that when I was a kid, after my sister told me Declan died, I was terrified that this is where she was."

I can see in his eyes that he's remembering everything anew, and a fresh wave of raw pain courses through me. "She's not, Charlie. She's alive. I can't explain it, but she's Dany." The thought of not telling him the whole truth now seems cruel.

"Dany?"

"Yes, Declan is Dany."

Instead of questioning my preposterous claim, he nods. And, more surprisingly, instead of asking me *how* or *why* or if we're both trapped in some insane dream, he not only accepts the idea but seems to acknowledge the coherence. "When I met Dany, I felt I knew her."

"You believe me?"

"I know what you're thinking."

"What do you mean?"

"I know what's in your head. Right now. I know about your mom and your dad ... and the guardians ... and who you are. Everything." His blue eyes meet mine and for a moment I see their depth again, no longer dulled by the shroud of heavy despair hanging over us. "Is it all true?" he asks.

I nod.

"This isn't a dream?"

I shake my head. "I'm sorry, but no ... it's real."

"We have to get out of here before he gets back," Charlie urges.

What's left of my heart breaks as our eyes meet again. "There's no way out, Charlie. I'm sorry. I'm sorry I did this to you. He promised me he'd take you out of here if I came with him. I'm so sorry."

"There is a way out," he insists. "Declan showed it to me in my dreams."

Chapter Sixty

Mira

A kernel of hope blooms within me. "She showed you?"

He nods. "She called to me and then she carried me out."

I shake my head. "No, Charlie. That's not what she told me. She said Avestan carried you out. She made him do it, but he's the one who carried you out."

"In my dream, Declan calls to me. I'm cold and moaning and drowning in pain and when I hear her voice, I feel hope." His eyes meet mine as he speaks. "She shouts at a man—the man with the ink black eyes." He pauses and stares at me strangely. "What was his name? Avestan?" He looks perplexed. "Was he my sister's *boyfriend*?"

I nod. I remember Dany saying that Avestan dated Molly to get close to Charlie.

"Figures," Charlie says flatly.

Humor in this soulless place is so unexpected and life-affirming that I nearly choke on my laugh. When we both manage to smile I know I'm not a wholly desiccated shell—I'm still me, in here somewhere, and there's still hope for us both.

I can see in his eyes, as he continues, that he's traveling back in time. "She orders him to release me. She won't take no for an answer. And he opens a wall of color and steps into it with me in his arms."

I nod. "He carried you out."

"But when I got home, I saw Declan, still stuck in the Land of No Light. She reached out to me—to the color, and the light—and I saw the connection between us. I saw how the portal opens."

He meets my eyes with an intensity born of conviction. "It's about connection, Mira. I've been in and out of both realms before, and I can get us back."

"That's an ambitious claim," Malentus's voice sneers from behind us. Before I can react, he circles around to our front and spews his venom directly at Charlie. "And I must admit it's precious that you, a mere mortal, thought you could save her. But Mira's not going anywhere. And now, neither are you."

Chapter Sixty-One
Declan

"I simply don't understand why she would go willingly," Edwin says, echoing all of our lamentations once again. We're sitting in Charlie's living room—the last place we saw Mira before she and Charlie disappeared.

"I understand about the hosts," Edwin continues, "although I can't explain it. No guardians, from either side, have ever been able to enter mortals in that way." He looks up. "But she knew what was happening. She knew it wasn't Charlie. Why would she go?"

"She said it was what she had to do," I whisper, breaking down again at the memory of the look of anguish and indecision on her face before she disappeared.

"She can't have pinned her hopes on Finn's theory," Edwin cries out, "she'd be putting the entire world in danger and she wouldn't take that risk."

Soren looks uneasy. "She might have, because of something I told her."

Edwin's head swivels sharply to face him. "What do you mean?"

"She insisted." Soren explains. "And I can't say I don't agree with allowing her to know all the options."

"What did she insist?" Edwin demands.

"That I tell her about the failsafe."

The room goes silent.

"What's the failsafe?" I ask with trepidation, but I think I already know.

Alexander turns to me, and the horror and sadness in his eyes tells me I'm right. "Soren told Mira how to destroy herself from within."

Chapter Sixty-Two
Mira

The despondence and depletion I feel in Malentus's presence is profound. I try to summon the pinpoint of energy I hid in the tip of my lightning bolt shield, but even if I could access it, I can't attempt to trigger the failsafe option with Charlie still here. I could never leave him behind.

Which leads me to my next, horrible, thought: should I try to destroy us both?

Immediately, I push the idea away. Self-annihilation is one thing, but taking the life of another? Even to put us both out of our misery? I'm sickened to have considered it even for a fleeting microsecond. There has to be a way to save him.

Charlie is in front of me, attempting to shield me from Malentus, and he's going to get himself killed if I don't do something fast.

I attempt to center myself, as Alexander taught me. It's difficult to concentrate through the pain and the panic I'm feeling but I imagine a ribbon of cool blue light guiding Charlie away from the darkness and illuminating a path for him far beyond the Land of No Light. I imagine finding the pinpoint of my energy I tried to hide. It feels hopeless, and ridiculous, but my love for Charlie and my determination to see him safe from harm urges me on. I imagine the light growing and I feel its warmth within me, and I feel it spreading through my limbs and expanding. I understand now what Alexander meant when he said it would feel infinite and I remember Uncle Finn's words: "the ultimate force." When I feel ready, I open my eyes and I see Malentus standing before Charlie, causing him pain, and I can take it no longer.

I summon every ounce of power within me and, as Dany described, I release it from my fingertips to explode with pinpoint accuracy, directly at Malentus's heart, if he had one.

Only it doesn't work.

Malentus staggers back, startled, and grips his chest, but the malevolent evil that draws over his face in the aftermath shakes me to my very core.

The small consolation for my efforts is that Malentus has stopped tormenting Charlie in this moment.

Now he's trained his wrath back on me.

Chapter Sixty-Three
Declan

"Charlie's talking to me," I say loudly over everyone's murmurings and fervid planning. We've called everyone here—my mom, Mark, Liz, and Finn—because this is an all-hands-on-deck situation.

The room falls silent and everyone's eyes are on me.

What do you mean he's talking to you?" Alexander asks.

"I hear him, right now, calling to me. He says he's in the Land of No Light and he's been here before." I look over at Edwin. "Could he remember?"

"Those who have been to Nusquam may retain some artifacts," Edwin answers, "unfortunately."

"But Avestan assured me he erased his memory," I insist.

Alexander shakes his head. "Knowing my brother's proclivities, I think he would have taken great pleasure in ensuring Charlie remembered Nusquam in some way."

"You told me I was there, too, but I don't remember it," my mom says.

I look over at her. "Are you sure?"

"I'm sure your father protected me from it, as best he could. I remember a vague feeling about that weekend when Malcolm—I mean Malentus—took me away, but nothing more. It's an uneasy feeling—it makes me ill to think of it—but I think Frank kept it at bay for me."

"Can't you go there and get them?" I ask Edwin. "Or you?" I turn to Soren.

Edwin shakes his head. "Guardians are forbidden there."

"But Alexander went. He saved me," I insist.

"If you remember, Declan, you opened a portal and reached out for him. He went at your invitation. And it cost him dearly."

I feel sick as Edwin reminds me of what happened. "I thought he was pulling me out. I never would have pulled him in."

Alexander takes my hand and squeezes it. "If I could have managed it any other way, I would have."

Edwin turns to me. "Declan, if Charlie is communicating with you, perhaps you can instruct him how to open a portal." He shifts his attention to my mom. "Declan is connected to Charlie because they were in Nusquam together. And Judy, you traveled there with Malentus, so you have a connection, too."

"But what can I do?"

"If Declan is able to communicate with Charlie, perhaps you can communicate with Malentus." Edwin's expression is conflicted. "I hesitate to ask this of you, Judy, but I don't see another way. I want you to concentrate on Malentus. Picture him as Malcolm, if that helps—the way he was when he took you there."

"What will I say?" she asks.

"Anything to distract him while we try to get Mira and Charlie out."

I look at Edwin. "But how can we get them out?"

"As guardians we can't enter, but as mortals you and Judy have traveled between the realms and that's the connection we need—you both have traveled in and out."

"But I went there in another life, as Declan."

Edwin nods. "There's a chance you may not have retained the ability to journey between the realms, but Judy traveled there in this life and she most surely has. It's a terrible risk to take, but perhaps she can pull them out."

"No," Mark says adamantly. "I won't let Judy risk herself like that. I'll go instead."

Edwin turns to him with profound sadness in his eyes. "Mark, I know you'd take her place. I would, too, if I could. But unfortunately that's not an option. We can't travel between the realms."

"And we don't have time to dither about any of this," Soren interjects. "In fact, it may already be too late."

Chapter Sixty-Four
Mira

Malentus grips his head with his hands, covering his ears. In that instant, Charlie turns to look at me. "I feel Declan talking to me," he whispers. "She's telling me what to do."

The last shreds of hope scattered within me pull together once more. The idea that we could see our loved ones again, and be together—the thought brings stinging tears to my eyes. It's too sweet a dream to try to hold onto in a place like this.

Charlie closes his eyes and after a long moment he opens them and swipes his hand across the air and I see a flash of color that quickly disappears. Malentus sees it, too, and the eruption of rage in his eyes literally sends rippling tremors through the air. He rips at his ears and then lowers his hand and points to me. "You," he growls ferociously. "You're doing this." Then he turns to Charlie. "If you try that again, you'll watch your girlfriend suffer a slow, agonizing, and *permanent* death."

In that instant, where the flash of color appeared, it opens again and I see my nan in the portal. She's leaning into our realm and her arm is colorless. Dany is behind her, gripping my nan's other hand and struggling to keep the rest of her firmly in place in the land of color and light. Charlie grips me with one hand and reaches for my nan with the other, but Malentus yanks me from his grip.

"I warned you," Malentus spits at Charlie. "And I promise you, this is going to hurt her more than it's going to hurt you."

My eyes meet Charlie's and I can still see the portal flickering behind him and threatening to close. "Please go," I beg. "Save yourself. Go without me. Please."

Charlie's blue eyes meet mine and his reply melts away my final shred of hope, because it's the same self-defeating answer Malentus's brothers gave, although this time it's out of love, not hate.

"Never," he swears with a determination that we both know is the making of his own demise. "I won't leave you, Mira." He makes the vow as I stare into his blue eyes for what I know will be the last time.

Malentus raises his arm to strike and the last thing I remember is Charlie screaming "No!" and charging in front of me as he grabs my hand.

Chapter Sixty-Five
Declan

Watching as Charlie takes the hit meant for Mira is agonizing. My mom managed to grab his arm before the strike hit his chest, and with his other hand gripping Mira's, somehow, someway, we manage to pull them both through. In the microsecond before the portal closes, I see the raging evil in Malentus's eyes, but then, just as quickly, he's gone.

Mira is lying on the living room floor, groaning, and Charlie is behind her, limp and unresponsive. My mom is gripping her head. I don't know who to tend to first. Edwin goes to my mom, Soren reaches Charlie, and Alexander holds Mira. "Are you okay?" he asks.

She groans, numbly, and looks from his eyes to mine. "Is Charlie here?"

I nod, but my answer feels deceptive because although he may be here, it's not at all clear that he's okay.

I look over and see Edwin and Mark tending to my mom along with Finn—she tells them she has a blinding headache but is otherwise all right, and then I quickly turn my attention to Charlie, whom Soren is tending to in earnest. Soren's hands move over Charlie with light radiating out from them and I feel the residual warmth when I join him at Charlie's side.

"Is he okay?" I whisper to Soren furtively so Mira isn't alerted yet. Charlie is lying on his back with his eyes closed and he's so still that I have to check for breathing. Surely Soren would be giving him CPR if that was the case? I check for a pulse and look up at Soren in a panic. "His heart's not beating."

Soren nods but continues what he's doing in a state of what looks like deep concentration. White light emanates from his hands as he moves them over Charlie's body, but it doesn't appear to be working. "I'm doing all I can," Soren states with calm urgency.

Liz joins us at Charlie's side. "Is he okay?" she whispers. She glances over at Mira and my eyes follow. Mira is still recovering with Alexander but soon she'll be sitting up and wanting to see Charlie. Eyes pleading, I say quietly to Soren, "When Finn's dog got hit by a car, Edwin saved him. I know he did. And Soren, I need you to do that," I plead. "I need you to work that kind of magic or whatever it is you guardians have—I need you to do that for Charlie. You have to save him. You *have* to."

Soren's eyes well up and the defeat in his voice nearly breaks me. "Getting hit by a car is one thing, but this is a direct strike from Malentus, with the force of Mira's energy behind it. I'm sorry, Declan, but I'm doing all I can."

Chapter Sixty-Six
Declan

"Edwin," I call urgently, and now that Mira is sitting up and has recovered sufficiently, she notices the flurry of activity going on around Charlie. Everyone quickly migrates over to Charlie until we're all surrounding him on the floor.

Mira turns to me in a panic. "Is he going to be okay?"

"They're working on him," I say, trying not to show my own fear. I look up at Edwin and the gravity in his eyes grips my heart.

Mira looks over at him, her eyes pleading. "Grandpa? Can't you do something?"

He joins Soren in placing his hands over Charlie and I see light emanating from both of their hands now. Edwin's light intensifies as his hands hover over Charlie's chest. Then the color from Edwin's hands starts to change and the white shade of Charlie's button-down shirt reflects the variation from white to blue before cycling through all the colors of the spectrum as Edwin settles his hands directly over Charlie's heart and closes his eyes to concentrate.

Mira's gaze is on Charlie and she takes his hand in hers. We all watch as Edwin's light surrounds Charlie's body.

"Charlie, wake up, please, Charlie," Mira whispers through tears. "I love you, Charlie. You have to wake up. You have to. *Please,* Charlie. Please wake up."

Edwin's ministrations seem to be having no effect and I meet his eyes as he continues to work but the message in his expression is grim. "I won't let this happen again," he says with a ferocity that gives me hope.

Mira is holding Charlie's hand and she bends to kiss his lips, her own lips slick with tears. She turns and looks up at me, "Isn't this what you did? You kissed Alexander and that brought him back?"

I nod with tears welling in my eyes because she's right, but it's not working this time.

"Keep trying," Liz urges her.

Mira looks me in the eyes. "Dany, he can't die. Not like this. Not for me."

I nod, tears flowing copiously now, not just for Charlie, but because I remember feeling the same way and the thought of having to repeat that kind of pain all over again is surely too much to bear. Mira can't lose Charlie.

She just can't.

Chapter Sixty-Seven
Mira

Grandpa Edwin directs everyone to sit in a circle around me and Charlie. I'm holding his hand in both of mine and I continue to kiss him to no avail. Grandpa Edwin asks me to place one hand over Charlie's heart and one hand over my own, and I look around and see everyone doing the same, only they have one hand on their heart and one hand on me.

Aunt Liz whispers to Uncle Finn to think of love.

"That's exactly and succinctly right," Grandpa Edwin says as he looks at Aunt Liz and then at all of us. "We're going to amplify Mira's power to replace what Malentus stole away."

We all nod.

I concentrate on Charlie with all the love in my heart and my hand feels warm against his chest. As I feel the love of everyone in the room flowing through me, my whole body grows warmer and I sense the strength of the power coursing into Charlie. I imagine the power sending a lightning bolt of electricity to his heart to get it beating. Surely that's all he needs to bring him back—that, and the love flowing in this room. As we continue, I feel it lifting me up and not only restoring what was lost, but expanding it more fully than I ever could have imagined. Surely a love like this can't be defeated by dark guardians—even one as powerful as Malentus.

"Charlie?" I whisper, as I kiss him once more. "Please come back to me."

There's no response.

I try again, kissing his lips softly. "Charlie," I whisper. "Please, Charlie. I love you. Please come back."

I turn to look at Dany, watching with tears streaming down her face; and at my nan, who looks much the same. "Tell him again," my nan urges softly. "If you have to say goodbye, tell him how you feel."

I turn back to Charlie, cradle his face in my hands, and lean down and kiss him once again through tears, with my heart aching inside because it may be the last time. "This can't be the way it ends," I whisper against his lips, "but if it is, then thank you. Thank you for saving me and thank you for loving me. If you're in pain, I'll let you go, but I won't ever forget you and, no matter what happens, I'll find you again."

Slowly I sit up, tears still flowing, but there's no response.

And that's when Aunt Liz hits him.

Chapter Sixty-Eight
Mira

"No!"

Aunt Liz's shout coincides with her fist landing on Charlie's heart. Something flies out of the pocket of his shirt upon contact and skips across the floor.

We're all stunned, but before we can react, the sound of Charlie sucking in air beckons our attention.

"Charlie!" I cry out, choking back a sob. His eyes are open, sending a spark of joy straight from his heart to mine. "Charlie," I whisper through a fresh wave of tears. "Charlie, you're back!" I'm laughing and crying at the same time.

His eyes scan the scene. "Did somebody punch me?"

Collective laughter fills the room, releasing all of our pent-up tension, and every eye turns to Aunt Liz.

She looks startled by her own action and shrugs sheepishly. "I saw it on TV once. I couldn't let the bad guys win."

We laugh again and Charlie, still looking a little dazed, runs his fingers over his chest and stops when he gets to the breast pocket of his shirt. He lifts the pocket, revealing that it's torn underneath and there's a bright red burn mark on his skin over his heart.

"Oh my God, what's that?" I ask. "Does it hurt?"

"Where's the penny?" he asks, looking surprised.

"Penny?" I search the floor where the object that flew out of his pocket landed. Grandpa Edwin picks it up and hands it to me. When I examine it, it's now clear that it's a hunk of melted copper and it's in the same shape as the mark on his chest—a small, rough lightning bolt. I look at him, questioningly. "This?"

He nods. "It's the penny you gave me."

"What?" My eyes are incredulous. "It is not."

He nods. "It was in my breast pocket. I've kept it with me every day since I met you."

I can't believe what he's saying. "You did? Why?"

"Because you said it was lucky. And meeting you was the luckiest day of my life."

I smile and he smiles back, and seeing the depth and love in his blue eyes that was missing before brings more grateful tears to my eyes. "It blocked Malentus's strike?"

He shrugs. "Or it helped at least. Pretty lucky, right?"

I smile and wipe the tears from my cheeks. "Or maybe it was fate."

Chapter Sixty-Nine
Mira

When I finish recounting the entirety of what happened, the room is silent and everyone looks astonished, but none more so than Grandpa Edwin.

"Stolvos and Mortegur are *gone*?" he asks.

"They were just a pile of ashes. I saw it myself."

Alexander appears equally floored. "That means their whole line is gone."

"And Malentus is the last one standing," Soren adds before he looks at me. "You lived up to your name in the story."

"What was the name?" I ask.

"The Destroyer," Soren answers.

I look over at Grandpa Edwin. "Why didn't you tell me that?"

"Because I wasn't certain what it meant—it could have been self-destruction or total annihilation. It was a terrible risk you took."

"I trusted Uncle Finn's science."

Uncle Finn's eyes go wide with alarm. "That was a mistake. It wasn't reliable." He glances at Aunt Liz. "I stated that clearly."

"But I knew I had the failsafe if it didn't work." I look over at Soren but he looks down, guiltily.

"You were going to sacrifice yourself," Dany says with sadness in her eyes.

"It's what you and Alexander did for me."

"But we did it so that you could *be here*," she answers. "So you could tip the balance for good."

I shake my head. "It was never going to end—everyone I loved would always be a target and always be in danger unless I did something to make it stop, once and for all."

Grandpa Edwin takes a deep breath in and exhales. "It was a risk I never would have condoned, but it worked in a way I never could have foreseen. The level of enmity between Malentus and his brothers caused them to act contrary to the Triumvirate's interests, out of spite." He shakes his head. "It's confounding, but as I've always said, never underestimate the stupidity of evil and hate."

Soren nods. "Malentus gained his power back—greater than before—but it amounts to a fraction of what he would have wielded with his brothers. He's the lone ruler left standing, but two thirds of his dominion has disappeared and that will take eons to try to rebuild."

"I still don't understand how I had that much power to give," I say, remembering my feeling of helplessness. "I was never able to summon much of anything to fight back."

"Quiet power is always stronger than bombastic, obnoxious shows of display," Alexander comments.

"Your vision about Mira has come true," Grandpa Edwin says as he shifts his eyes to Dany.

I turn to her. "You had a vision about me?"

She nods. "When you were born, I had a vision that you were safe and your birth had ensured the balance was tipped forever for good."

"And it was," Alexander says, "until I came back and brought Malentus with me."

I shake my head. "But that's the way it was meant to play out. The vision was right—it just took more steps than expected."

"And if you think about it," Dany says with a smile, "everyone here played a part in this working out the way it did."

Nan looks at Dany with tears in her eyes. "I'm just so grateful it worked."

"What did you say to him?" Grandpa Edwin asks her.

"Say to who?" I ask.

Nan turns to me. "Your Grandpa Edwin thought that since Declan and Charlie could hear each other that maybe I could communicate with Malcolm—Malentus—since I'd, unfortunately, been there with him before."

"You were talking to him? Is that why he was tearing at his ears?"

She nods. "Your Grandpa Edwin thought that I should try."

"What did you say?" I ask.

She places her hands on both cheeks and shakes her head. "Oh, it was silly, actually. I didn't know what to say—it just popped into my mind and I thought it was what would bother him the most. Just a short phrase I kept repeating over and over."

"What was it?"

She looks up at me. "I told him 'Love is stronger than hate.'"

The room is hushed and my eyes well up. "That's beautiful, nan."

"Simple and perfect," Grandpa Edwin agrees as he reaches over and squeezes her hand. Grandpa Mark has his arm around her and he pulls her closer and kisses her cheek.

She smiles. "It's the one thing I know to be true," she says softly as she wipes away tears of her own.

We all sit quiet for a moment and let the beauty of her statement sink in.

Aunt Liz breaks the silence. "Although sometimes being indignant helps, too."

We all laugh. "It does if you take it out on Charlie," I say with a laugh.

"Thanks, Liz," Charlie says with a smile as he rubs his chest and everyone laughs again. "And by the way, nice to meet you."

Aunt Liz laughs. "If it hurt, I'm sorry, but I'd like to proffer that any soreness you're feeling is more likely due to getting struck by a dark guardian and having a penny melted into your chest than from being hit by a middle-aged woman."

Everyone laughs.

"She makes a reasonable, lawyerly argument," Finn comments and the laughs build again.

When the chuckles finally die down, Grandpa Mark speaks. "I regret I'm the only one in the room who didn't play a part in all of this."

Dany shakes her head. "That's not true." She walks over and kneels in front of where he's sitting next to my nan on the couch and she takes his hands in hers. "You loved my mom. You took care of her after I was gone. You were Mira's parents when Alexander and I couldn't be. I see the love between all of you now and it makes me so grateful. Thank you, Mark, for being a part of our family."

I've never seen Grandpa Mark shed a tear in my entire life but his eyes are unmistakably wet when he holds Dany tight for a long hug and says, "We're glad you're back, Declan."

I'm starting to realize I'm the only one still calling Declan "Dany," but old habits die hard.

Someone orders pizza, and as we sit around talking and laughing and having an ad hoc birthday celebration, I marvel at how quickly we bounced back, and how comfortable and right this all seems.

Grandpa Edwin calls for a toast and we all raise our glasses. "To your twenty-fifth birthday, Mira. I'm sorry that I didn't realize until now that you've always been the wisest angel in the room."

I smile at him as we all clink our glasses and then I go over and hug him hard. "I'm sorry, too, Grandpa, for treating you the way I did."

He kisses my cheek. "I understand. You're safe and that's all that matters."

"It's Dany and Alexander's birthday, too," I say as I turn around to look at everyone. "Sort of, anyway."

Dany laughs. "I haven't decided yet which birthday I'm going to celebrate. Maybe I'll just have two every year."

Alexander nods. "I second that. For now, let's just toast everyone."

Grandpa Edwin raises his glass again and we all do the same. "To all of us being together again."

There's not a dry eye in the room when we all raise our glasses to salute that sentiment and everything it means.

Chapter Seventy
Mira

"That was quite a birthday," I say from my perch on the couch, legs curled under me, after everyone leaves.

Charlie smiles. "Your Grandpa Edwin was right—twenty-five was certainly momentous."

I laugh. "You think?"

"I know I should be reeling from everything that happened, but it's strange—it's as if I knew everything all along but just didn't realize it until now."

"You must be exhausted."

He shakes his head and smiles. "Not at all, actually."

"So, why didn't you do it?"

"Do what?"

"Leave without me."

"You have to ask?"

I shrug. "Tell me."

"For one thing, it turns out my girlfriend is an amazing, one-of-a-kind angel."

I smile. "Girlfriend?"

"I hope so."

I smile wider. "And for another thing?"

"For another thing, I'm in love with her."

His blue eyes meet mine. "You are?"

"I'm pretty sure I've been hopelessly in love with you since the first day you turned me down for a date."

I laugh. "I said yes at first."

"But then you said no."

"But then I said yes again."

He shrugs. "Better late than never."

He leans over and when his lips meet mine the happiness I feel is so overwhelming that I start to cry. He pulls back and looks into my eyes. "Hey, what's wrong?" he says softly as he wipes away my tears.

"I'm just …" I peer down before I manage to look back up into his eyes. "I thought you were gone … earlier … and I'm just so happy now to be able to kiss you again. I'm sorry I put you in danger. I don't want anything to ever happen to you."

He smiles and tugs open his shirt until I can see the scar on his chest. "Remember when you told me you thought of your scar as a shield? Well now I have a shield, too, and I'm protected forever. I don't even need the lucky penny anymore."

I laugh. "That's good, because it's a melted hunk of metal now."

"Well, I don't *need* it, but I'm still planning on carrying it around."

"Why?"

"As a reminder of how lucky I am."

"To have survived?"

"To have found you."

I smile, and the look in his blue eyes makes my heart melt. "We sort of match now," I say. "You have a mini lightning bolt and I have a bigger one."

"Saves us from having to get matching tattoos."

I laugh. "I think I'm ready now."

"For a tattoo?"

"For you to kiss me again."

He laughs and then his tone turns sincere. "I heard you, you know."

"Heard me what?"

"Tell me you love me, when you were kissing me."

"You did?"

He nods. "I was still in there—I just needed to find my way back."

"By being punched by Aunt Liz?"

He laughs. "And by being kissed by you. When you said you loved me, there was no way I wasn't coming back."

"I'm glad you made it … and you heard me."

"Me, too," he says softly. He cradles my face in his hands and when his lips meet mine, my heart is smiling.

Because my heart knows, just like the rest of me, that this was meant to be.

Chapter Seventy-One
Declan

"Can you believe it's over?" We're both brushing our teeth in the bathroom at Alexander's condo, after getting back from Charlie's house. "I still can't believe everything that happened."

Alexander shakes his head and looks at me in the mirror. "It's been a lot."

"Your daughter takes after you, you know."

"How?"

"She had a plan."

He spits into the sink and looks over at me and smiles. "And she kept it to herself. Now I understand why you find that so frustrating."

I laugh. "You finally get it! But, if she told us, we would have insisted she not take the risk."

"Emphatically, yes."

"But it worked, and now the balance is permanently on the side of good."

"As it would have been if I hadn't come back and brought Malentus with me."

I shake my head and spit in the sink and then I turn to him. "You can't mean that. Two thirds of the Triumvirate remained before, and now it's down to one third. Plus, we're both back and we get to be together and see our daughter and–"

He raises his hands in the air. "You don't have to sell me on any of it."

"Well stop chastising yourself for enabling Malentus to come back, then."

"The fact is, I broke the rules. And there were consequences."

"Mira broke the rules, too, and I'd argue it turned out better than it would have otherwise. Sometimes you need to break the rules—you can't just blindly follow tradition or the way things have always been. Haven't you read *The Lottery* by Shirley Jackson?"

He laughs. "That's an extreme analogy, but I get your point."

We rinse our toothbrushes and put them next to each other in the holder and I follow him into the bedroom. "I wish you could warm up my feet," I say as we slip under the sheets.

"Your feet are cold?"

I nod. "You used to be able to just put your hands on them when we were surfing and toast them right up."

He smiles. "I regret I don't hold the same powers. But I do have the ability to warm up your entire body."

I meet his gaze and the glint in his eyes makes me laugh. "Is that right?"

His reply is a slow nod.

"Aren't you tired?"

He shakes his head. "Not at all." The look in his eyes is unmistakable.

"In that case, maybe we should move forward."

"Move forward?"

"It's a euphemism."

"Not one I'm familiar with. Enlighten me."

I smile and shake my head. "You always make me say it."

He laughs. "I like it when you tell me what you want."

"Okay, I want you to make love to me."

"You don't want to wait any longer?"

I shake my head. "Now that we know Mira's safe, we can get our heads in the game ... and, like you said, waiting twenty-five years is long enough."

He smiles. "Get our *heads in the game*?"

I laugh. "Didn't you say you wanted to be able to focus?" The memory of his words that day still makes my body tingle every time of I think of it.

"Oh, I'm focused alright. I'm deeply focused on this conversation and getting our heads in the game."

I push his arm. "You don't mind doing it now, then? You don't have some grand plan that we'd be thwarting?"

"*Mind?* No. I can definitely attest that I don't mind."

I smile. "You don't want more build-up?"

His eyes shift to sincerity. "Declan, after all these years, getting the chance to reconnect with you in that way ... to rediscover how intensely good we make each other feel ... all I can say is, it's been a long time coming." He holds my gaze and when he speaks again his voice is low. "I don't need any more anticipation." His eyes darken and the heat between us builds with seductive promise.

"Do you think it will still be as good?" I whisper.

His eyes hold mine. "I know it will be."

"We're both mortals now, so you won't have to hold anything back."

He shakes his head slowly. "No holding back." His voice is rough, barely above a whisper.

I swallow hard and he kisses me, softly at first, his lips parting mine. Then he pulls me closer and as his tongue teases mine and the kiss deepens, I feel a familiar bliss course through me. I arch my body into his and sigh softly and he groans, deep in his throat, in return. Slowly, we remove our scant bedclothes, smiling and kissing the entire time, and when I feel the heat of his body on mine, it brings a rush of pleasure that I remember as clearly as if we were never apart. Our hands roam and he kisses me everywhere with a languid artfulness that coaxes sighs from me at every turn. When the anticipation becomes almost too much to bear, he pauses and our eyes meet, dark with longing, before he enters me, achingly slow and deliberate. His deep groan of pleasure and the satisfying fullness of having him inside me again brings me to a level of euphoria beyond words. "You feel so good," he groans hoarsely as his lips meet mine. We gaze into each other's eyes and the intimacy between us deepens until I can almost see the string of light connecting our hearts. "I love you, Declan," he whispers as he kisses me once more. "I love you, Alexander," I breathe out in return, basking in the feeling of being connected again. We continue to move in slow, rhythmic harmony as a swell of pleasure builds within me, intensifying and concentrating as it climbs, our breaths getting faster, until the delicious tension finally erupts in a powerful detonation of white light and pure, sensual bliss. We cry out together and Alexander grips me tight as wave after wave of exquisite rolling pleasure overtakes us until eventually he comes to rest in my arms.

As we lie still, savoring the glow of our connection, our breathing slowly equalizes and Alexander lifts his head and kisses me once more. "It's the same," he says with a slow, sexy smile.

I laugh. "Yeah, it is."

"It might even be *better*," he says with a laugh, "if that's possible." He reaches his hand up to caress my cheek and tucks my hair behind my ear. "With you, it always gets better and better."

I smile as he holds my gaze. "I can't believe we get to do this all over again."

"Give me five minutes."

I laugh and push his arm. "I mean *this*," I say as I point back and forth between us. "Being together—we get another chance. And this time we don't have to worry about evil dark guardians trying to take our souls."

He nods. "We get to live a normal, mortal life together."

"Which means we get to grow old together this time."

He smiles. "And I have it on good authority that we're going to live to over 100 years old, die holding hands in bed, and then become guardians together for eternity."

"You're making that up."

He laughs and shrugs. "I said I have it on good authority."

"But you always said there are no guarantees."

"Maybe, but we both know a love like ours bends the universe." He smiles and his green eyes crinkle and, in this moment, I know that it's true—and all is right with the world.

Chapter Seventy-Two
Two Months Later
Declan

"Woo hoo! Woo hoo!" Niko's whoops of delight as he rides his bike over the gentle slopes in the sidewalk in front of his house crack me up.

"I know, right?" Liz says as she watches me laugh. "You'd think he was jumping the Grand Canyon with the thrill he gets from riding over these." She points to two Magnolia trees in front of the house. "Their roots are starting to buckle the sidewalk and we know we'll need to do something about it eventually but right now I couldn't bear to fix it and take away Niko's daredevil thrills."

I laugh. "He's adorable. And he loves bike riding, just like Finn."

"Did you see how high I went, Aunt Dany?" Niko asks excitedly when he circles back around.

"I did, and it was amazing," I say with a laugh.

"It's like a roller coaster!" he shouts as he lines up his bike to go over the two bumps again.

Liz and I watch him crest the gentle slopes many more times until he eventually decides he's thirsty and we head back inside to join everyone else for dinner.

When we walk into Liz's large kitchen I see Charlie and Mira with their arms around each other, laughing and talking with Alexander and Finn. Alexander is chopping carrots and Finn keeps telling him that Liz likes them cut smaller. The happiness in my heart as I take in the mundane scene overwhelms me and I feel my eyes welling up.

Liz throws her arm around my shoulders and gives me a hug. "If I didn't believe that it was you before, I would now—you've got a marshmallow heart, just like you always did."

I smile and look at her as I press my fingers to the inside corners of my eyes. "You've got a marshmallow heart, too. You just cover it up better."

She smiles. "True."

"I just can't believe sometimes how lucky we all are to be here again, together."

She nods and I can see the emotion welling in her eyes, too. "We'd better go help these jokers prepare dinner or we'll all be crying about it soon."

We both laugh and join the others and, after everything is prepared and in the oven, we all sit down around the large dining table with our drinks to chat and catch up. Although there isn't much to catch up on since we see each other every Sunday at my mom's for brunch—along with Edwin and Soren, too—and we all go out together or make the rounds to our various houses for dinner regularly.

"I was happy to see that the hospital vote went your way," Liz says to Mira as she refills her drink.

Mira looks at Charlie. "Yes, apparently someone pledged a large anonymous donation to the hospital with the stipulation being that it remain a non-profit." Then Mira's eyes train on me. "And apparently others knew about it, too, but didn't say anything."

I smile. "It was off the record. What could I do?"

Charlie turns to Mira. "I couldn't say anything to anyone before the vote. And I wanted it to remain anonymous afterwards because otherwise the media would have a meal with the 'brother against sister' angle. Plus, I didn't think calling the new expansion "The Bing Wing" sounded good anyway."

We all laugh. "You could call it the CDS Wing," chimes in Finn.

Charlie nods and then his expression turns thoughtful. "Actually, that brings up something I want you all to know about the name of my company." He looks over at me. "Do you remember when I told you during our interview why I chose the name Candle Data Systems?"

"You said it was a metaphor for shedding light on data," I answer.

"I also said it had another more personal meaning—from my childhood."

Mira looks at him. "You never told me that."

He nods. "I never told anyone. In the dreams that I had, when I was in the Land of No Light, I was always rescued by Declan." He looks over at me and smiles. "You brought me into the light in my dream, and I don't know if you realize it but when you would come over to babysit when I was a kid, it was like the sun shining inside the house whenever you entered."

I smile. "I felt the same way about you."

"When I had to come up with a name for my company, I wanted something that conveyed a positive meaning broadly, but also had a more personal meaning—to keep me motivated and to remind me to stay positive."

"So it was about shining light on you, too," I say with a smile, "not just on data."

He shakes his head. "No. I mean, yes, in a way, but it's more than that." He pauses and meets my eyes across the table. "It's an anagram. If you rearrange the letters in *Candle*, they spell *Declan*."

The room goes quiet.

I'm so stunned I feel frozen to my chair. "You named your company after *me*?"

He nods. "I hope you approve."

My eyes well up and I hear Liz mutter next to me, "Here we go again," and that breaks me out of my gobsmacked stupor and I laugh.

"Charlie," I say as I wipe away an escaping tear, "I'm so honored that I don't even know what to say."

He smiles. "It brought me luck. Look at CDS now."

"Or maybe it was fate," Mira says next to him.

Charlie nudges her and they both chuckle and he kisses her sweetly, and it makes my heart radiate warmth to see them so happy.

"Or maybe it was just a lot of hard work," Finn says and everyone laughs.

"Or maybe it was all of the above," Liz chimes in. "What's that saying? 'Luck is when preparation meets opportunity.'"

"If that's luck, then what's fate?" Mira asks.

"Fate is when love is involved," I answer.

And I smile when I say it because I believe it's true.

Chapter Seventy-Three

Six Months Later
Declan

"This is a beautiful view up here," I say to Alexander when we get out of the car. We've driven twenty minutes out of downtown into an area dotted with sporadic houses in the San Mar Mountains.

"You like it?"

"How could you not like it?" I say as I breathe deep under the sunny blue sky and spin around in a slow circle in the middle of the large, flat expanse of grass. "Breathtaking views of the mountains and the trees, and a clear view all the way to the ocean. It's gorgeous."

"I was hoping you'd say that."

"Are we going to have a picnic here?"

"No," he answers. "I mean, yes, I was planning for us to have a picnic, but I'm glad you like it because I think we should buy it."

My jaw drops. "*Buy* it?"

"I have an offer in, pending your approval, and I'm designing a house for us to build on it."

My heart melts when I meet his eyes, nervously awaiting my reaction. "That's what you've been working on, late, all these months?"

He smiles. "I told you I was planning something."

If hearts can smile, that's what mine is doing now as I pause a moment to let the news sink in. I spin around in a slow circle again, taking in the ocean and the trees and the mountains once more, but this time from the imagined perspective of being inside a house—*our* house—and looking out on what will soon be our view.

"Are you serious?" I ask as I look into his eyes.

He nods, smiling.

"And you're going to build us a house here?"

He nods.

"Like the cabin you built for me once."

He smiles. "Well, this time around, mortal construction workers will be doing the actual building," he says with a laugh, "but yes, it is a similar view to our plateau on the mountain. I was hoping you'd see the connection."

"I love it."

"You do?"

I nod.

"It's going to take some time. Years, actually, but it's a good goal and someday we'll have a house here that we can share with everyone. I'll show you the plans and I want your input, too—there'll be loads of guest rooms for family, plus rooms for kids."

"*Kids?* Plural?"

He nods, smiling. "Of course I'll need your input on that, too."

I laugh. "You'll need more than my input if we're talking multiple pregnancies."

He laughs. "First we can start with a dog, like the song, and go from there."

I take his hand. "I love you. This is so beautiful and perfect." I turn to look out over the view to the ocean again and the feeling in my heart is overwhelming. "I love you so much."

He smiles. "Hold that thought." He drops my hand and walks back to the car and opens the trunk. When he returns he has a blanket on one arm and a cooler in the other hand. He spreads out the blanket on the ground and sets the cooler down in one corner and then he turns to me and reaches out with one hand.

I smile and step forward onto the blanket and take his hand and it's only then that I realize what's happening, because he bends down on one knee and looks up into my eyes.

"Declan, you know how much I love you, but I don't know if you also realize how much I love just being around you. I love talking with you and laughing with you and just *experiencing life* with you—I even love arguing with you over stupid things like what color the shower curtain in our apartment should be."

I laugh and he smiles and his eyes are filled with sincerity.

"I fell in love with you the moment I saw your true aura at San Mar High—all white light and sea blue, and purely beautiful, just like you are inside. And I loved you again when I met you as my best friend Dany and we kissed by the river. And I have no question that no matter how many times we come round, we'll always find each other and we'll always fall in love all over again. Because you're the tomato soup to my jaffle, and I tore apart the universe to come back to you and I know we're meant to be together, for eternity and beyond."

Tears are flowing down my face as I look into his green eyes.

"Declan Jane—or Dany Jameson—or any other name you'll ever go by, will you marry me and make me the happiest man in the universe?"

"Yes," I whisper through my tears. "Yes."

Alexander rises up and we both smile, staring into each other's eyes, and when his lips finally meet mine, I know in my heart we'll never be apart again.

Because true love stories never end.

Thank you to my readers

Dear Reader,

I truly hope you enjoyed Declan and Alexander's story! This brings the *Guardian Series* full circle and I thank you so much for following their journey.

If you liked this book, or any of my other books, I hope you'll post a quick rating and/or review on Amazon, Goodreads, or your favorite forum for fellow readers. Every post is sincerely appreciated and I thank you for helping others discover a new story!

If you enjoyed this series, look for more titles coming soon. I have several new books in the works. You can sign up for my newsletter (to be the first to hear about new releases) and you can connect with me online at:

Facebook: facebook.com/ajmessengerauthor
Instagram: instagram.com/ajmessengerauthor
Twitter: @aj_messenger
Website: www.ajmessenger.com

I appreciate you more than you could ever know and I love hearing from you!

A.J. Messenger

Sign up for new releases info!

Be the first to receive information about new releases and also to receive *exclusive bonus material and stories* available only to mailing list members!

Sign up now

To sign-up, please visit **ajmessenger.com** or **facebook.com/ajmessengerauthor**.

More titles coming soon!